Growing up Hadley

Dana Harp

B. Kat
PUBLICATIONS

To anyone who lacked the confidence to follow their dream but did it anyway.

Contents

Part Two: The Determined Years

Prologue

1992

Everything was different now. Hadley was home. Though after years of staying away, she hardly considered this her home anymore. She never planned to come back, but after a curious phone call, here she was. Driving down a perfectly paved road, surrounded by equally spaced cookie cutter homes with manicured lawns and identical mailboxes. Growing up, this was a rough dirt road that split an expanse of beautiful, rolling fields. Long gone were the green acres Hadley once loved.

She had no intention of prolonging this visit. She planned to sign whatever paperwork she was handed and head right back out of town. The woman who called yesterday divulged no details, she simply informed Hadley there was outstanding paperwork that must be signed in person. She could only imagine what kind of mess her father left behind.

Desperate to get the day over with, her foot pressed against the pedal while her fingertips tapped on the steering wheel. After rounding a corner, she noticed a small open field bordered by a wooden fence on her left. It looked out of place, but it was something finally familiar to Hadley, so she decided to pull over and get out. She spent a few minutes slowly walking along the fence, inhaling the perfume of a nearby magnolia tree and listening to the old leaves and broken branches crunch beneath her feet. She shoved her reddened hands into her coat pockets, which did little to warm her against the icy wind that stung her cheeks and knotted her hair.

After a few minutes, Hadley felt an unexpected warmth spread across her chest when she saw a chestnut-colored gelding appear from around the bend. Her cold muscles softened at the sight; it was the first time she'd seen a horse since growing up. After the initial moment of joy, Hadley looked around the small field that was set in the corner of a massive in-progress housing development and cocked her head to the side. Her eyebrows furrowed and her steps slowed as she approached the out-of-place horse. Hadley noticed his eyes wouldn't cross hers, so she was careful to not spook him. Captivated by the handsome creature with a white blaze pattern on his face that matched his white stockings, Hadley suddenly remembered an old trick. She dug around in her faded leather handbag until her fingers felt a red and white swirled peppermint candy. She always kept a few handy for whenever a headache was form-ing. The mint did wonders for her. She grabbed one, slowly unwrapped the plastic and placed the candy on her flat open palm. She extended a shaky hand over the fence, smiled, and stood patiently. The horse looked at Hadley, as if he was deciding if she could be trusted, before he leaned his long face over the fence to grab the treat. Once he took the peppermint, he let out a relaxed snort and slowly turned back toward the houses.

Hadley took a deep breath in, eyeing her surroundings, and ex-haled against the cold air. She leaned against the old wooden fence and watched the horse walk away. Suddenly memories of her childhood flooded her senses. She tasted both buttery cookies and stale dinners. Smelled the horses and the sting of bourbon. She felt the wind in her hair. All at once overwhelmed by freedom and fear. She remembered the love and the loss. She was definitely back, she thought. Back in the place she once called home.

Part One: The Formative Years

1979 - 1982

B. Kat
PUBLICATIONS

The Pink Ladies

Laughter echoed up the staircase as Hadley stared at herself in the mirror. She tried to smooth her golden hair, but her fingers kept getting stuck in the knots. Despite her best efforts, she remained a twelve-year-old twig, with pale skin and questionable fashion. What she lacked in friendships she made up for with her relationship with her mom. Her mom, who turned their living room into Studio 54 every Friday, was currently downstairs dancing and gossiping with a group of free-spirited women. Hadley, who couldn't wait to join her, abandoned the mirror and ran down the stairs, waving at the women with a toothy smile.

She grabbed a wide rimmed martini glass from the kitchen, filling it with milk before she slid onto the couch. As she sat, she focused intently on every move the women made while dancing, noticing they never spilled a drop from their martini glasses regardless of twirls and hops. Hadley on the other hand spilled half of her milk last Friday when she was tucking her feet underneath herself on the couch. Her mom had laughed, making a joke about how Hadley had one too many before quickly cleaning up the spill with a smile and a wink.

Tonight, Hadley held her glass carefully while she made mental notes of hip sways and sophisticated phrases to practice later. Her hand covered a laugh when Christine and Francie tried to bump their hips to the beat but instead Christine bumped too hard and Francie lost her footing, sending her three steps backwards. When Francie steadied herself, she burst into a deep laugh that made Hadley giggle even louder. She was transfixed by the way the ladies finished each other's sentences during a story and the way they held hands and sang into each other's faces during their favorite songs. Hadley absorbed these moments, committing them to memory so that when she had her own friends she'd know exactly what to do.

Hadley shifted her focus to her mom's best friend, Jeanine. She had a heart-shaped face with mossy eyes, all framed perfectly by loose auburn curls. She watched Jeanine push up the sleeves of her maxi dress and turn up the radio. Jeanine's dress was stamped with bold yellow flowers that looked to be waving in the wind as her moves grew bolder. Almost immediately all the women were dancing to Night Fever by the *Bee Gees*. They moved their hips, with one arm swaying in the air while their other held tight to the drinks they just refilled.

Jeanine and Christine twirled, their dresses flaring, their heads tilted back so their laughter floated right up to the ceiling. Hadley's mom, breathless and a little pale, took a break from dancing to drop onto the couch next to her. There was a haze to her mom's eyes that Hadley didn't understand. She worried for a moment as she set her faux milk martini on the end table, but then her mom wrapped an arm around her shoulders and they tilted their heads together. Hadley melted against her mother with a smile and trailed her fingers through her mom's hair, which felt brittle, not like the silkiness she was used to. A series of thoughts distracted Hadley as she tried to figure out what could've caused her mom's perfect hair to change. She settled on the idea that her mom probably bought a cheap shampoo from either the clearance section at Almac's Supermarket or maybe even the Dollar Tree.

What Hadley didn't yet know was that her mom, Elizabeth Martin, a 36-year-old woman with a jaw dropping physique and an unparalleled kindness, was recently met with the unfortunate fate of a stage 4 lung cancer diagnosis. The rarely discussed outcome of smoking for the past fifteen years. Since Hadley's mom stayed home and didn't work, the sole family income came from her father, Michael. He was employed by a large construction company in the center of town. After ten years of employment, it became obvious that he would never earn a foreman label or senior position, however his general labor skills kept him busy with a variety of assignments. Hadley never understood much about what her father did for work, only that he was really handy around the house. They maintained a relatively frugal lifestyle. When her parents found out about her mom's cancer, her father sat down and figured out a plan to cover the treatment copays. A plan which Hadley's mom turned down, knowing her likelihood of survival was extremely low. Hadley never knew that treatment was even an option. By the time she was told, it was explained that her mom didn't want to live like she was dying, she just wanted to live. Hadley watched her mom smoke, drink, and socialize. *She can't be that sick, she seems fine.* The only thing that changed in her mom's life was the amount of time she spent resting, which was at least 14 hours a day.

When her mom wasn't resting, and when it wasn't Friday night, she always seemed to keep busy. She would flutter gracefully from laundry to mopping to washing dishes, never leaving something for later. One day later wouldn't come, and she wasn't the type to leave behind a mess. Each day she made sure the house was tidy, the pantry stocked, the cookies baked, and Hadley's father happy. She worked through her chores while Hadley was at school, so that she would be ready to bond with her after a quick afternoon nap.

Even while doing housework, Hadley's mom always wore a form-fitted dress and maintained perfectly pinned hair. Her friend, Jeanine, liked to tease her and call her a perfectionist, but she'd waved her off, knowing she was simply doing what was necessary to keep her husband happy. Hadley, on the other hand, adored her perfect mother, often imagining she was the main character, Sandy, from the popular movie of the year, *Grease*. She didn't think her dad would have made a great Danny Zuko, because unless she focused on flaws, she had a hard time drawing any similarities. Her mom, however, was the ideal leading lady and would look amazing in a tight black leather outfit and teased up hair. That's why her mom smoked, she figured, because Sandy did and anyone who was anyone seemed to.

Would Hadley take up smoking when she was older? She thought she might, because she idolized her mom. She didn't understand, yet, that her mom was dying from the habit.

Gimme that night fever, night fever...
we know how to show it

Hadley refocused on her mom's friends, who she dubbed The Pink Ladies. Even though they never showed up wearing tight pants and pink satin jackets, they could turn the heads of even the politest of men with their ankle length brightly patterned dresses and perfectly painted faces. Hadley smiled as she watched them sing to each other with a carefree energy, their voices louder than intended. Her mom started humming along gently into her ear. She melted against her mom, her smile softening as she relaxed to her mom's beautifully perfect pitch, despite the out-of-tune singing surrounding them.

"Hadley Ann," her mom finally said in her sing-song voice. "Don't you think it's about time for my little girl to get some sleep?"

I'm not a little girl. Hadley kept this thought to herself. She hated to leave the fun but always listened to her mom. She hopped off the couch, smiled at her mom, and waved to the dancing queens. She wondered if one day she would look just as beautiful in the kelly green and teal patterned dress that currently hugged her mother's curves. Lost in thought, Hadley snuck off to her parents' bedroom instead of her own. Her dad was down the road at a local bar with his coworkers, so she had the second floor to herself.

Their bedroom seemed spacious compared to her own, which barely fit a twin sized bed and dresser. The walls in her parents' room were painted a light blue and the furniture coffee colored. Hadley walked over to her parent's large wedding portrait, which was displayed on the side wall in an ornate gold-tone frame. *They're so young.*

She studied the way her mom's shiny hair was twisted into a voluminous low bun and how it drew focus to the cerulean sparkle of her mom's eyes. She stared at how the copper and bronze makeup brightened her mom's olive skin and the way it all popped beautifully against the bright white of her satin long sleeved wedding gown. *Wow.*

Hadley's eyes trailed to the other pictures framed on the wall. On the right was a smaller framed photo of her mom's parents, who lived in southern California. She missed them. They rarely got to see each other because of how expensive cross country plane tickets were. Hadley looked like her nonna, with the same light features. She frowned as she looked at how handsome her grandfather once was. *I wish I was that tan. Mom looks so much like him, except for her eyes. We both have Nonna's eyes.* Hadley smiled and shifted her gaze. Her father's parents were framed to the left of the wedding portrait. *Grandma and Grandpa kinda look alike,* Hadley giggled. Her father's parents lived in the Midwest but they both passed away before she was old enough to know them, but based on the photos they looked as ordinary as her father, with skin neither light nor dark and muted brown eyes the same color as their thin hair.

Hadley walked over to the Victorian vanity set that sat across from the king-sized bed. *I wonder if Dad would build me one for my room.* It had a tarnished silver mirror with ornamental detailing throughout. She pulled out the plush stool, petting the soft white fabric, before kneeling gently on it. Staring at herself in the mirror, she pretended she was a Pink Lady. "Turn up the beat, Jeanine," Hadley said, drawing out the vowels. She sipped an imaginary martini and with great theatrics said, "You'll never guess what Bruce said last week." Her shoulders moved one at a time, forward and backwards, as she attempted to look fancy. Hadley giggled at the ridiculousness.

Hadley's joy faded as she paused to really evaluate herself. She hated her pale skin and her string bean legs with knobby knees seemed pathetic. *No way was Mom ever this awkward.* Hadley shrugged at her reflection. *At least my hair is pretty.* She imagined if her mom let her wear makeup or use a curling iron, she would look more like Sandy. While most girls coveted bright blue eyes, Hadley thought hers paired predictably with her flaxen hair. *Boring.* When she looked at her mom, she saw the same sky blue, but when juxtaposed by her olive skin and dark hair, it was truly stunning.

Not quite the Pink Lady, Hadley thought of herself, stepping down from the cushioned stool. But maybe one day; *I can't wait to grow up.*

Forced to Grow Up

One year later, Hadley grew up.

"Are you ready to go, Had?" She hated how empty her father's voice sounded. *Is he mad?* At the last second, Hadley ran toward her parent's room, tripping over her feet to stop before crossing the threshold. For the past three days, every time she tried to walk in, she broke down and a wave of nauseous redirected her to the bathroom.

Suddenly desperate, she braced herself and went in. A woody, floral fragrance hung heavy in the air, instantly suffocating her. *Something black,* Hadley panicked through quickened breaths. She shuffled through the collection of vibrant dresses until she reached her mom's black shawl toward the back. She grabbed it and shut the closet doors. Halfway out the bedroom, she turned back and stepped up to her mom's vanity. She closed her eyes and spritzed herself in the same perfume that moments ago clogged her throat. She took a sharp breath in. *Please be here, Mom. Please be here.* Slowly releasing her squeezed eyelids, she saw only the empty space around her.

Hadley turned toward the hallway and stepped down the stairs to meet her dad at the front door. He, like her, was drenched in black. She tugged at her mom's shawl, keeping it draped over her sunken shoulders as she wiped her tear-stained cheeks. She hid her puffy eyes behind a pair of black plastic sunglasses. Outside there was a driver standing against a 1970 Monte Carlo waiting for them. Her brow creased as she tilted her head, wondering why her father wasn't driving. If Hadley had been allowed to lean into her dad for support, she would have felt the harsh burn of bourbon lingering on his hot breath.

Hadley opened the door and slid into the back seat. She started to scooch across the bench seat to make room for her father, when the door shut, and she was left alone. She swallowed hard watching her dad get into the front seat. She wanted to ask him to sit with her, but all that came out when she opened her mouth was a tiny gasp as tears collected at the back of her throat. She stared at the back of his head, willing him to turn around and check on her. She waited and waited, but he never did. She needed him. Needed to lay against his chest and feel some sense of grounding, but he was too busy making small talk with the driver to notice.

She sank against the door, another piece of her heart cracking. She shifted away from the window, hating how the world around her remained vibrant despite her all-consuming dark cloud. She tried to close her eyes but the darkness overwhelmed her. Her mom was no longer there to comfort her after a bad dream, and as much as she wished this to be one big, bad dream it was her heartbreaking reality. It felt much too big and all too real. Instead, she took a deep breath and held it for as long as she could, feeling the pressure push against her lungs until she had no choice but to exhale. She did this a few more times, trying not to burst, until the sound of her heartbeat echoed in her ears. Only then could she finally release the tension holding up her shoulders. She separated her clenched teeth and stretched out her fingers while her father spoke in a hushed monotone voice to the driver, unaware of her anxiety. *Why did you have to go, mom?*

As they drove toward the church, Hadley wondered what her future would look like now that the family's rock was gone. She wished she could rest her head on her mother's lap like she'd done so many times before. Before she knew it, the car pulled up to the entrance of St. Anthony's Cathedral. Hadley was used to attending St. Anthony's every Sunday for services with her mother but today was Saturday and it felt very different. She walked up the front steps, as she had so many times before, but this time gripped the black metal railing to steady herself.

She stood outside the white doors, looking at the colonial brick façade and ornate white pillars in front of her. She once loved rushing inside, tugging at her mom's hand, hurrying to sit as close to the Italian marble altar as possible. She was mesmerized each week by the intricately designed stained-glass windows and the countless rows of stunning red mahogany pews.

Today was breathtaking in a different way. There was no hand holding and definitely no rush to get inside. Her feet, heavier than her heart, refused to move until her father placed his shaky hand on her back and pushed her forward. She slowly unraveled her left hand from the railing, knuckles white, and wiggled feeling back into her fingers. She sucked back the emotion and took her steps slowly until she was inside and sitting in the once coveted but now dreaded first row.

The service was long. Hadley never stood up, even after her father whispered in her ear that this was her last chance. "You'll regret it," he scolded. When she shook her head, he shrugged and got up without her. She sat and stared at her folded hands, when suddenly she felt the twitch of a smile and heard echoes of her mom's angelic voice singing

"We Go Together" from *Grease*. She sat in the memory, content with her decision.

After the recessional, family members that she never met walked up to Hadley and placed their hands on her shoulder. Their condolences were generic and half-hearted. *I wonder if I'll see any of these people again.* "Dad, can we go home?" Hadley whispered. Her father paused his conversation only long enough to wave her off with a disgruntled look. Despite the summer heat, Hadley wanted to crawl under her blankets and hide until this feeling of dread and loss somehow disappeared.

Looking for a way out, she spotted the Pink Ladies standing together in the back corner of the cathedral. Hadley approached them and gave each lady a hug. Unlike the forced condolences from a few minutes ago, the ladies' words coated Hadley with comfort. She leaned against Jeanine who was wearing a black wide-legged jumpsuit, and listened to the memories they were sharing. She felt, just for a moment, like she was back in her living room, holding a milk martini, instead of a prayer card.

***

For the next week, Hadley laid in her mother's bed. At some point the tears stopped but still she felt like a shell, ready to crack. Every morning she sprayed the musky floral scent of her mom's perfume into the air, allowing the soothing scent to envelop her while she held tight to a pine green teddy bear. She spent hours replaying memories in her mind until she could hear her mom's melodic laugh and feel her warm embrace. She pictured the curve of her mom's profile, the upturn of her nose, the sparkle in her oceanic eyes. She did this over and over, desperate to remember.

She felt a pang of guilt whenever she thought back to her birthday celebration last month. Her mom had been so excited. "I know you're thirteen now and you're much too grown for silly stuffed animals," her mom had teased. "But you'll always be my little girl. I had to buy this when I saw it."

Hadley had thought the bear was stupid and childish and planned to toss it into the pile of outgrown clothes and other stuffed animals in the corner of her messy bedroom. She rattled off a flippant thank you with a quick side hug to her mom and shifted immediately to the other present her parents had set on the table. She opened this second gift with a squeal, instead of an eyeroll, noticing a pair of bold plastic sunglasses. It was the style that former first lady, Jackie O., was always wearing in the newspapers and fashion magazines. Hadley wanted to look and feel older, stuck in her boyish body, and her new oversized frames with round black lenses did the trick. She thought it was cool, no, the *neatest gift ever*. She never gave that stuffed animal a second glance. Not until now. Now, she wouldn't let go of it. While the sunglasses sat forgotten on her dresser, the bear was clutched tight against her chest. *I'm sorry, Mom. I'm still your little girl.* Hadley hoped her mom could somehow hear her.

***

Hadley hardly ate that first week even though there were plenty of tuna casseroles, lasagnas, and ham and cheese quiches in the fridge from worried women around the neighborhood. While it was a nice gesture, she just wanted to wake up from this nightmare to the smell of her mom's homemade meatloaf and parsley potatoes. Instead, when she walked into the kitchen, she saw a table that no longer had a centerpiece of fresh flowers and a countertop that was slowly becoming cluttered with her father's junk. Since she no longer felt the joy that usually lingered in the air, she started to avoid the kitchen entirely and the Tupperware meals in the fridge were left untouched. She simply couldn't stomach the idea of sitting alone and eating a meal made by someone else's mom. Instead, she chose to ignore the gnawing ache that grew in her stomach.

It didn't help that Hadley's father seemed to come home after dinner more and more often. She sometimes noticed receipts left on the counter for orders of bar wings or McDonald's burgers. Hadley used to hate whenever her father brought her home a happy meal, *why can't I have a Big Mac, too*, she'd complain. Now she'd give anything for him to show up with a kid's meal in hand. She'd give anything just for his attention.

She could tell he was finding reasons to avoid her; she thought maybe he didn't want to deal with her perpetual sadness. He was often out at the bar but when he was around, he seemed to slip out of the room the moment she walked in. "Dad, let's play crazy eights like we used to," she asked in a moment of hope. She used to love those Sunday card games. They'd play after finishing whatever household project he was working on. A few months ago he let her help him and she remembered feeling so proud when he complimented how evenly she painted the pantry door.

"Why would I want to play cards, Hadley? You think I have nothing better to do?"

Hadley tucked the deck of cards into the back pocket of her pants and walked away quietly. She wasn't used to being alone like this. Before losing her mom, they had family dinners and shared stories from their days. Her father always cared about what Hadley and her mom had to say. *Why doesn't he care anymore?* He never went upstairs to check on her and certainly never offered to reheat a meal or play a game. He rarely even looked at her anymore.

Lately, Hadley noticed something else. There seemed to be more and more days where her father seemed to barely be able to stand, losing the battle between his balance and a bottle. He took camp in the velour chair at the edge of the living room with the lights off, making the maroon painted walls seem black in the evening. Hadley never knew what her father was thinking about when he sat in the shadows. The only thing she felt sure about was without her mom's unconditional love and support, and without her light to brighten her father's darkness, things would never be the same.

Reality is a Nightmare

Two months later Hadley shot up in bed to the muffled sounds of her father's voice accompanied by a loud crash. *What was that? Was Dad yelling?* She squeezed her eyes shut, feeling the sleepy burn behind her lids, before forcing them back open. Shifting her groggy gaze to the alarm clock on her nightstand, she squinted with confusion, realizing it was the middle of the night. 3:15 to be exact. *Why is he awake?* A pit in her stomach formed quickly as she tried to piece together what the avalanche of sound a minute ago could have been.

Hadley shoved her pink paisley comforter away from her body and swung her feet over the side of her small bed. Setting her teddy bear down on her pillow, she quickly stretched her arms above her head before standing up. She crept on the tips of her toes across her room, praying she wouldn't cross over a creak in the wood flooring beneath the thick shag carpeting. Even though she knew her father was awake, making his own noise, she was still afraid of disrupting him. She never felt anxious like this when her mom was alive, but lately it seemed like anything could set him off.

She stopped in place as she remembered last night. Like most nights, Hadley woke up around this time, except instead of from a shattering sound downstairs, last night she startled awake from the pounding of her heart as it tried to break free from her chest. Last night she fought for air in the same way she had dreamt her mom did while she suffocated to death.

She hadn't been there when her mom passed away, so her nightmares often played out the most gruesome of possibilities. She anxiously prayed that the blood dripping from her mom's nose and the foam coating the corners of her mouth were nowhere near reality. To help regain control of her heart, she sat and visualized her mom in a peaceful sleep, postured comfortably on the couch with her favorite blanket. She focused on this visual until the bloody nose and rabid mouth disappeared.

On nights, like last night, when she feared falling back into a nightmare, she'd soothe herself by pacing around her room clinging tight to her beloved teddy bear. She started holding her breath for as long as possible, a forlorn attempt at replacing the emotional pain with the physical lack of oxygen. It never helped. All it did was disturb her father, who was usually strewn across the dusty-rose-colored couch with a tumbler full, or empty, of bourbon. The floor creaking often sent him into a Boeing 747 tailspin.

Last night, in an enraged stupor, he stomped up the stairs, stumbling twice and sliding against the wall for support. Hadley ran to her bed and pulled the comforter up to her chin, gripping it in place. Her breathing grew ragged as she heard his clunky footsteps grow louder. He swung her door open, batting at it a second time when it ricocheted off the permanent indent in the wall.

Hadley being in bed hadn't fooled him. Instead of recognizing she was in pain and consumed by grief and fear, he focused on his own vexation – her *incessant pacing*. "If you don't keep your ass in bed and go to sleep like a *normal* child, Imma start takin' away those precious books."

"I'm sorry, dad..." Hadley had kept her eyes low to avoid his glare. Instead of offering her the help she desperately needed, he bullied her, which only worsened her anxiety. It wasn't always the books he threatened to take, sometimes it was her food, her comforter, and once even her entire bed. *If you aren't going to sleep, why have a bed*, he had spit.

She worked hard to memorize exactly which spots on her floor were noisy and mastered the art of walking on tippy toes aided by a chest full of suspended air. Tonight, she blew out a small breath and rolled her shoulders back, wanting to forget the night before. She knew her father was awake and while she didn't want to provoke him, she also didn't know what the commotion was or if he was okay. *Just go downstairs,* she told herself after she decided it sounded like he fell and broke another lamp or maybe a glass bottle. *Mom would've checked on him.*

Once she crossed her bedroom, successfully avoiding every creak, she slowly opened her door and inched down the stairs. When she didn't see her dad in the living room, she continued her journey to the kitchen. Sure enough, her father was lying there surrounded by shards of broken plates and bowls. It looked like a few remained intact, but Hadley was instantly destroyed by the visual. It wasn't her inebriated father that caused tears to collect under her eyes, but the realization that most of her mother's plates and bowls were now broken. More and more pieces of her mom were fading away and it was because of her father.

Hadley stood there paralyzed with renewed grief.

"I slipped on the damn mat," he griped impatiently. Hadley's eyes shifted behind him and took in the scene. He must have fallen reaching for a plate and grabbed at the cabinet shelves on his way down, causing a huge mess. "A-a-re you gonna help me or what?" Her father's words slid together as he laid there slack jawed, haphazardly jabbing his finger in the air in her general direction. *I should leave you here,* she thought while looking down at him. She knew, however, that her mom would have guided him up, made him a cup of hot coffee, and quietly cleaned up the mess. She wouldn't have yelled or shamed him at that moment and the next day they both would have acted as if nothing happened. *Was he always like this and Mom just covered it up? Doesn't matter, just be like Mom.* She reached her delicate hand out to her father and helped him get to a sitting position. She used every muscle in her body to help him stand up and slowly guided him to the kitchen table so he could sit on one of the old wooden chairs.

"You really made a mess, Dad," she whispered. She knew he heard her because he released a frustrated groan. She turned on a pot of coffee and cleaned up the pieces of broken chinaware while her father dimly watched the coffee trickle into the glass pot. His head slowly dipped toward the table until eventually his forehead made contact and his eyelids fought to stay open. Hadley allowed herself to stay on the floor, legs crossed, as she gripped a large piece of a broken plate. *I'm sorry, Mom.* She tried to hold her breath, but it did nothing to stop the streams of silent tears that fell onto the porcelain. *Why did Dad do this? There's not even any food out, why did he need to go grabbing at the plates?*

Feeling like she was losing another part of her mom, she wiped at her wet face, and placed the last of the broken dishes into the trash. She poured a mug of coffee and quietly set it next to her dad, ignoring his grumbles and made her way back to her room.

At least he would get some sleep that night.

Finding a Way

After school, Hadley fell into the routine of eating a snack and completing her homework, which often included civil war history worksheets, complicated math word problems, or persuasive essay prompts on topics that didn't interest her. After her homework was done, she spent the afternoon pointlessly waiting for her father to get home, never knowing what she should or shouldn't be doing. Sitting on the couch always stressed her out, as if her father would burst through the door at the exact moment she turned the television on, roll his eyes, and call her lazy. Instead, she took to aimlessly meandering, lost in her thoughts. *I miss Mom.* As she made laps around the main level of her house, she would notice dishes left out, pillows askew, or junk piling up. She did her best to tidy up, though never quite certain where things belonged or the right way to clean.

Her father was scheduled to work until 5 pm daily but it was not uncommon for a job to keep him late into the evening. Other days she clocked him arriving home much earlier than expected, sometimes before school let out. *I wonder if Dad gets in trouble or if he's being mean at work so his boss makes him leave. He never used to be so angry, but if I ask why he's home he'll probably freak.*

Ultimately, Hadley no longer felt a sense of security without the support of a stable parent. When alone, the walls started to close in around her and the overwhelming silence rang loud in her ears. She was drowning in grief with no one to care.

She wished she could walk next door, to where her best friend Sadie used to live, and hide until the pain went away. That house was full of happy memories, many of which included her mom. Hadley and Sadie grew up together. As a toddler, Hadley would waddle alongside her mom who couldn't wait to show up next door with two mugs of coffee and a round of morning gossip. Sadie and Hadley would giggle at their moms' feet while they played with a Fisher Price Little People barn set or a chatter telephone pull toy. As they grew up, they became inseparable. Where Hadley was quiet, Sadie was boisterous. Where Sadie led, Hadley followed.

Hadley's first heartbreak came two summers ago when Sadie and her family moved to North Carolina. It was only then when Hadley realized she had no other friends. Too shy to make new ones, Hadley clung to her mom and the Pink Ladies that much more. Now, without Sadie, her mom, or Friday nights with the Ladies, she felt a loneliness that constantly churned in the deepest part of her stomach.

That churning intensified when walking down the school hallway or while sitting on the bus. She was used to sitting alone, but while her classmates used to smile politely as they passed her row, they now avoided her entirely. No one knew how to interact with the weird, sad girl with a dead mom. She used to sit at the aisle and eagerly wait for an opportunity to be included, but now she sat against the window, with her backpack filling up the empty space beside her.

She would ignore the fun everyone was having, pretending not to notice she was always excluded from the stories and laughter. One afternoon her head, often resting against the window, lifted when a small farm came into sight. Farms in Rhode Island were rare, so it was weird she never noticed this one before. In the days that followed she started to look forward to seeing the horses freely roaming across the fields. *I wonder if their coats are as soft as they look.* The drive by was always brief and every day she longed for more.

One Tuesday, after she walked down her gravel driveway toward her barren house, she decided she would drop her backpack in the hallway and head out for a walk to that farm. *I wonder if I'm allowed to leave. Dad never said I couldn't... I'm pretty sure Mom would've wanted to come with me so I'm not alone, though, but Dad isn't home. Plus he definitely wouldn't want to walk with me. What were Mom's rules when we used to leave the house? Look both ways. Lock the door. Don't talk to strangers. Don't walk up to someone's car.* Pausing in the doorway, Hadley focused on the rules on repeat in her head before she stepped out onto the concrete front porch.

She followed her bus route until she walked up to a wooden fence that bordered the rolling acreage of farmland. She climbed up and sat on a section of beaten wood, her feet gently resting on the middle rail of fencing. She took in the scene before her.

When she squinted her focus, she spotted a few cows grazing further back in the field near an open style wooden shelter with a green tin roof. There were four horses roaming near an old wooden barn in the center of the field and two dark brown horses grazing on a patch of grass near her. She wanted to slide down the fence to be closer to them, but decided to stay put just in case they weren't friendly.

Breaking her gaze from the horses, she noticed a beaten dirt path that bordered the inside of the wooden fence that seemed to encompass the entire farm. There were a few oak trees scattered throughout the expanse and a patch of apple trees behind a small white ranch house. On the side of the house, Hadley spotted two vibrant flower gardens, one a sea of purple and the other a mix of pinks and reds. She sat on that fence for what felt like hours taking it all in.

Hadley walked to the farm the next few days after school, finding solace sitting on the fence and watching the animals roam. The fresh air felt restorative and led to the occasional fleeting moment of weightlessness between her otherwise harrowing grief.

By day six, Hadley decided to head down the grassy field toward the old red and white barn. The grass smelled fresh and as she approached the barn; her hand gently traced the top of the various pieces of spare fence posts leant against the building. Looking around, she noticed three small kittens, all white with gray patches, drinking milk from a metal saucer that was set under a wooden overhang along the barn. She smiled and whispered, "Omigosh you're so cute." She reached down to pet them but stopped herself. Up close they looked fluffy but delicate, small enough to be crafted from a thin glass that would crack if touched. She knew the feeling.

Her eyes wandered until they settled on the small house adjacent to the barn. The house, with peeling white paint, had faded yellow shutters and a screen door that hung crooked on its hinges. She slowly walked over and with an unexpected courage, walked onto the porch. She stood in place, debating what to do next. She held her hand up to knock before quickly pulling it back against her body. *This is crazy; I should go.*

"Why, hello there." Hadley startled and spun around to see an old woman with long gray hair wearing an oversized burgundy button-down shirt and mud-stained Levi jeans. "Can I help you?" the old lady asked as she pulled off her gardening gloves, shoving them into her back pocket. Her voice was inviting, and Hadley sighed with relief.

"Hi, um, I'm sorry to just walk onto your farm like this," Hadley stuttered. *Why the heck am I here? She probably thinks I'm lost or can't find my parents. If only she knew.* She hoped she wouldn't have to explain since the wounds on her heart were still raw.

"Not to worry, dear," the old lady said. "I just finished tending to my lavender verbena patch and was gonna put a pot of water on the stove for some tea. Why don't you come in a while. I'm sure I can find a packet of hot chocolate to make you."

Hadley's eyes lit up. Her mom used to make her hot chocolate on occasion before they snuggled up to watch an afternoon wintertime movie. Her mom called them day dates. Hadley loved when a lazy day came around, with the hope that a day date would form. They had a lot of them toward the end, since her mom was too weak to do much else. It wasn't too cold for October, brisk at best, but hot chocolate sounded perfect.

Hadley thanked her and stepped inside the small farmhouse, which smelled like burnt wood and chocolate chips. *This is way cozier than it looked from the fence.* She peered around the corner to see green shag carpeting and two overstuffed beige couches in a sunken living room. There was a small box television sitting to the right of a large rectangular window and a cast iron wood burning stove to the left. Along the back wall was a bookcase with books stacked haphazardly and several framed black and white photos.

Hadley turned back toward the front door and slipped off her cherry patterned Dr. Scholls sandals, a departure from her usual white Keds, and set them on the braided burnt orange mat. She picked them out with her mom before seventh grade last year and planned to wear them, faded soles and all, until they broke down entirely. She walked tentatively straight ahead toward the boxy kitchen. The walls were a dirty white with a blue checkered wallpaper along the top. Hadley approached the sun faded table and pulled out a chair with a yellow floral-patterned cushion tied to it. She sat down as the old lady poured her a cup of hot water and handed her a spoon and a packet of Swiss Miss.

Hadley jumped when she felt something rub against her bare leg, but quickly giggled when she realized it was just a cat. She reached down to pet the fat gray furball, who pressed its head into her palm wanting more.

"So, dear, what brings you 'round these parts?"

Looking up from the cat at her feet, Hadley noticed the old lady's eyes were a calming chestnut shade and her skin was wrinkled and spotted from the sun. *She looks a little older than Grandma and Nonna would be.* "Well, um, my mom died a few months ago..." Hadley mumbled as she poured her cocoa packet into the water. *Why did I say that?* "She had cancer. And, um, I thought I would try taking a walk, you know, to help clear my head. I can't stop missing her." Hadley was relieved to see the woman nod along as she listened with a gentle smile on her face. "I walked from my house across the river and up the dirt road that leads to your farm. I ended up sitting on the fence and watching your animals."

Hadley stopped stirring her drink and immediately panicked. *Oh no. Is that trespassing? Why would I say I sat on the fence?* "I hope you don't mind! I swear I was careful and never got too close to any animal or anything." Hadley awkwardly reached down seeking comfort from the fat cat only to find the space around her feet unoccupied. She looked back up, wrapping her hands around the heated mug, and continued, "Um, so how many animals do you have?"

The old lady let out a gentle chuckle that matched the kindness in her eyes. "Oh, about six horses, I reckon, and four dairy cows. We used to have chickens when Harold, my husband, was alive, but I eventually had to sell them."

"That's so cool! I mean, not the part about your husband or the chickens, but the horses and cows. They seem so carefree."

"Oh yeah," the old lady responded. "They're amazin' creatures. Sure are exhaustin' though without the help of my Harold," she sipped her tea, fogging up the space between them. "Anyway, I'm Dorothy, dear, what might your name be?"

Hadley was embarrassed that she never introduced herself. "My name is Hadley. I live right up the road. I guess I already said that part." She watched as Dorothy leaned in slightly with a wrinkled brow. "I just turned thirteen and don't worry, my dad knows I'm here." She knew better than to lie, but she didn't want to worry Dorothy, or worse, have her ask to call her dad. The old lady seemed content with her white lie and they continued to talk for the better part of an hour. Hadley thought about how nice it was to be talking with a woman again, even though it made her miss her mom even more. She was happy to have found someone who wasn't actively avoiding her.

She learned that Dorothy's husband, Harold, died two years ago, so she was also mourning. She even started wearing his old work shirts to help keep him near to the heart. Dorothy shared how they never had kids of their own so they invested their livelihood into the farmland. Dorothy used to show horses when she was younger but now spends her time maintaining the land and animals, offering horseback riding lessons on the weekend, and selling homemade pies at a local market on Tuesday and Thursday mornings. Her husband's family made a name for themselves as dairy farmers out west and gifted them cows for their wedding. "You'd think it would be one weird wedding gift, but Harold was thrilled. I was excited, too, to grow our farm. It was a process to learn dairy farmin' though." Dorothy smiled sentimentally as she took another sip from her hot tea. "Well, Miss Hadley, it's been lovely talking to you, but I better get back to work before the sun dips." Dorothy stood up, collected their mugs, and walked them to the sink.

"You, too, Ma'am. My dad's not much for talking and I don't have any aunts or sisters, so you know..."

"Us ladies have to stick together," Dorothy responded with a wink and a smile that deepened the lines bracketing her mouth. "First things first, though, none of that ma'am business. Ma'am was my mama."

Hadley giggled as she shook her head, "Got it. No ma'am." She stood up from the table and gently tucked her chair back in place.

"If you're lookin' for some gal time, I'd love to have some help 'round here. Sure doesn't get easier as you get older." Hadley saw at that moment Dorothy had a slightly bent frame. "I could even teach ya how to ride the horses if that'd interest ya."

"Oh! I would love that!" Hadley wore a toothy smile on her face at the thought of regular interactions with the kind old lady.

"If it's okay with your dad, why don't you stop by on Thursday and we'll tour ya 'round them horses," Dorothy said. "He could come, too, if he wants to see where you'll be hangin' out."

"Awesome, thanks so much. My dad will probably be at work, but I'll let him know. I can't wait to come back after school on Thursday."

Hadley slipped her sandals back on and left with a slight pep in her step. She had no intention of asking her dad for permission, knowing that when she got home, she'd quickly become invisible again. The reality of it all sent anxiety coursing through her veins like water from a spigot.

Stuck, Hadley took a sizable breath in and held it. *Just count. Count and you'll be okay.* She held her breath past twenty as the lack of oxygen pierced her lungs. She forced herself to exhale and start moving, making her way back through the grassy field toward her house one step at a time.

Hadley's first wave of anxiety crashed through her after her mom and dad sat her down to explain why her mom had been so sick lately. Shortly after that, Hadley started counting how long she could hold her breath, trying to cling to and feel the fullness for as long as possible. She thought it would help her stay calm but eventually she started to need to feel the pressure in her chest that built with every held breath. It wasn't until she felt lightheaded and often saw streaks of blue behind her shut eyes that she would convince herself to exhale.

Focusing on her breath, she looked at the horses and wondered which one she would be riding in a few days. *I wonder what kind of help Dorothy is going to need,* she thought, after regaining her composure. *It can't be too hard if Dorothy's been doing it by herself. Maybe spending time away from home will help me stop missing Mom so much. Maybe it'll be fun.*

With the smallest of smiles, Hadley decided she would learn how to feel happy again.

A Boulder of Doubt

Soon enough it was Thursday. Hadley hugged her backpack on her lap and mindlessly tapped her white Keds against the floor of the bus. She gazed wide-eyed out the window, staring intently until Dorothy's farm came into focus. She only had a fleeting view but in those few seconds she counted four horses of varying coats. Closest to the road was a rose gray mare, grazing easily on the pasture that surrounded her. Hadley also saw one white horse and one covered in a beautiful khaki patchwork. *The other two must be the dark brown ones I spotted the other day. Were the horses related? Did they have different personalities? Will they like me?* She perked up with each question that popped into her head.

As soon as she stepped off the bus, she broke into a slight jog to her front porch. Fumbling with her house key, she opened the door and reeled with kinetic energy. She carried her backpack up to her bedroom, dropped it by her bed, and quickly turned around, ready to leave. She stopped moving for a minute and started to worry if she'd get in trouble for leaving the house. She wasn't sure when her father would get home or if he'd even notice if she wasn't in her room. *I could leave him a note maybe, so he knows where I am. But if I were to write the wrong thing, he'll fume.* She stretched and clenched her fingers a few times, releasing her nerves. She decided against the note and left for the farm, hoping her dad wouldn't notice.

***

Ducking between the wooden fence rails, Hadley crossed onto the farm as a new reason to worry settled in her chest. Maybe Dorothy was only being polite by offering for her to come back. Her energy shifted from buzzing to nervous as her gait slowed dramatically. Looking around, she realized she didn't see any horses in the field. *Where is everyone? Maybe Dorothy's hiding with the animals to avoid me.* Feeling hesitant, she started to wring her hands as she walked toward the farmhouse. "You're being ridiculous," Hadley whispered.

She did her best to ignore the growing boulder of doubts and insecurity forming in her stomach when suddenly she heard a loud creaking to her right. Startled, Hadley's right hand swung to her chest, covering her pounding heart. Looking around nervously, she didn't see anything or anyone, until the barn door swung open to the tune of rust-covered hinges. Dorothy stepped out and Hadley took a deep breath, dropping her hands anxiously to her sides.

"Hadley, dear, I'm so glad you made it." Dorothy's melodic tone allowed Hadley to release the tension lodged between her shoulders.

She waved and called out "Hiya, ma'am!"

"Now, don't go startin' again with that ma'am business, dear. Dorothy is just fine." Dorothy blew out a puff of air, releasing a slight razzing noise, and waved Hadley off with a big smile. "Well now, come on. I have some horses for you to meet."

***

The horses, munching on green hay and alfalfa, stared at Hadley as she approached, particularly interested in the small woven wicker basket in her hand filled with oversized bright orange carrots. Dorothy encouraged her to hand feed one to each of the horses, explaining it would help establish trust.

Despite her shaky hand, she slowly offered a carrot to the first mare, holding it with the tips of her fingers. Her hand snapped back like an over-extended rubber band the moment the horse took a bite. "Whoa. Sorry, their teeth are so big." Hadley let out a nervous laugh.

"Not to worry, dear. They only want the carrot."

Hadley nodded, placing all of her faith in Dorothy's smile as she offered the next few horses the same treat. Her hand steadied as they progressed.

An hour later, Dorothy had introduced Hadley to five horses, taking her time to explain the nuances between each animal. Some were older, some friendlier, and a few who preferred to roam alone. "Three of the horses get particularly proud whenever they're chosen for a ride. They love any kind of human interaction. Those are the gals that usually help me with my riding lessons."

"Makes sense." Hadley tried her best to take in every fact Dorothy shared, though she already forgot the first horse's name. *Was it Buttercup or Butterscotch?* There was so much Hadley was ready to learn. For the first time in a while, it felt as though she were happy, joyful even.

She smiled easily as they approached the final stall, occupied by the white horse she had spotted from the school bus earlier that day.

This horse, who was smaller than the others and had a stunning dark brown mane, let out a soft nicker as they approached. Hadley glanced at Dorothy, who reassured her of the horse's friendly intent. Hadley turned her attention back and raised her arm to offer up the large carrot, like she had with the others. She giggled as the mare pranced her slender front legs in place as she ate the treat. "I remember this one time my mom told me I used to dance as a baby whenever she fed me strawberries. I guess they were my favorite."

Dorothy let out a chuckle. "Oh yes. This here is Miss Snow White. She's actually a light gray, but don't go tellin' her that. If you couldn't tell, she *loves* carrots. Almost as much as she loves peppermint candies."

"I didn't know horses ate candy," Hadley responded. She reached her hand out instinctively and rubbed Snow White's neck.

"Well now, not all candy, dear. But peppermints are good for diges- tion. Though they'll eat as many as you offer, so it's important to not give out too many. Imagine how you'd feel after too much candy."

Hadley hadn't had any candy since her mom passed away. It wasn't a treat her dad thought to bring home, and she knew better than to ask for any. She saved her requests for things like shampoo or toothpaste. She did remember, though, being younger with bellyaches after sneaking too many of her mom's chocolate covered cherries. Her mom would rub her back and remind her that less is more when it came to indulgences.

Smiling at Dorothy, she nodded her response, "So what else does Snow White like?"

"This girl loves to prance around and can pick up some speed when the mood strikes. She's my smallest horse. She was a tiny foal, and her original owner didn't want her. It looked as if she'd stay a runt, but she was bred for a competition circuit. I was afraid of what might happen to the pretty pony, so I purchased her and brought her back here."

"She doesn't seem *that* small." Hadley tilted her head quizzically.

"You're right. She grew up well with that big appetite of hers. Sure, she's still the smallest I've got, but her larger-than-life personality makes up for her short stature."

After learning about Snow White, Hadley followed Dorothy back outside and stepped into the sunlight. The horses were content, left to finish their food piles.

"Is it hard to ride them?" Hadley questioned, trying to mask her eagerness, but hoping her question would lead to an offer to try. She knew exactly which horse she would choose if Dorothy allowed.

Dorothy chuckled, "It's easy so long as you listen and respect the animal." Hadley nodded her agreement. "Unfortunately, we won't be riding the horses this afternoon."

Hadley tried to contain her disappointment, but she was sure it showed on her face. "Oh, okay."

Insecurity clogged her throat like a thick, cold mud as she ran through the last two hours in her mind, trying to figure out what went wrong and why Dorothy didn't like her after all. Her shoulders sagged. Feeling the dense mud spread through her gut, she decided to politely excuse herself.

As if on cue, Dorothy spoke up. "Not to worry, dear. Thing is, I fed the horses later than normal. I thought it best to have them stalled for your first introduction. I didn't want to overwhelm you or them." Hadley's eyes lifted with renewed hope. Before she could respond, feeling silly over her moment of dejection, Dorothy continued. "Now that they've eaten, they should rest up a bit. You see, dear, it's dangerous to force exercise after eating because of pressure on their lungs and in their gut. Horses can get colic easily."

"Cah-lic" Hadley slowly repeated. She cocked her head as her voice lifted.

"Yes, it's quite bad for them. I'll teach you more about that stuff next time." Dorothy said as she waved away the very idea of colic. *Next time.* That meant she would be back! Hadley felt like Snow White, wanting to prance around. "If you would like, come on 'round tomorrow after school. They'll be roamin' 'round freely."

Hadley let out a fast "thank you" for the invitation. The mud cleared and was quickly replaced with lightweight butterflies. After exchanging a few more pleasantries, Hadley waved goodbye and started her journey back home. Dorothy called out to remember to get her dad's permission. She looked over her shoulder and let out a "I know, I will." Hoping it sounded more convincing than it was honest.

***

Her dad's car was in the driveway as Hadley approached her house. She hesitated before walking inside, anxious over the unknown state of her dad, but luckily slipped inside without so much as a creak. She crept up the stairs and grabbed her school books and assignments from her backpack. She sat against her window, where she normally did her homework, rushing through the assignments that would normally have been done by now. The harder she focused on her civil war map of battles the more her mind drifted to today's adventure. She caught herself lost in a few horse-centered daydreams.

She was debating how early she could go to bed so she could wake up, get through school, and go back, when she heard her dad's deep voice from downstairs. She sighed with relief when he was only hollering to say he threw dinner into the oven. As far as he knew, she was upstairs the whole time. She opened her bedroom door and responded evenly with a "thanks, just finishing my homework and I'll be down." There was no response back.

Hadley mainly finished her assignment, leaving a few questions blank, and hurried down to eat. It was rare for her father to join her for dinner. Usually she made her own french bread pizza or Stouffer's meal whenever she felt hungry. Any other time she would have cherished this rare moment and tried to convince her dad to share a memory or even talk about work, but tonight she didn't engage. She felt protective of her new friendship and didn't want to let it slip or say anything that might upset him.

She looked across the table and noticed the tumbler three fingers deep with bourbon sitting next to his Stouffer's classic meatloaf tray. *Of course.* Since he didn't offer her any conversation, they sat and ate in silence. Every so often a smile twitched at the corners of her mouth that she hid behind a drink of water. Once done, she gulped down the rest of her water with the same speed with which her father did his bourbon. Aluminum trays empty, she obediently collected them for the trash and placed their forks and her water glass in the sink. She'd wash them in the morning with her cereal bowl. Her dad stood up, ready to refill his tumbler as she let out a hasty "Thanks dad, night." She was already halfway through the living room by the time he turned around to nod.

Ready for tomorrow to come, she laid in bed, grabbed her teddy bear, and forced her eyes shut. She eventually nodded off, dreaming of cantering horses and wind in her hair.

Lay of the Land

The next day, Hadley sat patiently on her school bus waiting to pass Dorothy's farm. Today she noticed Snicker and Dakota, a pair of brown horses, standing near the roadside fence. She could see more animals deeper in the field, but her view was fleeting. She sat straight-backed, feet pointing toward the aisle, knowing soon she'd hop off the bus and be able to walk to the other side of the fence.

When the bus stopped in front of her house she all but flew down the aisle, down the steps, and across her empty driveway. She continued her haste once inside her house, tossing her backpack onto her bed and before sprinting back downstairs, excited to see more of the farm. She didn't bother with a snack or a change of clothes, and instead sped-walked toward Dorothy's. As she ducked between the fence and started her trek toward the farmhouse, she attempted to brace herself for the possibility of still not getting to ride a horse. The horses and cows appeared to be peaceful companions, unphased by their differences while intermingling throughout the expansive green fields. She noticed the khaki patchwork horse, whose name escaped her, was grazing in tandem with a big black and white cow and wondered if they bonded over their similarly shaped patches.

Hadley approached the ranch house just as Dorothy was stepping outside. Her hair was pulled back in a soft silvery bun, and she wore loose blue jeans with one of her husband's old shirts. Dorothy waved at Hadley as she pulled the main door shut behind her before lifting the crooked screen door slightly, allowing it to latch properly. Hadley wished she knew how to replace hinges so she could make the door easier on her new friend. *My dad could fix it within minutes,* she thought, but then she'd have to tell him where she's been.

"Hi, Dorothy! Thank you for letting me come back today."

"You're welcome, dear." Dorothy wore a friendly smile that was bracketed by deep set wrinkles. "We'll see just how thankful you're feelin' once I show ya the help I need." Hadley noticed the humor behind the old woman's brown eyes, as she let out a giggle in response.

Dorothy spent the next forty-five minutes walking Hadley around the perimeter of her property. She wanted the young girl to learn the lay of the land and where the exit gates were located. It was critical to always double check that the gates were secure, otherwise the animals might accidentally wander off.

The duo eventually lapped around to the horse stables. It was one of two large buildings on the property, Dorothy's small house not included. The other building which was at the far end of the farm housed the cows. It had a shed extension off the side that functioned as storage for excess hay and grasses for the animals to eat. There were also a variety of tools and farm equipment toward the back of the space, but many of them now collected dust. Not long after her husband passed away, Dorothy hired a farm hand, Jeremy, to come by occasionally to tend to the land. While it was an expense she hated to spend, she eventually realized she spent enough years doing the back breaking work and enough was enough. She swallowed her pride and hired Jeremy once it started to hurt to get out of bed in the morning.

Dorothy paused outside the stables and shifted her body to face the young girl standing next to her. "I have plenty more to show'ya, dear... I could really use some help in this here stable but want to make sure I don't keep'ya here too late."

"My dad won't mind, Ma'a–Dorothy." Hadley quickly corrected her polite habit to not offend the woman. Her eyes bounced from the dirt and sheepishly back up. "Sorry, habit..."

"Like I said, ma'am is my mama." Dorothy chuckled as she placed her hand gently on Hadley's shoulder. "Well, alrighty, then. Let's head in and see what we got." Hadley stayed on the heels of Dorothy, anxious to learn and eager to please. She was nervous of saying or doing the wrong thing, knowing that she could easily be asked to leave or not get invited back. Dorothy walked to the back corner of the stable where a myriad of tools were hanging. She pointed next to a wheelbarrow where there was a pitchfork, a broom, a shovel, and a stiff-bristled scrubbing brush.

"These here are the basic supplies needed for cleanin' a stall out." Hadley nodded and waited for more information. "Now, I don't have much cash laying around to pay'a but if you help maintain these six stalls, I will reward'ya with horse ridin' less–"

"Yes!" Hadley interjected with a huge smile plastered on her face. "Do you want me to start right now? Just tell me what to do." Her words tumbled quickly out as she tried to contain her joy.

Dorothy laughed, entertained by Hadley's youthful energy. "How about I walk'ya through it now and then you can start on Monday."

"Okay!"

Dorothy walked Hadley through each step in the process from removing wet straw to using the pitchfork to scoop up manure. The clean dry straw fell between the tines and the rest could be tossed into the wheelbarrow. She showed Hadley how she could also use the shovel to scoop up large clumps of soiled straw and fling it against the sidewall so the dry straw would release, and the manure would separate. She told her it wasn't the most efficient way to clean but it definitely worked out any frustrations.

"So, you can throw the poop at the wall?" Hadley was giggling but her eyes were wide with curiosity.

"Well, it's certainly more fun than weeding through it with your hands," Dorothy elbowed Hadley playfully.

"Definitely." Hadley giggled again before Dorothy continued to explain how she would then need to spread out the existing straw and add more to the bedding where needed. There was a stack of straw from floor to ceiling in the front left corner of the barn to pull from. Her last step, after cleaning the stall floor, would be to rinse out the water buckets. She would give the bucket a scrub with the brush before she'd refill and replace it. Hadley had already learned yesterday that the horses aren't left with food all day long, but rather have feeding times followed by strict periods of rest.

"Alright, dear," Dorothy glanced outside to clock the sun. "You should get home for dinner. Come back on Monday and we'll get through these six stalls together. I can then show'ya 'round a horse so you can get comfortable with one."

"That sounds great! I can't wait!" Hadley was animated with her response, already wishing for Monday.

"To get on a horse or to clean the poop?" Dorothy questioned, with a sparkle in her eyes.

"Both," Hadley retorted, feeling goofy. This made them both bend in laughter as they walked out of the barn side by side. After regaining composure, they said goodbye, exchanging contagious smiles. Dorothy headed toward her much-too-quiet ranch house while Hadley made the walk back to the anxiety-trap she called home.

It's Not a Living

Hadley generally kept to herself during the weekend, except for Fridays when the Pink Ladies maintained their routine of stopping by, except now they'd bring a hot dinner instead of fruity adult drinks. Excitement bubbled as she noticed her empty driveway and started to wonder what the Ladies would have in store for her. She paused, confused to see the light on in her living room, but shrugged and dug around her school bag for her key. *I must've forgotten to turn it off.* When she walked in, her stomach knotted, and she swallowed hard. Her dad was yelling at someone, but she could only see the back of him from where she stood in the front entrance. She debated running up the stairs and hiding in her room, but her father must have heard the door open because he swung around.

"Bout time you showed up."

"Dad? Is someone else here?" Hadley crept slowly into the living room but it was otherwise empty.

"Is someone 'posed to be here?" Hadley watched him blink so slowly she thought he fell asleep for a second.

"No, I just mean... I thought I heard you talking when I walked in."

"Ya'did."

Hadley waited for more, but when her father didn't elaborate, she just nodded and turned to walk upstairs. Hadley looked forward to Friday nights, but now the whole night felt wrong. She wasn't sure the Pink Ladies would want to come over. Usually they had the house to themselves and would eat and dance around for a while until inevitably her father came home drunk. It would be *then* when he would embarrass her, often mumbling to himself and blatantly ignoring the Ladies.

She peered down the steps and watched her father. He was parading around the living room, loudly reenacting an argument he must have had earlier. That must've been what she heard him doing when she first walked in. She sighed and tiptoed to her room, taking a seat on the bench attached to her bay window. It was nice weather, so she opened the window to let the fresh breeze calm her nerves. She anxiously awaited the Pink Ladies' arrival, which would be any minute. She wondered if her father would retreat to his room or if maybe she should invite the Ladies to hang out in her bedroom. *Is he going to let them come inside? Would they even want to?*

Hadley looked up when she heard Jeanine's burgundy Oldsmobile Cutlass Supreme pull into the driveway. She was about to jump up, wanting to meet them at the front door, but froze when she heard their voices travel from the driveway right through her window.

Francie: "I don't know how long I'm going to last if Michael is home."

Jeanine: "We don't even know if he's home. The driveway is empty. We made Elizabeth a promise. Let's at least get Hadley to eat a decent meal and then we can make up an excuse to head out early if we need to."

Christine: "You girls are acting like he wasn't always this bad."

Jeanine: "He was bad before, you're right... but he's insufferable now."

Francie: "I don't know how Elizabeth put up with him. Always covering up for him and acting like he was the husband and father of the year."

Christine: "Turns out he's as big a jackass as we thought. Frank hates that I spend Fridays around Michael. Makes him uneasy. Let's just get through this for Hadley's sake."

Jeanine: "For Hadley's sake. Poor girl lives with the man, surely we can put up with him for an hour..."

The conversation was a kick to the stomach. Not wanting to embarrass the Ladies, she took a deep breath before she bounced down the stairs, prepared to act like she wasn't utterly crushed. After a quick glance around, finding the living room empty, though her father's whiskey tumbler still sat on the coffee table, she let the ladies in. She spent the next half hour acting almost too happy, not wanting to make the situation worse or make the Ladies feel guilty. She scarfed down the homemade lasagna and garlic bread that Jeanine brought, praising every bite, before lighting up over the blueberry cupcakes Francie brought.

After they finished eating, Hadley started to act tired, yawning dramatically. "We should probably let you go, you seem really tired," Jeanine said while rubbing her arm. "Are you sure you're okay?" Jeanine asked again, to which Hadley lied and quickly replied, "Yes, of course. Just tired from school." Noticeably relieved to not have to make up their own excuse, the Ladies left, waving concernedly on the way out. Usually they'd turn on music and convince Hadley to dance around the living room. It was the fun end to the school week that she always loved. Today there was no dancing. Once they left, she snuck up to her bedroom where she stayed all night, not wanting to further aggravate her father, who had stormed out to the backyard for some "peace and quiet" once the Ladies showed up. Hadley and her father continued to avoid each other for the rest of the night and all day Saturday.

***

"Greg's picking me up so I can get the car before work tomorrow."

"Okay." Hadley nodded. "Do you want me to get dinner ready for when you get back?"

"Did I say I was comin' right back?" He rolled his eyes and walked out, leaving Hadley standing there feeling stupid. *That was rude.* She decided to put dinner in the oven and hunker down on the couch. She often stayed in her bedroom when her dad was around, so it was nice to be back in the living room. She had some of the best memories with her mom on this couch. She grabbed the folded orange and brown afghan resting on the back of the couch and set it on the cushion. Before she settled, she quickly ran upstairs and randomly plucked *Trying Hard to*

Hear You by Sandra Scoppettone from the bookcase in her room before returning to the living room. She decided if she didn't find anything decent on television that she could read instead.

She grabbed the kitchen timer and twisted it to the twenty-five-minute mark. Once it started ticking time down, she picked up the remote to turn on the television, placing the timer and the book next to her. She wrapped the blanket around her body as she curled against the couch for a quiet evening alone. She landed on the series *It's a Living*, which was new that year, so she'd only seen it a few times. The sitcom surrounded a group of waitresses in California and it always made her wonder what her first job would one day be. *I could be a waitress.*

When the timer went off it startled Hadley, who was focused intently on the show. Shrugging the blanket off her shoulders, she stood up and padded to the kitchen. She grabbed a set of oven mitts and carefully took out her meal – an aluminum tray split into three triangles. The largest triangle held macaroni and cheese and the two smaller sections held peas and glazed carrots. She pulled out a fork and balanced it on top of her dinner before slowly walking back to the couch. She sat down immersing herself in the television program while mindlessly eating her subpar dinner.

***

Slam! Hadley must have drifted asleep. She shot up to a seated position after hearing the front door slam shut and locked eyes with her very angry, very drunk father. Quickly surveying her surroundings, she realized she never threw out her dinner. It was laying on the floor next to the couch with a few stray peas scattered.

"Hey, dad," she muttered slowly. She wasn't sure if she was supposed to say she was happy to see him. It would have been a lie but maybe it would assuage his temper. Before she had a chance to continue her internal debate, her dad let out an angry, "What the hell are you doing."

Hadley felt her cheeks burn. "I'm sorry, dad, I guess I fell asleep."

"Pick up this mess. Immediately."

"I will, I'm sorry..."

"Sorry. Yeah, you're sorry alright. Brat." Her father was swaying but his feet were planted firmly in place. He towered over his daughter.

Hadley quickly turned off the television and stood up. She bent down and collected the loose peas along with her tray and fork from the floor. She made her way to the kitchen to throw the trash away. She tried to keep busy by washing the fork when she felt her father's hot breath on her neck. Hadley delicately placed her fork at the bottom of the sink and turned her body around in what felt like slow motion. She was facing him now, trying to muster courage, but instead found herself leaning backwards away from him. *Please don't hurt me.*

"Let me make this clear," his voice was low and rumbled against Hadley's ears. Tears brimmed her frightened blue eyes. She tried to blink them away, but it only led to one escaping down her cheek. "This is my house." His voice grew. "That is my television and those are my meals." He was pointing around the room at everything that belonged to him. "I work hard to pay for this shit, and I don't need your greedy hands all over it."

Hadley felt panicked at this moment. She looked for a way to slip free but her father had her cornered against the sink with little room to wiggle free. Tears were quietly streaming now, and she prayed her mom would somehow show up. The prayer was left unanswered, of course, but her father did eventually step back.

"Suddenly you got nothin' to say?" He shouted.

Hadley felt paralyzed.

After a moment of silence, her father rolled his eyes, spitting out a sardonic laugh while walking to his bar cart.

Hadley took this opportunity to run. She darted to the staircase, tripping over her feet halfway up. Her knee slammed down on the edge of a step, but she quickly recovered and continued her hasty escape. Once in her room, she shut the door and her body slid down the wooden barrier until she was left crumbled on the floor in a pile of tears. *This is not living.* She felt lost and confused. She held her throbbing knee while the walls closed in on her.

Panicking, she squeezed her eyes shut, sucking in the surrounding air, waiting to feel a release that never came. She started to feel an intense tightening within her chest as her vision turned blue. She tried to convince herself to exhale but couldn't. Moments later her body collapsed.

She wasn't sure what happened, but she woke up what felt like hours later with a gasp, wiping at her wet cheeks. She pulled her body upright and placed both hands on her chest, focused on calming her breath until it felt natural. Hadley repositioned herself first to be kneeling then to a standing position. After a moment in place, she walked quietly, navigating around the known creaky spots, until she made it to her bed. She laid on top of her comforter, not bothering to tuck herself in, and fell into a bleak exhaustion.

Spiral of Uncertainty

Hadley woke up Monday morning feeling like she was buried under a pile of bricks. It took a few extra minutes of stretching before she got out of bed. She was nervous to go downstairs, after a harrowing night, but after glancing out her window and seeing an empty driveway, she felt relieved. *He must have left for an early job.*

She trudged downstairs and noticed a mess scattered across the kitchen. She recognized the irony of her father yelling at her over her accidental tiny mess when he had left behind a colossal one of his own. She quickly tidied the table and moved the dishes and tumbler into the sink. She washed them and set them on the drying rack to put away later. After sweeping the floors and wiping down the table and counter, she realized the bus would be arriving soon. She no longer had time for cereal so snagged a granola bar from the pantry on her way out. She would eat it on the walk to her bus stop; better than nothing.

***

School dragged for Hadley. Too preoccupied to worry about her slipping grades or lack of friends, she cycled through waves of doubt and giddiness. Her lungs compressed when she thought about having to see her dad later, only to crack a smile when she thought about seeing the horses again. *Would I have had this chance if Mom was still alive?* The thought stole her smile and left a sour burn in her stomach. She could barely hear her teachers.

If her father had shown up to last month's eighth grade parent-teacher conference, he would have learned that she stared vacantly out the window or into the distance more often than not. Her teachers would have shared with him their deepest condolences for his wife but also their concerns that Hadley's hand never sought to participate and her voice wavered when she spoke. It seemed no one heard Hadley - not teachers, nor friends, nor did she have an outlet at home. Hadley's teacher would have suggested that he look into the support of a grief counselor for the girl who had lost her mom and withdrawn deep into herself. Their concerns, however, would've fallen on deaf ears. Her father did not go to the conference, spending his time only in the bottles of dimly lit oblivion that made his life tolerable.

The final bell rang and Hadley tossed her books into her backpack on the way to the collection of buses waiting idly on energetic preteens. Weaving through the buses a slight smile poked through as she remembered her banter with Dorothy over cleaning poop. She thought about how her mom would've found it just as funny. She also thought about how her mom would've rolled up her sleeves to lend a hand. Perfect didn't even begin to describe her mom. Hadley approached her bus right as her excitement was cycling back to grief. Her emotions had been a rollercoaster all day, but, not wanting to get sucked into heartache, she sat in her seat and began to recount the steps required for cleaning a stall.

Hadley wasted no time getting back to the farm and walked directly to the horse shelter, knowing the work she'd have to complete. The barn doors were open, so she walked over the threshold and immediately spotted Dorothy. She was in the corner pulling fresh straw from the towering mound and creating smaller stacks. With Dorothy facing away from Hadley, she noticed a few sections of hair in Dorothy's pony tail still held a jet-black tinge. *That must have been her natural color. Pretty.* "Hi, Dorothy!"

"Hey, dear," Dorothy said as she turned around. "Did you get a snack after school? I can grab you some cookies I baked earlier today if you're hungry. You'll use up a lot of energy gettin' these stalls tidy." The question was laced in a consideration that Hadley wasn't expecting. Her mom would've also made sure she'd eaten. It was different with her dad since it seemed like he never cared much about her wellbeing. Just last night he screamed at her claiming she ate *his* food. "Hadley?"

"Oh, um, sorry..." Hadley shook away the fresh sting from the night before. "I didn't grab a snack, but I had a big lunch today. Maybe later, though. Thank you for the offer." Hadley felt guilty for lying but it was easier than the truth. She had hardly eaten since her morning granola bar. The acid in her stomach churned all day and the thought of eating was nauseating.

"Alright, dear. Well, you let me know if that changes. I made oatmeal raisin." Dorothy smiled and wiggled her eyebrows.

Hadley nodded and slipped on the spare pair of muck boots that Dorothy set aside for her after noticing her white Keds the other day.

Hadley had apologized and explained she didn't have any old shoes or boots but didn't mind getting her sneakers dirty. "Nonsense, dear. I have plenty of old boots layin' around. Just be careful walkin' in them as I reckon they'll be a size or so too big on ya." Hadley appreciated the generosity and was relieved she wouldn't have to hide muddy shoes from her father.

She and Dorothy spent the next two hours thoroughly cleaning all six stalls. As they progressed, Dorothy took on a smaller and smaller role, allowing Hadley to do the majority. At one point, Hadley looked up to see Dorothy sitting on a small hay bale. "It must be a relief for you to get a break," Hadley said as she continued to work.

"I try to push through, but it gets harder each week," she admitted. "I do what I hafta to keep this place runnin'. My spare change is spent on Jeremy runnin' the larger equipment from time to time, so the rest falls to me."

"That sounds exhausting."

"It sure is, but now I got some youthful energy to help me out."

Hadley smiled before grabbing some extra straw for the final stall.

Out of the corner of Hadley's eyes, she saw Dorothy's eyebrows furrow. She shifted nervously and quickly looked around trying to figure out what had displeased Dorothy. "Do the stalls look okay? I made sure to clean out all the wet straw and collected all of the manure in the wheelbarrow." Hadley pointed as she hurried through her words. "I just have to move this last pile around back where I laid the others. It might be a little heavy for me, but I can try. I don't know why I made this one so much fuller. More full. I'll make more trips next time. I'm sure this one is fine, though." Before Dorothy could respond, Hadley continued her spiral of uncertainty. "I scrubbed the water bowls really carefully, too, so the water should taste fresh. I wasn't sure if I put too much straw down for bedding. Um, so if it's too much, I can go back through and remove some." Hadley's eyes looked everywhere but at Dorothy's.

Dorothy watched the fragile girl. "Take a deep breath, dear. You did a wonderful job. It's such a tremendous relief to be able to take it easy today. These old bones move slower than they used to." Dorothy motioned for Hadley to take a seat next to her on the haystacks. She rotated her body to face Hadley and laid a hand gently on her knee. "I was just sitting here thinkin' that you should feel proud of yourself, dear. Cleanin' a stable ain't an easy task."

"I think I put too much straw in Butternut's stall..."

"Don't be silly. The stalls are perfect, dear." Dorothy's voice was steady and kind. Hadley slowly lifted her eyes to meet Dorothy's. She released the start of a smile, but it never fully spread. "It's time to get'ya onto a horse before the sun sets. First, I wanna hear'ya say it," Dorothy nudged.

"I'm sorry." Hadley lowered her gaze back to her feet.

"Don't be silly. That's not what I wanted to hear."

"It's not?"

"No, 'course not. You gotta say you worked hard and you're proud of yourself. You do that, and we go grab you a pony to sit on."

Hadley saw the challenge behind Dorothy's eyes. Feeling silly, but wanting to ride a horse, she nodded. "I worked hard... and I'm proud of myself."

"My, my, quieter than a church mouse, are we?" Dorothy teased.

This made Hadley's smile fully appear. "I worked hard, and I am proud of myself," she repeated, louder this time.

"Atta girl! That's a start, anyway. Now let's go find'ya a horse."

"Okay!"

"First, let's find a helmet for ya. I have a few over here. Hmmm," Dorothy looked at her collection before reaching for a medium-sized matte black helmet. "This oughta fit," Dorothy decided. Sure enough, when Hadley placed it on her head, it fit perfectly. She snapped the strap together under her chin and looked up at Dorothy with a smile. "Perfect! Now, can you grab the saddle hanging on the far left?" Dorothy pointed at a collection of saddles, in varying sizes. She kept a variety since in the warmer months she offered beginner riding lessons for some supplemental income.

Hadley walked to the wall and pointed toward the end at a chestnut-colored saddle with a black padded leather seat, weathered steel stirrups and a prominent horn. When Dorothy nodded, Hadley grabbed it and brought it back over. "This is heavier than I expected." Hadley did her best to hold the saddle in her tired arms.

"You got that right," Dorothy smiled. "I reckon you'll be slingin' that over your shoulder in no time if ya keep up the hard work in here." They walked to the entrance of the clean stables where Dorothy told Hadley to set the saddle until they brought a horse over.

"Dorothy?" Hadley summoned the little courage she had inside of her to get the next words out. "Do you think maybe I could ride Snow White? I mean any horse is okay, I don't mind... I just thought Snow White liked me best." Hadley was rambling again, afraid if she stopped talking she would be met with rejection.

Dorothy let out a soft laugh as she grabbed a bridle and happily obliged. "Well now, I had a feeling you'd pick my little beauty. That there saddle fits Miss Snow White perfectly. Let's find her, shall we?" Hadley and Dorothy walked into the fields, weaving between the roaming horse and cattle. Dorothy spent the brief walk explaining what a bridle was and how they'd secure it on Snow White. She explained how it could be used to guide the horse back to the barn so they could cinch the saddle. After that, Hadley would be able to use the step stool to help boost herself onto the horse. The conversation flowed easily as the duo approached and greeted the beautiful white horse, who was standing under a tree ready and waiting.

Walk Before You Canter

Hadley was beyond excited to be sitting on top of Snow White and watched closely as Dorothy secured the saddle and clipped a lead rope to the bridle. She was eager to learn, and hoped eventually she could set up and mount the horse on her own. Her feet sat comfortably in the stirrups, and she held the horn with both hands as she listened closely to Dorothy's explanation of what to do. "Okay, dear. Does it all make sense to you? It's important to feel confident 'cause a horse can tell if you're afraid or nervous and it could make them nervous, too."

"I think I got it all. How will I know if she is feeling nervous?"

"Well, horses can be hard to predict but I say if she starts to shake or tremble a bit you'll know. She could also plant herself in place and be nervous about walkin'. Butterscotch, on the other hand, takes off running when she's nervous. Lucky for you, Snow White is an extremely calm girl. If you treat her nicely and with respect, she should do the same right on back."

"Okay. Got it." Hadley made a mental note to always check that Snow White wasn't shaking or nervous.

"Snow White here is used to taking young'uns on rides during the summer so she should be okay."

"Are you ready to walk around?" Dorothy held the lead rope in her right hand and motioned with her left toward the surrounding land. She didn't have a designated corral since it was something Harold always meant to build but never had the time. When teaching lessons, Dorothy stuck to one general small area of the farm and so the horses have grown used to making their own circles when ridden. Snow White was a great horse for Hadley to be riding since she listened well and was patient. She also loved to navigate the beaten path surrounding the whole farm, but this is something that Hadley would have to wait to experience.

"Yes!" Hadley yipped out her response, filled with elation. She quickly placed her right hand over her mouth, eyes big and added, "Whoops, sorry... I have to remember to stay calm, right?"

"Yes, dear. Calm and loving is best. Best in life, really. But like I said, she's used to the little ones, so I reckon she can handle a little excitement."

"I can be calm!" Hadley laughed; fully aware she was anything but calm. She was ready to go.

"I'm sure you can, dear. Alright, I'm gonna hold on to the lead rope so that we can take it nice and slow. You go ahead and when you're ready give her a gentle little knock with your feet. Not too hard. She'll know it means to start." Hadley locked her eyes on Dorothy's and nodded her agreement. She wiggled her body slightly, to make sure she was secure and held the horn with both hands. She took a deep breath in and on exhale, she pressed her feet gently against Snow White's thighs. Just like that, they were moving.

Hadley gripped the horn tight, feeling her body tense up. She was afraid of falling off even though Snow White was walking quite slowly. Dorothy guided the pair by the lead rope as they made their way around the open land. After a few minutes, the tension melted from Hadley's body. Her shoulders dropped and her grip lightened. She felt comfortable and safe on top of the beautiful horse. She tested brief moments of lifting one hand off the horn. There was a slight breeze in the air enough to keep her hair behind her shoulders without blowing wildly.

Dorothy must have picked up on Hadley's ease because she gradually loosened her hold on the rope. "How's it feeling up there, Hadley?"

"Ohmigosh, this is so cool! I was secretly a little afraid, but this is *so* cool!" Hadley giggled and smiled wide.

"Want to try on your own?"

"Really?" Hadley's eyes widened, not used to this level of trust.

"Yes, dear. I can tell that Snow White already trusts'ya. I'm gonna take this rope off and leave ya go. Try not to kick up too much speed, my running days are long gone." Dorothy carefully unlatched the lead and reminded Hadley how to speed up, slow down, or stop. "All you, dear," Dorothy said, waving her on.

Hadley pressed her feet against Snow White again and they restarted their walk. *You got this.* Hadley's heart was pounding but her muscles remained relaxed. "Okay, Snow White. This is my very first ride so please be gentle with me. I think we're doing great. Don't you think so?" Hadley questioned the horse and almost expected a response. She giggled to herself and continued to talk quietly to the horse. Hadley eventually felt confident enough to signal the horse to increase their pace. She took a moment to remember the details about how to post trot. *Here we go,* Hadley thought.

Suddenly their pace doubled. *Ohmigosh, this is fast.* Hadley moved her body up and down in tandem with the horse's movements. It felt okay but she quickly grew afraid of this pace. *That's enough of that.* She pulled gently on the reins to slow back down. Back at a comfortable walk, she guided Snow White to turn left and back toward Dorothy. She impressed herself when the turn actually worked.

Hadley felt like a natural extension of the horse. She continued until she approached Dorothy and then successfully signaled for Snow White to stop. "Did you see that, Dorothy! Was that a trot? I felt like a rocketship!"

"Yes, it was," Dorothy chuckled. "A beautiful ride, overall. You did a great job guiding her to turn around." Hadley's smile grew as she stretched her body forward and extended her arm to pet Snow White's mane. "I really like her, she's amazing." Hadley worried and hoped Dorothy didn't mind that she was sharing her feelings. When she tried to express herself with her dad, she would be chastised or dismissed. She could feel the heat build in her cheeks as she straightened back up and avoided eye contact.

"That's good, dear. I really think she likes'ya, too. She wouldn't have listened so well otherwise." Dorothy's words eased Hadley's self-doubt. "We got about twenty minutes until I gotta tidy up. If'ya got the time, why don't you keep'on riding. Just keep it to an easy slow walk while my eyes are distracted. I'll flag'ya down when I need'ya to head toward the barn." Dorothy's offer was a question, but it sounded matter of fact to Hadley.

"Are you sure you don't mind?"

"Of course not, dear. I think Miss White will love it even more than you will. Pretty thing loves the attention." She smiled at Hadley and waved her into motion. Hadley watched as Dorothy started to walk back to the barn, but then turned around. She listened to Dorothy holler out a reminder to trust the process. Hadley paired a confident "got it" with a big smile as she guided the horse into the field. A few minutes into the walk, Hadley decided to practice stopping and starting with Snow White. She also worked on turning left and right, wanting to feel confident in her ability to communicate with Snow White.

Feeling the chill in the air, and noticing the sun start to dip, she redirected their walk back toward the barn and enjoyed their last few minutes together. She spent the time talking to the horse in hushed tones, sharing her inner thoughts as they moved through the field. Hadley felt in control and confident. She felt like a totally different girl while on the horse compared to at school or at home. She hadn't expected to talk to the horse as much as she was, or at all, but really enjoyed having the freedom to speak without judgment. She felt like this horse was the friend she'd been missing and just now realized she needed.

Looking up, Hadley spotted Dorothy waving at her from a distance. "Okay, Snow White, looks like our fun is over. This has been the absolute best day ever, pretty girl. Thank you for trusting me. I really needed this." Hadley removed a hand from the horn and gave Snow White a gentle rub next to the saddle. "I can't wait to come back," she whispered as they approached Dorothy at the barn and slowed to a stop. Dorothy guided them into the barn and had Snow White pause next to a small bundle of straw. She walked Hadley through how to safely dismount, instructing her to step down onto the straw to make it easier. Once Hadley reached the ground, she walked around to Snow White's muzzle. She placed her hand gently against the horse's snout and was surprised when she nuzzled into her hand. "I'll miss you too, girl."

"You won't need to miss her for long," Dorothy interrupted. "You're welcome to come back any day after school so'long as your dad's okay with it and you keep your grades up. Oh, and help me with the stable some'ore."

"I would love that! I really had a great time and didn't mind the cleaning part, either."

"Excellent. Well, you better head on home before it gets dark out. Make sure you tell your father I say hello. I'd love to meet him sometime if he's ever free."

"I'll let him know." A white lie that Hadley hoped would go undetected. She left feeling a sense of peace; her anxieties from earlier completely dissolved. Walking across the field, she paused to look back at the barn and noticed the dusky sky transition into a beautiful pink ombre as the sun started to set. Twisting forward again, she continued her walk back home. She sucked in a few big breaths of fresh autumn air before she ducked between the fence posts and continued her walk. She wasn't sure what tonight would bring, but for now she felt completely at ease.

***

Star Speckled Sky

Hadley forgot her worries on the back of a horse. Once she became comfortable, she started riding most days after school. It had been a particularly mild winter, so there were only three snowy days that she couldn't visit. Her time on the farm was really helping her balance the dread she felt while at home. Lately, even when her father wasn't home, the air still felt tense.

Since summer break started last week, she began to head straight from her bed over to Dorothy's. She'd grab a cereal bar on the way out the door, offering a half-hearted wave to her dad if he happened to be home. They usually didn't exchange any words and it was not uncommon for her wave to go unanswered. He never stopped her to ask where she was going so she eventually realized he must not care.

On the farm, Hadley loved to take on new responsibilities. She cleaned the stables, washed and brushed the horses, fed, and rode most of them. She sometimes helped feed and care for the dairy cows, though milking them was not her favorite thing to do. Hadley found the udders totally gross and classified the whole process as awkward. *Is this really how they get the milk that I add to my cereal?* She especially hated whenever she needed to clean the udders off before beginning to tug on them. Every so often an udder would have mud or poop on it that needed to be wiped off with a warm, wet towel to avoid contaminating the liquid. The practice was enough to have Hadley holding her breath for an entirely different reason – the smell! Whenever Dorothy asked for her help, though, she stepped up and never complained. It was important to not disappoint Dorothy.

Whenever she could, she stuck to the horses. Her favorite horse was Snow White. Hadley loved to run her fingers through the horse's chocolate mane, which laid like satin across the top of the beauty's pale gray coat. Snow White looked as majestic as her name suggested and Hadley chose her for her rides whenever possible. When inside the stable, she spent extra time grooming her and brushing out the mare's head-of-hair, which reminded Hadley of her mother's stunning locks, at least before the cancer changed the texture. Before the life shattering diagnosis, her mother's hair was a waterfall of dark brown, hand-spun silk and the Pink Ladies often teased her over its constant perfection. "Blue eyes and silk for hair," they'd playfully scoff. A few times Hadley noticed the women appeared jovial while poking fun, but would also subconsciously finger their own dull, dry, or frizzy strands. Hadley never blamed them since she also tended to stare in the mirror, comparing herself to her mother's effortless perfection.

Hadley wondered if she loved this horse more than the others because of this connection. Regardless of deeper meaning, she grew dependent on their rides. When she could, she'd bring a peppermint candy or an apple, knowing how much Snow White loved a surprise treat. Over time Hadley slowly learned to trot and cantor without Dorothy's supervision. They would travel around for hours at a time, sometimes staying within the fenced in fields, though Hadley preferred to travel along the narrow dusty roads outside of the farm.

There were days she would talk to the horse like a friend and others as if Snow White was her therapist. She shared stories of the time spent with her parents during her early childhood and how much fun she used to have with her mom and her dad. Her memories were always filled with a light that was now missing from her life. She always felt like this special horse understood exactly what she said. With Snow White, Hadley breathed easy and smiled often, slowly starting to feel like herself again.

Once or twice a week, Hadley rode down the hill to her house. It was a less than five-minute trot and Snow White seemed to know the path by heart. Occasionally Hadley would see her dad's rusted old Buick in the driveway. *I wonder why he's home again,* she often thought, worried he would lose his job. On their walk back to the farm, Hadley talked openly with Snow White about her growing concerns and rambled on about all the possibilities for what could happen if her father lost his job. She wondered how easy it would be to find a new one and what it would mean for their house.

***

One unusually balmy July afternoon, Dorothy told Hadley that she was expecting company at the end of the week and asked her not to come by on Friday, but that she was fine to come back over on Monday morning. It was only one day, but after getting accustomed to cutting across the grassy field each morning, Hadley felt so disappointed. She would miss watching the rising sun break across the blushed sky as she traveled through the morning dew. It was her favorite way to start her days in the summer and she would miss it on Friday and even more so once school started back in the fall.

Hadley wanted to ask if she could instead come over on Saturday, but knew the weekends were when Dorothy and Kimberly gave riding lessons to beginner youth. She wondered if Jeremy and Kimberly were the guests that were visiting Dorothy. She never heard her mention anyone else but also didn't want to pry. She of course acted understanding of Dorothy's request and promised to be back bright and early Monday morning.

On her walk home that day, however, her mind rattled. She wondered if her dad would be working Friday or if she'd be home all alone. She wondered if she would sleep in or if her body would wake up thinking it was time to leave. She wondered if the day would go by as quickly as she hoped. Would the Pink Ladies show up that night? They used to show up every Friday, but after several awkward run-ins with her drunk father, they started to show up less and less. She wondered the whole way home.

***

Hadley woke up the next morning bright and early. She almost jumped out of bed to get changed before remembering her agreement with Dorothy. Having nowhere to go on a Friday morning, she perched in bed to relax. Her birthday was tomorrow, but she didn't expect her dad to remember or acknowledge it. She was too embarrassed to tell Dorothy about the day, not wanting her to think it was meant to be a guilt trip. Hadley planned to take Snow White on an extra fun ride on Monday in place of a Friday celebration. Since she was stuck home for a long weekend, she decided she'd pick a new book from her mom's bookcase to start reading. She pulled out *The Bluest Eye* by Toni Morrison and *Speedboat* by Renata Adler. After reading the descriptions, she decided to start with *The Bluest Eye*, opting for a full novel over the collection of vignettes. She hoped this book would take her through the weekend.

Hadley was soon invested in the main character, Pecola, who was only a few years younger than she was. As the book unfolded, Hadley learned Pecola's father was an abusive alcoholic. Curiously, the words on the pages started to feel familiar. She started drawing parallels to her own life when suddenly she heard the distinct sound of an engine shutting off. With the slamming of the front door, she knew her father was home. *Wait, why was he home?* She glanced at her alarm clock to see it was only 1:15.

Soon Hadley heard music echoing off the living room walls. A half hour after that, she heard a shattering noise and a loud thud. Hadley quickly marked her page in the book and stood up, once again forced to make sure her dad was okay. She started moving, thinking it would be nice if for once he was checking on her. She walked downstairs and noticed one of the living room lights was broken on the floor. That explained the noise. Her dad was lying on the couch with a bottle of Jim Beam in one hand and his other hand draped across his face. At first, she wasn't sure if he was asleep or dead, but a loud groan reassured her that he was alive. Hadley walked over and turned down the stereo before shifting her eyes back to her father.

"Dad? What are you doing?" she asked hesitantly. "Why aren't you at work... it's like 2 o'clock." Hadley was as confused as she was concerned. She started to think about all the days that she had ridden past her house during the school year and saw his car in the driveway. *Is this what he leaves work early to do?*

"Leave me alone, Had. I was asleepin' before your loudmouth woke me. Wh-why do you care, Had-ley? Why are you here, shouldn't you be out, God knows where?" His voice was harsh but his words slurred sloppily together. Hadley didn't understand what was going on. She grew up around drinking, but not like this. When the Pink Ladies drank, they had blushed cheeks and contagious laughter. They would joke and sing and were always happy. They didn't act like this. She even remembered when her dad would come home from grabbing drinks with his friends. He sometimes had a short fuse, but not often. He was still his normal self – a self she barely remembered now. Now he was distant or mean, sometimes, somehow, he'd be both. It was normal to find him in a drunken stupor by sunset, but not by midday. He was getting worse as the days went on and she no longer thought it was from grief.

Hadley reluctantly went into the kitchen and got her father a cold glass of water. By all definitions, she was a young girl, but in moments like these she felt like she was the parent, not him. It was hard for her to process, especially since all she really needed was to feel a parent's love again. She brought the water out to her father and placed it on the floor next to the couch. She grabbed the broom next to clean up the shards of glass from the broken lamp. "What happened, dad?"

"I was swatting a damn fly." Michael said, sounding annoyed that she couldn't figure that out herself. Once the mess was cleaned up, Hadley retreated to her room. She rested her head against her window with a blanket draped around her. Every so often she heard her father yelling indiscriminately but she never got up to hear what he had to say. Instead she sat there and stared at the night sky. She never picked back up *The*

Bluest Eye, knowing it would be too difficult of a story for her to read immediately following her father's outburst. Tomorrow she would pick it back up only to learn of Pecola's dreadful rape. She'd shed a tear for the girl and a tear for herself, relieved for not having read this scene the night before.

For tonight, she eventually grabbed a tattered soft cover version of *Romeo and Juliet* from her mother's three-shelf bookcase. She used to beg her mom to read it over and over at bedtime, entranced by the way her mom used different voices to bring the story to life. She walked back to the bay window in her tiny bedroom and settled in to read what was one of her favorites. She read it so many times that she could probably recite it from memory. This was what she needed tonight – a book with familiar phrases and definitely no unexpected traumas or heartbreak to spin her already enervated mind.

Shifting her eyes from the book to the view outside her large window, Hadley tried her best to mimic the feelings of a young Juliet. Despite her efforts she knew it was impossible. Still, she tried.

> *"Give me my Romeo; and, when*
> *he shall die, take him and cut*
> *him out in little stars, and he will*
> *make the face of heaven so fine that*
> *all the world will be in love with*
> *night, and pay no worship to the*
> *garish sun."*

Would she look out her window to the star freckled sky and see her love scattered in the brightest of lights? Would the sun the next morning seem dull just as it did to Juliet? She feared never finding the type of Romeo she often read about. She sometimes wondered if this is how her mom had felt about her dad. She didn't think so. From Hadley's perspective her parents were happy together, but happier apart. Her mom seemed happiest with the Pink Ladies and her dad with his coworkers at the local hangout. At such a young age, Hadley assumed this was normal. Marriages were functional and friends were loving and fun. Every day when her dad got home from work, instead of her mom rushing to the door to greet him in the excited way she did when her group of friends arrived each week, she would smile, pat her hand on his chest, and take his thermos to the kitchen. It was functional. Was Shakespeare exaggerating?

Hadley was content with the thought that maybe her greatest love was already scattered across the sky. While her parents may not have shown Shakespeare level love with one another, Hadley experienced a love so deep with her mom that she knew it would never be matched. Her mom was her idol, her sun and her stars. She liked to think that the bright lights outside her window were her mom twinkling down on her. Maybe it was her mom who made up the stars. *I could live with that.* She curled up against the window and closed her eyes.

Fourteen Candles

The next morning, Hadley was woken by the sun pouring through the window her head was pressed against. She must have fallen asleep reading *Romeo and Juliet*. She scooted to a sitting position, rubbed her eyes, and reached her arms toward opposite walls as she rotated her core slightly back and forth. She did her best to stretch out the kinks, after a cramped but full night of sleep. Making quick work of cleaning up her space, she decided to head downstairs for a bowl of cereal. She almost forgot today was her birthday until she noticed a gift bag, a wrapped box, and a card sitting on the kitchen table. Hadley stopped in her tracks when she noticed it, and glanced up to see her dad standing there with a mug in his hands. He leaned against the counter and looked right at her with a sad smile on his face. "Happy birthday, Had."

"I... um, I didn't think you'd remember," Hadley stuttered.

"I remembered." Her father sighed through a clenched jaw.

"Right, of course. I didn't mean to make it sound like you'd forget, dad. I just meant..." Hadley paused. She wasn't sure what to say. She didn't want to anger her father, but she was being honest when she assumed he'd forget. He seemed to accept her pause for what it was.

"I know. Listen... I know this is your first birthday without your mom and well..." his eyes fell shamefully to the floor. He knew how much he had been failing his daughter but wasn't sure how to pull himself out of the hole he fell into. He didn't know what to say or do next. If Hadley's mother was alive there would've been pancakes on the table, balloons tied to the chair, music in the background, and pure joy in the air. Today the air felt stale. "Anyway, sit. Let's check these gifts out."

Hadley cautiously walked to the table and sat down. She watched her father take a sip of coffee and simultaneously suppress a hiccup. She looked curiously behind him and noticed the coffee pot seemed untouched. He either filled his mug and promptly cleaned the pot, *yeah right*, or he wasn't drinking coffee. She returned her eyes to her father and gave him an uneasy smile before she looked at the gifts in front of her. She gasped. "This...w-wait, this is mom's handwriting." Her statement came out as a whisper as she picked up the envelope and held it between her hands. She stared at it for what felt like eternity. She looked up at her dad who nodded in her direction. He took a sip of his coffee but even though the mug covered his face Hadley swore she saw a mist in his eyes.

She slowly opened the envelope to find a Hallmark card inside. The front of the card had a floral bouquet and read *Gathered these wishes especially for you...* The sentiment continued inside, to the right of the fold. *...for happiness, good times, and dreams that come true.* Hadley hadn't noticed the printed words, though, because as soon as she opened the card her eyes landed on beautifully swoopy cursive handwriting.

Dear Haddie,

I can't believe you are 14 now! I am sorry I can't scoop you into the biggest hug and help you celebrate. I hope you know

how much you mean to me. You will always be the most
cherished part of my life and my greatest accomplishment.
I know how hard this past year must have been for you. I
hope you are finding ways to keep happy. Please don't be sad
over me. Look around, my pretty girl. Wherever you go, I
go. I will live on in your heart forever. Please remember to
smile. Here is one last gift from me, my sweetheart. I love
you completely. Happy Birthday.

Love, Mom
P.S. take care of your dad for me.

Hadley read the card over and over as a few tears gently trickled down her cheeks. Her pointer finger brushed gently over the ink, wishing for something, anything, that would bring her mom back. She finally set it down as carefully as she would a glass egg. She shook her head at the last part of her mom's note. *If only you knew, Mom.* She looked up at her father, who was pulling out the chair to sit down across from her. He took the cream-colored box patterned with orange and brown flowers and pushed it across the table to her. "I promised I would give it to you today."

Hadley stared. "Should I open it?" Hadley was suddenly very nervous. This is the last gift from her mom. Ever. She felt her heart race and her stomach flip. She wasn't sure if she should open it or leave it preserved for a while longer.

"Of course... that's what gifts are for. You know your mom, Had. Always thinking ahead." His voice cracked slightly. Hadley nodded. She gently opened the lid and parted the white tissue paper which revealed her mom's green and teal patterned dress. Hadley's favorite. She pulled it from the box, bringing the material up to her face. She took a deep breath in, unraveling into the fading scent of her mother. This gift is one she would cherish forever. She couldn't wait until she grew into her body enough to be able to wear it.

"I loved when Mom wore this dress," She sighed. "I always used to try it on and walk around the house pretending to be her. It used to crack Mom up, probably because of how much this dress drowned me. She used to tell me to slow down and that one day I'll be all grown up and the dress would fit then. I wanted that day to come so badly because I just wanted to be like her. She was so beautiful."

"You're the ivory copy of her, Hads."

Hadley looked up from the dress, her eyes meeting her father's. She couldn't remember the last time she opened up to him let alone the last time he said something soft hearted. She was used to harsher words - if any at all. "I don't know about that, Dad," she smiled softly. "I'm not sure I'll ever be that pretty."

"She stole my breath, that's for sure. The most loving woman I've ever met. I'm actually not sure why she put up with me sometimes." He let out a low-spirited chuckle. Hadley smiled at her father, not wanting to comment on his admission. "Anyway," he shook his head and looked back at Hadley. "This one's from me." He pushed the gift bag across the table and told her to open it.

Hadley pulled the tissue paper out of the bag, setting it delicately on the table. She saw something shiny inside and as she lifted it out, she was surprised by what she held. It was a carved alabaster horse figurine that stood maybe 3 inches tall. The translucent white horse felt smooth against her fingers and looked to her a bit like Snow White. "I love it, dad, really," she said with a genuine smile.

"I know I haven't been the parent you're used to having, but I do notice when you're gone. Mostly, anyway." He hid his shame behind another long sip from his mug. Hadley tensed up immediately. This was the moment she'd been waiting for. This was the moment her dad snapped. "Dad –"

"I just mean I know you've been hangin' out at Wellington Farm." Hadley let out a shaky breath, still waiting for the shoe to drop. "I saw you riding a white horse on my way home from work one day. I wasn't sure it was you, actually, but the next day I saw you again."

"Oh," Hadley shifted her eyes around the room, not sure where to look. "Yeah, that's Snow White. She's actually a light gray," she said dumbly.

Her father nodded at her but didn't press her to share any details. "I didn't know what to get ya and then I saw this at a store in town." He was pointing at the figurine in Hadley's hand.

"It's really neat, dad." She set the gift down on the table and started to push her seat back to stand up and hug him. Before she stood, her dad continued talking.

"Hey, there's something else in that bag for ya."

"Oh, whoops! I didn't notice. This was more than enough already..." He waved his daughter off, motioning her to check inside. Hadley peered into the bag and sure enough she spotted a photograph that was leaning against the side of the bag. How had she not noticed? She gingerly lifted out the faded black and white polaroid. She looked closely at the teenager standing next to a beautiful spotted horse. "Is this Mom?"

"Yeah, when she was sixteen. That's the year we met." Leaning back in his seat, he stretched his arms out before continuing. "She grew up in Montana down the road from a riding arena. Her uncle worked there in the stables and so she spent most of her summers on the ring."

"She never talked about horses..." Hadley desperately searched her brain for any memory of horses.

"Nah, she wouldn't have. She had moved on from that part of her life." Hadley watched as her father picked up his mug before noticing it was empty and setting it back down. She saw his eyes bounce to the bar cart then to Hadley then back down at the table. "I, uh, I think once we got married and moved up here, life changed. We got married young, made new friends, made *you*. And, well, horses never really fit in." Hadley nodded. There were a million questions swirling in her brain, but no words came out. She wondered why her mom never visited Dorothy's farm. Maybe it was too hard for her. Hadley stared at the photo when her father suddenly cleared his throat and pushed his chair back so he could stand up.

Feeling the shift in energy, Hadley also stood up. "Thanks again, dad. I love my gifts." She debated approaching him for a hug, but he was standing at the bar cart adding whiskey to his mug – probably what he was drinking the whole time. He kept his back to her while he waved halfheartedly in the air. Hadley quietly grabbed her gifts, careful to not mess anything up, and carried them to her room.

Once upstairs, she set the carved alabaster horse on her dresser. She slid the box with the dress under her bed, anxious for the day it would fit. She then climbed on top of her bed, old photo in hand. She spent the next twenty minutes mesmerized. She decided her mom definitely skipped over the awkward teen years entirely. She was less curvaceous in her youthful body, but her beauty was almost unbelievable. Hadley stood up and walked to her dresser. She rested the photo carefully against her new figurine. It slid down a few times, but eventually she got the angle right for it to stay put. Stepping back, she admired the set up. She grabbed the book she started the day prior and retreated to her bay window. She sat for a few minutes against the panels daydreaming about her mom. She felt even more connected now that she knew her mom loved horses. She couldn't wait to get back to the farm to tell Snow White all about her birthday. Satisfied with her morning, she settled in and opened *The Bluest Eye* to the earmarked page.

She spent the rest of her birthday paging slowly through the devastating novel. *I guess things could be worse.* She was thankful her father had never laid a hand on her, even if his words did pack a powerful punch. She couldn't imagine going through what Pecola had. She smiled thinking about this morning's conversation with her dad. Maybe he was turning a corner and would be nicer now that she was getting older. *Maybe.*

Come, Sit Down

"Hey, Snow White," Hadley crooned as she walked through the stables on Monday morning. She brushed her hand along the stalls of the other horses, garnering attention from all, but her eyes were locked on the beauty at the end. The petite horse began to pitter her hooves in growing excitement as Hadley approached her stall. She giggled as she reached her hand up and gave the horse a gentle rub on the neck. "Happy to see you too, Pretty." There was so much Hadley wanted to tell Snow White before she released the herd into the fields. She had fallen easily into the routine of shepherding the horses out of the stable, thoroughly cleaning the stalls, and then wandering about until she found Snow White for a quick ride before sunset. On occasion, she would keep Snow White tied up to the fence while she cleaned so she could start their ride right away instead of searching the field for her. Most often, she let the horse wander around with the others until she was ready.

The last few weeks, she saw Dorothy less. She was proud of how much Dorothy must have trusted her with the maintenance and care of the horses and their home. With time, and much reassurance, Hadley also learned to trust herself and be proud of her work. She figured Dorothy was in the house or over by the cows today since she was on her own in the stables. "Snowy, I know I have to turn you all out to the field, but guess what?" She paused as the horse let out a friendly huff. "Saturday was my birthday, but don't tell Dorothy! I didn't want to tell her and make her feel bad since she was so busy this weekend." Hadley was twirling the horse's silky mane as she spoke. "Anyway, my dad actually remembered. I was shocked. And not only that but he got me a gift. Omigosh, first he gave me this box and it was actually from my mom! Not in a spooky way, just that she had thought all those months ahead and wrapped up my favorite dress of hers. Oh, I would swim in it now, Snowy, but one day I'll look just as beautiful as she always looked. Well, maybe not *as* beautiful..."

The horse interrupted Hadley's monologue with a gentle snort. It was as if Snow White was disagreeing with her self-doubt. Hadley smiled as she rubbed Snow White's neck in appreciation. "Okay, okay. Anyway, my dad got me a gift. When I opened it, it was this beautiful little white horse made from stone. It looks just like you; it's perfect. I set it in my bedroom so when I look at it, I can think of you." Hadley had a big smile on her face, loving her time with Snow White. She decided to focus on this part of her birthday, reluctant to admit her dad drank himself into another stupor. "Anyway, Snowy, let's get you and the others outside so I can start cleaning." She detangled her fingers from Snow White's mane and reached toward the stable latch. She opened the gate and let the horse walk freely while she progressed around the stable guiding the others out one at a time. Once the barn was empty, she walked to the first stall and got to work.

***

Once the stalls were cleaned, Hadley began her walk into the field, bridle in hand, eager to find Snow White, who was usually over by the large tree midfield, so they could enjoy a belated birthday ride. She spotted the stunner of a horse in the field and headed in her direction. Her steps quickened as she grew excited to tell Snow White about how her mom also loved horses; a fact she forgot to share earlier.

Halfway through the field Hadley paused when she heard Dorothy holler out her name. She pivoted to see Dorothy waving from the front porch of her small rancher. Hadley waved back, uncertain if she should change directions or continue deeper into the field. As if reading her mind, Dorothy called out, "Can you come on over for a few minutes before your ride, dear?" Hadley smiled and nodded her head in agreement, though deep down she was a little disappointed. She was looking forward to her time with Snow White, but shifted directions toward the house so she wouldn't upset Dorothy. She set the bridle down on the small front porch before walking inside.

"Come, come, sit down. I'll grab us some sweet tea and be right over."

Hadley slipped off her shoes near the door and walked to the kitchen table. She settled in and watched Dorothy move from the fridge to the counter. Lately Hadley spent the majority of her time focused on the barn or out in the field, so this was the first quiet moment she had with her in a few weeks. Now that Hadley was really looking, she suddenly felt guilty. *Was her back always that hunched? Did she always move that slowly?*

"So, um, how have you been? How was your weekend?"

"Well, dear, that's actually why I called you in." Dorothy carried over two glasses of cold sweet tea, handing one off to Hadley before sitting down.

Hadley's stomach immediately tightened. Feeling her anxiety build, she picked up her glass and took a giant gulp of the icy drink. "Oh, um, is everything okay?"

"Yes, dear, I don't mean to worry ya like that." Dorothy waved the air between them. "I just wanted to let'ya know of a change comin' soon on the farm."

"A change?"

"Yes." Dorothy's eyes had a wetness to them, but her soft smile remained. "This weekend I had an old friend of mine come visit. He's much younger than me... probably 'round your fathers age actually."

Hadley nodded, waiting for the bad news. It was always bad news.

"Anyway, he's also a farmer. His property is two counties over. We came to a deal this weekend where he's gonna buy my cows. Now before you panic, the horses aren't goin' anywhere. I know you don't spend much time with the cows, but I didn't want you to get alarmed seeing random haulers. The cows are startin' to become too much work for me. I think they'll have much fuller lives over with Daniel."

"Oh." Hadley wasn't sure how to react. She was relieved to know the horses are staying but wondered for how long. "Is there anything else I can be doing to help you out?"

"Oh please, Hadley, you're already the rock around here. If it weren't for your hard work and love in the main barn, I mighta had to sell them horses, too. You're the reason they are so content here at this little old lady's farm."

Hadley smiled as she listened.

"I just wanted you to know, dear. You're an important part of this farm so you deserve to know the good and the bad. And hey, this means I won't need to trick ya into milkin' them anymore."

Hadley let out a soft laugh.

"Anyway, you'll see him come and go over the next few weeks and he'll collect the cows with his trailers at the start of fall. Just the cows."

"I understand. I'll miss watching them roam the fields, but I'm really glad the horses can stay. I promise I'll keep taking great care of them and their stalls."

"Oh, I don't doubt that. Speaking of horses, dear, don't you have a date with one of them?" With that, Dorothy collected their glasses and slowly walked them to the sink.

"Is there anything I can help with first? I can do the dishes," Hadley felt uneasy about walking away from Dorothy. She didn't want her to think she was selfish or uncaring.

"I might be old and slow, dear, but I can handle a few dishes. Go on, now. Snow White is probably looking for you." Dorothy smiled and practically shooed her out the door. What Hadley didn't see was after she walked away, Dorothy set the glasses down slowly in the red enameled cast iron sink, dipped her head, and closed her eyes. She allowed herself one moment of pause before she lifted her head back up and started to wash the glasses. A few tears slipped free in the process, a silent tribute to her long life lived despite the changes soon to come.

Meanwhile, outside, Hadley collected Snow White's bridle and walked into the field, deaf to the surrounding nature as her mind spiraled with what ifs. Now that she saw how feeble Dorothy was becoming and knew the cows would be leaving, she worried what the future might hold.

She didn't realize she was holding her breath until she approached Snow White. Meaning to offer her a friendly greeting, she instead let out a breathy sigh as the trapped air finally released from her lungs. She placed a hand on Snow White, resting her head on the horse's side, and collected herself. She softly patted the horse then secured the bridle. Taking a deep breath in, she guided her companion in silence toward the barn where she would attach the saddle and climb on, using her usual straw stack for leverage. Once steadied, they took off into a steady trot. Hadley completely forgot to tell Snow White about how her mom once rode horses, too. Instead, the duo silently navigated the open fields, which allowed the fresh air to surround Hadley, granting her solace.

***

Hadley walked home quietly; head slung low. She walked inside, noticing the living room was empty but *Simple Man* was playing from the stereo. As she slipped her shoes off in the entryway, she saw her father walking in from the hallway. He swayed against the wall slightly before he walked toward the couch with tunnel vision. The drink in his hand sloshed when he plopped onto the cushion. "Great song, in'it?"

"Yeah. Lynyrd Skynyrd, right?" Hadley took a seat on the chair opposite the couch.

"Yep."

Hadley fiddled with the hem of her shirt, trying to muster some confidence. She could really go for a treat after the news Dorothy had shared. After the amenable birthday she had on Saturday and the calm Sunday that followed, Hadley was hoping her dad's better mood was here to stay, despite the glaze in his eyes. Once the song ended, she decided to go for it. "Do you think we could order pizza?"

Silence.

"With it being my birthday the other day and all, I thought maybe we could order a small pizza to split. As a treat."

"Was Saturday not enough for you?"

"It was great," Hadley replied quickly.

"And now you need pizza on top of that?"

"I just thought it would be fun since we normally just eat the freezer stuff."

"Too high and mighty for a frozen meal? Suddenly you're entitled to make plans with *my money?*"

So much for finding comfort in a hot slice of pizza. "You're right. I'm sorry. I'll go get dinner started for us instead."

Hadley's father nodded dramatically, his neck as functional as a baby's, before settling his head against the back of the couch. His eyes closed and he tapped the fingers on his free hand along to the music that filled the otherwise quiet house.

Yesterday and Forever Ago

When Hadley approached the fence, she noticed multiple cattle haulers set on the gravel drive attached to Dorothy's farm. Picking up her pace, she ducked between the fence posts, and pivoted toward the house instead of following her normal path toward the barn. She knew this day was coming, but her stomach still churned with sadness for Dorothy, knowing how big a change it will be to have the cows leave. Hadley also selfishly worried that the horses would be next. Ever since Dorothy sat her down, she had been trying, and failing, to imagine what life without Snow White might look like.

She walked into the house, slipping her shoes off by the front mat, and moved toward the kitchen. "Dorothy?" Her voice bounced around the narrow room. She continued looking around the small rancher's main rooms until she determined Dorothy was not there.

"Oh, duh," she mumbled to herself, realizing Dorothy was probably out with the cows. She quickly slid her feet back into her shoes, securing the door behind her as she walked out.

Walking toward the cow enclosure, Hadley felt lousy with guilt. She spent the walk searching her memories for changes in Dorothy. Had she slowed down? Yes. Was the arch in her back more pronounced? Yes. Had her positivity and uplifting demeanor changed? Definitely not.

She worried that Dorothy was hiding the effects of aging from her. She was so preoccupied with her own home life struggles that she hadn't paid close enough attention to her friend and how she was doing. Hadley heard voices as she approached the west side of the farm where the cows reside.

"These are some of the best dairy cows on the whole east coast so don't go gettin' any ideas, Daniel," Dorothy jokingly chastised.

"No ma'am, no ideas. I promise I will treat these cows as my own. My current herd will be plenty welcoming, I'm sure. Ranger, my blue heeler, will be the most excited, I imagine." The response came from a deep but gentle voice. He sounded younger than Hadley expected since she had envisioned someone as prematurely aged and curmudgeonly as her father. When she rounded the corner she saw the total opposite. He easily could be around her father's age but he was healthy and bright where her father was beaten down and dull. Wearing well-fitted jeans with a thick leather belt and brass buckle, dark brown boots, and a tucked in plain white t-shirt, Daniel leaned against an old wooden support beam showcasing an easy smile.

"Ma'am is my mama," Dorothy retorted right as Hadley came into view. She winked at Hadley who was looking between them with a nervous smile.

"Right." Daniel said through a chuckle as he followed Dorothy's line of sight over to Hadley. "This must be the amazing Hadley I heard so much about." Hadley's eyes went wide. *He knows me?*

"Well yes, of course," Dorothy confirmed. "This ray of sunshine is who saved my horses."

"Wait... I, what?" Hadley stammered.

"Come on in here, dear. This here is Daniel. He's bringing the cows to their new home today."

Hadley walked up next to Dorothy, suddenly overly aware of her sweaty palms and responded in a quiet tone. "Hi, Daniel. It's, um, nice to meet you."

"And yes, dear," Dorothy interjected. "You saved my horses. I just can't handle this farm on my own and I can't afford to bring in Jeremy to help more. You are the lifeline I needed with keepin' those horse stalls spic 'n span." There was a mist to Dorothy's eyes that her big smile could not hide.

"Oh, I mean I don't do much. I probably could be helping a lot more if I wasn't always off riding the horses," Hadley's eyes focused on a stray piece of straw on the floor as she rambled on. "I'm surprised you haven't told him I've been taking advantage of the whole situation..."

Dorothy smiled at Daniel before saying, "see, I told you she was a whirlwind." She shifted her gaze to Hadley, placing a wrinkled hand on her shoulder. "You sell yourself short. I thought we were workin' on that. You do a stellar job in the stables and them horses need to be ridden for the exercise, so that's just as helpful." Hadley looked up and nodded at Dorothy, wanting to believe her. "If you weren't here to help, Daniel would've been getting an even better deal today."

Hadley smiled and looked over to Daniel. "Um, do you need help moving the cows toward the haulers? I saw them out front."

"I should be just fine, Miss Hadley. I'll let you get to the horses, but I know where to find'ya if I need any help. How does that sound?"

"Okay, sounds good. It was nice to meet you." She shifted toward Dorothy, lowering her voice, before continuing. "I'll stop by the house after I'm done with the stables, okay?"

"Yes, dear. If Snow White allows it, that sounds quite nice."

***

Hadley took extra care today with cleaning the horse stables. While she always did a thorough job, she felt doubly responsible today. She never realized she was the sole reason the horses weren't also sold. After making sure the stables were clean and the horses were peacefully wandering the open fields, she redirected toward the house. By now the haulers would be full, the cow barn empty, and Daniel long gone.

Hadley walked through the front door in the same manner she had earlier in the day. She slipped her shoes off by the mat and walked into the kitchen as she called Dorothy's name. Unlike earlier, this time she heard a response. "I'll be right out, dear. Have a seat." Was that a sniffle Hadley heard? She wasn't sure how Dorothy would be doing after the cows left, which is why she wanted to stop in to visit. Dorothy appeared moments later with a forced smile on her face and an apron around her waist.

Hadley took a seat at the table while she watched as Dorothy busied herself rolling cookie dough and arranging the balls of batter on an old cooking sheet. She reached down to pet one of the cats that had approached her even though she never knew who was who with the barn cats. Dorothy's nervous energy filled the room and it made Hadley's stomach sink. Dorothy put the tray of cookies in the oven before wiping her hands on her apron and turning to face Hadley. "Let me get us some tea and then we can catch up, dear."

Silence filled the air for a moment before Hadley gained the confidence to speak. "Thank you. The cookies smell so good already." She did her best to sound positive. Dorothy smiled at her as she set two glasses of iced sweet tea onto the table. She settled into the chair opposite of Hadley and let out a slow exhale before placing her hands on the table.

"Well now, that's that, I guess," Dorothy decided.

"How are you?"

"Oh well, I'm just fine, dear. Just fine."

"Really?" Hadley pressed, knowing there had to be more to Dorothy's feelings than she was sharing. She had cows before Hadley was even born, so selling them must've been hard.

"Shoo, dear. When did you get so perceptive?"

"I'm definitely not *that*, I don't think so. I'm not sure if I know what that means but I know this has to be hard. I get caught up with my stuff and with Snow White... and well, I forget that other people can be going through things, too." Hadley's eyes searched the room.

"It's okay to be focused on your own stuff, dear."

"I know... but I want to focus on your stuff today. So, are you okay?" Hadley watched as Dorothy took a long sip of her tea. She wasn't used to speaking up and was afraid Dorothy was annoyed. She pressed her fingertips together nervously and was about to apologize for overstepping, when she saw Dorothy's shoulders drop.

"I'm about as good as you can imagine, dear." Hadley nodded for her to continue while anxiously wiping at the water droplets forming on the outside of her tea glass. "It's hard to explain. Life is weird. One day I'm married to the love of my life and we're closing on this farmland. Young an'in love. Livin' our dreams out. We never could have kids so we poured our love into them animals and into eachother. Days go by and suddenly I'm a widower. A few more days and somehow my bones are all crickety and slow and it's all too much to keep up with."

Hadley nodded. "Time is weird. I feel like one day my mom was here and then suddenly she wasn't, and I can't even believe it's been a year and a half already. It feels like yesterday and forever ago at the same time."

"That's a keen observation on life, dear. That's exactly right... yesterday and forever ago." Dorothy and Hadley sat quietly at the table for a few moments, each drinking their tea and letting the time pass. When Hadley sat mutely with her father it felt tense and stressful, but here with Dorothy it felt comfortable. The oven timer eventually broke the silence. Dorothy pushed herself up from the table, grabbed an oven mitt off the counter and pulled out the baking sheet. The rich smell of melted chocolate chips filled the room. Dorothy set the tray aside allowing the cookies to cool down but first lifted two onto a plate. She brought the warm cookies to the table and sat back down. Hadley was entranced by the sweet, nutty smell of the cookies before her. "Oh wow, Dorothy, these look incredible."

"Normally I'd let them cool down first, but I say today calls for some ooey gooey." She put one of the cookies on a napkin before pushing the plate in front of Hadley. They both broke off a piece of their cookies and began to enjoy the treat. Sighs of comfort washed over both of them as they looked across the table and laughed.

"These taste even better than they smell." Hadley covered her mouth once she realized she should've swallowed before she spoke.

"There are no manners when it comes to fresh cookies, dear." They laughed again. Once they finished eating they rotated between enjoying the silence and sharing bits and pieces of their lives. Dorothy admitted to Hadley how comforting it's been to have her around. "It gets quiet 'round here without my Harold and without any grand nieces or nephews to dote on. The cows kept me busy when it got too quiet. "

"I don't mind the quiet." *It's better than dad's yelling.* "There's no other kids in my family, either. At least none that I know about. I think both of my parents were only children, just like me."

"Harold and I, too. What're the odds?" Dorothy smiled.

"Did you ever wish you had a sibling growing up?"

"I'm quite sure at some point I did. Though it does no good to wish about things outta your control."

Hadley nodded, not wanting to admit just how many wishes she'd been making about things she had no control over.

"It's been a true delight to have you 'round." Dorothy said, interrupting Hadley's thoughts. "There's kids here on the weekends when me or Kimberly are teachin', but they're usually a bit younger and aren't much for conversation."

"How many kids do you teach?"

"A lot more now that I have Kim helpin' out." Dorothy slid Hadley another cookie before continuing. "As soon as Jeremy let it slip that his wife was a former equestrian turned elementary school teacher, I knew I had to meet her. She's been great. The back-to-back lessons were really harrowing, but with Kim steppin' up, it's helped us both. They're a young couple tryin' to save up for their own family, and I'm an old maid just tryna get by." Dorothy chucked out a sigh.

She continued to explain how working with Kimberly helped Dorothy slow down without having to turn away interested kids. She didn't have the funds to build an indoor ring or create a dirt ring on the farm, so they generally taught only the fundamentals. It was limiting

financially, since inevitably the children would transfer to a more professional equestrian center but was better than nothing.

The whole time Dorothy talked, Hadley soaked up the information. She was overwhelmed knowing that Dorothy loved having her around as much as she loved to be around. Eventually they started talking about the horses. Hadley told Dorothy how she recently learned her mom grew up around horses and how she feels a connection to her mom now whenever she's out with Snow White. Dorothy told her that with Hadley's help she was confident the horses would be able to live a happy life here for years to come.

The back and forth felt so natural to Hadley. When the sun started to set, Hadley asked if she could stop in more often for tea time. She was relieved to see the smile on Dorothy's face grow. "Of course, dear."

It's Not Your Fault

Ever since the cows left a few months ago, Hadley made it a point to stop in a few times a week to visit Dorothy before taking Snow White for a ride. She felt obligated at first, but after several months it became her favorite routine. Twice a week turned to daily as obligation turned to easy contentment. There was always a glass of sweet tea waiting for her – hot cocoa now that it was winter – along with cookies or biscuits baking in the oven. She knew Dorothy looked forward to their time together just as much as she did. While her happiest moments were still on the back of Snow White, her conversations with Dorothy were a close second.

Today, however, was different. The air felt stripped of joy, as Hadley's thoughts were rattled from the rough night she just had. Instead of walking into Dorothy's place, as she normally would, excited to share memories of her mom, or a summary of what she was reading, she entered feeling disheveled. She did her best to keep quiet and appear normal, despite the fear from last night still searing in her gut. She wanted to tell Dorothy what happened, but was afraid Dorothy would side with her dad, seeing the faults that Hadley worked so hard to hide.

"What's wrong, dear?"

"Oh, uhm, nothing." Hadley attempted to hide the storm in her eyes by looking at a suddenly interesting knot in the wooden table. She debated saying more but the words didn't come out.

"Hmm, doesn't look like nothin' to me. You know, dear, it's okay to have a bad day 'n even more okay to talk 'bout it." She fixed her eyes on Hadley.

Hadley didn't feel pressured to respond, knowing Dorothy wouldn't push the topic. The silence wasn't laced with intimidation or tension, it simply filled the space between them. All the same, the anxiety within her was rising in her throat like a shaken soda. She wanted to talk. Needed to. But what would she say? It was easier to hold it in. How does she explain that her dad was so drunk and angry that she spent half the night hiding. How does she make sure Dorothy knows it isn't her fault her dad gets so angry. That bits and pieces of her resolve kept breaking apart. That her father's outbursts kept causing cracks in her shell. How he never missed an opportunity to remind her that everything wrong in their life was her doing.

All the questions swirling in Hadley's mind led to the dam breaking. She released a dramatic breath, unable to hold it in any longer. She tried to wipe at the stream of tears, but it only made her cry harder.

"Oh, Hadley," Dorothy whispered. "I'm so sorry. Come here." She motioned for Hadley to come to her, wanting to hold her but she was glued to her seat. Eventually Dorothy rounded the table and knelt next to her chair, placing a hand on her shaking arm. "It's okay to feel this way." Her voice was gentle.

Hadley lifted her eyes to meet Dorothy's. She sniffled and wiped her cheeks. "I'm so embarrassed. I'm sorry, I didn't mean to cry," she mumbled.

"You should never apologize for having feelings, dear."

"I know, but I didn't mean to bother you with it."

"Never been a bother before. What's goin' on, dear?"

She took a slow deep breath in and after holding it for a moment, she forced herself to exhale. After a few more deep breaths, she felt a little better. She looked over to see Dorothy had set a box of tissues on the table and was heating up milk to make her cocoa. It was exactly the comfort that she needed. A few minutes later, Dorothy set a mug of peppermint tea on her side of the table before placing a steaming cup of cocoa in front of Hadley. Hadley, wiping her nose with a tissue, smiled when she saw the mini marshmallows floating in her mug. "Thank you."

A few minutes passed before either spoke again. They sat in their normal seats, both blowing and sipping on their hot drinks, despite the unusually warm March weather.

"My dad drinks," Hadley blurted.

"I see..."

"A lot, I mean. He gets drunk all the time." Hadley squeezed her eyes shut.

"How's his mood when he's drunk, dear?" Dorothy treaded lightly.

Hadley slowly opened her eyes but fixated on the floating marshmallows. "That's the thing. Um, so my mom and her friends used to drink, and they would dance around, and joke and it was so fun. My dad... it's... different when he drinks." Hadley considered her words as she spoke, not wanting to paint the wrong picture. She glanced at Dorothy, who looked like she was about to respond, and decided to add one more thought. "I think he can just get a little annoyed if I'm bothering him or haven't done something that he was wanting me to do. It's actually no big deal. I'm being dramatic." Hadley choked out an unconvincing laugh, which did little to move the concerned line of Dorothy's mouth.

She watched Dorothy take a slow sip before responding. "It's not your fault, dear."

Hadley looked up, unconvinced.

"It's not your fault."

"But my dad tells me it is. He says I cause a lot of stress and that's why he drinks. Sometimes I'm supposed to do a chore and forget to or don't get to it fast enough. That really makes him upset." *And sometimes I think he's going to hurt me.* She looks at Dorothy, desperately wanting to say more. But she knew if Dorothy saw the overflowing laundry or dishes in the sink, she'd only agree with her dad.

"Him drinkin' is on him. That's not on you."

"I guess..."

"Does he know how upset you get when he drinks?"

"No, I don't think so. I spend a lot of time in my bedroom, so I don't bother him."

"You should talk to him, dear. Maybe you can catch him before he starts drinkin' and talk to him then."

"I don't know..."

"I know it's scary, but it'll help if you talk to him. He shouldn't be treatin' you that way, dear. You're all he has left, and I bet that's hard, but it sounds like he's not dealin' with life so well. You need to know that's not on you. You don't deserve to be upset or feel this way."

"Maybe..."

Hadley's words hung in the air a minute before Dorothy pressed for more. "How long has this been goin' on, dear?"

"Ever since my mom died. I guess he drank before, but I never noticed because everything always felt happy and easy with mom around." A fresh tear fell. "It's gotten worse though. My dad, I mean. Last night he got real mad at me. I didn't mean to do anything wrong... but yeah, he was mad and stumbling around... and anyway, I am just more upset today than I thought I'd be." Hadley's eyes fell to the table.

"What happened?"

Hadley fidgeted with her fingers while debating her next words. "I was supposed to wash the dishes... and, well, I did," she explained quietly. "But my dad wasn't home, so I left them in the drying rack so that I could watch some television." Hadley swallowed the dry knot in her thought. "I usually stay upstairs when my dad is home, so it's fun to spend time on the couch. Anyway, I forgot to get up and put the dishes away before my dad got home. When he went into the kitchen to grab a tumbler, he tripped into the drying rack, and it caused a plate to fall out and break. He got really mad, and I know I was wrong so, you know, he reacted." Residual fear clouded Hadley's vision as she chewed on her lip.

"Sweetheart, you know accidents happen, right? A plate breakin' ain't your fault."

"It *was* my fault. I left the dishes out."

"Unless you took that plate and smashed it yourself, it wasn't your fault."

Hadley looked at Dorothy but didn't respond. She wasn't sure what to say. She knew it was her fault.

"You said your dad reacted. How, dear?"

A nervous heat crept up Hadley's neck. "It was nothing, really. I don't know why I'm being so dramatic about it. I ruined our tea time..."

"I reckon you're not bein' dramatic at all 'n nothin's been ruined. So keep talkin'."

Ringing her hands, Hadley took a deep breath and continued. "Well, he was reaching for a glass but stumbled and the plate fell and broke. It didn't completely shatter but it broke in half kinda. Anyway, I heard the noise and hurried into the kitchen to apologize. I knew right away what happened. My dad was so mad. He spun around to face me with half of the plate in his hand and threw it at the wall by me. Or I think it was meant for the wall... It shattered when it hit the wall and that only made him angrier. I panicked and ran. I got to my room and shut my door and stayed there all night. I don't think he ever came up the stairs after me, but he was yelling for a while. I eventually fell asleep against the door. And, um, when I woke up the next day and went downstairs the plate pieces were still there. I cleaned it up so it's fine now. I think he will be okay when he gets home, he usually acts like nothing happened. But I don't know. Things have broken before but he's never thrown something like that."

"That does sound scary."

They sat in a shared silence. Dorothy extended her arms across the table, resting her hands on top of Hadley's. Hadley wanted to withdraw but stayed still. She sat there, enveloped in sadness, and allowed Dorothy's warmth to comfort her.

After a few minutes, Dorothy continued. "You can always come to me, and I will be here to listen. Maybe you could catch your father before he drinks and get him talkin'. Maybe that could help. I'm sorry I don't have better answers." Dorothy smiled, but it fell short.

"Thank you. I'm sorry I got upset. I just have to do better at home..."

"There's nothin better to do, Hadley." Dorothy grabbed her hands and gave them a small shake. "You are a great young girl. You work hard. You're smart. You're caring. You are everything you need to be. Your father's drinking, grief or not, that's on him. His demons should only be his. I hope he finds his peace but please remember, none of this is your fault."

Hadley nodded with a small smile as she wiped at a few rogue tears. She wanted to believe Dorothy, but it felt too easy. When she saw the clouds behind Dorothy's eyes, she knew even Dorothy wasn't convinced. "I think I'm gonna go find Snow White, if that's okay."

"Of course, dear. She'll be excited to see you."

Hadley got up from her seat at the table and walked toward the door. She paused halfway and turned around. Looking at Dorothy she said, "Thank you for believing me."

"Of course, dear. I believe you but I also believe *in* you. Remember that."

Hadley smiled as she turned back toward the front door ready to find Snow White.

What About Last Night

After her talk with Dorothy, Hadley decided she would try to talk to her dad about how she's been feeling. She decided she would wake up early, setting her alarm for 5 am, to talk with him before breakfast since she noticed that lately, if he was around, he was drinking by lunchtime. She paced her room and reached for her alarm clock several times, debating if the possible outcomes were worth the attempt. Her mind nagged with doubt but she knew something had to change. She always felt better after talking to Snow White or sitting down with Dorothy, so she hoped a conversation with her dad would be just as helpful. Deep down she knew better, but she had to hope.

Exhausted from the anxious circles she was making, Hadley decided she should get in bed and prepare herself for tomorrow's confrontation. *Not confrontation, just a conversation.* She squeezed her teddy bear tight to her chest as she tried to fall asleep. The harder she tried, the more awake she became. Her mind, and her gut, were swirling. She's never approached her father before and was afraid all she'd do is start a fight. Dorothy seemed so reasonable and understanding when Hadley expressed how she was feeling. She made Hadley question whether things really were her fault.

Hadley grew restless lying in bed. Once she realized she wasn't falling asleep any time soon, she decided to get up and walk off more of her nervous energy. After restarting her laps, she tiptoed to the bathroom where she attempted to rehearse a whispered speech in front of the mirror. She wanted her words to be perfect. Direct but not accusatory. Kind but not soft. She wanted her dad to actually hear what she had to say. She cut off every sentence after the first few words, never satisfied with what was coming out. Nothing in her head sounded right out loud. She eventually gave up and decided tomorrow she would wing it.

***

Hadley was sitting at the kitchen table with a bowl of cereal when her father came down. He looked surprised to see her up so early but didn't immediately acknowledge her. Instead, he moved tiredly toward the coffeemaker. It wasn't until the machine began to percolate, that he turned around. Facing Hadley, he stated, "You're up early."

It wasn't much of an opener, but it was better than silence. Hadley mustered up every ounce of courage in her body and took a deep, slow breath before responding. "Yeah, I was actually hoping to maybe talk to you for a few minutes before you left for work." Hadley wavered and felt small against her dad's gaze. She added a quick, "If you have time."

He stared at Hadley for what felt like eternity. He then turned around and poured himself a cup of coffee. With an audibly annoyed sigh, he turned back and pulled out a chair. "Let's have it then."

Hadley tried to not let his deadpan response affect her. She took one more deep breath in and suddenly the words vomited right out. "I want-

ed to talk to you about drinking. I mean, not me drinking, obviously…
I just mean, your drinking. You drink all the time and you're mean a lot
and it's just hard for me." Her eyes bulged and she immediately stared
at her bowl of soggy cereal. *So much for being subtle.*

"Oh, I'm mean now, am I?"

"Sometimes, yeah…"

"I guess it's *mean* of me to work as hard as I do to pay for all the things
around you, like that cereal you seem to find so interesting. It's *mean* of
me to make sure you have ev-ery-thing you need."

"No, of course not." Hadley was losing the conversation quickly and
wasn't sure how to turn it around.

"Well, apparently I'm mean. That's what you said, right?"

"Yeah, that's what I said but I don't think you're *always* mean. Just
sometimes you get really mad at me or like last night…"

"What about last night, Hadley?"

She gulped down her racing heart when her dad pushed his chair
backward and stood up.

"You, um, you threw that plate, and it really scared me."

"And why did I throw the plate?" He stepped toward her.

"Because I left the dishes in the drying rack."

"Is that where they were supposed to be?" When he bent down to
meet her eyes, his stale breath on her face caused her to lean back.

"No. I forgot to put them away."

"Right. So how is you neglecting to do your chores suddenly my
fault? I wouldn't have to act *so mean* if you did the very basic chores
you're supposed to be doing." His words were punctuated with growing
anger and he placed air quotes around 'so mean'.

Hadley's cheeks flushed. She had no idea how to make her dad understand how she was feeling. All this conversation was doing was showing her that maybe it is her fault after all.

"I'm sorry about the dishes, dad, but your reaction really scared me."

She watched the disgust wash over his face. "You know, your mother always got the housework done without forgetting. Even when she was sick she didn't forget. And she never complained."

"I know."

"You could stand to be a bit more like her. She'd be disappointed to see how little you do to help around here."

His words speared her in the heart and a few tears broke free. Her body deflated and she was left half her original size. "I'm sorry..."

"Right. Well, until you get your act together I guess you'll have to deal with a *mean dad.* You get what you give and right now you're not giving me shit's worth of help."

"I'm sorry."

"Right." He rolled his eyes and walked his coffee cup over to the sink. In deliberately slow speech he added, "I'm putting this cup into the sink. This is your *friendly* reminder to wash it. Then dry it. Then put. It. Away."

Hadley didn't lift her eyes. She was too ashamed to face her dad. Instead, she let his sarcasm consume her as she tried to shrink in her seat. She stayed still as he walked out of the room, looking up when she noticed he stopped abruptly halfway through the living room. He turned around to face her and make one last point.

"And Hadley?"

"Yeah?"

"You're too young to even understand drinkin' so stay in your lane. Don't you dare accuse me of something you don't understand. I drink to deal with all the shit around here." Hadley nodded. "Now if you'll excuse me, I have a job to get to so maybe we can afford to keep having these wonderful family moments." With that he walked out the front door, slamming it shut behind him. Hadley, always on edge, jumped at the noise. She continued to sit at the table staring at her cereal that had turned into an unrecognizable pile of mush. Exactly how she felt.

I Feel Better

"I feel so stupid," Hadley admitted to Snow White as they trotted together through the open field. "I wanted to believe Dorothy but my dad is right. I forget to do things sometimes and that's why he's angry. It's me. I'm the reason." Even though Hadley was opening up to Dorothy more, she still kept her deepest thoughts and biggest secrets for Snow White – her silent confidant.

"The thing is, Snowy, he said something awful and I can't stop hearing it. It keeps playing in my head over and over and over." She let out an exasperated sigh before stuttering through her next sentence. "He told me my mom would be disappointed in me." Hadley slumped her shoulders forward as tears fell onto the saddle.

Snow White came to a stop and stood patiently in the field as Hadley folded on top of her. Tears were streaming down her face as she gasped between sobs. Hadley didn't try to contain her emotion. Instead she let herself feel every ounce of the confusion that seared through her.

Eventually Hadley straightened up. She took a deep breath in and released it slowly. Her breath still trembled on exhale, but she was calming down. She wiped her tears and shook out her arms, releasing the tension from her body. Her hands flew to the horn when she almost lost her balance. She shook her head and blew out a shaky breath before giving Snow White a thankful rub on the neck.

Hadley gently squeezed her feet against Snow White to signal that their walk could continue. The duo proceeded to silently walk and then canter around the field. The bitter wind wiped away Hadley's tears that continued to fall with each new thought she had. Once back to a walking pace, Hadley decided to start talking again. "It's just that whenever I think about my mom, I imagine her looking down on me. I stare out my window at night and see her in the stars. I always think she's watching over me with pride but now I'm afraid she's let down. That's what my dad thinks." Silence filled the air for a few moments. "He's right, you know. My mom was really sick at the end and she still kept the house spotless. She would've never left the dishes in the rack or dropped food on the living room floor. She was perfect. She was perfect and I'm not. I'm not sure I'll ever be as good as her. If you think about it, Snowy, it makes sense that my dad is so mean all the time. He had perfection and now he doesn't."

The horse stopped again but this time it seemed like a protest. "It's okay, pretty, you don't have to stop." Hadley pressed her legs together to encourage the horse to restart. "It's just the truth. It was stupid to talk to my dad as if anything would change. Things won't change until I do." As they meandered toward the barn, Hadley noticed Dorothy waving at her from the old wooden rocking chair on the front porch. "What do I tell Dorothy, Snowy? She believed in me and gave me all this hope. Once she finds out I messed up the talk with my dad, I think she'll be disappointed. I don't think I have it in me to disappoint any more people."

Hadley dismounted the horse with a heavy sigh. She spent a minute with her forehead pressed against the side of Snow White's neck and allowed herself to feel the raw emotion that squeezed her stomach. She whispered to her favorite confidant to forgive her for the lie she planned to tell.

***

"I'm so glad to hear you talked to your dad, dear." Dorothy smiled as she set a plate of snickerdoodle cookies between them, next to a glass carafe of milk and two etched petal patterned drinking glasses. Hadley poured a little milk into one of the glasses and smiled feebly. She wasn't sure what to say, so quickly took an oversized bite of a warm cinnamon sugar cookie.

"I hope he took to heart what you had to say."

"Yeah, I think he did." That part wasn't a lie. Hadley felt sure her dad felt the impact of her words. He just didn't agree with her. He made sure she understood just how wrong she was.

"Good, dear. Are you feelin' any better about all of it?"

Hadley took a long sip of her milk before responding. She tried to look thirsty but really she was buying time. *I should be honest.* She wanted to change her mind and tell Dorothy just how awful the conversation went. But looking across the table, she saw the hope in Dorothy's eyes and the smile on her face. She could feel Dorothy's pride. To tell the truth now would definitely disappoint her. She needed at least one person to be proud, even if it was under false pretenses.

"I feel better," Hadley said with every ounce of conviction she could muster. She paired her lie with a big smile. The immediate guilt caused rising bile to burn her throat. She swallowed loudly before clearing her throat and grabbing more milk.

"You sure, dear?"

"Oh yeah, definitely. I think I just drank too quickly. I feel better now. Thank you for suggesting it. I think things will be okay."

Dorothy didn't look convinced, despite her words. "That's great, dear. I am always here for'ya if you ever wanna talk more. Don't ever be afraid to tell me things."

"Thanks, Dorothy," Hadley said with a smile.

Dorothy glanced over at the clock. "I reckon you better start headin' home so you're not late for dinner."

Hadley didn't want to tell Dorothy that there was no chance of her missing dinner since dinner only happened if she made it. "You're right. I should head home before I'm missed." Dorothy and Hadley stood up together, tucking their chairs in and collecting their glasses for the sink.

"I can handle a few dishes, dear. Go on home. I'll see'ya tomorrow?"

"Okay. Tomorrow for sure." Hadley waved as she shifted toward the front door. Once outside, Hadley fought her lungs for the fresh air surrounding her. She held onto the little air she drew in. She rubbed her clammy hands against her winter jacket and shuffled her feet toward the fence. She eventually found herself forcefully exhaling a few moments after she grew dizzy. She focused all her efforts on breathing. *Just breathe.*

She didn't realize she had walked to the fence line until she nearly knocked into it. Hadley paused, realizing this section of fencing was completely out of view from Dorothy's house. Since she was hidden, she decided to sit for a few minutes to calm down before finishing her walk home. She sat and watched the field and the few roaming horses she could see. The sun was starting to set which painted the sky a beautiful ombre. Hadley barely noticed, instead she rested her head in her palms and stared at her shoes.

She wanted so badly for someone to feel proud of her. She had that from Dorothy but it wasn't sincere. She had lied. There's no way Dorothy would've been proud of Hadley if she were honest. She thought lying would feel better, but it didn't. She now added the weight of a guilty conscious on top of the already too-heavy weight of her parents' disappointment. Parents. Plural. She knew her mom would be as let down as her dad described.

Drawing in one last deep breath, Hadley hopped off the fence and walked home with her head slung low. She ignored the songs of the goldfinches and the whines from the downy woodpeckers perched in nearby trees. She ignored the babbling from the stream that paralleled the road, where she used to hunt for newts and salamanders with her mom. The internal conflict building inside her drowned it all out, leaving her with a swirling brain. *Where did everything go wrong?* She was once her mom's favorite sidekick. They were always happy together. Now she was the thorn in her dad's side. *I can fix this. I can be better.* She decided she would set her alarm clock an hour earlier than normal. This would give her more time to clean the house before her day started. She could stay up late, too. If her mom could be perfect, so could she. Then maybe she would find the peace she desperately needed.

Time to Grow Up

Over the next few months Hadley settled into her new routine, often waking up a few minutes before her alarm clock rattled. With the extra hour each morning, she had no excuse not to keep the house pristine. She would mop the kitchen floor, often kneeling down to hand scrub the caked-on mud that her dad's work boots left behind, before moving on to vacuum the other floors. Next, she dusted and wiped every surface she could reach. She made sure any dishes or glassware left behind from her father's night were washed, dried, and put away, stacking them all in evenly spaced uniformed rows. Lastly, she would carefully clean and wipe down the bar cart, throwing away any used napkins and returning the cap to the bottle. She wouldn't let her shoulders drop until everything was in perfect order.

Every evening, when Hadley set the oven for her dinner, she would use the preheating time to collect laundry. Whenever her father wasn't home, and normally he wasn't, she would go into his room to pick up his strewn laundry, toss it into a basket, and bring it downstairs to the washing machine. After starting the wash cycle, she'd take out a frozen dinner and put it in the oven. While her dinner cooked, she would return to her dad's room where she'd spend the next ten minutes cleaning the space. Before this new routine, she never realized quite how messy her father was. Her mom really did do a lot.

Each night after dinner and before bedtime, Hadley went through a mental checklist and made sure her morning efforts were repeated. She took a few minutes to walk from room to room and tidy up anything that fell out of place. The house was as clean as it had ever been. Now when her father came home from work, or the bar, he was greeted by evenly spaced and fluffed couch pillows, dishes neatly stacked behind closed doors, and freshly folded and put away laundry. She was determined to eliminate all opportunities for her father to get angry. She tried her best to become the perfect daughter. She hoped her mom was looking down on her with pride. Despite the nervous thread in her chest, waiting to be pulled loose, Hadley felt accomplished. However, between waking up early, cleaning the house, attending school, working on the farm, riding the horses, doing homework, and cleaning up again in the evening, she also felt exhausted.

Hadley's eyes grew heavy as she laid in bed and thought about how school would let out in a few weeks. She couldn't believe it was already almost summer again, though it would be a nice change to have some downtime. She missed reading at night, a luxury she could no longer afford. She imagined she'd have the time over the summer. She rotated in bed, shifting her gaze to her mom's bookcase. She squinted to see the titles better. There was a whole shelf of books she hadn't yet read. Unable to clearly read the titles, she decided she would pick one in the morning and place it on her nightstand for when school let out.

Moments after drifting to sleep, Hadley was startled awake by the sound of her dad's voice. It took a minute to realize that she wasn't dreaming. She heard her name twice before realizing it definitely was not a dream. She quickly got out of bed and walked toward her door. She grabbed her bathrobe off the hook on the back of her door, slipping it on, before walking into the hallway and down the stairs.

"Dad? Were you calling my name?"

"Yes. Jesus. What took you so long?" Hadley's father was sitting on the couch wearing old, torn jeans and a dirty neon yellow shirt. His mud-caked work boots were lying under the kitchen table. Hadley noticed the tracks on the floor she'd have to wash in the morning. She sighed as she finished surveying the area. Her eyes landed on the half empty glass of bourbon rattling in her dad's hand.

"Sorry, Dad. I was asleep so I didn't hear you right away. Is everything okay?" Hadley wondered if her dad realized how late it was. The look on his face made her think otherwise.

"Asleep?" He glanced at the clock on the wall. "Must be nice." Hadley stared at her dad waiting for more. "Sit. We need to talk." His voice was thick with demand.

Hadley walked over and sat on the nearby chair. She tucked her feet up, tightening the bathrobe around her waist, and faced her father.

"You're going to be fifteen soon."

Hadley wasn't sure what his point was. Her birthday last June was one of the last nice moments she had with her father. Maybe this year will be the same. Maybe he was feeling sentimental. For a moment she started wondering if her father was about to suggest they do something special. That bubble burst quickly.

"Are you deaf or stupid?"

"Neither." Hadley said quietly as she wiped her sweaty hands against her bathrobe. "Sorry. Yes, my birthday is in two months..."

"Right," he said as he took a long pull from his tumbler. "Which means you need to start pulling your weight around here."

"Oh." Hadley was confused. She thought she was already doing that. Especially compared to last year.

"You don't just get a free ride for life, Hadley."

"I know. I don't expect that. I have been doing a lot though, around the house I mean."

"You think because you sweep the floor and wash a few loads of laundry that you're suddenly Alice Nelson?"

"Who?"

"The housekeeper. Brady Bunch." Hadley watched as he rolled his eyes and let out a gruff sigh.

"The Brady... Oh... No of course, not... I know I'm not a housekeeper. But I've been trying hard to make sure the house is clean."

"Oh yeah, it's simply a-maz-ing." His sarcasm left Hadley defeated. She was constantly exhausted from her efforts and he still didn't care. It wasn't enough.

"What are we talking about? With my birthday, I mean," Hadley questioned timidly.

"It's about you growing up and doing something around here." He spoke pointedly. "Once you turn fifteen, you're getting a job. I'm not gonna be the only one around here held responsible."

"A job?" Hadley stared wide eyed at her father.

"Again. Deaf or stupid?"

"I know what a job is. But am I even old enough to have one? I'm only a freshman."

"You only need to be fifteen to work. So, once again, when you turn fifteen, you're getting a job. You can find one that works around school."

"But what about –"

"I do not care about your little farm or whatever else is about to come outta your mouth. When you turn fifteen, you're getting a job. Plain and simple. I expect to see the money, too. It's high time you start contributing. Washing a few dishes ain't gonna cut it. That's called a chore, Hadley. Time to grow up."

She went to open her mouth again but stopped. She stared heartbroken at her hands.

"That's all." He waved his hand in the air, a clear indication that she was to leave the room so he could enjoy his night. Without her.

Hadley stood up and made her way back upstairs. Once in her room, she held her door handle twisted until the door was flush to the frame. She gently released the handle so that it wouldn't make a noise. She tiptoed into her bed, slid under her comforter, and curled up against her pillow. She buried her face against her teddy bear and cried until she eventually fell back to sleep.

While asleep, she dreamt of galloping the open land with Snow White. The wind was gentle, the sun bright, her mood elevated, and her smile wide. She woke up the opposite. Devastated.

She immediately wondered what would happen to the horses if she was forced to get a job somewhere. She knew Dorothy couldn't afford to pay her. She also knew Dorothy was too old to manage the horses without all the work that Hadley voluntarily did. *Now what.*

She decided to ignore the thumping in her chest and the sweat that dampened her palms. Instead, she would enjoy the next two months, until her birthday, and worry about it then. She couldn't bear to tell Dorothy her dad's demand. She was hoping she'd be able to balance it all. The house, school, the farm, a job. *I can do it.*

Determined to make the best out of it, Hadley got out of bed and started her day. She went downstairs and began her routine, spending an extra ten minutes on the path of mud her father left last night. She didn't have the nerve to ask him to leave his boots on the door mat. Instead, she obediently, defeatedly, cleaned up any mess he left behind, including the one currently rising in her throat.

Make a Wish

Hadley's birthday came and went without a whiff of acknowledgement from her father. She expected as much. What she hadn't expected was for Dorothy to remember since she only mentioned her birthday once, which was months ago and in passing. When Hadley showed up to Dorothy's that afternoon, for their regular tea time, she saw a small box and a dark chocolate cupcake sitting on her placemat with a single lit candle.

"Ohmigosh…"

"Come, come. Make a wish before the candle starts dripping."

Hadley moved toward the table and pulled out her chair. She started to sit but then stood back up and twirled around to face Dorothy. She rushed over and pulled her into a tight hug, nearly breaking her with the embrace. "Thank you."

"You're welcome, dear. Now make your wish before it's a waxy mess."

"Oh, right. Okay!" Hadley took a seat and admired the homemade cupcake. It didn't take much thought for Hadley to know what her wish would be. Focusing on the pink striped candle flickering before her, she closed her eyes. She mustered all of her positive energy, took a breath in, paused briefly, and blew out the candle. When she opened her eyes, Dorothy was sitting across from her with a big smile.

"Now, I know it's bad luck to say your wish out loud, so don't spoil it. But I hope it comes true." Dorothy picked up her own cupcake before continuing, "There's only one thing left to do."

"What's that?"

"Eat the cake. Always eat the cake," Dorothy laughed.

Hadley chuckled while she picked up her cupcake and thoughtfully removed the candle and peeled off the liner. She smiled at Dorothy before taking a big bite. "Ohmigosh," Hadley gushed with a mouthful of fudgy cake. She took another big bite, careful to not let any bits drop to the table, before telling Dorothy it was the best thing she'd had in a long time.

"Thank you, dear. It's a great occupier of time. I have a lot more of that now with the cows rehomed. Speaking of, I heard from Daniel the other day. He said the cows fit right in. The herd is fully integrated and gettin' along perfectly with the others."

Hadley felt a pang of guilt. She almost forgot how much Dorothy had given up. Hadley's father hadn't mentioned a job lately, but she knew it was coming. She also knew what it would mean for her time with Dorothy. Choosing to ignore the worry, she focused on the moment. Dorothy looked content and so she decided, for now, she would be content, too. "That's great. I'm so relieved that it worked out okay. I was afraid the cows would be treated as outsiders."

"Wouldn't that be somethin'. Cows actin' catty!" The duo giggled together as they continued eating their decadent treat. "I think you politely ignored that box nex'ta ya long enough, dear. Why don't you open it."

Hadley looked at Dorothy with a sheepish grin. "I wasn't sure if it was for me or not."

"Well, it's not *my* birthday. Go on, dear. It's meant just for you."

Hadley smiled again and centered the wrapped box in front of her. She slowly peeled off the paper to reveal a plain brown cardboard box. She proceeded to lift the top of the box off and push aside the white tissue paper unveiling a used horseshoe. She stared at it in awe, never having seen a shoe that wasn't still glued on a horses' hoof.

Before Hadley had a chance to comment, Dorothy spoke up. "Okay, so here's the story, dear. I don't have much spare change layin' 'round the house, so I couldn't go out and get ya a formal gift. But I had this idea. Last week the farrier was here changin' out them shoes. He normally collects them to recycle at the scrap yard one town over. Anyway, I let him know you're a big fan of Snow White and asked him to set aside one of her used shoes. I thought you'd like to have it as a decoration."

"That's really neat." She picked up the shoe and ran her fingers along the perimeter. "I love it."

"Do you know what they say about horseshoes?"

"No, I don't think so..."

"Well, they're supposed to be good luck. When you hang it pointing up, it's said that it keeps the good luck. When you hang it pointing down, it's bad because all the good luck pours right on out."

"Wow, really?"

"Yep. Now, I don't know if it's all mumbo jumbo, but if I were you, I'd hang it pointing up. Ya know, just in case," Dorothy said with a wink.

"Anything that brings good luck sounds good to me! Thank you, Dorothy. This is so special. Is it really the shoe Snow White was wearing?"

"One of them anyway," Dorothy smiled.

"Thank you... for this and for the cupcake. And for remembering my birthday. This was a really cool surprise."

"No need for thanks, dear, but you're welcome. Why don't you go find Miss Snow White and enjoy a birthday ride. Don't forget to head back here before leavin'. You can grab the horseshoe then, but I also have extra cupcakes to send home with ya."

"That sounds great. Thank you again, Dorothy. I'll see you in a bit!" She waved behind her on her way out the door.

***

After enjoying a long ride with Snow White, Hadley walked back toward the house. She felt renewed by their exploration of the land along the dirt roads just outside the fences. She thought back to when she lacked the confidence to leave the pastures. Now it was a common path for her to ride. She walked into the front door and slipped off her shoes.

"Dorothy? I'm back!"

Dorothy rounded the corner and came into sight. "Hello, dear. I was just packaging up the cupcakes now. How was the ride?"

"It was great. The weather was perfect. I took Snow White down the road a bit. I think she secretly loved breaking free from the fenced in grass. She's so funny."

"Oh, I reckon you're right. That little girl loves an adventure. Especially when it's with you." Hadley's smile grew. "Come, come. I know you gotta get going so here's your gift box and some extra cupcakes."

"Thank you! You made today really great."

Dorothy waved off the compliment. "I hope the rest of your night is just as great." They smiled at each other as Hadley collected the goodies and slid her shoes back on.

Hadley smiled the whole way home with a slight spring in her step. When she approached her house, she noticed the empty driveway. Home alone on her birthday. Most people would probably feel sad, but Hadley was relieved. She looked forward to a quiet evening.

After she walked inside and slid off her shoes, she set the cupcakes on the kitchen table. She placed one on a napkin for herself and left the rest covered. She grabbed a second napkin and a pen so she could leave a note for her dad, knowing it was likely he'd show up once she was already asleep.

Hope you enjoy!
xo Hadley

After scribbling the note, Hadley poured a glass of whole milk and grabbed some caramel popcorn from the pantry for her dinner of sweets. Balancing it all in her hands, she made her way to her bedroom. She set her snacks and milk on her nightstand, then realized she left her horseshoe downstairs on the table with the cupcakes. She ran down, grabbed the gift, and ran back to her room. She didn't think she could hang the horseshoe on her own, so she set it on the floor, standing against the wall, making sure the horseshoe was pointing up, just like Dorothy said.

Hadley spent the rest of the evening cozied up on her bay window seat. After she indulged in her treats, she grabbed an unread book from the shelf and finally started to read. Eventually she fell asleep, book in hand, chest rising and falling steadily against a backdrop of stars, feeling completely satisfied with her fifteenth birthday.

A Little Horseshoe Luck

The next morning Hadley walked downstairs to grab breakfast. She noticed the cupcake container was empty and there were crumbs scattered across the table and onto the floor. She also noticed fresh ink on the napkin she left for her father.

15 = job.
Get one.

Hadley read and re-read the short words. No happy birthday. No thank you. No nothing. Just a demand. *Okay, then.* She sunk into her chair, forgetting to grab the cereal. Her mind rattled with thoughts. How would she find a job? How would this affect Dorothy? The horses? She'd only been fifteen for a few hours and yet everything had already changed. So much for birthday wishes and horseshoe luck.

She placed a hand over her chest, realizing at some point during her inward spiral she had stopped exhaling. *Breathe. Just breathe.* She tried. Her lungs didn't cooperate. She felt paralyzed as her heart thumped desperately beneath her hand. The anxiety building made the thumping faster. Louder. She forced her mind to quiet as she managed a few staccato breaths. She removed her hand from her chest and watched as it trembled. The distraction of studying her quivering hand helped her calm down. After a few minutes, she felt stable and was breathing normally. Lightheaded, but breathing.

Hadley looked up at the kitchen clock and noticed the morning was almost over already. *There's no time for this,* she thought. She was mad at herself for allowing her father to wreck her so easily. She realized if she was going to balance a job with maintaining housework and helping on the farm, she'd have to get moving. She quickly gathered the crumbs into her hand and did a fast sweep of the floor.

She went upstairs and changed into a pale pink blouse and the only pair of jeans she owned that didn't have holes and weren't too short. She debated wearing a nice pair of shoes, but ultimately slid on her white sneakers since she'd need to keep her feet comfortable. She washed her face, brushed her teeth, and smoothed her golden hair into a straight ponytail.

She grabbed a small bag from her closet and ran downstairs. She picked out a granola bar from the pantry, despite having lost her appetite, and filled up a bottle with sink water. She dropped both into her bag. Determined to find a job that would not impede her time with Dorothy and the horses, she walked out the front door. This would be a much trickier balance once school resumed, but for now she could make it work. She would make it work. She knew if she left her driveway and turned right, it would lead her to Dorothy's farm. So instead, she turned left.

There was a small strip of stores in this direction that would be her only chance at getting a job. It's not like her father would be dropping her off or picking her up each day. She'd need to be able to walk there on her own.

Twenty minutes later, Hadley approached the cluster of stores. She stood on the sidewalk and evaluated each shop, reading their signs. There was a dry cleaner, a florist, and a general store. The shop on the end past the general store had no sign and looked abandoned. *Okay. Three chances.* If she couldn't make one of these work, she'd end up needing to walk another twenty minutes to the nearest Walmart.

Hadley decided she would start with the dry cleaner and make her way down the strip. She paused in front of the entrance to take a deep breath and wipe her clammy hands on her pants before pushing the door open, sounding an electronic bell. On cue, a short Chinese woman, with dull black hair, wearing a faded purple apron and large wire-rimmed glasses, approached from the back room.

Hadley introduced herself, awkwardly clearing her throat in the middle.

"Do you have your slip or order number?"

Hadley realized since she wasn't holding any dirty clothes that this woman must have thought she was picking clothes up. "Oh, um, actually I don't have anything to pick up. I was hoping that maybe you'd be hiring? I have decent grades in school and learn quickly. I'm also great with cleaning. Just ask my dad." She was aiming at making a joke, but her words came out jumbled.

"How old are you, Haley?"

"Hadley," she quietly corrected. "I just turned fifteen."

"Sorry. Hadley." The woman ran her eyes up and down Hadley. "I wish I had something for you, but I pretty much run this shop alone. I don't really get busy enough to hire help. You're young; you should be enjoying your youth anyway." The woman smiled despite her deadpan voice.

"Are you sure? I could really use the money. It's just me and my dad at home and –"

"I really am sorry, sweetheart. Maybe try next door. Majority of the cars that pull into this lot walk into his shop instead of mine."

"Okay, thank you," Hadley said as she focused on the counter, avoiding eye contact.

"You're most welcome. I really should get back to the clothes. Stains won't remove themselves." She waved at Hadley before retreating to the back of the shop.

Hadley walked out and stepped toward the next door which belonged to the flower shop. She wiped her hands again before pushing open the door. This time she heard a jingle from bells knocking against the glass door. She took a quick glance around, noticing how much livelier this store was compared to the boring dry cleaners. This store was full of vibrant flowers and smelled like strawberries.

There was an elderly black man bent over a bouquet of orange, pink, and yellow flowers standing toward the back of the store who Hadley assumed was probably close in age to Dorothy, since his hair matched the gray t-shirt he was wearing under his dark green apron. Hadley had no idea what kind of flowers he was piecing together but found the colors beautiful.

Noticing her presence, his copper-colored eyes glanced up. "Hello, there! How can I help ya today?" Hadley was surprised by the tenor in his voice. She was used to a deeper male tone which often intimidated her. She found the absence of gravel a relief.

"Hi, my name is Hadley." She made it through this time without awkwardly choking on her words.

"Hey, Hadley. I'm Steve. Have you been here before? You look quite familiar." He walked around the counter to get a closer look at her.

"No, I don't think so."

"Hmm. I could swear I've seen you before. Are your parents in the car?"

"Oh. Um, no. I actually walked here by myself. I don't live far and it's so nice out," she said with a slight quiver.

"I see. Are you looking for any specific arrangement today?"

"Oh, actually, I don't need flowers. I was hoping I could find some part time work. I'm fifteen and it's just me and my dad at home. I wanted to help out while I could. Is there any chance you'd be hiring? I don't know all that much about flowers, though. But I've always loved them. I follow directions well and I learn quickly..." She knew she was rambling. If she kept talking, he wouldn't have the chance to reject her.

Steve listened patiently, not wanting to interrupt. "It's mighty generous of you to want to work at your age to help your dad out." He paused again, observing her bright blue eyes. "Are you sure I don't know you?"

Hadley shrugged.

"Hmm. Well, I hadn't planned on hiring but I suppose a lil' help never hurts. It is starting to get busy around here."

"I would really appreciate it! It's summer so I'm free whenever. Once school starts, I would need to take the bus home and then walk here after."

"That sounds just fine. We can work out fall once it rolls 'round. How about you work a couple hours each morning until, say, lunchtime? I think it would be useful to have you help open up the shop. Then I can teach you how to organize upcoming orders and how to write down phone orders."

"I would love that! That sounds perfect."

"I can set you up for minimum wage, but that's about all I can part with right now." He tapped his finger against his lips, and Hadley stood still, hoping he wasn't about to change his mind. "If you would want to work under the table I could bump up the pay a bit."

"What's under the table mean?"

"It just means I won't put you on the insurance or payroll. I'll just hand you cash from the drawer at the end of each week."

"Oh! I get it… I think. I mean, that's fine with me. Whatever is easiest for you, really. I don't want to cause any issues. I would appreciate anything."

"How about $3.20 an hour in cash, that's about thirty cents over minimum wage. You can start each morning at 8:30. I open at 9, but it takes a bit of time to make sure the shop is ready for the day."

"I can do that! When should I start?"

"You can come back tomorrow. You said you are already fifteen, right?"

"Yeah. My birthday was yesterday, actually. Is that okay?"

"Happy birthday. Yes, that's just fine. So long as you're fifteen we're good to go. I don't think I caught your last name."

"Oh, I'm sorry. I should have started with that. It's Martin. Hadley Martin."

Steve was jotting down notes on the pad of paper by the register when his hand froze. He lifted his gaze back to Hadley and studied her closely. "Hadley Martin?"

"Yes…" Hadley saw something click behind the old man's eyes. She immediately worried Steve knew her father. Chances are that would ruin everything. Her dad wasn't exactly known for his pleasantries lately.

"Well, I'll be. That's how I know you. Your mom is, or I - uh, was, Elizabeth, right? Elizabeth Martin?"

Hadley's eyes widened. "You knew my mom?"

"I sure did. She was one of my favorite clients. She was always in here ordering elaborate table displays. She was the sweetest lady. Always had the best stories to share. I was so sorry to hear about her cancer and how it all ended. I'm so sorry for your loss."

"Thanks. It was really hard, but I'm figuring it out. With it just being my dad at home, this job will really help."

"Glad to hear it. Any daughter of Elizabeth is a friend of mine," he said warmly. "Anyway, it was quite nice to meet you, I'll see you tomorrow morning, okay? I gotta get back to these arrangements before the pick-up rush begins."

"Thanks, again." With that, she left the shop and started to walk back home. She was elated that she'd be able to work all morning and still make it to the farm to clean the stalls and ride the horses. She could even enjoy sweet tea with Dorothy. She'd just have to handle most of her housework in the evening, instead of the early morning. She hoped her dad wouldn't mind. He should be happy enough that she found a job. She was a bit worried about what would happen in the fall when she had school during the day. For now, anyway, she found the perfect solution.

With the stress of finding a job behind her, she noticed her stomach was rumbling. She reached into her bag and grabbed the Quaker chewy chocolate chip granola bar that she packed and ate it while she continued her walk home. With excitement in her step, her return only took eighteen minutes, two faster than her earlier walk. Her steps quickened as she grew eager to get to the farm, happy to have the whole afternoon ahead of her. *Maybe that horseshoe had a little luck saved up after all.*

She decided the outcome of today was the best possible one for her and hoped her dad would agree. *Yeah right.* Hadley quickly walked inside and changed her clothes. She grabbed a handful of Goldfish and ran back out, this time turning right toward the farm.

Daisy & Daffodil

Hadley was filling the coffee pot for her father when he walked into the kitchen. "Morning, Dad. Coffee will be ready in a minute."

"You drink coffee now?"

"No, but I was up and saw you hadn't come down yet so thought I'd help."

"I see. Thanks."

"You're welcome." Hadley quietly navigated the kitchen, mop in hand. Her father sat at the table with the daily newspaper and an Otis Spunkmeyer blueberry muffin. Every few minutes Hadley noticed her father would rub his fingers together, releasing crumbs onto the floor. The floor she was actively cleaning.

When the coffee pot beeped, they both looked up. "I'll get it," Hadley offered. She moved to the cabinet and grabbed a mug. She prepared the coffee the way she knew her father liked it and walked it over to him. He nodded his acceptance before promptly returning to the sports section.

Hadley never got used to the silence that fell between her and her father. When her mom was alive, the space between them was filled by music, laughter, and love. With her father, it was either deafening silence or anger. Sometimes both. Hadley debated her father's seemingly neutral mood while she prepared herself a bowl of Rice Krispies in milk.

She decided now was as good a time as any to tell him about her job. "So, I wanted to tell you something," Hadley said, with a mouth full of crackling cereal.

"Ah, the catch for me takin' this cup of coffee?" he set down his newspaper and wiped his hands, causing more crumbs to fall to the ground. He looked at her and gave an exaggerated roll of his hand, indicating for her to start speaking.

"No, there's no catch," Hadley mumbled.

"Then, speak up. Get on with it."

"I got a job yesterday. Well, I start today. I have to leave in a few minutes, actually."

"Is that right? Where is this job at?"

"At Daisy & Daffodil, the flower shop. It's close enough that I can walk there. I am working in the mornings now, but the owner offered to change my schedule once school starts."

"The coon's flower shop? For God knows what reason, your mother loved it there."

"Oh, um, do you mean the owner? I don't know his last name. He just said his name was Steve." Hadley was confused. Did her father know Steve's last name or was he saying something rude that she didn't understand. She assumed from the disgust in her father's voice that it was the latter.

"Whatever. How much?"

"How much what?"

"Money. How much money, Hadley?"

"Oh. Right. Um, I think he said $3.20 an hour. I'm not sure how many hours I'll be working though."

"You're not sure?"

"I can ask again today. He mentioned a few hours a day, until lunchtime."

"Don't mess it up. Don't be tryna leave early either. You should be pushin' the limits and offering to stay late. You gotta pull your weight around here. I'm not joking, Hadley." With that, he stood up and left the room. His muffin wrapper and coffee cup still on the table.

Hadley sat there dumbfounded. He didn't seem as pleased about her finding a job as she expected. She was worried her hours wouldn't be enough. She thought if she worked hard enough for her new boss, maybe he would want to keep her around longer. Only time will tell how this arrangement will work out.

Hadley heard the front door open and close a few minutes later. *Okay, bye.* She rolled her eyes. Immediately a sense of dread washed over her as if her father somehow saw her. She shook the fear from her mind and collected herself. She stood up and gathered her father's mess along with her empty bowl. She wiped down the table, cleaned out the coffee pot, and washed the dishes. Once the kitchen was clean, she rushed upstairs to change her clothes for the day. She grabbed an old t-shirt and a pair of jean shorts and folded them into her bag. She didn't want to dirty her nicer clothes so figured she could quickly change once she got to Dorothy's. Grabbing her bag, she hurried downstairs. She tossed in a few snacks from the pantry to keep her satiated throughout the day since she planned to walk directly from Daisy & Daffodil to the farm.

After completing a cursory inspection of the house, making sure everything was in place, she walked out the front door. She spent the next twenty minutes wondering what the day would look like and hoping Steve was as friendly as he was the day before.

Hadley was relieved to have reached the strip mall at 8:25; five minutes early. There were only two cars in the parking lot. Both empty. She grew nervous when she reached the flower shop's main door and noticed the lights were off. She turned to scan the parking lot again right as a third car pulled in.

"Hey, Miss Hadley," Steve said as he stepped out of his car, thermos in hand.

"Hi, Steve," Hadley waved.

"I hope you haven't been waiting out here long. I'm usually a few minutes earlier but I had the darndest time gettin' out of bed this morning," Steve chuckled. "Nothing this here thermos of coffee can't fix." Hadley matched his smile with her own and assured him she had just shown up. "Alright, then, that's good. Let's get us inside and I can show you the ropes."

"Sounds good."

Steve spent the next fifteen minutes walking Hadley around the store, pointing out the different sections. He showed her how he organized his flowers by variety and not by color. He also showed her the row of floral display fridges on the side wall of his shop. He explained how the coolers were designed to utilize high humidity to help protect the petals and leaves from drying out and the appliances were designed to hold a mild temperature, so the flowers never get too hot nor too cold. He demonstrated how to do temperature checks on the coolers, which would be an important responsibility of hers.

Once the tour ended, Hadley and Steve stood at the cluttered front desk. Hadley took a mental inventory of everything surrounding the register: notepads, loose paper clips, rubber bands, small scissors, a collection of pens, and random notes scattered over the desk. Behind them was a telephone attached to the wall. Hadley would be responsible for answering the phone and writing down the order. She would then confirm the contact information and required pick up date and time.

"Sometimes you'll get a customer who is not sure what they want or who has a ton of questions. If you ever are unsure, just ask them to hold and flag me down. I'm always here to step in and answer the tricky stuff. You'll learn more than you think and be able to answer some questions yourself eventually. For now, feel free to grab my attention."

"Okay, I can do that. So, write the order down and get all the information. What do I do then?"

"You can take the paper and place it on the left side of the register. That's what these other papers are. One of these days I'll get a better system in place. For now, the phone orders placed on the left haven't been started. Once I grab the order and pull the arrangement together, I'll stick the paper on the right side of the register. Once a customer pays and picks up the order, the paper goes into a big bin in the back. Once a week, I'll take the papers and organize them alphabetically in case a customer ever wants to order the same arrangement again." Hadley nodded along but was surprised to hear how disorganized the ordering process seemed and wondered if papers ever got lost. It was especially surprising since yesterday the lady at the dry cleaner told her this place was always busy. *I should think of some ways to help Steve get a better system in place.* Caught up in her thoughts, she startled at the sound of the phone ringing.

"Perfect timing. I'm going to flip our door sign to Open. Why don't you try your hand at answering the phone. I'm right here if you need me."

Hadley looked at Steve with wide eyes but with the sound of the next ring, she quickly pivoted to answer. "Hi, this is um, sorry, uh, D- Daisy and Daffodil. Sorry. How can I – may I help you?"

"Jesus. You'll be fired in no time."

Hadley's heart pounded. "Wh-what? Hello?"

"It's your father, moron."

"Oh. Hi. Are you ordering flowers?"

"Clearly not. I was checking to see if you were lying about the job. I'd work on that introduction, or you'll be kicked out before you know it."

Click.

Steve looked quizzically at Hadley as she gently placed the phone back on its hook. "Wrong number?"

"It was just my dad." Hadley forced a smile. "He wanted to wish me a good first day." Her cheeks flushed hoping that Steve hadn't overheard her father's harsh words.

"How nice." She could tell he was being genuine. She smiled and gave him a slight nod, not wanting to correct him.

Hadley continued to answer the phone each time it rang. She stumbled through the first few, her dad's words on replay in her head. *You'll be fired in no time.* By the fourth call, Hadley's voice steadied. By the fifth, she had a seamless interaction. Her confidence grew as she fell into the routine and started to feel less self-conscious.

Steve stayed busy creating beautiful bouquets and arrangements. Hadley watched in awe as he pieced together different types and colors of flowers from the tables around the store. Each arrangement was better than the last. She leaned against the desk and wondered how he managed to think up such vibrant combinations. Steve only came over to the desk to grab an unfulfilled order or when it was time for someone to pick up or pay for an order. He told her he planned to teach her how to operate the register but wanted her to become comfortable with one task at a time.

She appreciated that he wasn't trying to push her too quickly, but wanted to make sure he knew she wasn't lazy, so when the phone was quiet, Hadley worked on straightening the written orders to the left side of the register. She sorted them by which order was due the soonest. Once that was organized, she used the slow moments to sweep the floors and dust around the displays. Whenever she passed a cold case, she peeked at the thermostat to confirm it was the right temperature. She tried to stay as noticeably busy as possible. She didn't want Steve to think she was slacking. She didn't want her father to be right.

At 11:30, Steve walked over and told Hadley she could wrap up for the day. She was in the middle of dusting a small table of pale blue and purple hyacinths.

"Okay, if you're sure. I can keep dusting if you want."

"This place is already cleaner than it's been in months," Steve said with a smile. "I appreciate your hard work, Hadley. You did great today."

"Thank you. It definitely took a few tries before I managed to get a phone order correct."

"That's just part of learning. No one is perfect ever, but especially not in the beginning. You gotta let yourself learn first." Hadley nodded, with a growing smile on her face. "Go ahead and finish that table but then you can call it a day. You'll have put in three hours which I think is pretty great for day one. Especially at your age."

"Okay, that sounds good. I appreciate the chance to work here. I hope I organized the front desk okay."

"It looks great actually. I'll see you at the same time tomorrow?"

"Definitely!" Hadley finished cleaning the display table in front of her before hanging up the duster and grabbing her bag. "Thanks, again, Steve. I'll see you tomorrow." Steve smiled and waved back at her before returning his attention to the bouquet of dark pink roses, white asiatic lilies, and lavender set before him.

As she walked, Hadley peeled back the wrapper of her oatmeal granola bar and gulped down the water bottle that Steve offered her. She planned to pass her house and continue straight to Dorothy's farm. She was buzzing from a successful morning. She decided she didn't care whether her father was home and if he'd see her walk past the driveway. She doubted he would rush out the door to stop her. She was too excited to tell Snow White all about the different flowers she saw today.

Twenty minutes later, she was passing her house, with its very empty driveway. Despite telling herself she didn't care, she still breathed a sigh of relief. A few minutes after that, she was at the farm. She practically jogged across the field to Dorothy's front door so she could change and get to her happy place: the horses.

***

"Well, don't you look nice. Come on in, dear."

"Thank you!" Hadley rushed through the door and grabbed the spare clothes out of her bag. "Do you mind if I use the bathroom to change?" Hadley was already halfway through the house.

"Of course not. I'll pour you a cold glass of tea before you head to the stable."

"That sounds great, thanks!" Hadley changed quickly and met Dorothy in the kitchen. She gratefully picked up the glass of iced tea and finished it with a few loud gulps. "Oh man, I was definitely thirstier than I thought."

Dorothy chuckled at the girl's reeling energy. "What has you lookin' nice today?"

"It's a long story but basically my dad told me I needed to get a job. You know, since I'm old enough to be working."

"Hardly old enough, dear. It's bad enough you're doing so much work here on the farm, now a job, too? Are you sure you can balance both? You really should be out playing with your friends and enjoying your childhood." Dorothy focused on the strawberry shortbread cookie dough she was mixing, though her concern was hard to hide.

"Yeah, it's okay," Hadley shrugged. "I actually found a job that's only for a few hours in the mornings. You know that flower shop down at the strip?"

"I sure do. He puts together some wonderful flowers."

"Yeah! That's where I got the job. Steve, he's the owner, he seems really nice so far. I just started this morning."

"Well, you sure seem happy," Dorothy said as she turned to face Hadley. She handed her the cookie dough spoon as a taster.

"I think it went pretty well. It took me a few times to not mess up the phone orders, but I got it by the end."

"Good on you, not giving up."

Hadley smiled hearing Dorothy was proud of her. With a slight nod to herself, she stuck the spoon in her mouth. Her teeth scraped off the bit of raw dough as she let out an immediate groan of appreciation. "Mm, strawberry! This combination is going to be so good, I can tell."

"Thank you, dear. We'll see! Now, I'm sure you're excited to get to the horses but promise me one thing first?"

"Sure..."

"If it gets to be too much, the job and the stables, you need to tell me. It's great if you can balance both but you're still just a kid. Please remember to have fun. Don't let it start to overwhelm you. I know your dad's wantin' the job for ya, so if you need to come here less, that's okay."

"I can do both," Hadley blurted.

"Just promise me."

"Okay. Yeah, I promise. But I think it'll be easy to balance. Really. Steve is kind so it makes the job easier and it's not a far walk to here. It's like you said, I'm just a kid. Kids are full of energy!" Hadley let out a giggle and displayed a wide smile, meant to assure Dorothy.

"Yeah, yeah. You enjoy that endless energy while you got it. Shoo, I know firsthand it doesn't last forever. Go on now, don't let me hold ya up. Just remember to talk to me. And keep that promise. If you start to get overwhelmed, we'll find a way for you to slow down. Deal?"

"Deal." They smiled in agreement before Hadley skipped out the door in pursuit of the stables. She wanted to keep her promise to Dorothy. It was a nice thought to be able to slow down. But it wasn't reality. Not the reality Hadley knew anyway. In Hadley's world she was never doing enough. She never *was* enough.

As she approached the stables, she paused. Before trading her clean white shoes for the old muck boots by the door, Hadley turned around. She took a deep breath and stared out at the expansive green. This was Dorothy's home. It was where she made her memories. The ones with her husband and the ones after. Hadley believed if she didn't pull her weight, like she was made to at home, then Dorothy would lose all of it. The thought sent a chill down her spine. She couldn't let that happen. Wouldn't.

Hadley felt determined. She would work at the flower shop to appease her father while continuing to help Dorothy on the farm. In a month, she would add in school and homework. She could do it. She shook out her arms, releasing the heaviness from her shoulders. She chose to ignore the pressure on her chest and instead rallied the endless energy she claimed to have and entered the stables.

She would find a way to balance her job, her homelife, the farm, and eventually school. No matter what.

Plenty of Sunlight

For the next five weeks, Hadley felt on top of the world. Tired, but happy. She kept her promise to everyone, including herself. She started each morning with a big stretch before she dragged herself downstairs to fill the coffee pot for her father and make herself a bowl of cereal. After a quick sweep of the floors and wipe of the counters, she'd grab her backpack, which she'd pre-pack the night before with clothes and snacks and start her twenty-minute walk to work. She spent three to four hours every morning at the flower shop, never leaving before Steve formally dismissed her. She would then walk straight to Dorothy's house to change and get started with her barn work. After getting home in the evening, she would throw a frozen dinner into the oven and use the bake time to clean up the house.

This past week Hadley noticed Dorothy started setting out more hearty snacks like fruit-filled muffins instead of cookies for when she arrived. She looked forward to seeing what would be set out for her, especially since the granola bar she'd eat after leaving work hardly bridged the gap from breakfast until dinner. "Thanks for always having something yummy out for me," Hadley said with a mouth full of a blueberry and lemon muffin that she was trying hard to not completely scarf down.

"You're welcome, dear. It's been a while since I played with my muffin recipes, so it's been fun to mix up new flavor combinations. You let me know when you find a favorite."

"So far they've all been my favorite. You're the best baker ever."

"Well, aren't you the sweetest."

"It's the truth. I could sit here and eat this whole platter."

Dorothy let out a chuckle as she wiped her hands on her apron. "If you do that, you might get too full to ride Snow White."

"Nothing could stop me from riding her. But I bet *she* wouldn't appreciate having to carry me around if I ate a dozen muffins."

They laughed together as Dorothy waved her off. "I don't think you need to worry about that. I'm pretty sure a strong wind could still knock you over. You enjoy your metabolism while you got it."

"In that case, do you mind if I have another? I can eat it while I head over to the stables. I need it for energy... you know, for all the poop slinging I'm about to do."

Laughing again, Dorothy nodded. "You're a funny girl. Go on, help yourself." Hadley grabbed a second muffin and made her way to the barn.

***

Three hours later, Hadley was wheeling the last pile of manure around to the back of the stable. She used to finish the work in two hours but lately her lack of energy, despite Dorothy's muffins, was obvious. Once she dumped the last barrow, Hadley took a minute to lean against the side of the building where she released a long, slow breath. *Phew. Okay, still plenty of sunlight.* Resisting the urge to lay right there in a pile of hay, Hadley pushed off the wall and walked back inside the stable. She did a quick inspection to make sure everything was clean before collecting Snow White's gear. At the entrance of the building she swapped out Dorothy's old muck boots for her sneakers. She was happy to see Snow White was roaming nearby and not all the way out by the big tree.

A short walk later, Hadley retrieved Snow White and guided her toward the side fence. She secured the gear to her favorite mare before sliding the reins over the fence post. Using the wooden fence rails to help her gain the height needed to swing her leg over, she safely sat on the saddle. She never could figure out how to step up from the ground without assistance. Once on top of Snow White, Hadley felt renewed. She lifted the reins from the fence post and loosely held them in her hands. With a quick grip of her legs against Snow White, they began to move, navigating the fields lazily for a while. Hadley enjoyed the slight breeze they created as she soaked up the sun, which was especially warm, even for August. She was relieved to have the clouds block some of the rays that were otherwise causing a steady drip of sweat down her back.

As the sun started to dip, so did the temperature and the sweat that dampened the back of Hadley's shirt caused her to let out a slight shiver. She knew it was time to head back to the barn so she wouldn't have to walk alone in the dark, which sometimes spooked her. She guided Snow White back and made quick work of removing the gear and placing it back on the hooks in the stables. She gave the horses a kiss on the side of her neck before heading toward home. She walked sluggishly knowing she still had to vacuum, sweep, and do laundry before she could go to sleep. *This walk is taking forever.* Her feet dragged and her focus started drifting. A few minutes later she turned and walked down her driveway, relieved to be home. Even more relieved noticing the empty driveway. She wasn't sure what time it was, but with any luck she could get the housework done and her dinner heated up before her father stumbled in.

She walked through the door and slipped off her shoes. Her hand moved against the wall until it hit the light switch. Flicking it on, the overhead light fixture cast a yellow glow over the foyer. She dropped her backpack at the bottom of the staircase as she glanced at the clock on the wall. 7:00. No wonder she was exhausted. She rested the back of her head against the foyer wall as she took a few deep breaths. She found herself holding the last breath as she pushed her body forward and padded toward the kitchen and it wasn't until the freezer chilled her hand that Hadley thought to exhale. Her hot breath whistled out of her as she took a few follow up breaths to steady herself. *You can do this.*

She grabbed her dinner without even looking at what it was and closed the freezer door with the heel of her foot. She placed the meal on the counter as she programmed the oven to start preheating. She decided to sit down just while the oven got hot, deciding once she put her meal in to bake, then she would get moving on her chores.

***

Shoot!

Hadley bolted from her chair and immediately rounded the corner into the living room. With a tentative breath, she squinted her sleepy eyes at the hanging clock. 8:58. She must have fallen asleep waiting on the oven to heat up. Luckily, the house was quiet. It was also completely dark, aside from the warm lighting in the foyer. Hadley was thankful her father hadn't returned home yet. She wasn't sure what would've outraged him most. Surely he would be pissed she was asleep at the table, but he would also be livid to learn she wasted money on the electricity powering the empty oven. She envisioned her father throwing the spoiled, defrosted dinner in her direction as she stood on the threshold between the kitchen and living room. The thought sent a chill down her spine as she felt the rage in his bloodshot eyes.

She shook the nerves from her system, stretched out her fingers, and bounced her thin body on the balls of her feet for a few seconds as she created the energy needed to get back on track. Since the oven was already hot, she dipped into the freezer and grabbed a Swanson turkey meal and slid it into the oven. She took extra care in burying the wasted meal deep in the trash. She couldn't risk her father noticing.

She twisted the kitchen timer to the twenty-five-minute mark before setting it on the counter and taking a quick lap around the house to turn on a few lamps to brighten the quiet space. The lit-up house helped trick her brain into thinking it wasn't already past her bedtime and with nothing but the ticking of the timer to accompany her, Hadley moved to the closet and pulled out the feather duster. After that she would fluff up the couch cushions the way her father preferred before exchanging the duster for the Hoover vacuum.

Her stomach grumbled as she cleaned as quickly as her tired body allowed. When she finished, she checked the timer and saw only two minutes to go. *Thank goodness!* She weighed her options for a moment before deciding she could grab her father's laundry and hide it in her hamper until tomorrow. There was no way she'd be able to keep her eyes open long enough to get through washing, drying, and putting it all away. Considering her father still wasn't home, she knew he'd stumble in and pay little attention to how full or empty his closet was.

She ran back down the stairs after hiding her father's dirty clothes right as the timer started to ding. She turned it off with a sigh of relief and grabbed her dinner from the oven along with a glass of milk. She took a quick inspection of the kitchen to make sure everything was turned off and cleaned up. Grabbing her drink and dinner, she flipped the light switch down in the kitchen and foyer as she made her way up the stairs to her bedroom.

Finally, she could sit. Hadley crossed her legs and leaned back against her pillows while she quickly ate her dinner with no appreciation for the bland flavors. She still felt hungry when she was done but made no motion to move. Instead, she slid the aluminum tray under her bed to hide it just in case her father opened her door before she had the chance to properly clean up. Knowing her mess was hidden, she switched off her lamp and unraveled her tired body under her comforter as her eyes fluttered shut. After a few short moments she was deep asleep; utterly exhausted.

It's Been Great, But...

Hadley slept soundly but woke up tired. That happened often, lately. This morning she stole a few sips of her father's coffee. Not enough where he would notice but hopefully enough to jolt her nerves into action. Her nose scrunched up as the surprisingly bitter taste still lingered on her tongue, even as she set her backpack down under the desk at Daisy & Daffodil an hour later.

"It smells different in here," Hadley commented as she walked toward the coolers to check the thermometers and hygrometers, ready to start her week.

"You have a keen nose."

Hadley smiled. "Hmm, I smell lilacs and... jasmine? But there's something new... not sure. It smells sweet. Did we get a new flower? Oh! Is it the sweet alyssum you told me about?"

Steve smiled at this, proud of Hadley's memory and growing interest in flowers. "The alyssum should be here by Friday. They'll smell like honey, right now what you're smelling are fresh glazed donuts. There's a shop down the road that makes 'em piping hot on the spot."

"Oh, wow! That's so much better than more flowers," Hadley giggled.

"Equally as good anyway."

"Right..." Hadley cringed. "So, what's the occasion?"

"I thought we oughta celebrate your last week of summer."

"Is that this week? I didn't even realize..." Hadley tried not to panic. She knew exactly what that meant. It was definitely not a reason to celebrate.

"You haven't been school shopping yet? Do you need any school supplies? There's plenty of notebooks and pens in the back room if you need."

"That's super nice of you, but I'm okay. I have left over from last year." Hadley smiled. *Don't freak out.*

"If anything changes, help yourself."

"Thank you." Her smile was small, but she did her best to look appreciative.

"Speaking of helping yourself, don't be shy."

Hadley, startled out of her thoughts, glanced up at the old man.

"You can grab yourself a donut, I mean. They're best when the glaze is still warm. There's a milkshake, too. I wasn't so sure you were old enough for coffee so played it safe."

"Turns out I'm not a fan of coffee, so well played," she giggled as she shook away the memory of the acrid drink. She turned the corner to find the cardboard box of donuts with grease already soaked through around the corners. She pulled one out and couldn't help but grow wide eyed. "Whoa, they definitely look as yummy as they smell." Her smile cracked wider when she spotted the milkshake, complete with whipped cream and little bits of chocolate shavings. She took a big suck in from the straw and let out an elated sigh.

"Shake okay? It's a fudge ripple flavor."

"More than okay! This is good. Like, crazy good."

"Happy to hear. You enjoy the donuts and shake. I'll take the lead on opening the shop."

"Are you sure?"

"Yes, quite sure. I already snuck a few donuts before you got here." He patted his stomach and winked at Hadley before beginning the shop's morning routine.

Hadley polished off her first donut allowing herself to enjoy the creamy vanilla and strong cacao flavors of her shake, before grabbing a second glazed donut. Guilt blossomed inside her knowing that her boss was doing the entire morning routine alone. She scarfed down the end of her second donut and took one last long slurp of her milkshake.

Whoa. The cold froze her throat and gave her an immediate brain freeze. In that moment, overwhelmed by the temporary pain, Hadley realized just how significant the day was. If he knew she started school next week then he probably knew what he wants to do with her. Will he fire her? Change her hours to after school? She didn't know which option sounded worse.

She took a deep breath and while her brain defrosted, she decided to ignore the weight on her chest and get to work. She wouldn't bring anything up unless Steve did. Instead, she spent the whole shift distracted but busy. She cleaned every table, wrote down every order, and hyper-focused on every single detail. She was determined to find balance. She thought if she moved faster, maybe she could leave faster, but no such luck.

All the same, the morning flew by and before she knew it, it was time for her to pack up. She took a deep breath in and a slow breath out. Time to get to the horses. Everything's better with the horses.

"Before you head out, I wanted to check with you on what you plan to do for the school year."

Of course he would bring it up. Now what. "Oh?" Hadley kept her voice light almost like she hadn't heard him.

"Have you talked with your pare- uhm, I mean, your father about it? Is he on board with you working during the school year or would you rather keep this to a summer job?"

"Not recently but I know he wants me to keep working."

"How about you, do you want to keep working?"

No. "Yes... It's been great, but I'll have school until 2:30 and then need to walk here. I wouldn't be able to start until 3:30. Which I know is late, so I understand if that's not good for you." Hadley was rambling, partially wishing to get fired, even though it would infuriate her father.

"Nonsense, that would be fine. We can swap you from morning duties to the afternoon. That'll work out for me anyway. Now that you're a pro around here, it'll be nice to have you for the afternoon rush."

"Okay, that sounds great," she lied.

"How does 3:30 until 6:30 sound? I usually flip the sign around 6 or 6:15, but it takes a few minutes' worth of cleaning before I lock the doors and head out."

"That works!" Lie.

"Great. We can keep you working in the mornings this week and make the change on your first day of school. Does that sound alright?"

"Sounds good." Another lie.

"Wonderful. You're free to go for the day. Thank you for the help!"

"You're welcome." Hadley waved at Steve as she stumbled out the front door. She tripped over her feet a few times as her pace picked up, desperate to get to the farm. Desperate to see Snow White. She slowed down after a few minutes until she completely stopped. *Why am I rushing?* She knew when she got to the farm she'd have to tell Dorothy the update. If Steve remembered the start of her school year, then she felt certain that Dorothy would have, too.

She took the rest of the walk slowly. Practicing different versions of the conversation in her head. She thought about the possible outcomes. Could she help on the weekends? What time did it get dark? Could she help before bed during the week? Or maybe before school in the mornings? Do horses sleep in?

Calm down. A few cars flew past before Hadley realized she wasn't moving. Her breath was lodged deep in her throat, unwilling to pass through. *Just breathe.* Nothing. It wasn't until the next car zipped past her that her senses reacted. She let out a loud exhale and a few audible gasps for fresh air. She bent slightly and placed her hands on her knees.

Th-thump. Th-thump. Th-thump. She focused on the fast vibration of her heart until the sound slowed down.

As her heart rate regulated, so did her breathing. She straightened up and resumed her walk. She spent the rest of the journey convincing herself that she could balance it all and by the time she approached Dorothy's front door, she had her speech mastered. She was ready to convince Dorothy of the same lie she told herself. She could still do it all. You'll see! It'll be easy. Just give me a week to settle into the routine, she'd tell Dorothy when questioned. *You got this.*

Plastering a big smile on her face, Hadley pushed the front door open and let out an excited "Hey Dorothy!"

Everything Would Change

Hadley failed. She tried endlessly to get Dorothy to understand that she could still do it. She could sleep when she was dead; she heard that once. She's young, remember? Full of energy! Still, she failed.

Dorothy gently explained to her that there was no way she could go to school all day long then work after and still have time to help on the farm. There's not enough daylight before school or after work. Plus, homework only gets harder as you get older. It wouldn't be manageable for anyone, not even Hadley. It would be okay, Dorothy assured her. Everything would be just fine. No need to worry.

Except nothing would be fine. At the end of this week Hadley would stop going to the farm. She'd stop cleaning the stables, stop riding Snow White, and stop bonding with Dorothy over fresh baked goods. Everything would change and nothing would be fine. Tears streamed out as Hadley curled against her bay window, clutching her stuffed animal with a blanket draped over her. She made no attempt to control her emotions, letting her sadness overflow and soak the neckline of her t-shirt. Her eyes burned from the stream and her breathing came out ragged. Every few minutes a gasp would accompany her crying as she reached for oxygen.

After what felt like hours, she heard her father's engine roar as he turned into the driveway. The squeaking of the breaks let her know he would be parked and inside shortly. She tried to take a few calming deep breaths, but nothing worked. She felt too broken. The best she could manage was one deep breath in. She welcomed the rising pressure on her chest that crept into her throat. Her tears stopped but the burning did not. She could feel her heart slamming against her chest. Her thoughts became fuzzy and her surroundings drained of color.

Slam!

The front door swung open and closed with enough force to jolt Hadley. She let out several wheezing breaths as the colors around her reappeared. She wiped the blanket against her face while her heart still jackhammered inside her chest. She looked down to find a series of red crescent shaped indents on her palms. She must have been clenching her fists without realizing. After a few more gulps of air, Hadley stood up. She placed her teddy bear gently against the window and neatly folded the blanket. She rubbed her hands down her outfit, smoothing invisible wrinkles. She wiped under her eyes one last time, hoping it eliminated the sight of sadness.

Hadley walked across her bedroom and placed a hand on the doorknob. She debated turning around and bundling herself under her covers for the night. Maybe her father wouldn't notice she went to bed early. Maybe he would. *Everything would be fine.* Dorothy's words rang in her head over and over. She used the mantra to get herself past her bedroom door and down the stairs.

"Hey Dad."

"Well aren't you a sight."

"Oh, um, I was working on my summer book report, that's all."

"Is that so?"

"Yeah. How come?" Hadley was taken back by her father's doubt. Surely her father knew that all kids had summer assignments.

"I'm just saying. Your eyes are awful bloodshot and puffy for *doing a book report*." Hadley watched as her father took a few steps toward the kitchen and glanced at his bar cart. Did he think she was drunk? After witnessing her father's rapid decline, Hadley promised herself she'd never try a sip. Even if she wanted to, she'd never be dumb enough to steal alcohol from her father. Of all the things he freaked out over, she knew this would be the worst.

"Oh. I mean it was just a long day," Hadley mumbled. Hadley kept her eyes trained on her fingers as she felt her father get close again. She assumed he didn't blatantly accuse her because he had no idea how much bourbon should be in the bottle in the first place.

"What kind of long day can a kid even have," he gruffed. Hadley wasn't sure if her father was looking for a response or stating the obvious: his life was harder than hers. He stared at her momentarily and then walked with annoyance into the kitchen and this time reached for a glass tumbler from the cabinet. After he filled it with two fingers of bourbon, he turned back around. "Well?"

"Oh. Um."

He rolled his eyes impatiently as he waited for her to speak.

"It's the end of summer, that's all."

"What's your point? I thought you liked school."

She hated school, even in elementary school. Why didn't he know that? "It's not school starting. Well, not exactly. Um, it's just with working —"

"That monkey's not firin' you because of the school year, is he? I swear to God, Hadley, I'll walk my ass right down there and cause real problems if that's what you're tellin' me."

"No, no," Hadley blurted. She could tell his question had nothing to do with protecting her and everything to do with making sure she would still be handing over her money every week. "He actually offered to switch my hours. I'll be able to work after school."

"Good. Then what's the issue?"

"It's nothing, really. I'm being dramatic." Hadley tried to wave it off, but her father was like a dog with a bone.

"I'm about to be dramatic if you don't spit it out."

"I won't be able to help on the farm anymore. With school and the flower shop and then having to do my homework and chores around here. There's no time left," Hadley said with a shrug. She tried to sound casual and like she hadn't spent the last few hours crying.

"Always the farm. If the worst thing in your life is that you can't play pony, then you're fine. Like I been saying, it's time to grow up."

"I'm only fifteen."

"Your point?"

"I guess I don't have one," Hadley said as she walked back toward the staircase.

"Just where do you think you're going? Don't think I haven't noticed this house ain't been cleaned up yet. My clothes are overflowing the basket, and the oven isn't even preheated."

His ranting didn't affect Hadley as it normally would.

She felt numb.

She felt bold.

"I don't care! You do it, you jerk!"

She ran up the stairs and slammed her door shut. She used the adrenaline coursing through her to push her dresser against the door. She didn't want her father tearing in and grabbing her. She took a deep breath once the barrier was in place. She walked, not caring which floorboards creaked, toward her bed and sat on the floor. She stretched her legs out and felt the cold metal of her bed frame press against the middle of her back.

She turned her head toward her door and waited a few minutes. She could hear her father cursing and slamming cabinets, but it didn't sound like he was getting any closer. Maybe he wouldn't chase her after all. Maybe he was just waiting until she stopped being scared, then he would set off on a rampage. He probably wanted to catch her off guard.

Assuming she was alone for now, she tilted her body against her bed and reached her arm underneath. She slowly, quietly, pulled out the cream-colored box patterned with orange and brown flowers from her fourteenth birthday. She opened the lid to see her mother's dress, perfectly preserved for her. Hadley's fingers hovered gently over the material as a few tears started to fall. She lifted the dress and set it gently next to her. She then collected the money she had hiding underneath.

Every week when she was paid, she pocketed a few dollars for herself. It was never enough for her father to notice. As she counted up her savings she realized she was making progress. If she could keep hiding money away until she was eighteen, she could leave. She felt confident she could escape this house and her father. She wouldn't need him anymore. She hardly needed him now. Satisfied with this thought, she neatly placed the dress in the box and slid it back under her bed.

She grabbed her bear that was laying by the bay window and collapsed into bed. Hadley burrowed her thin body into the bedding, wishing she had opted to do that from the start. Hadley brought the stuffed animal, which she occasionally spritzed with her mom's perfume, up near her face. She rested her chin on top of it and let the comforting scent envelop her. After a few minutes she started to gently cry into her pillow. She cried because she missed her mom. She cried because she was afraid of her father. She cried because she didn't know what else to do.

***

The next morning, Hadley looked around her room as she stretched her arms above her head. Dread washed over her when her eyes landed on the dresser blocking her door. She had stayed up for hours waiting for her father to push through and whip open her door. She imagined he would rip her from her bed to shake the sass right out of her. Overpower her. Defeat her. Instead, nothing happened. The silence. The anticipation. It was just as frightening. Knowing she was now okay, she stepped out of bed. She padded sleepily to her window and saw the empty driveway. *Phew.* Hadley walked toward her door and started to lean her body against the dresser to slide it back in place. She was startled by how heavy and difficult it was to move. It was barely budging. Wasn't this easy last night? Once she struggled it into place, she wiped her brow and continued on her way.

Oh, okay. Hadley stopped on the bottom step of the staircase. Her eyes slowly shifted around and her mouth popped open. Her father may not have hunted her down, but he still set out to teach her a lesson. She looked around the main level of their home to find the couch pillows thrown, laundry scattered, a can of half-eaten chili beans on the mantle, the dirty fork abandoned on the coffee table, and multiple water rings wherever her father rested his tumbler. *He took the time to toss the laundry around?*

In spite of herself, she hung her head and accepted defeat and let out a frustrated sigh as she started with the clothes. She grabbed the empty basket, tossed on its side in the corner, and started to fill it back up before she dragged it to the laundry machine. She made sure to reach into every pocket before tossing the clothing into the machine. She thought back to the time when a stick of gum was left in her father's jeans pocket and how it made a complete mess. He all but killed her for that. Ever since, she double checked. Today she pulled out a chocolate wrapper, a few old receipts, a napkin, and a peppermint. She tucked the peppermint into her own pocket before throwing everything else away. She was sure her father wouldn't notice a missing candy and thought it would make the perfect treat for her favorite horse.

Once the washing machine kicked on, she went back to cleaning. She reconstructed the couch, cleaned up the food, wiped away the water marks, and dusted the surfaces. Lastly, she grabbed the Hoover and gave the floor a quick once over. She checked the clock and estimated another 20 minutes until the laundry could be moved to the dryer. She'd have to walk quickly to make sure she'd get to work on time. As she waited, she made fast work of the dirty dishes. Once they were clean, she laid them in the drying rack. She then grabbed an english muffin and poured a glass of milk before sitting at the kitchen table. She stayed there, sulking, until the washing machine buzzer came to life. With that, she quickly washed her milk glass and rushed to the laundry room. The moment her father's clothing started tumbling in the dryer, she dashed toward the front door.

She opened it - then closed it. She spun around and ran up the stairs to grab her backpack. She didn't have time to grab a snack but at least she'd have a change of clothing. Backpack in hand, she ran down the stairs and flew out the front door. With any luck, and some quick feet, she would arrive at Daisy & Daffodil with seconds to spare.

Here Makes Me Happy

Hadley had been dreading today ever since she ate those delicious glazed donuts. Over the last few days, her sadness transformed into resentment. She hated her father. Hated him for forcing her to give up the farm. Hated him for making her work. Hated him somehow for her mom's death. For turning her into a fifteen-year-old adult. She understood enough to know this was a deep seeded hatred she'd developed. It wasn't the type that other kids her age shouted after minor inconveniences. This was a true, real hatred. She tried to ignore it but it festered like a slow burn. One that would leave its marks on her for the rest of her life.

Despite her frustrations, she made sure to do her best at the flower shop. If she was forced to keep working, she wanted to make sure she did a good job. It would end worse for her to lose this job and have to find another one, knowing her father would terrorize her if the money stopped coming in. She bottled up her emotions and swallowed them down. As far as Steve or any customer was concerned, she was the picture of happiness.

Yesterday, Steve unknowingly pulled Hadley out of her wallowing with a surprise. He reminded her Friday is her last day of freedom before the school year and told her to go enjoy it. He handed her the full week's pay and told her he'd see her Monday afternoon. Hadley couldn't wait to tell Snow White they'd have a full day together. She was overwhelmed by her boss's unprovoked kindness. She almost wrapped him in a hug before she remembered he wasn't Dorothy. She'd grown to trust him but a little butterfly in her stomach always reminded her that if she didn't do enough, he could still fire her. She wished she would have bonded with him the way she did with Dorothy, but it just felt different. Instead, she thanked him several times and continued to make sure he was certain before she finally left.

***

Without needing to work today, Hadley had the entire day to spend on the farm. She woke up at her usual time so as to not raise suspicions and made sure to grab the peppermint she stole from her father's dirty laundry before heading out. She followed her normal routine, except for the direction she turned at the end of her driveway.

As she approached the farm, all frustration with her father melted away. She took a cleansing breath as she ducked through the fencing and walked toward the small ranch one last time. Was it really the last time she'd visit the farm? She promised Dorothy many times she'd visit, but would she? She wasn't sure. She wanted to maintain the relationship she formed with Dorothy but had a hard time believing she'd actually be welcomed back. Once Dorothy realized she had been abandoned, she would probably be disappointed in Hadley and would resent her. If Dorothy had to give up the horses, it would be Hadley's fault. It was always her fault.

She paused in place, feeling the turmoil bubble up in her stomach. That overwhelming peace she felt by the fence was fleeting. She stood in place and did a slow 360 degree turn. The farm was always bewitching despite the fact that the buildings, including Dorothy's house, all showed signs of deterioration. Dorothy used to joke and say the buildings weren't rundown, they were just well loved in and well lived in. She'd say those aren't cracks, that barn's just burstin' with memories. She would say if you think that's bad, I'd hate to know what you think about *my* wrinkles. That's just aging, dear; a beautiful thing. Hadley caught herself smiling as she moved her eyes around. Dorothy always had the best perspective on life. Her farm wasn't run down, it was seasoned with love. Hadley hoped one day she would have her own life and like Dorothy find the best in everything. As contentment washed away her apprehension, Hadley continued her walk. She approached the dusty white ranch and pushed open the door. She slid her shoes off, as she always did, and hollered out her customary greeting.

"Hello, dear, come on in." Dorothy was standing in the corner of the kitchen, undoubtedly baking. The house smelled like fresh bananas and warm vanilla spice.

"You're not already baking are you?"

"Who, me?" Hadley giggled at the twinkle in Dorothy's eyes. "Take a seat, I made us breakfast."

Hadley promptly sat down and fiddled with her fingers as she waited for Dorothy to approach with two stacks of pancakes. Each pile was covered in banana slices, miniature chocolate chips, and an oversized pad of half-melted butter. "We've got whipped cream and syrup. Take your pick."

"Ohh. Syrup, please!"

"Comin' right up."

"These look so delicious. I know I told you yesterday I could come all day but I was not expecting you to have breakfast for us. This is nice... Thank you." Hadley's appreciation was genuine, despite the tears in her eyes.

"Us girls gotta eat, right?" Hadley smiled. Dorothy returned to the table with a plastic bottle of Aunt Jemima's as she continued her thought. "I wanted to talk with ya too, before I lose you to Snow White for the day."

The words 'lose you' hit Hadley hard. Dorothy said it lightly and didn't mean it in the final sense. Did she? Either way, it stung. "Oh, okay," Hadley said slowly. She focused on the syrup she was swirling onto her pancakes instead of on Dorothy. She was afraid to look up. Afraid to make eye contact.

"Don't go worryin' yourself, dear. I just wanted to catch up with ya. Nothing bad. You have a lot going on next week and I know your daddy ain't the most thoughtful so I wanted to make sure you had someone to talk to. This is your sophomore year coming up, right?"

"Oh," Hadley sighed with relief. "Yeah, starting my sophomore year."

"Are you nervous? Do you have everything you need?"

"I'm a little nervous, I guess," Hadley said as she chewed through a forkful of fluffy pancakes. "I have everything I need though. I'm just not sure what to expect. Last year was hard. I mean, I passed everything but I'm definitely not a star student."

Dorothy smiled at Hadley as she began to cut into her own stack of pancakes. "It's okay to not be the star. It's impossible for everyone to be the best at everything. Wouldn't make sense. I mean logically, only one person can be the best. It's okay if it's not you. One day you'll find the thing that you're the best at. Takes time." Hadley nodded. She never considered that but it made sense. "So, tell me about your new schedule. Are you going to be okay?"

Hadley wiped at a tear. "I don't think I'll ever be okay without my afternoons with Snow White. She feels like my best friend. Silly, right..."

"No, dear. Not even a little silly."

Hadley shrugged. She pushed her forkful of pancakes through the syrup on her plate before taking another bite. "I mean, I guess it's fine. I'll walk to the bus stop in the morning, make it through the school day, then take the bus home. I have to figure out if I'll have time to stop home first or if I will get off the bus and head to work right away. The flower shop is like a twenty minute walk past my house. Once I get there, I'm there until it closes... then I walk home and start dinner and homework and chores..."

"That's quite a busy day, dear. Are you sure you can handle it?"

"I don't think I really have a choice. My dad said I have to work no matter what."

"I wish I had the money to pay ya here as a job. Even with the extra money that Kimberly brings in, there's just nothing left in the pot at the end of the day."

"It's okay," Hadley said while shaking her head. "I wouldn't have expected you to pay me. This isn't a job to me. This is honestly the only place that feels like home anymore. I don't think my dad means to, but he makes things hard there. But here, it's easy. Here makes me happy. Made me... here *made* me happy, I guess." Hadley's eyes welled up. If today was her last day, then this was also the last day she'd get to feel the peace and freedom. The last day the wind would brush against her, carrying away her anxiety.

"You're not banished, dear."

"I know, I'm just sad about it all."

"I'm sad, too. But you promised you'd visit when you can. I know Kimberly and I teach on the weekends but if that's your only free time, I'm sure we can figure that out. You still promise to visit, right?"

"I promise…"

"Good. Now that that's settled, go on and finish your breakfast. I'm sure Snow White is waitin' on you."

"Thank you, Dorothy." They locked misty eyes and smiled at each other before finishing their plates in a shared silence.

***

"Hey pretty girl," Hadley said as she entered the barn. Snow White let out a loud nicker and pranced in place as Hadley approached her stall. The dance move usually made her laugh but today all she could manage was a weak smile. "I'm glad you're excited to see me," Hadley said with a gentle tone. She reached out and rubbed the side of Snow White's neck. "Look what I have for you." Hadley pulled the candy out of her pocket and Snow White responded by swishing her tail and letting out a snort. "Can I take you on a ride? We have catching up to do." Hadley asked, letting the silence linger between them, momentarily forgetting the horse didn't speak. She took the continued pitter patter of the horse's front hooves as a sign of agreement.

Hadley guided Snow White to the entrance of the barn and went through the usual motions for saddling up and safely climbing on the horse. Once on the back of her favorite horse, she sucked in and released a deep breath of fresh air before squeezing her legs against the mare to indicate her readiness and the duo moved as one, slowly at first, toward the center of the field. Hadley took this time to mentally debate where to start. She was used to talking with the horse and sharing her secrets, however this conversation felt different. Of course the horse wouldn't respond, but she believed that Snow White would understand. She wanted to be careful to not say the wrong thing. She didn't want to upset her best friend. She had already let down so many people.

Hadley wiped at her eyes. "So, school starts on Monday. It's going to change things a lot." She let out a heavy sigh as her head dropped. She stared at the horn on the worn leather saddle as she fought back a full-on cry. After a few moments, Hadley lifted her gaze. She shifted into a cantor, thankful to the wind for clearing away her tears. Once they reached a comfortable pace, she continued to explain how she would need to work after school and wouldn't be able to get to the farm everyday anymore.

"I love these rides, Snowy. You're my best friend. I'm honestly not even sure how I'm going to survive without you. Dorothy told me to keep visiting whenever I can but I'm afraid she'll change her mind. She'll be really mad at me once the barn work piles up. I don't think she can pay Jeremy to come more. And, well, don't tell her I said this, but I think she's too old to clean the stalls herself. You wouldn't mind being cleaner would you?" Hadley tried for a joke but it fell flat. She wiped at her tear stained cheeks as she admitted the hardest truth. "Oh, Snowy. Even on my worst days, you make things easier. You remind me what happiness is. You remind me how it felt before my mom died. Before my dad became so mean. He expects so much from me now. I'm never going to be good enough for him. You make me feel good enough. You're always happy to see me. Thank you for that." Hadley let her words linger, unsure what else to say. She spent the next half hour roaming the farm in a trot. Hadley took in every moment of the ride, noticing how easily Snow White responded to her every move.

Finally, despite how hard Hadley tried to avoid this moment, the barn was back in sight. "Well, pretty girl, I guess this is it." A fresh set of tears spilled out of Hadley as they slowly moved toward the barn. "I don't know what's going to happen, Snowy. I'm so mad at my dad for this. I think I'll always be mad. But I've been hiding away money and when I turn eighteen, I'm going to leave. I'm going to go far, far away. Maybe I can take you with me. I mean, I doubt Dorothy would let that happen... But wouldn't it be fun? Someday everything will be better. For now, Snowy, I'm just sorry. I'm sorry I can't come back on Monday. Maybe one day I will... until then, please look after Dorothy for me. Keep her as happy as you've kept me."

Snow White let out a rumbling nicker as she nodded her head.

"Thank you," Hadley whispered. Tears poured from her swollen eyes as she folded forward and wrapped herself around the horse. Snow White stood patiently and accepted the hug. Hadley wondered if she understood this was the last ride they'd share. "Okay, girl," she whispered. "Let's get me dismounted so I can get you back into your stall for some rest."

Snow White snorted and lined herself up to the pile of hay bales outside the entrance of the barn. One last time, Hadley threw the guide rope onto the fence post before carefully stepping down. She peeled the equipment off the horse and set it gently on the hay. Hadley smiled as the beautiful, white horse nestled against her neck before resting her muzzle on Hadley's shoulder. Hadley would take this memory with her. She would hold on to this feeling and use it to keep herself working toward a better tomorrow. One without anger or expectation. One where she would be enough.

"Thank you," she whispered again, this time into the horses' neck. The pair nuzzled one last time before Hadley shook away her emotions and guided the horse back into her stall.

Hadley couldn't bring herself to move. Instead, they locked eyes for what felt like hours. Eventually, Snow White broke the gaze and moved to another corner of her stall to chew on a pile of alfalfa. Snow White moved on from the moment. It was time now for Hadley to figure out how to do the same. She choked out a quiet goodbye, turned around, and left.

***

Part Two: The Determined Years

1989 - 1992

Seven Years Later

Hadley never moved far, far away like she once had hoped. In fact, she didn't move away at all until shortly after her twentieth birthday. She wanted to escape countless times but was afraid her father wouldn't survive without her, and as mad as she was, she couldn't stomach losing another loved one. No matter how loose the term. Her father had grown increasingly dependent on her cooking and cleaning and relied on her to obey whatever he could think up and demand. She felt responsible for him in a way a child never should. She felt bad for him, but mainly she felt angry. So angry.

Even worse, he knew how to press her buttons and never missed the opportunity to remind her to grow up and stop playing pony. She had to pull her weight, then pull some more. To hell with the farm. He made sure of that. She had built up so much resentment toward her father, but afraid of making things worse, she kept it buried deep, gnawing like an ulcer in her gut.

Hadley, laying with her legs sprawled across her perfectly made bed, thought back to that day seven years ago when she showed up on Dorothy's front steps in tears. She wouldn't be able to balance everything the way she promised she could. She remembered noticing how much slower Dorothy moved and how much her face had aged, her skin a thin crepe paper. It all had made Hadley feel that much worse to be abandoning someone who actually needed her.

She would never forget how kind and understanding Dorothy was in that moment; explaining to her that she knew the day would come and how much she appreciated all the hard work she had done. Dorothy made her promise to stop by and visit when she could, no matter how rare. She would always be welcome. Hadley's promise back was as thinly veiled a lie as she believed Dorothy's open invitation was. There was no way, in Hadley's mind, that she would be welcomed back.

Still, in the months that followed, Hadley woke up on Saturdays and walked to the farm, planting her feet on the outside of the fence to watch the horses. Often she would see Dorothy or Kimberly teaching a small group of seven or eight-year-olds the basics of how to interact with horses and watch them guide the lucky children around in slow circles. Whenever her eyes found Snow White, her heart would race with a desire to duck between the fence posts and run toward her. She'd visualize Dorothy pulling her into a tight hug while Snow White pranced in place and the children clapped with excitement over the unexpected reunion.

Or. Hadley's mind always wandered to the 'or'. Or Dorothy and the children would be annoyed by the interruption, Snow White would give her the cold shoulder, and her father would wake up and angrily notice she was not at home. The 'or' always made her back away from the fence and sulk home. She failed every time, deciding the next Saturday would be the day she'd re-find her peace.

Back then, when not at school or cleaning the house, her time had been spent working at Daisy & Daffodil. While she successfully hid away a few dollars each week, the majority of her earnings went toward supporting her father's drinking habits. Each week he was quick to snatch the cash from her hands and even quicker to glare at it, and her, disappointedly. He always expected more. If she had more, he'd expect *even* more. It was never going to be enough.

It took a long time for Hadley to hide away enough money to be able to leave and even longer to work up the courage. She froze every time she tried to tell her father she was leaving. Over the years Hadley realized he was what a doctor would classify as a functioning alcoholic. Eventually he progressed to chronic alcoholism, which directly affected his everyday life, and led him to have frequent aggressive outbursts. It was these outbursts, the unwarranted strings of insults, that made her afraid to say she was leaving. She knew once she was out of the house she'd be safe, but still she feared the emotional chokehold that he would threaten. Regardless of how normal it was for someone her age to move out, she was stuck in an endless loop of staying home and pretending it would be okay.

Hadley knew he was only out for himself and incapable of feeling love. She no longer wondered, like she did as a child, if her dad truly loved her mom, in the way she often watched in a movie or read in a book. She knew better now. The grief her father experienced wasn't over the loss of her mom; it was for losing his way of life. He no longer had someone who provided him unconditional love, offered him easy forgiveness, and surrounded him with the brightness and joy that her mom so naturally exuded. He existed, through her light, as the man of the hour, perched on his easily fractured pedestal. With her gone, he was left with Hadley, a reminder of all he lost. Ultimately, he served the same for Hadley.

***

When Hadley finally told her father she was leaving two years ago, he laughed in her face. A mist of hot spit covered her as his disapproval slurred loudly from his mouth. He told her she would fail and be back within a month and then she'd have hell to pay. She packed a few boxes the following week and left quickly without saying goodbye. She was utterly terrified of failing, hoping she'd never have to face her dad's told ya so looks.

She spent those first two years in a small, rundown studio apartment in Cumberland. It was the only place she could find that was low maintenance and close to the flower shop where she started working full-time after high school. For the first few months, she walked forty minutes each way to work, but in a rare moment of kindness, that Hadley still didn't understand, her father had given her his car. It was a lifesaver. Though, she sometimes wondered if he did this to keep a finger on her pulse. He knew, as much as she did, that he could take the car back whenever he pleased. In his constant state of half-awareness, he rarely drove, usually relying on one of his co-workers to pick him up whenever he was assigned to a job. It blew Hadley's mind how her father was even employed at this point. She thought maybe his boss felt sorry for him. He was demoted to general labor, at the most basic level, during Hadley's junior year of high school.

Shaking the memories from her mind, Hadley took in the fresh scent of her cozy new apartment while she lounged comfortably in her bedroom. Was cozy the word? Quaint? Tiny. The walls were a dull white, and the carpet beige. The space felt brightened by the assortment of wall hangings and knick knacks she collected from thrift stores since moving out.

Above her couch was an orange and pink sunset printed on a stretched canvas, to the left she hung a *Grease* movie poster and in the narrow hallway were a pair of floral prints. Her mom's bookcase in the living room was topped by two white resin sculptures of faceless women reading, which were practically free at the Salvation Army because of their chipped exterior. A few steps away in her kitchen, she placed a mustard colored hand towel by the sink and on the back counter a garage sale blue and white ceramic chicken cookie jar and a set of hand painted floral salt and pepper shakers.

In her bedroom, where she currently sat, a muted print of a brown pinto horse standing front and center with a wooden barn in the snow-filled background hung above her head. Her nightstand held a small alarm clock, the alabaster figurine from her father, and the photo of her mom as a teenager, now secured in a slightly tarnished silver frame.

She admired her hodge podge of decorations and smiled whenever she saw Snow White's horseshoe above her front door. She got up from her bed and walked around her apartment barefoot. On occasion she'd step heavier than necessary, just to prove to herself that nobody cared how loud her feet were. The carpets were installed right before she moved in, so her feet sunk into the fresh plush with each step. Often, she found herself standing in place and wiggling her toes until they got lost in the fibers.

Hadley's closet-sized bedroom was only three feet away from her narrow kitchen space but she didn't mind being cramped as long as she had space for her mother's bookcase, which she did. The finish on the wood was faded and the shelves had warped, but she cherished it and the collection of books it held. Hadley's father had surprised her mom with the handbuilt piece when they first got married. It was the first thing

Hadley unpacked and set up. It sat immediately to the left of the kitchen, across from a small couch. Whenever she walked past it, she made a new promise to start reading again. The bottom two shelves held the books she hadn't yet touched and the top shelf stored all of her favorites, most of which have been read multiple times.

Just past Hadley's bedroom was a narrow window and a small bathroom. Inside the bathroom was a sink, a mauve colored toilet and a narrow stand-up shower. She only needed to take one step inside and could then pivot in place to face the sink, use the bathroom, or step into the shower. Hadley was glad to have maintained a slender shape since she wasn't sure she would've otherwise fit.

Another positive of this new apartment, compared to her last place, was that the heating and air conditioning worked. *And no unidentifiable odors.*

Whenever she paused to look out of the window at the end of the hall, she'd see the busy city streets lined with trees. Every sixth tree was paired with a dark green lamp post. The view sent a burst of fresh air through her system. She felt safe knowing there were always women, clad in legwarmers and oversized t-shirts, walking their dogs or strollers on the half-lit concrete sidewalks.

Late at night, that same window showcased a beautiful display of bright, scattered stars. The stunning night sky often caught in her throat as she stared in awe. Her heart bloomed whenever she imagined it was her mom cascaded across the sky and she hoped her mom was proud to see how grown up and responsible she'd become.

She decided that first evening after moving in, while standing at that window, that this was exactly the move she needed. The rent, $430 per month, would be covered with a minimum wage job and the layout had everything she needed at an arm's length. *Literally*. This would make a great home with the perfect backdrop for a new beginning. Next up, a new job.

Placers Staffing

Hadley spent two weeks filling out applications for stores and small businesses around town and browsing the *Classified* section of the local newspaper. She applied to every job that sounded remotely interesting and that would take someone young with limited professional experience. She was excited to hear back about a receptionist position with an industrial employment agency. It was only slightly above minimum wage, offering $3.90 an hour, and while Hadley wouldn't have much left at the end of the month, it would at least cover her rent and basic groceries. She wasn't sure what running a front desk as a receptionist entailed but was just happy to have found something that was hiring immediately. Her first real adult job. She stared in the mirror and smoothed her hair behind her ears, feeling proud of herself for this big step.

Despite her initial excitement, as Hadley drove toward the edge of town, she grew nervous. She was offered the position after two phone interviews, and this would be the first time she'd see the office and meet her new manager. There was a small part of her that was convinced it was an elaborate prank she'd show up to an abandoned building.

She approached an intersection, stopping at the red light, and was relieved to see the faded navy lettering for Placers Staffing on a sign across the street. *Phew.* When the light turned green, she took a deep breath, holding the air in her lungs while she pulled into the parking lot, squinting to make out the almost nonexistent parking lines. She lined herself up the best she could and parked her dad's old 1968 Buick, feeling thankful it was still running twenty years later.

Slowly exhaling, she eyed her surroundings, first noticing that the concrete sidewalks were cracked with weeds sprouting between each slab. Placers Staffing was a narrow building nestled in a faded strip mall; its once vibrant signs now hard to read.

Well, at least my car fits in.

Hadley quickly checked her reflection in the car mirror, and then stepped out, locking the doors, and heading toward the entrance. It rained earlier that morning, so she was careful to sidestep the puddles of water that collected in the low spots of the gravel lot. She wore a cherry red dress patterned with tiny white flowers and a pair of brown leather wedges. The dress had long sleeves, but she was now second guessing if she should have grabbed a sweater. She hoped she wouldn't be required to wear a blazer, because that was a step too professional for her current wardrobe.

Hadley walked into a faded pink room, eyes falling to the row of cracked vinyl chairs. There was a coffee table in the middle with old magazines scattered across the top and a water cooler in one corner that opposed a dusty, fake lemon tree in the other. She slowly approached the front desk, set behind a sliding glass window, and smiled at who she assumed was Mary, the woman she had spoken to on the phone. Mary was an imposing figure, her broad shoulders and strong frame dwarfing Hadley's slender form. Her face, unremarkable in its plainness, seemed to fade into the background.

Mary introduced herself and ushered Hadley behind a door that separated the pink room from a cramped back office with unforgiving fluorescent lighting and undecorated white walls. The unremarkable woman, with short straw hair, had a strong handshake that made Hadley feel small.

With a quick glance around the space, Hadley noticed a navy-blue blazer that matched Mary's slacks draped across the back of one of the computer chairs. Her eyes darted to it, registering it with slight panic, before she forced herself to refocus on the incredibly brief office tour. She nodded intently when her new boss pointed here and there, all the while anxiously holding her breath. Her heart, a trapped bird in her chest, reminded her to breathe. She turned her body away from Mary, pretending to look closely at the nearby desk, allowing her the chance to release a slow, almost-casual exhale.

Turning back to face Mary, Hadley learned her responsibilities and the culture of the company. She would be the first face that the primarily male clientele would see, and it would be her responsibility to welcome them, hand them a comprehensive packet, and collect and photocopy their proof of identification. Most jobs Placers offered were temporary, with a few becoming permanent, and were with construction, out-door maintenance, or production line companies. She wouldn't need to worry much about that part, as Mary was in charge of securing the partnerships and positions.

Mary explained that everyone who comes to Placers Staffing is un-employed and in need of help. Some of them seemed to be in a bad place, really down and out, while others just seemed to have lost their motivation, wanting to completely pivot their lives. Hadley felt a surge of empathy, their struggles resonating with her own. She had grown up in a dysfunctional household, her childhood marred by alcoholism and neglect. She understood the feeling of being invisible, of being lost in the shadows of her own family. She also understood the desire to escape and the determination to find a better way of living.

While she stood in the center of the room, Hadley did her best to engage with her new manager so that she would have an idea of who she'd be working alongside. It turned out Mary was an open book and freely shared insight into her personal life.

"I have two children, a son in high school and a daughter in middle school," she shared. "I've been married for eighteen years but if you were to ask my husband what an ideal weekend looked like to him, he would pick Sunday night football over our family dinner night every time." Mary huffed and rolled her eyes. "Anyway, I've been the manager here for the last three years but have been working here for over a decade. Like I already mentioned, I handle all of the account management which is why I'm not always in the office. I spend a lot of time on the road. I'm usually only here Mondays and Fridays because that's when Meg is off."

"Meg?"

"Right. Guess I should've mentioned that. Meghan also works here but only three days a week. She has a cute little daughter, who she shares with her ex. I'm not really sure what happened there. If you ask me, I would've hung on to that man for dear life."

Hadley smiled, unsure how to respond. As silence filled the room, Hadley looked around, taking inventory of the cramped surroundings. She nodded when Mary told her to not be shy if she thought of any questions. She watched as Mary returned to her desk and promptly opened the latest edition of Cosmo magazine. Hadley, still standing in place, felt a flick of hope ignite within her. This would be her first grown-up job and while she fell into an easy groove at Daisy & Daffodil, even accepting a store manager promotion, she knew this would be so much more. She felt a newfound sense of purpose and felt proud to be joining a woman-led company. This was a big step for Hadley, one that had the potential to change her life and help her move on from the past.

***

At the end of the day, with her head held high, Hadley decided she'd stop at the pizza place around the corner from her apartment. She normally wouldn't splurge knowing she had a stocked freezer from a recent grocery store sale, but decided a successful first day at a new job was reason enough. She pulled into her parking lot and walked the block to Franco's. She ordered a slice of pepperoni and a garlic knot, momentarily hesitating when realizing her dinner cost her an hour worth of work at her new job. She stuck her nose in the brown bag the cashier handed her, inhaling the garlic scent. *Worth it.*

She walked down the block and up the staircase in her apartment as her stomach eagerly rumbled. As she approached her door, she noticed a yellow sticky note a few inches above her door handle. She pulled it off and stuck it to the pizza bag in her left hand, using her free hand to finagle her key until the knob finally unlocked. Once inside, she traded her wedges for slippers and slid her dinner onto the kitchen counter. She pulled out her meal, enjoying the brick oven aroma, as she read the note that was left on her door.

***Name:** Michael Martin*
***Time:** 2:35 pm*
***Message:** Donation pick up*
Wed.
If you want anything, come before
then.

Well that was unexpected. She wondered what exactly he was planning to donate and why now. She leaned against the counter, breaking off chunks of her garlic knot as she considered her options. She could go tonight, or she could go tomorrow after work. She rolled her eyes and decided she'd go tomorrow, not wanting to waste the $3 spent on a celebratory dinner. Whatever was to come would surely ruin her appetite.

She licked the garlic grease from her thumbs before grabbing a paper napkin to wipe the rest of her fingers. She dropped the note into the garbage with the orange-stained napkin before she filled a glass with tap water and carried her paper plate of pizza to the couch. She curled her legs under and smiled at the salty taste of pepperoni. *So worth it.*

Meeting Meghan

The next morning, Hadley was first to arrive. After successfully using her new office key, she turned on the lights and sat at her desk, which was made from a cheap combination of fake brown wood and black metal. She started to organize her new workspace, which was covered in scattered loose papers and a bouquet of mostly dead flowers. She threw away the flowers, which must have been from the previous receptionist, and piled up the papers into a neat stack. *I'll figure those out later.*

Hadley carefully pulled out a photo from her handbag and placed it next to her computer. It was a sepia toned photograph of her with her mom on her sixth birthday. The edges of the photograph were torn but Hadley loved it with her whole heart. *I'm gonna make you proud, mom.* She stared and reminisced, wishing she could go back in time and hug her mom one more time.

"You must be the new girl."

Hadley skyrocketed out of her seat, banging her thighs on the bottom of her desk. She spun around in her gray worn-down swivel chair to see a woman with fire engine curls standing in front of her. The woman wore a silky green blouse that perfectly matched the shade of the beautiful round eyes that were staring expectedly at her.

Hadley stood up a little too quickly causing her chair to shoot backwards into her desk. "Oh, um, yes I am. My name is Hadley, I just started yesterday. Sorry for jumping, I must have been lost in my thoughts for a moment." *Great start, space cadet.* Hadley fought the urge to pressure test her lungs and instead extended her hand to the woman, who looked to be in her early thirties, with a beautiful black textured leather handbag draped over her left forearm. Thankfully she didn't seem to bring a blazer, which hopefully meant Hadley wouldn't need to waste her first paycheck on a shopping spree.

"Well, hey Hadley. I'm Meghan, I sit at that desk over there." Her emerald eyes glistened when she smiled. "I'm sorry I couldn't be here yesterday when you started, I have a little girl at home and only work part time right now." Instead of shaking Hadley's hand, Meghan stepped in for a hug that enveloped Hadley in an unexpected warmth. Meghan was a similar height as Hadley, except instead of Hadley's ballerina limbs, Meghan had a distractedly curvaceous figure. Her embrace rivaled Hadley's favorite weighted blanket. How could a stranger to Hadley make her feel so much comfort?

It was a sucker punch to the gut since Hadley generally avoided physical and emotional contact. She learned to avoid making genuine connections, since they always lead to heartbreak. First when her mom died of cancer when she was thirteen, later when the Pink Ladies stopped showing up, when she had to leave Dorothy, and most recently the divide she created from her father.

Hadley realized she was in her head again. *Shoot. Say something.* "How old is your daughter?"

"She's three years old," Meghan smiled. She continued their conversation as she walked to her desk to set her handbag down. "Her name is Amelia. She's a feisty little girl but cute as a button."

"I don't think I've met any Amelias before. That's a really pretty name."

"Thanks! It suits her. Hey, you drink coffee?"

"No. Well, honestly I only ever tried a sip once a long time ago. My dad always had coffee in the morning, but he wasn't the sharing type."

"Ah, men. Coffee keeps me going most days. You must still have that natural youthful energy in you. Mine has long since expired," Meghan giggled. Hadley laughed and shrugged.

Meghan took a slow sip from her thermos while her eyes lingered on the girl in front of her. "You have beautiful hair."

Hadley looked behind her, but the room was empty. "Me?"

"Don't look so surprised," Meghan laughed. "Yes, you. I could spend hours straightening my hair and it would never look like that."

"Oh, well, thank you." Hadley smiled uncomfortably.

Meghan chewed at the inside of her cheek before clearing her throat. "Did, uh, did Mary explain the job to you already and our usual clientele?"

Usual clientele? "Only the basics. She seemed pretty busy."

"With her magazines?" Hadley smiled but didn't respond. "Not surprising. She's great with contract procurement but not so great at being engaged in the office." Meghan shook her head. "Anyway, no big deal."

"I'm sorry, again, for not hearing you walk in. I swear I'm better than that."

"No worries, girl." Meghan's words were light, but Hadley saw the judgment on her face. "Mary doesn't hire just anyone, so I trust her choice in you."

"Thanks." *I think.* "I really will do better."

Meghan waved her off, her expression seeming to soften after she looked at Hadley's big doe eyes. "So, if you don't like coffee, how about lunch? My treat. I can fill you in on some of the goings on around here."

"Wow, that's, well, really generous. I would love that." Hadley smiled and sat back down, ready to go through the pile of miscellaneous paperwork left at her desk. She hated a mess. She made quick work of alphabetizing the stack before she started to file them in the cabinet that stood tall next to her desk.

Meghan also settled in for the day. Hadley couldn't help but watch as she gracefully navigated the office, moving from one task to another without ever breaking her smile. She spoke with an easy confidence that felt a bit overwhelming to Hadley. Meghan was everything she was not. She worked quietly, not wanting to draw unnecessary attention, but still, every so often, Meghan sparked a random conversation.

"I used to beg my parents for a younger sister."

Hadley looked over at Meghan and smiled, waiting to see where the conversation was headed.

"I have two brothers, but they could care less about their annoyingly frilly sister." Meghan chuckled. "I bet if I had a younger sister she'd be close to your age." Meghan squinted her eyes. "Hmm, maybe a little older. All the same, I think this will be fun. Me and you, I mean!"

"I look younger than I am," Hadley blushed. "It's been great so far working with you this morning. You're about the nicest person I've talked to in years."

"Aw, shucks." Meghan feigned modesty before laughing. "How about you? Do you have any siblings?"

"I'm an only child, but I would've loved an older sister growing up." Hadley sighed. "Could've really used one, actually."

Meghan nodded but didn't pry. "Well, you got me now. You should be careful what you wish for." She laughed right as the phone rang. "Looks like you're saved by the bell." Meghan winked before answering the phone.

Hadley suppressed a laugh and returned her focus to the paperwork in front of her. She hoped Meghan was as genuine as she seemed, though a small piece of her wondered if she was only being nice out of necessity. From what Mary told her yesterday, they'd been through several receptionists in the past six months. Surely Meghan was just trying to get Hadley to stick. Still, she smiled.

Lunch at Morty's

"I don't know about you, but I'm positively famished. Lunch?" Meghan asked as she closed the file in front of her. She stood up and grabbed her handbag before Hadley had a chance to respond.

"Oh, sure. Now that you mention it, I am getting hungry," Hadley smiled. She was actually starving but wasn't about to admit that. It was nice enough that her new coworker offered to buy her lunch, especially since she only packed an apple and a Nature Valley granola bar in her bag, which would need to keep her full until whenever she got back from her dad's house later. She was used to eating small, sometimes skipping an entire meal. She always made sure to pay her rent and utility bills before worrying about what was or wasn't in her fridge.

"Great! We can head next door for a sandwich. Give me a minute to lock up."

"Sounds good."

***

"I know this strip mall is pretty haggard, but Morty's is delicious. It's the only Jewish deli in the area and their meats are *fresh*. They wait to slice anything until an order is placed. If you like rye bread, I definitely recommend that. Though, I find myself leaning toward their kaiser rolls." Hadley nodded along as they stared at the chalkboard menu above the front of the counter. "Anyway, not sure why I'm giving a dissertation on delis. Get whatever you want!"

"Thanks, again," Hadley blushed.

"You got it, girl. Now that I've told you I prefer kaiser rolls, I think I'm going to mix it up. I'm going to get the pastrami on rye. You?"

Hadley eyed the menu. She'd never had most of the meats listed and was afraid of choosing the wrong thing. "Hmm, how about the turkey and cheddar?"

"Yum! Okay, I'll order while you grab a table. Sound okay?"

"Sure, thanks." Hadley chose a table in the back corner of the small delicatessen. She looked around while she waited on Meghan. The tables were made from beautiful beech wood and the matching chairs had comfortable burgundy vinyl padding. She noticed the padding here was perfectly intact, unlike the cracked cushions at her new job.

She enjoyed the style of this place, which was much nicer on the inside than the exterior suggested. The bottom third of the walls were covered by a green beadboard while the top of the walls were covered in photographs, some old and others relatively new. Her eyes bounced from one frame to the next, admiring the generations on display. She wondered if Morty was just a name or if he was the owner. Maybe one of these photos were of him.

Hadley's thoughts were interrupted when Meghan approached with their plates. Her eyes bulged at the height of both sandwiches. She couldn't remember the last time she ate such a big meal. It could keep her full for days. "Wow! Are the sandwiches always so huge?"

"They take their sandwich construction very seriously with the perfect combination of thick cut tomatoes and thin sliced onion," Meghan giggled. She placed a plate in front of Hadley before taking a seat across from her. "And don't forget the tangy kosher pickle on the side."

Hadley eyed her sandwich, determining where to start. Finally, she decided to just go for it and bit into one of the corners. "Oh wow, this is great," Hadley said, using her free hand as a curtain to hide her full mouth.

"This has been my go-to for a while. I usually come here once or twice a week. I'm pretty sure I would be as huge as this sandwich if I ate here as much as I wanted to, though." Meghan smiled before taking another bite, letting out a low *mmm* as she chewed. "I don't know what it is about food that is always so satisfying."

"I know what you mean. Honestly, I spent most of my life eating frozen dinners so whenever I have something real like this, it's heaven."

"Oh, yeah. I make those once in a while. Usually on nights after Amelia had an especially sassy day and I'm utterly exhausted." Meghan's eyes sparkled at the mention of her daughter. "I agree, though, it definitely doesn't qualify as satisfying."

Hadley smiled. "You're telling me. Thanks again for this," Hadley pointed to her half-eaten sandwich. "It's hitting the spot."

"No worries at all! I figured this would be a good time to give you some of the background on Placers and what you should know going into it."

Hadley wondered what she could mean by that. Wasn't it just a normal receptionist position? "Sounds good."

"So, of course you've met our manager, Mary. She focuses more on high level stuff, and her magazines," Meghan smiled. "You'll see her in the office, especially on Mondays and Fridays when I'm not there. Otherwise, she's on the road meeting with our contracted companies. She also works to secure new contracts. We need to keep good relations with the companies so that they give us placements for our clients." Hadley nodded along as she bit into the crisp pickle spear. "As for our clients... that's a different ball game."

Hadley set her pickle down, picking her sandwich back up, and watched the look on Meghan's face change. "Oh?"

"Yeah, they're not ideal. Before I get into that, though, I apologize... I meant to start by asking your background. Have you worked this type of job before? Mary let me know she hired you but didn't share too many details."

"I worked for a florist in my hometown. I worked there for seven years, starting in high school. It's a small-town flower shop but by the end of it I was managing orders and the majority of the store. It was part-time, until toward the end, but a great learning experience. Honestly, that's the only job I've had."

"I'm sure you're very organized, then," Meghan smiled before stealing a big bite of pastrami.

"I am. I also spent a few years helping a, uh, neighbor, with her farm. I cleaned the barn and stables and took care of the horses. It wasn't paid so I don't know if that counts but it's where I learned about the importance of hard work and responsibility. It was also a lot of fun."

"That's great. Willingly doing manual labor like that speaks to your natural work ethic. What about the customers at the florist? Were they mainly friendly or can you think of any difficult situations?"

"It was rare to have an angry customer. Customers were sometimes sad, wanting a bouquet for a memorial or to serve as an apology, but other than that..." Hadley shrugged. "On the rare chance we had an inpatient customer, Steve, the owner, stepped in."

"Got it. Okay, so this will be a whole new experience for you. These guys are not the best people you'll meet. It's important to remember that we're in charge and they are not. Most of them act entitled and occasionally come off downright rude. You'll never be alone with them, since Mary or I will be there, too. Just something for you to feel prepared for. Of course, we do get the nice ones, too. They're just rare."

Hadley's palms felt sweaty. Her only experience with angry men was through her father and she worked hard this past year and a half to distance herself from him so she could find her voice. The small pit in her stomach over knowing she'd see her father later today started to grow with worry that her new job would throw her into a similar aggressive environment as the one she worked so hard to escape. Swallowing a gulp of cold water, Hadley responded, "That's good to know. I've dealt with angry men before, I just prefer not to."

"I think we'd all prefer a gentleman. Realistically, the best case for most of these men is getting assigned to a short term, back-breaking warehouse job, most of which are third shift. They're not the golden egg they pretend to be. They get whatever low-level job we offer them. If they're rude on the job site, we'll hear it from the managers or foremen, and they won't be welcomed back. They get one second chance from us, assuming we have another vendor to send them to. If not, their file gets shifted to the back with a big red mark."

"Red mark?"

"Yeah, we're not subtle here. We'll take a red sharpie and literally write an X on their file tab next to their name. That's how we know they're problematic."

"Oh, okay. Got it."

"I don't mean to scare you. Like I said, they're not all bad. I just want to prepare you for the ones that are. Hopefully things will go easily for you. Once we finish up here, we should head back. We have an open interview period from 2 to 5 pm. I'll teach you more about our process as we go. I think for now, I've told you more than enough."

"Sounds good. I'm sure I'll learn as I go." Hadley and Meghan smiled and nodded at each other. They sat and finished their sandwiches before they cleaned up and walked back next door. Meghan was hopeful she shared enough to prepare Hadley since she'd hate to have this conversation yet again in two weeks with the next front desk girl.

Hadley, on the other hand, hoped Meghan was overly cautious in explaining their normal clientele. She never learned how to stand up to her father and was afraid she'd crumble with an angry client, too. *Everything will be fine,* Hadley thought, reciting her go-to motto.

When they settled back at their respective desks, Hadley began working on organizing the random files left on her desk. She chewed the inside of her cheek as she waited for someone to walk through the front door. Soon her mind wandered to what exactly her father could be donating. She tapped her fingers eager to get through the afternoon. A few relatively easy clients came and went and soon enough they were locking up.

"Nothing better than a quiet day," Meghan smiled.

"For sure. See you tomorrow?"

"You got it." Hadley waved at Meghan as they walked to their cars. *Okay. Let's get this over with.* Hadley turned the key in her ignition and set herself in motion toward her childhood home.

Being Thoughtful

Hadley felt a familiar relief coat her anxiety-burnt throat when she noticed an empty driveway. It meant her father wasn't home and she'd be able to go through the donation boxes without confrontation. Hadley shut off the engine and while unbuckling her seatbelt, she dropped her shoulders and blew out a frustrated breath. *Of course the driveway is empty, I have his car.* Hadley tapped her fingers against the steering wheel and let her head fall backwards against the headrest. She closed her eyes and worked to stay calm. There's no telling if her father was inside or even if her key still worked. The clock on that dashboard said 6:45, which meant it was actually 5:45 since Hadley had no idea how to adjust for daylight savings. *Now or never.* Wanting to get home before dark, she rolled her shoulders and stepped out of the car.

Hadley hesitated and decided not to use her key or walk in unannounced, aware this was no longer her home. Trying to forget that her father told her to never come back, she reminded herself that he left her a message telling her to come. She knocked on the door and quietly waited. *You are not a little kid anymore. You can do this.* She tucked her thumbs into her fists and squeezed nervously when she heard a shuffle on the other side of the door.

"The hell are you doing here?"

Hadley looked at her father, struck by how much thinner he was. His face had sunken, and his hair had both grayed and thinned. The whites of his eyes were now as yellow as his teeth and had red streaks that led toward his brown irises. He wore an oversized t-shirt, or perhaps a regular shirt that now seemed oversized, and a pair of stained gray sweatpants. "Hey dad. You left me a message about donation boxes yesterday, remember?"

"Course I remember, I'm not an idiot. I'm just surprised you decided to show your face after abandoning me." Hadley watched her father walk away from the door, but took the fact it wasn't slammed in her face as an invitation to walk in.

"I didn't abandon you, dad. I just grew up."

"Whatever. Boxes are in the corner. Don't make a mess."

Hadley nodded with big eyes and walked toward the pile of boxes, ignoring the layer of dust that coated every surface and the general mess that seemed to overtake the house. There were three big boxes and one small one. She knelt down, a potato chip fragment crunching under her knee, and unfolded the cardboard lid of the first box. She reached in and pulled out a beautiful blue paisley maxi dress followed by a brown and beige crocheted sleeveless dress. Hadley's breath hitched. "These are mom's dresses."

"Well they ain't mine. You're as thin as you've always been, so they're probably not worth your time."

"You can't possibly think I haven't changed at all." Her dad shrugged from his spot on the couch. "If it's all the same to you, I'd like to take them, even if they won't fit."

"Whatever. The donation truck comes tomorrow so you take it or they take it, either way it's out of here." Hadley nodded, and folded the lid of the box back together, excited to pull out all of the dresses later. She pushed the box out of the way and pulled forward the next one. She wondered what else her dad was getting rid of that would warrant needing a truck for pick up. She looked over her shoulder at him as he took a long swig of his drink, and decided it wasn't worth the conversation. Instead she refocused on the box in front of her which was full of books and old photo albums. She didn't bother sifting through the contents, knowing she'd want all of it. The third box pulled forward weightlessly compared to the box with books and when she opened it she saw it held a few colorful knitted afghans. She remembered them well and couldn't wait to drape one on her couch. She could store the others in her closet in case she ever became friends with someone who would want to keep warm during a movie or even spend the night.

She took a moment to stack the three large boxes by the front door before she picked up the last box, which was notably smaller, and looked like a box that her dad's work boots would've come in. She lifted the lid and saw a pile of mail and a few magazines. When she started sifting through the envelopes, she realized they were all addressed to her. The magazines, which seemed like free promotional issues, were also in her name. *What the heck...* "You kept my mail?"

"Hmm?"

"This box. It's full of unopened envelopes and magazines and stuff... it's all in my name. Why didn't you ever tell me you had my mail?"

"Not my mail, not my problem. You shoulda thought about a forwarding address before you hightailed it out of here."

"I don't even know who would've needed my address. It hasn't been that long since I left, though. This is a lot of mail for two years..."

"I don't know Hadley. I been busy keepin' myself *and you* afloat. Least til you left. Maybe some of that junk came in when you were still here, I don't know. You never asked about it so why would I have thought twice to tell you."

Hadley scoffed. "Are you serious, dad? How would I even know to ask about it in the first place."

"Again, not my problem. I didn't need to save it all but I was being thoughtful."

"You think this is thoughtful? Thoughtful would've been giving me my mail as it came, not tossing it aside in a random old shoebox."

"What do you even know about being thoughtful? You couldn't get out of here fast enough and haven't even bothered to come visit me. Guess I should feel *honored* you bothered to leave your address and phone number on the answering machine. Not *your* number, as it turns out, the lobby number."

Hadley set the box down on top of the others and took a deep breath before she stepped toward the couch. She watched as her father huffed at her and gulped the end of his drink. "First of all, I don't have a cell phone, so that *is* my number. Second of all, I stayed here until I was twenty. I didn't even bother trying to apply to college or go out with friends, since I was so busy working or taking care of the house stuff. I bent over backwards for you and it was never good enough."

"Since when did *you* have friends?" He jeered and stood up, brushing past her to refill his drink.

"That's what you got from that? I had friends," she lied. "I just couldn't do anything or go anywhere. I was only allowed to go to work. You were fine with that because it benefited you."

Hadley winced when she heard the bourbon bottle slam down onto the cart followed by three heavy footsteps. She braced herself as he appeared in the kitchen entrance. "Where do you get off talking to me that way?"

"Sorry," Hadley murmured.

"And for the record, working wasn't some huge punishment. It didn't benefit me; it benefitted the house. You know, the roof above your head, the food you ate, the heat and AC…"

"The alcohol," she mumbled under her breath.

"What was that?"

Hadley gulped and shook her head, starting again. "I was a kid, dad. That wasn't supposed to be my responsibility."

"You don't get outta responsibilities just because you're fifteen."

"Sure, dad." Hadley, defeated, just wanted to be home. Home meaning her apartment, not here in this shell of where she grew up. She walked toward the door then turned around, her father's eyes still boring into her. "Thanks for the boxes but I better get going before it's too dark to drive."

"That was fast. You didn't bring dinner or nothin." He rolled his eyes and leaned against the kitchen door frame.

"I'm sorry. I wasn't sure you'd be here or what you had going on. Do you want me to cook you something to eat before I go?"

"You got cash? I'll order myself a hoagie."

Hadley was startled by his blunt ask. She stumbled for a minute on how to respond but his eyes stared expectedly so she gave in, like she always did, and dug in her purse for her last ten-dollar bill. "This is all I have on me." She held the money in the air and watched him walk over and pluck it from her hand. She rocked nervously on her heels when she realized he wasn't going to thank her, his focus back on his tumbler.

"Well, it was good to see you, dad."

"Yup." He grabbed the television remote before he plopped onto the couch, clearly over the conversation. He got what he wanted and had no need for pleasantries. Meanwhile, Hadley stood there for a moment, feeling a deep ache in her heart. She missed the version of her dad that existed when her mom was alive and the good times they once shared. Tears threatened to fall so she quickly rambled a goodbye and moved the boxes to the other side of the front door. Once outside, she carried the boxes one at a time to her car, trying to ignore the tightening of her chest. She dreaded this visit. Even though she stood up for herself, something she never would've done before, she still couldn't understand why she had to. *It could've gone worse.*

Once the three big boxes filled her backseat, she set the shoebox on the passenger front seat before rounding the car and getting in the driver's side. She buckled up and started the car. While she waited for the engine to warm up, she popped the lid of the box and fingered through the stack of mail. She noticed a lot of the same yellow envelope and gasped when she read the name written in the top left corners. Dorothy Wellington.

Yellow Envelopes

Once Hadley carried the large boxes into her bedroom, turned the oven on to preheat, and set a frozen chicken pot pie on the counter, she carried the shoebox over to the couch and took a seat. She slowly lifted the lid and started to go through the contents. She stacked the People, Good Housekeeping, and Tiger Beat magazines into a pile, knowing they'd make good reading material for the office, even if they were outdated. She then set aside two Sears catalogs for the trash before pulling out the pile of mail. She counted three white envelopes and thirteen canary yellow envelopes. She started with the white envelopes, opening them one at a time.

The first one was a graduation card from her grandparents, on her mom's side, who she hadn't seen or heard from since her mom's funeral. Her father told her several times growing up that they lived on the west coast because they wanted nothing to do with them. With her. Hadley felt embarrassed to have believed him, but it made sense at the time. When she was fourteen, she would daydream about sneaking onto a plane and showing up at their home in San Diego. She wondered what it would be like if they took her in and showed her the same love that their daughter, her mom, had shown her. She always dreamed her life with them would be a better one, but, after her dad's constant reminders that they didn't want to be a part of her life, she stopped having those thoughts. Seeing this somewhat generic graduation card made her smile. Her nonna had the same swoopy cursive as her mom.

The next card she opened was from her mom's best friend, Jeanine. It was meant for her twenty-first birthday and had a 20-dollar bill and a one-dollar bill inside. She read the endearing note about how she hoped everything was going well and that she was sorry to have fallen out of touch. She wrote that she hoped Hadley's wishes were coming true and that she was able to live a fulfilling young adult life. *I'm trying.*

The third card was also a twenty-first birthday card, again from her California-based grandparents. There was no written message beyond *With love, Grandpa and Nonna.* Hadley set the three cards aside, grateful for the 21 dollars to add into her empty wallet. She pulled forward the stack of lemon envelopes right as the oven buzzer sounded. Hadley released a breath she didn't realize she was holding and stood up. She carried the empty white envelopes and Sears catalogs to the trash before she slid the frozen pot pie onto a baking sheet and into the oven. She set the timer for 32 minutes and proceeded to spend the first six of them pacing the room as she stared at the yellow envelopes that seemed to stare right back.

Once curiosity beat out anxiety, she sat on the couch and picked up the first card in the stack. She slowly read through card after card. It turned out ever since Hadley stopped visiting the farm, Dorothy started mailing her a card each year for her birthday and for Christmas. Each card had a kind message, an update on the horses, the farm, or on life in general, and a reminder to Hadley that she was always welcomed and to keep in touch. None of the cards ever felt mean or hateful and none of the cards made it seem like Dorothy felt let down. The last few cards in the stack were missing the hand-written updates on the horses and life, but still had a warm reminder to keep in touch.

Hadley fanned the Hallmark cards in front of her like a winning poker hand and stared, completely blown away. She wondered what Dorothy thought of her, for having never responded. Was it too late to reach out now? She sat and stared until the oven timer made her jump.

She walked over to the kitchen and when she pulled out the pot pie, she instantly wished for the smell of Dorothy's blueberry lemon muffins instead of the celery and savory gravy that billowed out from the oven. She frowned at her dinner but grabbed a plate from the upper cabinet along with a fork from the drawer anyway. After she filled a glass with water, she carefully balanced it all in her hands as she walked to the couch.

While she ate, she started to think about what she would say to Dorothy and how. She considered driving to the farm over the weekend, but then thought it would be too bold to just show up after seven years. She thought maybe she'd start with a phone call, but after she glanced back through the cards, she realized Dorothy never left her phone number. She could call the operator and ask for the Wellington Farm residence, but then worried that if Dorothy wanted her to have her phone number, she would've given it. She finally settled on the idea that she would write back to Dorothy. She had the address and clearly it was a form of communication with which Dorothy felt comfortable.

She closed her eyes as she chewed and thought about what she would write. She would definitely start with an apology paired with an explanation that she just now got the box of mail from her dad, who for some reason withheld her mail for years. She'd tell Dorothy how much she missed her baking and their conversations, how she just started a new job, and all about her new apartment. As she took her last bite of dinner, she looked over at the horseshoe tacked above her front door. Snow White. She'd definitely ask about Snow White.

She didn't have any stationary to start tonight, but decided she could use a piece of paper and an envelope from her desk tomorrow. Anxious to finally reach out, Hadley cleaned up dinner, wiped down the counters, fluffed her couch pillows – a neurotic habit after years of trying to please her father, and grabbed a book to read in bed until she grew tired enough to sleep.

It wasn't until she walked into her bedroom that she remembered the other boxes. Tomorrow she would write a letter to Dorothy explaining how she regretted not visiting or staying in touch. Tonight, however, she couldn't wait to dig into the box that held her mom's stunning dress collection.

Obvious Ogling

"Morning, Meghan," Hadley said through a yawn as she entered the office. She stayed up late last night, shifting from Dorothy's cards, to unpacking the collection of her mom's beautifully maintained dresses, draping them proudly on her bed as she associated each one to a specific memory. She shuddered when she hung her mom's vibrant and timeless wardrobe alongside her own thrift shop collection. The thought of tossing out her discount rack finds popped in her mind once or twice before she reminded herself they're only outfits and it would be wasteful to throw away perfectly fine, though dull, clothing.

While Hadley was eager to start wearing her mom's dresses, even though they would hang on her thin frame, today she wore one of her own. She smoothed her hands against the front of her dress before she sat. Touching the cheap modal fabric made her instantly regret not changing into one of her mom's more quality pieces. Up until now, though, the dress she slipped on this morning, which fit like a glove, made her feel pretty. The white dress had a pale blue trellis pattern and a slight flare ending at her knees with a bodice that formed snuggly to her waistline. The square neckline flattered her slender figure while the long sleeves kept it modest.

Meghan was standing at a small table against the back wall, stirring a packet of sugar into her coffee mug. Hadley watched from her desk as Meghan pushed her hair behind her shoulders, causing her glossy curls to bounce across the back of her emerald green dress.

The table Meghan occupied was just large enough to hold a small coffee maker, a red plastic container of ground coffee, a box with sugar packets, and a container of powdered creamer. Near the edge there was also a random collection of mismatched coffee mugs, one of which held plastic stirrers.

Meghan twisted her head around to make eye contact with Hadley and returned the friendly greeting. She then proceeded to finish messing with her coffee before returning to her seat. She took a moment to smooth her diamond printed maxi dress, in a similar fashion Hadley had, before she sat in her seat. Hadley marveled at how much more sophisticated the motion seemed when Meghan did it.

Meghan sat adjacent to Hadley's desk and immediately in front of her was Mary's unoccupied desk. On the other side of Hadley's desk, across from Meghan, were multiple black metal filing cabinets. The cabinets held client files, past and present, in alphabetical order. There were smaller versions of these rusty cabinets underneath each desk. Hadley's was somewhat empty but held copies of blank applications and tax forms. She wasn't sure what was kept in Meghan's two-drawer cabinet but knew all of the company contracts were kept inside of Mary's, protected by a lock and key.

Meghan blew at the steam from her coffee before she took a slow sip. She dropped her shoulders, closed her eyes, and released a quiet sigh. Hadley, on the other hand, futzed with the items on her desk, not all that sure what to be doing but afraid of looking lazy. "How was your night, Hadley? Do anything fun?"

Hadley let out a *pfft* noise in response, prompting a giggle from Meghan. "Girl, please. If that means you had a boring night, then I'm jealous. Amelia has no dial on her energy. It's like a switch, all on or all off. Last night it was all on. All. On." Her eyes round with emphasis.

Hadley smiled. "You say that, but it has to beat the dead silence I come home to. It gets eerie. I was thinking about getting a kitten but decided I better save my money for now. I just moved into my new apartment a few weeks ago, so we'll see. Maybe once I'm settled in."

"Cats are great pets and way less expensive than a dog. Less time consuming, too, since they tend to be self-sufficient."

"Yeah, very true." Hadley returned to the papers in front of her and mindlessly played with the corners. Avoiding eye contact, she continued, "So, this might be stupid, but I'm not sure what I'm supposed to be doing."

"No worries. And, that's not a stupid question... how would you know if we haven't told you?"

Hadley shrugged and lifted her eyes to meet Meghan's.

"So mornings are usually pretty slow for you. Please don't feel guilty about bringing a book or a crossword puzzle, or whatever you're into. There are definitely moments of down time. You'll just have to tuck whatever away when clients show up."

Hadley nodded, not wanting to admit she'd already planned to use the downtime to write to Dorothy. "Do they always have appointments or do people just show up?"

"Great question! We try to advertise 'open interview' periods. This means we designate a chunk of time for new people to come in and fill out applications and get screened by me. But, we also tend to get random walk-ins. We don't turn people away, so be prepared for unexpected people. Oh! And sometimes our repeat clients will stop by looking for new assignments. They never make appointments. They feel *much* too entitled to be sitting among the *squalor* of new clients." Meghan's words dripped with sarcasm.

Hadley appreciated her humor. "Right, of course."

"We take lunch from twelve to one daily. You are welcome to eat at your desk or leave for the hour. I try to hit Morty's once a week, at least, but otherwise pack my lunch. The receptionist before you used to go home for the hour. She lived nearby and would use the time to let her dog out and eat in private. Totally up to you! You just need to be back by one. Then, our open hours are from two until five. Once the last one is complete, we lock up and head home. That part is just like yesterday."

"Okay, got it. Thanks for explaining."

"No problem. Just ask me again if you forget, it's really no worry." Hadley smiled while she listened. "In the meantime, I'm going to enjoy this coffee and pretend it will actually jolt me to life. Yesterday was so slow, right? That usually means today will be busy. Buckle up!" Meghan laughed before she lifted the hot coffee she was cradling in her hands toward her mouth.

"I'm ready," Hadley said, eager to start on her letter. "Hey Meghan, do you think it's okay if I used a few pieces of paper? I don't want to take advantage, but I was really hoping to write a letter to... an old friend, during the slow moments."

"Oh of course. You don't even need to ask! We have more paper than we know what to do with. There's plenty of envelopes and stamps in that drawer in the corner you can grab once you're done."

Hadley looked over at where Meghan had pointed and nodded. "Thank you!"

***

Hadley greeted a few new clients throughout the morning, but overall it stayed slow. It took her longer than expected to find the right words to say to Dorothy and whenever she got into a groove, she'd hear the bells jingle and would quickly shift her focus.

Hadley found a rhythm with building the application packet and handing it through the window for the potential client to complete. While they were friendly enough so far, a few had eyes that lingered a beat too long. She regretted wearing a form fitting dress with a somewhat exposing neckline but did her best to ignore the obvious ogling, often finding reasons to temporarily step away from her desk. "So skeevy, right," Meghan whispered as Hadley walked to the coffee table, with no plans of getting coffee.

"Yeah," Hadley whispered, keeping her back to the window. "It's like they can see through my clothes." Meghan and Hadley both shook the thought off and made matching disgusted faces.

Hadley slowly made her way back to the desk and immediately felt eyes on her. She glanced over at the waiting room and returned the unwelcomed gaze with an uncomfortable smile. She then sat down and refocused on her half-written letter to Dorothy. She decided at that moment to stop at the corner market on her way home to pick up a word search activity book to keep in her desk drawer for future awkward moments. It was safer to appear busy, even if she wasn't.

"Miss?"

Hadley lifted her head at the gruff voice coming from the window at her back. She turned her attention to the man, sliding her draft under an empty manilla folder. "How may I help you?"

"Mmm, I can think of a few ways you could help me," the man said with a dirty smirk. He was short in stature and wore dirt-covered blue jeans and his bright orange t-shirt had an advertisement for a crane operating company across the front. His thin hair was tucked under an old baseball cap and his crooked smile was framed by chestnut and gray stubble.

Meghan was up out of her chair before the man uttered his next thought. She snatched the clipboard from his hands and looked at his name. "Is that so, let's see, *Mark* is it?"

"I was having myself a nice conversation with this here little bombshell. Jealous, *Ariel*?"

"First of all, not my name. Second of all, if you don't know how to respect a lady then you will not be working for Placers. Care to try again or should I remind you where the door is?"

Hadley was dumbfounded by Meghan's natural confidence, grateful she stepped in so quickly. Hadley sat like a statue, her eyes bouncing between her coworker and the man behind the window. She swallowed hard as silence filled the room. Meghan continued to stare at the man, unwavered.

Finally, the man responded. "My bad, ma'am. I was just having some fun." His eyes bounced down to his shoes before he shifted his gaze back up. "Miss?"

Hadley realized his words were directed at her. Nervous, she cleared her throat, and rotated her seat to face him. "Yes?"

"Sorry if I was rude. My packet is done."

Meghan gave him an annoyed head nod, rolled her eyes, and returned to her desk. She gave Hadley a wink of reassurance once she was out of view.

"Thank you," Hadley said to the man. "I just need your driver's license to photograph for the file."

"Here you go, Miss uh, Miss."

"You can call me Hadley," she responded. "Thank you for the license. Meghan will give it back to you once you've interviewed. You can have a seat for now."

Meghan had no other clients but still let the man sit in the waiting room for a few minutes before she called him back. In the two seconds it took for the man to pass by Hadley's desk, Hadley felt his dirt-colored eyes rake slowly across her body. Suddenly her dress felt paper thin. She was embarrassed by the vulgarity of his gaze and immediately turned her chair to face away from him so no one would see the heat that rose to her cheeks or the tears that threatened to escape. She forced herself to calm down not wanting to draw any more attention to herself. *You're being silly.* She held in a deep breath until she felt the pressure build, and then slowly, quietly exhaled.

She listened to the interview starting behind her, without turning back around. "Okay, Mark," Meghan began. "Let's take a look at your application, shall we?"

Hadley wasn't sure but she thought Meghan might have noticed the unwarranted body scan, too. She hoped it meant the guy wouldn't get a job. Or maybe he'd get a job somewhere where no women worked. She hated to think that someone else may get the same skeevy attention that she just had. On paper the interaction was mild, but to Hadley it felt gross.

***

"I guess that's what you meant," Hadley said once the office was empty.

"Actually that was fairly tame."

"Oh." Hadley's eyes went wide.

"Though I'm sure he would've pressed his luck if I hadn't gotten up to stop the conversation. I don't know what makes a man see a pretty young girl and suddenly think he's Don Juan. Totally perverse. Like no, thank you, dude... you don't even have a job," Meghan laughed.

Hadley laughed, too, as her shoulder muscles unwound. "It's not like he did anything but it felt so violating. His eyes were literally searing through me. I guess I should wear something looser tomorrow. I'm sorry if this dress isn't appropriate. I don't have a huge selection, but I figured the long sleeves made it okay for work. It *is* a little tight..." Hadley was spiraling. *This never would've happened in one of mom's dresses.*

"Girl, take a breath." Meghan bounced her eyes to Hadley's chair, motioning for her to sit back down.

Hadley sat. "I'm fine, I just feel silly showing up to work in this type of outfit."

"And what type of outfit is that? I think it's a beautiful dress. Perfectly appropriate for work."

"Okay." Hadley chewed at the inside of her cheek. "I just know it's important to dress correctly for work. I don't want to mess up, this job is really important to me."

"Well you're doing great so far." Meghan confirmed. "The receptionists before you never lasted long, if I'm being honest. The creeps that blow through here seem to scare them away. It's not a high paying or glamorous job, so it's easy enough to quit and move on. I am impressed that you are motivated and want to succeed." Meghan pivoted, hoping to convince Hadley to stay. "There's no reason to feel like you're to blame for other people's behavior. Yes, your dress fits your body great. Clothes are meant to fit us that way. We don't dress for anyone but ourselves. We shouldn't have to cover ourselves with potato sacks so men don't objectify us. It's *their* job to be polite and to remember their manners. What you are wearing is completely appropriate. Now, if you show up in hooker heels and a mini skirt, then we'll talk."

Hadley laughed. "Oh shoot."

"What's wrong?"

"Now I have to plan a different outfit for tomorrow. I had laid out my favorite hooker boots and a sequined mini skirt." They laughed as the tension in the air dissipated. After a few minutes, Hadley looked over at Meghan and smiled. "Thanks, again. I just don't want to mess this up."

"Stick around and before you know it, you'll see just how pathetic these guys are. You'll learn when to ignore them and when to bite back. I mean, we can keep hoping for the Mr. Rogers types to show up, but let's face it... those polite gentlemen don't need our help getting jobs."

Hadley nodded. "Yeah, good point." Meghan nodded back and let out a *mhm* noise before she returned to the papers in front of her. Hadley knew that Meghan would find Mark a job, despite the poor attitude, because that was what her job required. She watched Meghan flip through a file of open requisitions before she smirked and made a quick phone call.

"So guess what I did?" Meghan said, leaning back in her chair. Hadley looked at her curiously. "I assigned Mark to the waste station."

"That's awesome," Hadley chuckled.

"It's a second shift position that starts next week. He'll be stationed in the middle of a garbage heap for most of his day. He gets a few weeks before we get an evaluation on him and can go from there." Meghan giggled before adding, "Trash for trash, amiright?" Hadley joined in the laughter until they heard the jingle of bells at the front door. They quickly composed themselves before a young man approached.

"Hi, welcome to Placers Staffing," Hadley said, still smiling. "Have you been here before?"

"No, miss. I was hoping to fill out an application as I could really use the work." Hadley was relieved to hear manners. The young man, probably similar in age to herself, was wearing a clean pair of Levi jeans and a fitted light blue t-shirt. He stood tall with neatly styled wavy brown hair and a sincere smile. It was a stark contrast to the older man from earlier.

"Sure, give me a moment to grab a packet for you."

"Take your time."

Hadley turned around to compile a new packet and attach it to a clipboard. She paused to look over at Meghan who whispered a theatric *"As I live and breathe, it's Mr. Rogers,"* causing Hadley to stifle a laugh. "Here you go. Fill this out and hand it back once you're done. Then we'll call you back for an interview and go from there."

"Got it. Thank you."

"Honestly, thank *you*." The young man didn't understand why he was being thanked but still nodded an acknowledgment. *They're not all bad*, Hadley reminded herself. *They're not dad.* The scars on her spirit would always be there and her trust in men forever marred, but still she worked hard to find the good. The boldness of Mark scared Hadley but the easy manners and gentle smile of the next guy helped Hadley remember the balance.

I can do this, she thought before returning her attention to the letter in front of her. She was determined to finish it before the end of the day so she could drop it in the mailbox on her way home. She couldn't wait for the letter to reach Dorothy. She made sure to include her current address and the apartment's lobby phone number at the bottom of the letter. With a little horseshoe luck, and a lot of patience, she'd get a call from Dorothy soon.

I'm Just the Candy

Hadley's first week at Placers was coming to an end. She quickly noticed a difference between the days when Mary was in office and the days spent with Meghan. Meghan had a bubbly energy and made constant efforts to connect with Hadley whereas Mary sat with tension stored between her broad shoulders and a permanent frown on her face. She paid little attention to Hadley and barely lifted her head when handed a client packet.

At 12 o'clock, Hadley opened up her brown paper lunch bag and pulled out a plain bologna sandwich. She began to eat her lunch quietly but when she realized Mary was also staying in-office, she decided to try to find a connection. "So," Hadley began, waiting for Mary's attention before she continued. "I remember you said you've been here for ten years, right? What made you want to work at an employment agency?"

"Twelve actually. I don't think anyone *wants* to work at an employment agency. I mean, good for you if this is your dream. For me, it's a paycheck. Kids are expensive and while Carl makes decent money, we always seem to need more."

Hadley finished chewing before she responded. "Oh, yeah. I guess that makes sense. Same here, to be honest. This job pays for my apartment and for this delicious bologna," Hadley laughed. Mary nodded before returning her focus to the open Cosmopolitan magazine on her desk. *Ohh-kay then.* "Um, so what are your kids' names? You have two, right?"

"Yep. Patrick and Sarah. Pat is sixteen and Sarah is twelve. Turning the big thirteen in a few weeks so it's been party planning central in my house. She has a vision," Mary said with a playful eye roll.

"That sounds fun. Thirteen is when I lost my mom. She was pretty sick on my birthday, so we just had delivery lunch to celebrate. Never really celebrated my birthday much after that, it was never the same. Anyway, uh, I hope your daughter appreciates what she has."

Mary's face softened. "I'm sorry to hear about your mom. What a hard age to lose her. Not like there's ever an easy age."

"Yeah. Anyway, I'm sorry for oversharing, I don't normally do that. I'll stop chatting your ear off and let you enjoy your meatballs." Mary smiled at Hadley before she refocused begrudgingly on the magazine's cover feature, *What Wives Can Learn From The Other Woman*.

The rest of the day moved slowly. Any efforts to make small talk were abandoned so the pair sat quietly. Hadley worked on a crossword puzzle between clients while she wondered when she'd hear from Dorothy. She asked the woman who manned the front desk at her apartment building, Hazel, every day if she had any missed calls or messages. Hazel never had anything to say except to go buy a cellphone.

After forty-five minutes of silence, the bells sounded. "Hi, welcome to Placers Staffing," Hadley said with a smile.

"Damn. They're putting the candy on display to get people through the door, now?"

Hadley broke eye contact with the man in front of her. She understood she was the candy in the sentence but couldn't fathom how someone could speak so boldly to a total stranger.

"Oh, you don't gotta get quiet on me, sweetheart. Was justa joke."

Hadley's eyes flicked to Mary who remained consumed by the file in front of her. Up until now, Meghan had been working whenever Hadley received an unsettling comment. She always jumped out of her seat to shut it down. Hadley was confident Mary could hear from her nearby desk but she either thought Hadley could handle it herself, or she didn't care. Hadley cleared her throat and looked back to the man behind the window. "Are you a new client or a repeat?"

"I'm sure you'd remember me if I was a repeat. I'm new, sweetheart."

"You can call me Hadley. Here, fill out this application." She shoved the clipboard through the window.

"Pretty name for a pretty girl," the man grinned.

"You can have a seat while you fill that out." Hadley turned her chair around and ignored the whistle the man made before he walked toward the chairs. She looked over again at Mary, who was still staring at paperwork. Unsure what to do, she stared at her desk and allowed herself to unravel just the slightest bit. *It's okay, you're okay. It's just words. You're used to rude words.* Hadley worked on maintaining a steady inhale and exhale without drawing attention to herself. She knew if she started holding her breath, she would have a hard time releasing so instead she closed her eyes, counted to four, and exhaled, then counted to four again while she inhaled. *One, two, three, four, exhale. Again.*

"Sugar?" a raspy voice sounded behind her. She focused on her folded hands and didn't turn around. "Oh fine." He tried again, this time singing her name for her attention. She knew she couldn't ignore the clients; it was her job to interact with and welcome them so after one last exhale, she slowly turned her chair back toward the window. "Are you done with your packet?"

"Sure am."

"Okay, I need to make a copy of your license. I'll take it with your app and then Mary will be ready to see you in just a few minutes."

"Mary? I'd rather come back there and talk to you." The man had piercing blue eyes that should be attractive but instead bore through her. He had overgrown sandy hair and a healing cut along his left cheek. He was of an average height and weight, but hunched slightly in place and his yellow teeth were spaced sporadically and created an off putting smile.

"No such luck. Mary does the interviews. I'm just the candy, remember?"

"Ooo, a little sour with that sweet. Fine, I guess Mary will do." The man handed over his clipboard and driver's license before returning to his chair. He slouched in the seat, his legs shaking with impatience as his eyes remained fixed on Hadley through the window.

"Did you just call yourself candy to that man?" Mary frowned.

"Yes, I'm sorry. That's what he called me when he walked in. I think it was a cheap attempt at flirting. I was just trying to disarm him."

"Oh, I see." The scowl on Mary's face dissolved. "*Men*. Okay, give it a minute and call him back." Hadley nodded and returned to her desk. She counted to sixty before she turned around to face the window. His eyes were already on her when she did.

"Peter, you can come back." She opened the door for him, using it as a shield as he walked through toward Mary's desk.

"You sure I can't interview with the princess instead?"

"No, sir. One more comment like that and you'll be sure to stay unemployed. Am I clear?"

Peter leaned back in the chair and rolled his eyes. He looked over to Hadley and winked before conceding. "Yes, ma'am. On my best behavior."

"We'll see about that. Now let's take a look at this application, shall we?"

Turned My Day Around

Hadley couldn't wait to be home. The tension in the office, and in Hadley's chest, left with Peter and the rest of the afternoon was un-eventful, with a few easy-going walk-ins. With the office quiet, Hadley stepped away for a bathroom break. When she washed her hands, she heard Mary's voice along with a man's. She first assumed it was a client and felt bad that Mary had to answer the window herself, but when their voices started to thunder, Hadley instantly panicked. She was suddenly 15 again with her father screaming in her face.

She gripped the white porcelain sink and cowered, afraid to move. Afraid to breathe. When she looked up, her eyes met her own in the mirror and she felt ridiculous. She reminded herself she was no longer 15 and she was perfectly capable of standing up for herself. She held her own against her father the other day and kept Peter in his place earlier today. She could handle whatever, whoever, was on the other side of that bathroom door.

When she crept the door open and stuck her head around the corner, she saw Mary stumble backwards and fall into her chair. She also saw a gruff middle-aged man wearing a gravel colored utility jacket with an orange beanie that covered his stringy hair. For a brief heart-racing moment, Hadley thought it was her father. Snapping herself out of it, she jumped into action. Even though the man hadn't touched Mary, he yelled sloppily only inches from her. Hadley immediately decided he was a threat. She remembered many nights growing up being in the position Mary was currently in and while her father never blatantly put his hands on her, the fear was very real.

Without wasting time, she grabbed the phone closest to her, which was on Meghan's desk, and dialed 9-1-1. She rattled off their address, a description of the man, and the scene she walked into. As soon the man realized she was on the phone with the police, he spit out *Bitch* in her direction and took off.

Hadley hung up the phone and looked over at Mary who was wiping away the wrinkles in her blouse to avoid eye contact. "Mary, I'm so sorry I was in the bathroom."

"Oh, sweetheart, don't apologize."

"I heard you yell and I panicked but I should've come out faster to help. My dad, he uh, was, well I guess is, an alcoholic and I think hearing that man's voice brought me right back to my childhood. I was afraid to come out."

"I'm sorry about your dad. Honestly, I was hoping you'd stay in the bathroom, in case it escalated more."

"What happened anyway?" Hadley slowly walked back to her desk and took a seat, facing Mary who had also sat back down.

"Just a random drunk stumbling in. He wasn't here for a job. I don't think he even knew where he was. I know you've seen how we sometimes get rude guys in here but this, I can honestly say, is a first. I'm just glad neither of us are hurt and nothing got destroyed. Guy was just angry at life and happened to wander in here and direct it my way."

Hadley nodded then shifted her eyes to the front door where she could see red and blue lights flashing.

"Great job calling them so fast. That took guts."

"Thanks," Hadley said with a small smile before they stood up and walked to meet the police officers at the front door.

After the officers took their statements and let them know they'd be in touch, Mary decided to close Placers for the rest of the day. They were only an hour away from closing anyway and this way they could both go home and settle their nerves.

***

Hadley was thankful to be home, even though she was still in her parked car at the front of her apartment complex. Once the adrenaline wore off, Hadley felt drained and a little bit embarrassed. If she hadn't hidden in the bathroom, she could've scared away the guy faster, which would've put Mary at less of a risk for being attacked. *Everything was fine*, she reminded herself. She unbuckled, grabbed her bag, and made her way inside, ready for a pair of sweatpants and a frozen pizza.

Hadley headed straight toward the staircase when Hazel called out to her. "You're not going to ask me if you have any messages?" The receptionist, who reminded Hadley of a gossipy Betty White, was leaning on the counter with a Cheshire smile.

"Hey Haze. Sorry, long day. Guess I'm losing hope all around."

"Well?" Hadley shook her head confused so Hazel asked again, "Aren't you gonna ask?"

This made Hadley perk up, she suddenly realized Hazel had a point to her taunting. "Did I get any messages?" Hadley rubbed her fingers together anxiously as she walked over to the desk.

"Oh hm, I'd have to check."

Hadley rolled her eyes and begged Hazel not to torment her.

"Okay, okay, and *I'm* the dramatic one. Yes, you have a message. Hang on, I wrote the details down on my notepad for you." Hazel rifled through a few papers before she found her notepad and ripped off the top page. Hadley took the paper and stared, letting out a shriek of excitement.

"Hope restored?"

"Yes! This just turned my day around. I'm so excited."

"Well, who is this Dorothy lady? Does she owe you money? Gifting you her heirloom diamonds? Ooh, does she need a kidney? Do *you* need a kidney?"

Hadley chuckled at Hazel's theatrical hand motions and wiggling eyebrows. "You really need to cut back on those soap operas."

"And you really need a cellphone," she razzed.

"As soon as I can afford one, I promise I'll stop hogging the lobby phone." Hadley smiled as Hazel waved her in that direction. Not bothering to go upstairs first, she made a beeline to the community phone, and set her bag at her feet. She slowly typed the numbers in and held her breath as it rang.

"Brad Lee Danielson Care Facility, this is Rhonda. How may I direct your call?"

Hadley looked at the phone number on the sheet of paper and wondered if she typed it wrong. "Oh, I'm sorry, I must have the wrong number. I meant to call Dorothy Wellington..."

"You have the right number, dear. I can connect you. Who may I say is calling?" Hadley gulped and told her name, which led to being placed on hold.

Three hours, or maybe thirty seconds later, the line clicked, and she heard a familiar voice. "Hadley, dear, is that you?"

"Dorothy!?"

"The one and only," she chuckled. "I can't tell you how happy I am to hear from you. It's such a shame you didn't get my cards all these years but I'm so glad you have them now and know I've been thinkin' 'bout you. How are you?"

"I had a long day, actually, but now that I hear your voice, the drama doesn't even matter. I spent years being afraid to visit or reach out, and then with time, I was convinced you wouldn't want me back on the farm anyway. The cards really meant the world to me, even if I only got them a week ago."

"That's lovely, dear. I was so happy to read you're in your own place now. That Hazel's a real hoot. Had me cracking up."

"Oh yeah, she's the community gossip, probably taking notes on this call right now," she laughed and waved in Hazel's direction. "She's really sweet though and looks out for me in her own way. Speaking of being in my own place, are you not on the farm anymore? The person who picked up the phone said something about a facility?"

"Oh, well, I had to sell the farm a few years ago –"

"No! Dorothy, that's awful. I'm so sorry."

"Why are you apologizing? You didn't make me old. And do not even try to blame yourself for steppin' away years ago. Even if you stayed and helped me, by now I woulda had to sell the place. I'm practically an ancient relic." Dorothy's laugh blended with a dry cough.

"I'm sure that's not true. Is the facility nice? I guess you couldn't bring the horses with you," Hadley laughed, though her lips turned down.

"It's really clean and everyone's precious. The food's mediocre but that's the way it goes. Unfortunately, the horses couldn't come. They're with Daniel, remember him?"

"I do, he's the man who bought the cows, right? He was really kind."

"Sure was and still is. Enough about my stuff, we can talk more about that later. I want to hear all about this new job you have. Tell me everything. The most exciting stories I hear anymore are who won Bingo or who allegedly cheated at Pokeno."

Hadley laughed and slid her body down to sit against the wall with the phone to her ear and the metal cord rested against her shoulder. She positioned herself comfortably and then began to recite the most exciting story she could think of: the random drunk from earlier. She was about to start on another story, this one about her coworker Meghan and how she had learned a lot from her already, when Dorothy interrupted to say a nurse had arrived to give her medicine and then they'd have to head down to dinner. Hadley wanted to ask why Dorothy had a nurse and what kind of medicine she needed, although surely that was a normal part of aging, but before she had the chance, Dorothy had ended the call with a reminder to call again whenever she had time to talk.

"You look happy," Hazel prodded.

"Yep! Have a good night, Haze."

Hump Day at Morty's

It'd been three months since Hadley started at Placers. Her days with Mary were rigid and dragged and her days with Meghan were full of inside jokes and conversation. They quickly fell into a routine of heading to lunch on Wednesdays. Meghan called it Hump Day at Morty's, which made Hadley laugh now, though the first time she heard it, she was completely confused.

"Girl, please," Meghan had giggled. "I'm pretty sure Morty is like 80 years old. Do you really think he's hosting some weird humping event?" They both started laughing. Meghan went on to explain that hump day also meant Wednesday, since it was the middle of the week, which only made Hadley laugh harder.

She loved their fast, light-hearted friendship.

Today was no different than any other *Hump Day*. When lunchtime rolled around, the pair tidied their desks, locked up, and walked next door to the deli. "I think I'm going to get the brisket and pastrami melt. How about you?" Hadley asked.

"Have you ever had a whitefish salad sandwich?"

"Hmm, I'm not sure. Is that tuna? I've had tuna salad..."

"Honestly, I have no idea. I guess there's only one way to find out. I'll try it!"

Hadley nodded and stepped forward in line to place their order while Meghan walked off to find a table. They rotated weeks on who treated and who grabbed the table. Hadley was nervous at first, worried she wouldn't have enough spare change to cover two lunches, but after several months of consistent full-time work, she finally had slightly more in her bank than she needed to spend on essentials.

"Lunch is served." Hadley smiled as she placed their lunch baskets on the table. She theatrically crossed her right arm over her stomach as her body bent forward in half. They laughed as Hadley fell into her chair. Catching their breaths, they dug into their lunches.

"Whitefish salad was the right call! This is delicious. I can really taste the onion and dill... hopefully it doesn't linger on my breath and scare off the afternoon candidates."

"Maybe I should have gotten that. I could use a little repellent breath."

"Well, geez, I hope my breath isn't totally disgusting," Meghan said while breathing into her cupped hands. "Okay, it's not great. Repellent breath may be accurate," she chuckled.

"Oh my gosh, Meg, I obviously didn't mean *your* breath was gross." Hadley rolled her eyes.

"Yeah, I hear what you're saying. The guys don't ever seem to lay off, do they?"

Hadley shrugged.

"It seems like you're starting to get a little more confident with shutting them down, though. How is it on days with Mary?"

"She either doesn't notice or doesn't care. I sometimes feel like I'm left for the wolves."

"Yeah, if it's not written in her magazine, she's not paying it any mind."

"I usually feel dramatic. The guys aren't jumping through the window and attacking me. They're just creepy. I guess it just makes it hard to believe there are nice guys out there."

"You're not being dramatic. Words can hit just as hard as hands can."

"Yeah, you're not wrong."

"There are nice guys out there, trust me. You just have to keep believing there's good in people."

"Yeah, I don't know. In my experience, women are the ones who are kind and generous, but men... men are sharp and sour."

"Men and women are definitely different, and we are for sure the fairer sex... but not all guys are bad. I know I mentioned before that I have two brothers, one older and one younger. They're a big reason why I know good men exist. Although they were always equal parts nice and jerky to me, come to think of it," Meghan laughed. "I guess that's pretty normal for a brother though. My daddy was a strong, patient man. I searched for those traits and found them when I met Andrew. Even though we didn't work out as a couple, it wasn't for his lack of heart. I try to hang on to the good in people like that in my daddy, especially at work."

"I'll have to try harder to find the good in people, too. Dorothy keeps telling me to keep my heart open to the universe, whatever that means," Hadley laughed. "I think she's dying to play matchmaker, but I'm just not interested. I don't have any good references to go off of, my dad was all bourbon and anger, no real redeeming qualities."

"I'm sorry, girl. That's a shitty hand to be dealt."

"It's alright. Maybe one day I'll meet someone who's kind and patient and then I'll get to know him. Until then, I'm not interested."

"Wait. Okay, this is personal so feel free to tell me to mind my own business, but have you ever dated?"

Hadley blushed. "Nope."

"But you're, what, twenty-three, right?"

"Twenty-four next week, but yeah, I've never dated. I don't like to put myself out there. Plus, where would I even meet someone? In the lobby of my apartment? Hazel would *love* that."

Meghan laughed. "Hazel would live for that moment. Do you ever go out with your girlfriends? You gotta tell them to be your wing ladies."

"I would need to make friends, first." Hadley's cheeks reddened deeper. "I lived at home until a few years ago and when I was there, my dad had so many demands for me that I had zero downtime. I never had the time to keep friends in high school. I also was never that good at making them in the first place, I was a weird kid." Hadley's self-reflection hung in the air while she sucked back her soda.

"Anyway, after that, I was working at a flower shop which is not an easy way to make friends. At least not friends under sixty. Plus, like I said, my dad used up every minute of my time, he was hard to please." Hadley smiled sadly but kept talking. "I don't even know where to start," she sighed. "My mom had this fun group of friends and they got together every Friday at our house. I loved watching them dance around and gossip and I couldn't wait to be a part of my own group of girlfriends like that. Just never happened." Hadley shrugged and focused her attention on her last bite of pastrami.

"I'll be your wing woman."

"What? You mean like help me pick up a guy at a bar? You don't need to do that. I'm really not looking to date, I promise, and you have so much to manage already with Amelia."

"Amelia is exhausting, you're not wrong. But that's even more reason why I should be demanding this girl's night! I need it even more than you do. This is more for me than you."

Hadley watched Meghan's excitement grow. "I know what we'll do. We'll swear off even the most handsome of onlookers. Will that get you to come out with me?" Hadley giggled but wasn't sure what to say.

Meghan must have registered her hesitation because she tried a different approach. "Okay, how about if a girls' night out is not your thing, then we settle on a birthday party?"

"Oh, I don't really do anything for my birthday…"

Meghan burst into laughter. "I love you, but I meant for Amelia, silly. She's turning four so we're having a small get together. No eligible bachelors but a few fun ladies you would love. I'm quite positive they'd love you, too."

Hadley buried her face in her hands. "Ohmigod, that's so embarrassing."

Meghan chuckled. "Just say you'll come!"

"Okay, okay. I'm in. Is there anything I can bring?"

"Nope, just yourself. It's this Saturday at 2. I'll write down my address for you when we get back to the office. Which, looking at the clock, we better head back." Hadley turned around to check the clock on the back wall and quickly agreed. They shoved the scraps of their kettle chips into their mouths as they consolidated their trash and returned the sandwich baskets to the side counter.

Back at the office, Hadley spent the next hour staring blankly at her crossword puzzle. She was too preoccupied trying to determine how much money she could spare on a gift for Amelia. What did four-year-olds like anyway? Maybe Dorothy had some suggestions.

She'd head to the local Walmart on Friday with Dorothy's ideas and browse through the toy aisle.

Every so often, a jingle would break Hadley's daydreams and alert the ladies of a client. Luckily for them, they were all generally respectful and so the day passed easily.

***

On Friday, after work, Hadley stopped at Walmart. Dorothy didn't have any groundbreaking ideas, saying she was only ever around that age group from an introduction to horse safety perspective. Hadley thought maybe she'd find something horse related for Amelia. She browsed the toy aisle, passing by a bin of multi-colored Koosh balls, a display of easy bake ovens, and a shelf of unorganized Cabbage Patch Dolls. She lingered at a green plush Glo Worm toy before locking eyes on a My Little Pony rainbow display. She'd never heard of the toy but it was exactly what she hoped to find. Her eyes bounced between the six brightly colored plastic ponies that were lined up on the display shelf. She was about to grab the yellow one, named Butterscotch, when another caught her eye. Its name was Sundance and it had a white body with pale pink hair and a pattern of pink hearts stamped on its side. The white body immediately reminded her of Snow White, which caused her chest to flood with memories that she'd share later with Dorothy.

On the way to the register, she grabbed a small bright pink gift bag, white tissue paper, and a generic birthday card. She spent $2 more than she planned but was pleased with the gift.

During her drive home, Hadley cycled through memories of Snow White, deciding which she'd share with Dorothy first. Without meaning to, her thoughts drifted to their final ride. Her eyebrows crinkled and she quickly shook away the memory entirely. She was happy to have reconnected with Dorothy, but it broke her heart to learn that she did sell the farm and lose the horses. Sure, Dorothy was in great spirits, and they talked for hours at a time several days a week, but Hadley still felt like she had let her down.

Avoiding a guilt spiral over Dorothy, Hadley forced herself to head down a different memory lane. The Pink Ladies. It had meant the world to her that they kept showing up after her mom passed away, checking in or dropping off meals. She used to sit in the living room on Friday nights, buzzing in her seat until she heard that familiar knock on the door, knowing it was one of the Ladies with something hot to eat. She could still hear the beat of the music and see the twirling skirts when she closed her eyes. She could still feel the smile break across her face and smell the barbecue chicken and macaroni and cheese they'd bring her to eat.

Hadley knew this care wouldn't last forever but she truly cherished these fleeting escapes from her otherwise isolated life. Sure enough, after several awkward run-ins between the Ladies and her father, one Friday, the knock never came. After hours of waiting, Hadley realized she was on her own and that the Pink Ladies had moved on. The only other time Hadley saw them was when they surprised her a year or so later at her high school graduation. She remembered how fast the tears fell as she ran into their arms. It was only moments before that she had realized her father never bothered to show up, despite her reminders. Even though her summertime graduation was the last time Hadley saw the Ladies, she hoped they remained friends with each other. She liked to imagine them dancing around in living rooms on Fridays with wide mouth martini glasses in hand. Sometimes her imagination added Dorothy in with them, all dancing together. Maybe she'd tell Dorothy more about the Pink Ladies when she called, since she never really shared about them before.

Hadley longed for friends that she could dance with, though after her dad's downward spiral, she'd do it without a martini in hand. She wasn't someone who willingly put herself out there, and Meghan seemed to recognize that but pushed her anyway. When Meghan was first friendly with her at work, she assumed it was just a professional courtesy. Now that they've been bonding over weekly lunches, and Hadley was invited to Amelia's birthday party, she felt hopeful. Maybe this friendship was blossoming into one that would soon resemble that of the Pink Ladies.

Hadley pulled her car into a parking space with a smile on her face. She went to turn her stereo off, shaking her head when she realized it wasn't even on. She grabbed her Walmart shopping bag and purse off the passenger seat, locked her doors, and walked toward the main door, excited to get into her apartment and get the gift out to wrap. She couldn't remember the last time she had a reason to buy someone a gift. She planned to call Dorothy in the morning before the birthday party to tell her about the perfect gift she'd found. She also wanted to share her memories about the Pink Ladies and how she hoped to find a group of her own. She predicted Dorothy would be thrilled for her.

Hadley spent the rest of the evening dancing and singing along to some of her mom's favorite bands while figuring out what to wear to a four-year-old's birthday party. She settled on a simple outfit right as her oven timer went off. *I really need to learn how to cook*, she thought as she pulled out a bubbling Red Baron sausage pizza from the oven. She set it down on her oven top to let the cheese cool before attempting to slice into it. This would be her third pizza of the week, but she ate whatever was on sale and whatever required very basic oven skills.

She danced to one more song, giving the pizza time, before she turned the music down and cut off two slices. She sat with crossed legs on her living room floor, setting her plate on the coffee table. She didn't have a television for entertainment, but this spot against the wall gave her a beautiful view of the evening stars from the window down the hall. Though rare, she loved nights like these. Nights where it was her and the stars. Nights where she could see the life she was slowly building. The life she could barely even dream up ten years ago from her childhood home.

She smiled knowing there would be no broken plates or angry yelling tonight. Just her and the stars... and a mediocre sausage pizza. *Could be worse.*

Happy Birthday, Amelia

The next day Hadley wiggled into a pair of black high-waisted jean shorts and pulled on a shirt with thick red and white stripes and capped sleeves. The shirt was cropped to show off a sliver of midriff and was fitted to her small frame, a nice contrast to her wide legged shorts. She didn't have time to apply makeup or fix her hair, since she spent longer than she meant to on the phone with Dorothy that morning. Rushing, she threw her golden locks up into a simple ponytail held by a white scrunchie, grabbed Amelia's gift and the handwritten driving directions, and jogged down the stairs to her car.

Two wrong turns later, Hadley pulled up to a quaint single-story brick-front bungalow which was set back in a row of similar bungalows and cape cod homes. Hadley added her car to the row of vehicles parked along the road and checked her reflection in her rear-view mirror. She wasn't sure why but felt a sudden onslaught of nerves. What if Meghan was so busy occupying the other guests and the birthday girl that Hadley was left alone? As ridiculous as that sounded, it made her anxious. What if no one even acknowledged her. *Get a grip. This party isn't even for you, it's for a little kid.* She released a noisy exhale and wiped her hands down her face before getting out of her car. She grabbed the gift and made her way across the sidewalk and up three steps that led to a bright white front door.

Do I knock or walk in? Hadley stood in place unsure what to do, until the door swung open.

"Whoa! Sorry." A tall man with dark auburn hair blurted after narrowly avoiding her. "I clearly wasn't paying attention."

Hadley quickly stepped out of his way, but he didn't seem to move. She couldn't tell if she was staring at him or if he was staring at her. She jumped slightly when he cleared his throat. *It was definitely me staring.*

"Anyway, uh-"

Hadley tilted her head slightly, waiting for him to finish.

"I hope I didn't scare you any more than I just scared myself," he laughed. "Or, I mean, I hope I scared you less. Or, you know, not at all." She watched as he bounced on the balls of his feet and shook his head, producing a goofy grin.

"No, you didn't," she giggled. "I was actually just standing here wondering if I was supposed to knock or not. I'm glad you made the decision for me."

"Ahh, well, glad to be of service. My sister's in the living room with Meels." With that he scooted past her and down the sidewalk. He turned back and said, "Nice to meet you, by the way."

Hadley smiled and let out half a wave in his direction before she walked toward the middle of the house. *He seemed nice.* She followed the sound of laughter, until she walked into the living room, crowded with people and balloons.

"Hadley!"

"Hey Meghan! Thanks for inviting me," she said, as they wrapped their arms around each other.

"Of course. I'm so happy you came."

"Where should I set this?" Hadley lifted the gift bag into Meghan's line of sight.

"You're so kind! You didn't have to get her anything. Here let's put it on this table with the others then I'll introduce you to some people." Hadley nodded and followed Meghan's lead. They walked around the small house side-by-side as Meghan introduced her to her parents, her ex-husband Andrew, her older brother Liam, and her two closest friends, Helen and Cathleen. "My little brother is around here somewhere," Meghan said, looking around the room. Her eyes shifted to the bundle of energy bouncing her way. The young girl had wild light copper curls and wore a sparkly purple dress with a matching plastic tiara.

"You must be Amelia," Hadley smiled.

"Yeah! It's my birthday," the girl smiled while pushing her hair out of her face. "Are you my mommy's friend?"

"I am. Well, we work together. My name is Hadley. Happy birthday!"

"Thanks! Mommy, can we have cupcakes now? Pleeease?" Amelia folded her hands in the air and offered her mom her best doe-eyed look.

"I think we can arrange that. Why don't you have your friends head into the dining room and Miss Hadley, and I will corral the adults." Amelia skipped off toward her friends with a squeal.

Hadley let out a soft laugh, turning to Meghan. "Okay, I see what you mean about the endless energy."

"You're telling me! I'm sure the frosted cupcakes will tamper her down." Meghan chuckled and Hadley grimaced playfully. "Hey, can you let Helen and Cathleen know we're going to do the cupcakes now and I'll track down my brothers and Andrew?"

"Sure thing."

The Happy Birthday song for Amelia kicked off, and Hadley found herself looking around the room at the friendly faces, locking eyes briefly with the man she ran into at the door. She bit the inside of her cheek to keep from smiling at him and quickly diverted her attention back to Amelia. The palpable joy in the room caused a pang of grief to rip through Hadley. This was what she missed.

The room erupted with applause as Amelia blew out the number four polka dotted candle sitting on top of a chocolate fudge cupcake. Meghan carefully removed the candle and motioned for Amelia to dig in. Andrew walked around the table and placed a cupcake on each child's plate, pausing to kiss Amelia's temple when he passed her. He gave a friendly wink to Meghan before he announced there were bottles of wine open in the kitchen for the adults.

"Hadley, I found my other brother, Josh. Come, let me introduce you." Hadley walked toward her friend, happy to have avoided an invitation into the kitchen.

"Joshy, come here. This is my coworker, Hadley. I was introducing her to everyone earlier but then couldn't find you."

"I'm not twelve, Meg, you can stop calling me Joshy whenever you'd like."

"Big sister rules dictate that I cannot. Sorry, *Joshy*," Meghan laughed.

"Yeah, whatever," Josh smiled and turned his attention toward a wide-eyed Hadley. "Oh hey, you're the girl I almost took out earlier."

"What?" Meghan looked between Hadley and her brother.

"Yeah, that was me," Hadley blushed and waved him off. "He's being dramatic. He let me into your house when I first got here."

"More like I swung the door open and almost walked right into her. But, sure, I'll take the version where I have manners."

"Well, it's nice to meet you. Again."

"You too, Hadley. Now, if you'll excuse me, I'm off to chase some sugar babies."

"Be easy on them, Joshy. I don't need chocolate throw up on the carpets."

"No promises!"

Meghan turned back to Hadley, still laughing at her brother. "He's the baby of the family, if you couldn't tell. But he is the absolute best uncle to Amelia. She is obsessed with him."

"That's so nice," Hadley smiled, letting her mind wander for a moment to what it must have been like to grow up with siblings.

"Well, with Josh occupying Meels and her friends, I think I'm safe to grab a glass of wine before I rejoin the girls. Do you want one?"

"I'm good, thanks."

"Okay, if you're sure. I'll meet you over by Helen and Cathleen in a minute. You'll love them."

"Sounds good! They seem really cool so far."

"The coolest! Right, Joshy?" Meghan pressed her foot against her brother, who was squatting next to Amelia, causing him to topple onto his side. A bunch of tiny laughs floated in the air. "Smooth move," Meghan cackled as she made her way to the kitchen.

Hadley walked over to the women standing by the back window. They both had full glasses of white wine in their hands and seemed to be gossiping in a way only old friends could. She approached them with a small smile and let them know Meghan would be joining them soon. "Oh, you wanna bet," Helen said with a wiggle of her thin eyebrows.

She had leather black hair, cut neatly at her shoulders and wore a plain red t-shirt with faded straight leg jeans. Her lips were painted to match her top and left an imprint on her wine glass.

"Girl, stop," retorted Cathleen. Cathleen stood several inches taller than Helen and kept her long honey hair tucked behind her ears. She wore an oversized white Led Zeppelin t-shirt with electric blue bike shorts. She shifted to face Hadley before she continued. "Helen is convinced Meg and Andrew are still in love. She's just waiting for the day they realize it."

"Really? She never talks about him at work," Hadley considered.

"Ex-act-ly," said Cathleen. "That's because they're obviously *not* in love. Helen's just a hopeless romantic."

"Okay, then why are they standing so close to each other?" Helen nudged her head in the direction of the kitchen. The ladies shifted their focus in time to catch Meghan laughing a little too loudly with her hand resting on Andrew's arm. He looked at her with pure adoration.

"Hmm." Cathleen pursed her lips then took a long sip of wine.

"Like I said," Helen laughed. "Hey, Hadley, do you want a drink? I just realized you have empty hands!"

"No, I'm okay for now." Hadley said, dropping her gaze briefly to her white sneakers.

"If you say so," Helen smiled. The ladies gossiped for the next ten minutes, the topic of wine never coming back up. Hadley rolled her shoulders, releasing the tension, and immersed herself in the jokes and conversation.

When Meghan finally made her way back to the ladies, she was instantly met with three sets of suspicious eyes.

"Oh, let it rest, Helen! We just get along well."

"Mmm-hmm, says everyone who gets a divorce."

Hadley's hand covered her mouth, but a chuckle still slipped free.

"Oh no, not you, too!"

"No, no, if you say you're just friends, then I believe you. It's actually really nice for Amelia to see her parents are happy."

"Exactly. *See*, Helen? It's *nice*."

"I see what I see," she responded with a wink.

"Whatever you say," Meghan elbowed her friend. "How about we wrangle the kids so Amelia can open gifts before that sugar high causes a tantrum or a crash."

"On it!" the ladies declared.

Hadley settled onto the floor next to the couch, along with the other adults who didn't grab a couch spot or chair fast enough. Andrew handed out the birthday gifts, one at a time, to an overly enthusiastic Amelia. Hadley noticed he only took his eyes off his daughter long enough to watch his ex-wife react to the pure joy that radiated from their daughter with each gift she opened. Hadley sighed. The family dynamic, despite them being divorced, was something Hadley only experienced in her earliest years and many of those memories were now fuzzy.

Andrew handed his daughter the bright pink gift bag, which prompted Hadley to sit up a little straighter, nervous about her gift choice. Amelia tossed the tissue paper into the air and reached in to pull out the My Little Pony box. She shrieked and all but ripped the packaging in half.

"Did Meg give you insider info?"

Hadley turned her head in response to the playful whisper and noticed Josh was now sitting cross legged next to her. "No," she smiled. "I actually had no idea what to get but I spent a lot of time with horses when I was younger, and loved them, so I went with it."

"Meels *loves* My Little Pony."

"Really?" Hadley smiled. "Well that's good."

"Mhm," Josh smiled as he shifted slightly in his spot, ending up closer to her than he was a minute ago.

Hadley's eyes bounced down to the narrowed space between them, momentarily distracted. "Did you say something?" She kept her voice low so she wouldn't draw any attention, and after a quick glance around the room she was relieved to see all eyes were still on Amelia. All eyes except Josh's. His seemed to be focused on her. She wiped her fingers against the edges of her mouth in case maybe she had frosting on her face.

"Nope."

"Oh, okay, nevermind..." She focused forward to watch Amelia, as embarrassment crept up her neck.

"Was I staring?" Josh realized, his own eyes saucers.

Hadley shifted her look to the left. *Yep.* She nodded. "I thought you said something or that maybe I had something on my face," she laughed.

Josh turned his head back toward Amelia as he gulped down the rest of his wine. Glancing to his right, he mumbled, "I got distracted, I guess. Your eyes are pretty. They're, like, *really* blue. Like the ocean or something. I've never seen that bright of a shade in real life."

"Oh," Hadley replied, her cheeks burning. "Um, thank you." Josh's smile widened as he nodded, holding her gaze for a moment before Amelia's high-pitched voice broke the connection.

"Thank you, Miss Hadley!" She ran over and wrapped her tiny arms around Hadley's neck. Hadley hugged her back and gave her a quick tickle as she said happy birthday.

The rest of the gifts were opened as Hadley actively worked to keep her folded knee from bumping into Josh's. Despite her efforts, her heart jumped each time his leg accidentally brushed hers, even more so when he leaned slightly, and she could smell his eucalyptus and mint body wash. She focused as hard as she could on Amelia, not wanting to offend Josh by moving away.

After the last gift, Josh offered her a hand up and once standing they nodded awkwardly and went their separate ways. Hadley toward Helen and Cathleen, and Josh toward the wine in the kitchen. Hadley stole a look toward the kitchen once, but when she realized Josh was already looking her way, she quickly turned around and focused on the neatly gardened backyard on the other side of the living room window.

She enjoyed the next two hours with her new acquaintances, laughing at jokes she only half understood, and listening to gossip about people she'd never met. She was happier in this moment than she'd been in a long time. When the room started to clear out, Cathleen extended an invite to Hadley to join them for a girl's night on Thursday. They were going to meet up at the Royal Oak Bar & Grille for happy hour.

"I'm not much for drinking, but thanks for thinking of me."

"Nonsense! There will be appetizers, too. It'll be fun to have a fourth wheel," Helen encouraged.

"Yeah! We promise we won't hold you hostage if you end up not having fun," Cathleen giggled.

"I'll think about it," she said nervously. "Anyway, I should probably get going." The ladies nodded then surprised Hadley by taking turns moving in to wrap her in a warm hug. Through a smile, she turned to Meghan. "I'll see you Tuesday?"

"Definitely. We can talk about Royal Oak, then," Meghan winked.

"You got it," she said with a wave. Hadley left the party, reeling with energy as she walked to her car. The whole drive home she debated whether she should go to the girl's night. It *would* be nice to make new friends. *Any* friends. But a bar sounded like the worst idea possible. She spent the last few years removing herself from those types of people. Namely, her father. Her mind then wandered back to how everyone was drinking at this birthday party and yet they all were incredibly kind. She continued this back and forth, debating where to let her mind settle.

By the time she got home, she decided she would try. It's just one night out with three girls, how bad could it be.

The Girls at Royal Oak

"I want to, Meg, but I'm not sure I'll fit in," Hadley said through a mouthful of liverwurst, doubting her decision.

"What do you mean? The girls loved you," Meghan countered as she ripped off bite size chunks of her pastrami and rye.

"I don't know…"

"Trust me, they wouldn't have invited you if they didn't want to. They're pretty picky."

"Well that's reassuring," Hadley laughed.

"You know what I mean." Meghan sucked in a strawful of diet coke. "They both thought you were the sweetest and wanted to get to know you more."

"I'm just not sure a bar is the right place. I, um, I don't drink."

"That's okay. As long as you're okay with us drinking, but it doesn't mean you need to. It's more a chance for us to hang out and catch up."

"Yeah, I guess you're right."

"I have an idea, I mean, only if it makes you more comfortable. When I was in the beginning of my pregnancy with Amelia, before I told anyone, I would order a club soda with a lime. Everyone assumed it was a vodka tonic and I just didn't correct them. Why don't you try that?"

"Okay, I think I can manage that. It *would* be nice to leave my apartment for a change."

"Yay," Meghan squealed. Hadley rolled her eyes at Meghan's outburst but followed it with a genuine smile.

***

Hadley got home from work on Thursday with an hour to spare before she'd need to head back out to the Royal Oak Bar & Grille. She wasted the first twenty minutes staring at her closet without a clue what to wear. She thought back to Amelia's birthday party and what the women were wearing. It seemed like Helen and Cathleen both had distinct styles. What was Hadley's style? Thrift shop chic? *Ugh.* She finally settled on a plain v-neck shirt with an acid washed denim skirt. She secured the mid-thigh length skirt in place with a chunky white belt and slid on a pair of second hand tailored linen pumps. She gave herself a nervous once over in front of her full-length mirror. She wasn't positive her mossy green heels matched her dusty rose shirt but decided from a distance it worked, plus she didn't have a huge selection anyway, so this would have to do. She tossed her hair up into a ballerina bun and applied grocery store makeup before she grabbed her embroidered raffia handbag. The handbag belonged to her mom and though the style was outdated, Hadley loved the flower detailing and wooden handle.

She stood by her front door and squeezed her eyes shut wrinkling her nose and held her breath to the count of three. She released her muscles in tandem with her breath then opened her eyes and quickly left before she had the chance to change her mind.

She spent the entire drive to Royal Oak distracted by 'what ifs'. What if no one showed up? What if they didn't want *her* to show up? What if they know she's drinking club soda? What if they teased her? She considered the biggest 'what if' as she pulled into the parking lot. *What if this was a mistake?* She looked down at her white knuckles and peeled her fingers from the steering wheel. She turned off the engine and sat in her seat for a few minutes with her eyes closed, searching for a sense of calm. She pictured herself on the back of Snow White with the wind blowing her hair from her face. She pictured Dorothy pulling freshly baked muffins out of the oven. She pictured her mom and the Pink Ladies dancing around the living room. She could hear their laughter ringing in her ears. She opened her eyes as a tear slipped free. She gently patted her cheeks with the back of her palm, careful not to mess up her mascara and released a deep, slow exhale.

She entered the bar, clutching her handbag tight to her side. Her eyes searched, hoping to quickly find Meghan among the splattering of crowded high top tables. She finally spotted ginger curls bouncing back and forth in the corner of the room, and knew it was an animated Meghan sitting with her back to the door in a semi-circle booth. As if on cue, Hadley heard her name being shouted from that same corner. She squinted slightly to see Helen waving dramatically in her direction.

As Hadley approached, the ladies all welcomed her. Meghan scooched over giving Hadley room to sit. "Oh, I love your bag," Cathleen gushed.

"Thanks," Hadley beamed. "It was my mom's. I guess it's practically vintage now."

"It's so pretty and the embroidery is so detailed. I love it," added Helen. Hadley smiled and set it against her side. She noticed a drink already sitting in front of her.

Before she had a chance to panic, Meghan chimed in. "I got the first round of drinks just a minute ago." She winked at Hadley.

"Oh, so generous. Thanks!" Hadley took a tentative sip, relieved to be met with the fizz of a plain club soda. "Thanks for inviting me tonight, I haven't gone out...well, pretty much ever."

"Never?" Helen's eyes bulged. "Girl drink up!" Hadley giggled and took a convincing sip of her drink. "Do you like potato skins?"

"Doesn't everyone?"

"You got that right," Meghan responded. "Let's place an order before we get lost acting like a bunch of... what does Henry call us?"

"Chatty Cathies." Cathleen rolled her eyes.

"Henry?" Hadley's eyes were already tired bouncing from one woman to the next in their conversation.

"He's my lovely husband," Cathleen giggled. "You may have noticed, I'm a bit of a gabber so he called me Chatty Cathleen at first, but eventually it shortened to Chatty Cathy. Our daughter even has one of those dolls."

"Ohmigod, there's a Chatty Cathy doll?" Hadley laughed.

"Yeah, who was named after who, I don't know," Helen laughed as she tossed back the end of her french martini.

"Anyway," Cathleen continued, drawing out the word for emphasis. "He mighta thought I talked a lot but when he saw us all together in action – well, I'm pretty sure he went straight home that night, swallowed an aspirin and collapsed on the couch," she cackled. The ladies all laughed along. Hadley smiled, relaxing her muscles into the plush ink blue velvet cushion.

Meghan turned her attention to Hadley and explained how Cathleen is their resident wife. She's been married to Henry for eight years and they have a six-year-old son, Leo, and a three-year-old daughter, Lizzy.

"They *are* adorable, even if they wreaked havoc on my body," She laughed. "It's why I wear so many oversized shirts," Cathleen said, sipping her ruby red cosmopolitan.

"You can't mean that." Hadley wiggled her finger at the fitted burgundy low cut top that Cathleen was wearing and added, "plus, based on this, I would die for your curves."

"I'll trade you these big ol' curves for that ballerina body any day," Cathleen smiled. "But thank you, that's about the nicest thing I've heard all week."

"I'll cheers to that!" Helen said, before realizing her drink was empty. "In a minute..." The ladies all laughed at that as they fell into easy conversation. They ordered a few more rounds of drinks. Hadley, relieved the bartender recognized she was secretly sober, opened up more as the night went on. She participated in gossip over people she'd never met and became invested in several stories the women willingly shared.

As Hadley finished her soda, Helen flagged down the waitress and asked for a round of melon balls, also pointing to the empty plate of loaded potato skins. "Maybe more of this, too."

"I'm guessing she doesn't mean the actual fruit," Hadley whispered to Meghan.

"Oh, it's – I'm not even sure what it is actually. Something mixed with vodka. Definitely not fruit." Hadley tried not to panic. She didn't want to be the outcast but up until this moment had never even sipped alcohol before. She evaluated the ladies surrounding her. Meghan and Cathleen still had their wits to them. Even Helen, who seemed a drink or two ahead of them, seemed okay. Their laughter got louder and their lips a bit looser, but everyone was happy. Maybe this would be okay.

"You can just slide yours down to me if you're not comfortable," Meghan reassured as the waitress returned with another tray of potato skins and four bright green shooters. To Meghan's surprise, Hadley grabbed the fourth shooter and held it in her hand. She gave Meghan a small smile as she shrugged and looked back at the women across from her.

"Ohh, let's toast," Cathleen gushed, holding her shooter glass toward the center of the table. Hadley and Meghan followed suit, also bringing their glasses to the center.

Helen was the last to join, but the first to speak. "May all your ups and downs in life be between the sheets." Hadley's eyes bulged as a snorty laugh spilled out of Cathleen.

"Oh my god, Helen. Always with the classy toasts." Meghan shook her head. "How about we just toast to our friendship?" Meghan nudged Hadley as they shared a smile.

"To friends!" the ladies all exclaimed. One by one, they tossed their shooters back. While the women looked satisfied as the sweet drink hit their throats, Hadley reacted differently. Her cheeks and throat immediately burned as she swallowed hard. Her face contorted as if she sucked a lemon and she let out a huff. This drew the attention of Cathleen and Helen, as well as a sympathetic look from Meghan.

"So you can drink vodka tonics all night but a melon ball does you in," Cathleen giggled.

"Oh, um, it just surprised me. Not used to the whole shot thing," Hadley said. She had no idea if her cheeks were burning from the liquor or the embarrassment, but was relieved the ladies had already moved on. She picked up a potato skin and took a big bite, letting the cheesy potato soothe the burn.

Conversation returned to normal as Hadley looked at the three women surrounding her. After trying alcohol, even that tiny bit, she feared she'd unravel, but as she sat and waited, she realized she was fine. She smiled to herself, recognizing she was not her father and there was no anger building inside of her. While she didn't care to try another shot or a full drink, she was thankful to have made it past this hurdle, which allowed the weight of the unknown to finally lift from her shoulders.

With a sigh of relief and ears full of laughter, she allowed herself to think that maybe, just maybe, the next generation of Pink Ladies was forming. Could she have found the group of friends she dreamt her whole adolescence about? She smiled to herself as the women were fully invested in Helen's retelling of her latest escapades. Hadley thought Helen reminded her a bit of her mom's best friend, Jeanine. Jeanine was always the life of the party and never afraid to speak her mind. Helen definitely seemed the same.

Hadley shook away her thoughts when she felt Helen's eyes land on her. "So, enough about me and Lance..." She giggled. "What about you? Anyone settin' their boots under your bed," she asked with a dramatic wink.

"Oh, uh, no. I'm not much for dating. I usually just hang out by myself at home."

"Boo, that's no fun! There's gotta be someone you find cute!"

"I mean, I don't know, not really. I just moved into my new place so I'm still settling in."

"You stumbled in the beginning there a little. Who is it!"

"Who is who?" Hadley asked Helen as the other girls giggled but leaned in.

"The guy you just thought about as you were saying you didn't know."

"Oh. Uhh..." Hadley tried to buy time but had no idea what to say. Feeling the pressure as the ladies waited, she finally said, "I mean Andrew was pretty cute."

Hadley smacked her hand over her mouth. The table grew quiet for a minute and Hadley wanted to die right there in her seat. *Oh my god. Why's that the name you said? Why didn't you say Josh. Josh would've been better. Or just make a name up. Why didn't you make up a name?*

Cathleen broke the silence with a loud laugh. "Pshh! That's not even news. Just wait until you're on the receiving end of one of his little winks," Cathleen gushed. She leaned her head against Helen's as they swooned theatrically before they broke into laughter. "That's why Helen is waitin' on Meg to get back together with him. Never gonna find a hotter man than that guy."

"Hot or not, we're better as friends," Meghan laughed.

"Sorry, I don't know why I said his name," Hadley mumbled. "It's not like I'm actually interested."

"Because he *is* cute," Helen laughed.

"Preach."

"Yeah, yeah." Meghan smiled.

"That's low hanging fruit," Helen continued. "I want the scoop when there's someone new. We *all* have crushes on Andrew." The ladies clinked their glasses together in silent cheers to Meghan's ex-husband.

Hadley felt sure she ruined the evening and was afraid to look over at Meghan, who surely was mad. That's her ex-husband after all. Her father never missed an opportunity to remind her how difficult she was, and how she always said and did the wrong thing, and here she was, still saying the wrong thing.

The group however seemed to grow happier, not angry. Hadley released a deep exhale of relief as she looked over to Meghan who was sharing neighborhood gossip completely unphased by Hadley's comment. As the night continued, she relaxed her shoulders and sucked down her ice cold club soda. She let herself smile, laugh, and let loose.

The ladies started to quiet down after the second round of potato skins were polished off. "I better call Henry to pick us up," Cathleen said with a hiccup.

"Had-ney, you needa ride," Helen bumbled.

Hadley giggled before letting Helen know she'd be fine to get home. She thought Helen was a blast, even though she noticed her drink several more cocktails than the others. She had also learned, throughout the evening, that Helen was single by choice. Her exotic look and almond shaped eyes drew a lot of interest, even from passersby this evening, but there was never someone she wished to entertain for longer than a weekend. A true, free spirit.

The ladies all tumbled out of the booth and made their way to the front of the bar. They exchanged rounds of compliments as they waited on Cathleen's husband to arrive. As Henry pulled up in this Ford Escort, Hadley promised the group that she would join again next time.

An Unexpected Loss

Hadley and the girls continued the routine of meeting up once a month for a girls' night, almost always opting for Royal Oak, where they'd always request the same booth. To Cathleen and Meghan, it was the incredibly deserved mom's night out, to Helen it was an audience for her theatrical tales of who and what she's been up to, and to Hadley it was healing. She was thriving in every way that mattered to her, a steady income, a home of her own in the form of a small apartment, and a group of friends that she could rely on. She started to worry less and spent more time enjoying the moment. She also started to carve out time to read, an activity, easily neglected, that always brought her peace.

One Saturday, she sat on her couch, legs extended and crossed, with a library copy of *Morning Glory* by LaVyrle Spencer rested open, but face down, on her lap. Every time she started reading, she'd get to the bottom of the page and have to restart it, her mind distracted by one particularly funny moment from last week's girls' night. Helen was sharing a story, really gesticulating and getting into it, but Hadley and Meghan had a hard time hearing her from across the table since the live band had their speakers set too loudly. After a few failed attempts at reading lips, Helen grew frustrated by their "whats" and yelled out "Turns out I slept with his brother, too" at the exact moment the band finished their song.

A pin drop would've echoed, at least until all of them wheezed and hollered with laughter, as they fell over each other, unable to regain their composure for several minutes.

Hadley gave up on reading after the second time a laugh bubbled out of her. She wedged her bookmark into chapter four then closed the book and set it on her coffee table. Continuing to giggle to herself, Hadley decided she'd give Dorothy a call. She hadn't talked to her all week and was dying to tell her about Helen's embarrassing moment. Although, Hadley wasn't sure which part was most embarrassing, when she realized she slept with brothers or when she shouted it out in a quiet room. Shaking her head, Hadley stood up and slipped on her moccasins. She grabbed a thrifted navy-blue Frog and Toad sweatshirt from her closet, since the lobby doors always wafted in the cold air, before she made her way downstairs.

"Hey Hazel, how's it going?" Hadley walked over to the front desk instead of making a straight line to the phone.

"You sure seem happy today. Staying warm up there?"

"So far. I'm glad that hot air rises, even if I'm only two floors up, because it's a bit chilly down here." Hadley crossed her arms tightly as she smiled.

"You're telling me. People need to stay put and stop opening and closing the front door. Those gusts of cold air are no joke."

Hadley nodded.

"You down here to talk about the weather or to use that relic in the corner?"

"Guilty. I was going to call Dorothy since it's been a few days. Actually, it's been about a week... the last time I called her, the receptionist said she was at dinner."

"Well go on, get to it. I don't want to keep you from that sweet lady. Tell her to call the main number once in a while, she's a blast to chat with."

"She'd love that. Thanks, Haze!" Hadley rushed to the phone and dialed the number from memory. She giggled to herself, excited to catch up with Dorothy.

Moments later the room spun.

The joy on her face crumbled when the receptionist stammered through an explanation that Dorothy was gone. Hadley tried to understand and kept asking questions, but like the novel she was reading earlier, nothing sunk in. Eventually, frozen in place, unable to speak, the phone dropped from her hand. When the telephone's handset bounced off the wall, ricocheting noise, Hazel looked up and took in the scene. As a mother of five and grandmother of 12, Hazel had grown extremely empathetic toward others and therefore knew, without seeing her face, that Hadley was upset. It took less than a minute before Hazel ran to Hadley's side, placing her hands on Hadley's shoulders.

Hazel's embrace startled Hadley out of her trance. She turned around, mute, and with an overwhelming break in the dam, wrapped herself into Hazel's arms and cried. She cried until she felt raw, and only then did she slowly detach herself from Hazel, with a quiet apology for clinging so tight.

"Honey, I'm so sorry. Let me walk you upstairs. Can I call someone for you? I have Meg's number in your file, how about I call her?" Hadley nodded and wiped her wet nose against the sleeve of her sweatshirt. Two months ago she was so happy to have an emergency contact to be able to give Hazel, after she finally worked up the nerve to ask Meghan about it. Meghan was honored even though Hadley kept telling her it would never get used because why would an apartment complex ever need to call her emergency contact. It was clearly the last thing she expected to happen.

Once Hazel used her master key to let Hadley into her apartment, she guided her to the couch and wrapped a lime green and cinnamon crocheted blanket over her shoulders. She looked around the living room, her compliment on the decor falling on deaf ears, as she finally spotted a tissue box. She brought it over to the stunned Hadley and promised her she'd come back upstairs if she was unable to get ahold of Meghan. Hadley nodded at Hazel with big eyes that streamed tears and a mouth that wouldn't move and watched as she tiptoed away. Once Hadley was alone, she buried into the couch and let out a stomach wrenching, guttural cry.

Twenty minutes later there was a knock on the door. Hadley looked over, exhausted. "Hadley, it's me. Hazel said she left the door unlocked, so I'm going to open it, okay?" Meghan waited a moment before she opened the door. When her eyes found Hadley puddled on the couch, she ran over and scooped her up. Hadley sat wrapped in Meghan's arms and cried, relieved that Meghan hadn't tried to force her to talk. Eventually, the presence and embrace of her best friend was enough to calm her down and she took a deep breath. It was the first complete breath since being told the awful news.

"She's gone, Meghan. Dorothy's gone."

"I know babe, I'm so sorry. Hazel told me she called the care center and went over the details with a nurse because she had a feeling you might not have absorbed it all."

"Did Hazel tell you what she found out? I think I blacked out," Hadley sniffled through a hiccup.

"She did. Let me throw a pot of tea on for us and then I'll tell you everything. I hope you don't mind but I called the ladies and they'll be here in a bit. We thought we'd order some pizza, and you could tell us more about Dorothy, like a little memorial. I told Cathleen to hold off a few minutes before leaving, in case you rather be alone. I can call them off, you tell me."

Hadley wiped at her eyes and did her best to smile. "That sounds nice."

"Are you sure? I don't want to overwhelm you."

Hadley nodded.

"Okay, let me get this kettle on and then we can walk through what happened."

While the water prepared to boil, Meghan explained that Dorothy was diagnosed with aggressive colon cancer nine months ago, three months before Hadley reconnected with her. It progressed and spread quickly likely because of her family history of cancer along with her older age. She maintained great spirits with the help of a pain management regimen. Meghan also explained that the nurse who talked to Hazel wanted to make sure Hadley understood that her calls to Dorothy brought such a tremendous joy to her and that Dorothy often told the staff about how proud she was of Hadley.

"Wow," Hadley whispered, right before the tea kettle whistled. Meghan placed her hand on Hadley's leg before she got up to pour them each a cup of tea.

"I hope peppermint is okay, it's the only box of tea I could find." Meghan handed a mug to Hadley and rejoined her on the couch.

"It's perfect, actually." Hadley blew away the steam. "I got that tea because peppermints were Snow White's favorite treat so sometimes I make myself a mug just so I can smell the sweet spice and think about her. Dorothy would've gotten a kick out of me having peppermint tea now, in her honor." Hadley smiled again and wiped her cheeks with her tear-soaked sleeves. "I just wonder why she never told me she was sick. Whenever I brought up nurses or asked why she opted for a care facility, she'd quickly change the subject."

"Man, Had, I'm not sure." Meghan chewed at the inside of her cheek as she thought of what to say next. "You did say you first started visiting her shortly after your mom had passed away, right?"

"Yeah…"

"Well, it's possible Dorothy considered how hard it was on you when your mom was sick with cancer and didn't want you to go through that again. Or maybe she just wanted to enjoy the last few months she had and have normal, light conversations with you instead of filling both of your time with sorrow."

"Yeah. When you put it that way, it makes sense. I was broken when I first met Dorothy and she worked so hard to get me to believe in myself. It took a while until I did, or tried to, anyway. I'm glad I reconnected with her even if it was just for a short time. If I'm being honest, though, it makes me that much angrier at my dad than I already was. Imagine if I had those cards in real time and I never lost touch with Dorothy in the first place. Things could've been so different."

Right as Meghan was going to counter and remind Hadley there's no point in dwelling in the what ifs of life, there was a knock on the door. "Must be the ladies. Are you sure you're okay with them being here? It's not too late to turn them away. Everyone grieves differently."

"It's okay, really. It's another thing that Dorothy would've gotten a kick out of. I always talked about and grew up wishing for a group of girlfriends like my mom had, and here I am, with that exact thing."

"It's good to see you smile, Hads." Meghan set her tea mug on the coffee table as she walked to the front door to let the ladies in. Cathleen held a large white and red cardboard box from the pizzeria down the road and Helen held a brown bakery bag.

"We rallied as soon as Meghan told us what happened. We're so sorry, girl." Helen collected Hadley into a tight hug. "Cathleen grabbed a pie; I hope you're hungry. It's okay if you're not, though, we all know how good cold pizza is."

Helen pointed to the brown bag that now sat on the kitchen counter. "I stopped at the bakery that's near my house because I remember you mentioned once how much you missed Dorothy's muffins. These obviously will pale in comparison but wanted to grab you some anyway. They're lemon coconut."

Hadley's smile wavered and she burst into tears.

"Oh, my girl, don't cry. The muffins were a stupid idea, I realize that now. I didn't mean to upset you more. I can throw them out!"

"No, it's not that..." Hadley shook her head and took a deep breath and held it for a moment before she pushed the air out slowly. The ladies watched her nervously but patiently, granting Hadley the moment she needed. "My emotions are on high alert right now, I didn't mean to cry like that. It was actually incredibly thoughtful of you to bring muffins." Hadley paused to blow her nose. "It's funny, Dorothy kept telling me to keep my heart open to the universe and I thought she meant so I could find a guy to fall madly in love with." Hadley's eyes welled as she gently swatted the air in front of her, which felt clogged with sadness.

"She started dating her husband when she was a teenager and they were wildly in love until he died." Sniffling between words, she continued. "She stayed devoted to him and the life they built for all of her years after him..." The ladies smiled as they listened. "Anyway, I'm just, uh, realizing she wasn't talking about finding a man." Hadley blew out a breath. "She was talking about–". Hadley's voice cracked as she pointed around this room. "This. She meant this. Opening my heart to *this* kind of love."

Meghan wiped a tear from her own eye and grabbed Hadley's hand. "It's the best kind isn't it." Hadley nodded as they walked deeper into the apartment. Meghan, Helen, and Hadley shared the couch while Cathleen sat on the chair next to them. "Okay, here's what we were thinking. We wanted to help you honor Dorothy with an impromptu mini memorial. Granted we know you only just found out, so we may have jumped the gun a little and probably should've given you space to process. But that's not how we work."

Helen wrapped her arm around Hadley and added, "We, of course, didn't know Dorothy, but we're great listeners."

Hadley pulled her sweatshirt's sleeves over her hands and brought them up toward her mouth. She fidgeted with the material as she wondered where to start. "I know we have pizza, but I was thinking we could start with the muffins. I spent many afternoons sitting at Dorothy's kitchen table and talking with her, always in between bites of her freshly baked goods. Do you mind if we start with dessert?"

"I think that sounds lovely." Cathleen, who sat closest to the kitchen counter, got up for the bag and handed everyone a muffin. They were larger than Dorothy's but had the same coarse sugar crystals coating the top, which was Hadley's favorite part.

Hadley ripped a small chunk and popped it into her mouth, surprised by the tang of lemon mixed with the nutty richness of coconut. She tore another bite off before thanking Helen. "They're not Dorothy's but they're still pretty delicious." The ladies nodded enthusiastically as they dug into the treat. After a few moments of shared silence, Hadley knew where to begin. "I could probably talk about Dorothy and Snow White all day. Especially Snow White, she was the absolute best," Hadley sighed. "But before I get to that, I think I should start with the day I first walked onto Dorothy's farm."

The ladies leaned forward and clung to Hadley's every word. Some stories brought tears and others caused them to bend in laughter. Hadley, destroyed only hours ago by an unexpected loss, felt grateful for the love and sympathy that surrounded her. She knew it would take time, and that her grief would come in waves, but after hours with friends she knew the sharp pain in her heart would one day subside.

Cold Weather Companion

A week later, Hadley woke up freezing. She kept her apartment's heat system turned off for as long as possible, hating to waste money when she could just use an extra blanket, but this morning it felt like the temperature had plummeted. She sat up in bed, wrapping her blanket around her body, and let out a shiver. She slid off her bed with her blanket cocooning her, shuffled down the hall to the thermostat, and reluctantly turned it on.

Once it kicked into gear, she walked to the end of her hallway where the window was to check the weather and was delighted to see the first snowfall of the season. *That explains the chill.* She loved wintertime and the natural beauty of the season, even though she hated the cold. She stared at the sidewalks that were covered in the same fluffy white flakes that continued to fall steadily from the sky. Thankfully, the roads seemed wet but mainly clear. She stood in place, holding her blanket tightly, and lost herself in the beautiful scene. It felt, to her, like Dorothy was painting her world Snow White as a reminder to smile.

A few minutes later she returned her blanket to the bed and rushed into the shower, ready for the hot water to warm her body. She opted not to wash her hair since it took forever to blow it dry, and she knew she'd be that much colder if she left it wet. Instead, she wrapped her day-old locks into a high bun and threw on a gray cable knit sweater and a pair of faded black leggings. She slid her feet into an old pair of fuzzy pale blue slippers before she walked into the kitchen. She placed a small pot of milk onto her stovetop, deciding hot chocolate made a suitable breakfast on a morning like this.

She sat on her couch with her steaming hot mug, a blanket, and a copy of *Little Women* by Louisa May Alcott. After she moved out she treasured the silence of her apartment and enjoyed weekends like these where she could relax in peace. She enjoyed knowing she could leave her empty mug on the coffee table all day and nobody would yell. She never actually brought herself to do it, but she *could* if she wanted to.

Lately, however, the silence felt loud. After weekly lunches with Meghan and several Girl's Night adventures, Hadley started to flourish. She still had no interest in drinking but had opened up to Cathleen and Helen and shared the truth about why. It was another weight lifted when they weren't at all phased. Turns out they could care less if she drank or not and simply enjoyed her company. Last week when the ladies rushed to her side after she found out Dorothy passed away, she truly understood the importance of a group of girlfriends and why her mom always seemed uplifted after those Friday night gatherings. Hadley certainly cherished it and had come out of her shell. So much so that now her weekends felt lonely. The silence and freedom she relished after moving away from her father, now taunted her.

Knowing she couldn't constantly surround herself with friends and could no longer call Dorothy to catch up, she decided she would find a companion. She definitely did not want to tackle the dating scene for the sake of companionship, but maybe she'd finally adopt the cat she'd been debating all year. As she swallowed her last warm sip, she decided the affection from a small animal was exactly what she was missing.

She placed her book on the couch to continue later and carried her mug to the sink. After washing and placing it on a drying mat, she walked down the hallway and into her bedroom toward her small bedroom closet. She reached to the back and pulled out a pair of lined black boots, checking that the treads were still present enough to keep her from slipping. Satisfied with the boots, she grabbed her bag and left for the shelter.

Twenty minutes later, Hadley pulled into the Hopeville Animal Shelter's parking lot. The building, a rectangle of gray painted bricks with three oversized blue painted paw prints, had a perimeter of shrubbery. As Hadley crossed the concrete sidewalk and approached the glass front doors, she took a deep breath in feeling nervous but excited. She wondered if she should have stopped first at the local PetLand for cat food and supplies, but decided she could stop on the way home.

Hadley walked into the lobby and was captivated by the hundreds of paper paw prints with names that covered the walls. She walked up to the first set to see the turquoise ones were for the names of pets who had been adopted whereas the purple ones held names of people who had donated money. Hadley smiled at the sentiment before she approached the main desk. There was no one behind the counter so she tapped her finger on the chrome service bell. While she waited for someone to appear, she went to the side wall to peruse the pamphlets on display. She picked up a lavender colored pamphlet with the headline *Why Spay or Neuter?* and began to read the information.

"Sorry to make you wait, miss." Hadley turned around and was surprised to see a familiar face.

"Hadley?"

"Josh? Hey, I didn't know you worked here."

"Oh, I don't. I mean, I do, I guess. I volunteer. On Saturdays," he said while organizing papers that were already pretty organized.

"That's so cool. How do you stop yourself from taking all the animals home?"

"Trust me, the temptation is real. If only my apartment allowed pets... it would be game over."

Hadley let out a small laugh and shook her head.

Josh cleared his throat before continuing, "Anyway, um, so you want to see the animals? Are you looking to adopt?"

"Yeah, that'd be great. I've been thinking about getting a cat for a while and this morning I was curled under my blanket, drinking hot chocolate, and the room was *so* quiet. Too quiet. I realized something was missing."

"You had hot chocolate for breakfast?"

"Yeah. Is that weird?"

"No, It's amazing. I love hot chocolate," Josh said with a wide grin. They stood awkwardly facing each other, neither knowing what to say.

"So, the cats?" Hadley lifted up and down on the balls of her feet anxiously.

"Right, right," Josh said quickly. He waved his hand toward the door to the back room and said, "Right this way, m'lady... I mean ma'am. Miss? Ugh... Hadley. Right this way, Hadley."

Hadley burst into laughter. "I never thought I would meet someone more awkward than I am."

"Thank god my sister isn't here to see this, she'd be on the floor."

"You guys seem close," she giggled as they walked into the back room.

"Yeah, I'm six years younger than her so I think growing up she treated me like I was her own baby. She always loved playing house."

"That's so cute."

"If you say so," he said as he chewed his bottom lip. "Okay, my suggestion is to walk up and down the room and check out all the cats. They have little tags on the crates with some basic info. If there's any that catch your eye, we'll take them out for you to hold. There's a pen around the corner for them to play in so we can set a few in there too for you."

"Awesome, sounds good." she beamed.

"I'll hang back but I'm here if you have questions." Josh leaned casually against the back wall. Hadley nodded as she started to walk down the room, looking at each cat and thoughtfully reading the related informational tag. A few times she paused to stick her fingers through the grates, but she stayed silent until she came across a crate holding two kittens.

"Ohmigod, these are so cute!" She turned around to get Josh's attention only to realize he was already standing right behind her. She stumbled slightly in place and let out a tiny gasp.

"Sorry about that. Darn quiet feet. Ahh, Daisy and Donald are the new babies of the shelter."

"Who neglects tiny kittens?" she questioned with sad eyes.

"They were actually found because a woman heard a weird noise coming from under her front porch, so she had her grandson stop by and check it out. Turns out it was these two lil' ones. We think the mom was a feral cat who gave birth under the house then ran off."

"Oh wow. I guess it's good she heard them crying."

"Definitely. Kittens these young need a lot of attention, so it was smart the grandson brought them here as early as he did. They're strong enough now to be adopted but we're trying to keep them together. They're bonded."

"They're like tiny little snowballs," Hadley gushed. "But I've never had a pet before so I think I probably should start with just one," she sighed.

"Yeah. Not to worry, I bet they get adopted quickly with those big blue eyes."

Hadley smiled and nodded. She continued her journey down the room and lingered in front of another crate. The orange cat purred against the crate as soon as she approached to read the name tag.

'Littlefoot'
Female, Approx 3 years old
Loves milk & to sit on laps

"Littlefoot. Like the Land Before Time?"

"Yeah, exactly," Josh smiled. "Can you guess who was visiting when we got this little rescue in?"

"Amelia?"

"Ding, ding ding." He laughed.

"Wait, you get to name the animals?"

"Sometimes. We take turns." Hadley nodded before quickly returning her attention to Littlefoot.

Joshed smiled at the enamored look on her face. "Do you think you might like this one? We can take her to the play pen so you can interact with her without the barrier of the crate."

"Yes, please!" Hadley anxiously watched Josh unlock the crate. He carefully lifted Littlefoot who immediately rested against his chest. "Ohmigod," she melted.

Josh let out an awkward one syllable laugh as he carried the medium sized cat over to the pen. Hadley spent the next fifteen minutes sitting with her legs crossed in the middle of the playpen. Within the first minute, the cat had walked up and brushed herself against Hadley's leg. When she looked up at Josh, he nodded encouragingly so she reached her hand out and whispered hello. Littlefoot responded by pushing her head into Hadley's palm and within the next few minutes had found a home on her lap.

Josh chuckled as the sleepy purrs became rhythmic and the cat's eyes fluttered shut. "I think she likes you," he said softly. "But do *you* like *her*? We have a lot of other rescues we can bring out, too. It's a big decision."

"A really big decision," Hadley swooned her response to the cat instead of Josh.

"However..."

Hadley looked up at Josh with a big smile. "It *is* a big decision," she debated. She glanced back down to the sleeping animal on her lap as her smile grew. "However, I think she's perfect."

"I think you guys are a great match."

"Me too!"

"Littlefoot's a lucky cat, that's for sure."

Hadley looked up again and laughed, "We'll see. I've never had a pet before so I might mess this up."

"I doubt that. Come on, you can carry her to the front if you'd like. We have a little pen by the desk she can lay in. There's some paperwork for you to complete before you take her. Normally we ask for a reference but if I had to guess you'd write Meg's name and I already know how much she loves you."

Hadley laughed. "You're correct, that was my plan."

"Okay, we can skip that step. Plus, I'd gladly vouch for you, too."

"You would?"

"Of course," he smiled. They walked together up front before Hadley handed the sleepy cat to Josh to put in the pen. He gathered the application and a clipboard and handed it to her. Hadley took a seat in the lobby and worked on completing the questionnaire. She thought she'd be more nervous, but she felt completely content. She felt like this decision really solidified how far she'd come with her freedom.

Hadley answered the last question and signed her name. She brought the clipboard back to the desk and slid it over to Josh. His eyes quickly browsed her responses before he nodded his head in approval. "All set then. Do you have a carrier?"

Hadley's eyes dropped to her hands. "Um, no... I wasn't sure if I was actually going to pick a cat, so I didn't stop at PetLand yet. I don't have food or a litter box either. Oh my god, maybe this is proving I'm not a good fit after all." Hadley slapped her forehead.

"Oh," he said, surprised by her lack of confidence. "Please don't worry, you wouldn't be the first person to adopt a cat or even a dog without having anything ready. Here, we have a carrier you can borrow. Would that work?"

"Are you sure? You probably need that..."

"We can do without it for a few days. You can bring her in the carrier right to Pet Land and have some fun picking out what she'd like. We, or I mean I, I guess, can send you home with a few samples of wet food, too."

"Thank you so much!"

"I normally recommend mixing the cans of wet food with dry food. Or doing one in the morning and the other in the evening. Cats like the variety and also the dry food is a bit cheaper and lasts longer."

"That's a great tip, thank you so much. I'll make sure to bring back the carrier as soon as possible, too. I don't want you to get in trouble."

"What about tonight?"

"Oh, yeah... sure. I can make that work. How late is the shelter open?" Hadley wasn't expecting to have to come back so quickly but didn't want to seem unappreciative.

"We close at 4, but um–"

Hadley glanced at the clock. "I'm not sure I could make it back in time," she worried, interrupting his thought. "I'll hurry though and try."

"I actually didn't mean to bring it back here."

"Oh?"

Josh started to busy himself collecting the carrier and cans of food before picking up Littlefoot. Avoiding eye contact he continued, "I meant maybe dinner? Like, I could take you to dinner? And you could bring the carrier then."

"Oh." Hadley froze, her eyes growing big.

"You don't have to," he rambled. "I just thought this way I could get the carrier back and we could spend more time talking about Littlefoot and what to expect, and whatever else."

"Oh." They stared awkwardly at each other.

"Super casual," Josh tried to convince.

Hadley smiled, just now realizing she hadn't said much of anything. "That's. Yeah, okay. That sounds okay."

"Really?" Once Hadley nodded, he released a deep breath. "Do you want me to pick you up? Or meet you at the restaurant? Whatever you prefer?"

"I can meet you there."

"Ah yes, a solid plan in case you need to flee the scene."

Hadley laughed, "Exactly."

"How about seven o'clock at McCafferty's." Hadley nodded and smiled. Josh walked the carrier and plastic bag of food samples around the corner and handed them to her. "You're all set. I'm so excited for you and Littlefoot."

"Me too," she beamed. "I'll see you later."

"Yeah, later," he said with a goofy smile.

Hadley made her way to the exit, as Josh leaned against the front of the counter, a smile still plastered to his face. She looked over her shoulder at him, so he'd see her hands were full, but instead he waved dumbly.

"Could you give me a hand?" Hadley laughed.

"Whoop...yep, I'll get that," he said as he jogged to the door.

"Thanks, see ya."

A Non-Date Date

"What was I thinking," Hadley whisper-shouted into the lobby phone as she turned her back to Hazel, who was practically hanging over the counter trying to listen. *I really need a cellphone.*

"Girl, calm down. Hanging out with Josh is like hanging out with a less mature version of me. You'll be fine."

"You know I don't date!"

"Then don't date."

"But I already said yes, and I don't wanna be a flake."

"You can still go to dinner with him. Just keep things friendly and talk about neutral topics and if you run out of things to say, default back to Littlefoot, who I can't wait to meet by the way."

"Okay, okay. You're right."

Meghan chuckled into the phone. "Always. I can't believe he even worked up the nerve."

"What do you mean, the nerve? The nerve for what, Meghan?"

"Just that he told Andrew you were cute after he met you at Amelia's party. But that was like half a year ago."

"What!"

"Yeah, Andrew couldn't wait to tell me. I didn't tell you because I figured he'd never do anything about it. Good for Joshy."

"No, not good for *Joshy*, Meg! We literally just agreed I wouldn't date."

"Calm down, Had. If you want to keep things friendly, he will totally pick up on that."

"If you say so."

"I do," she laughed.

"If this blows up, Meghan, I blame you."

"Understood," she giggled. "Call me tomorrow. And order the shepherd's pie! It's delicious."

"That I can do. Thanks, Meg. Okay, let me go head upstairs before Hazel turns this conversation into one of her soap operas."

"You know there's a simple solution. If you just got a cell, you wouldn't have to whisper in the lobby."

"Too bad I just spent all my extra money on cat food, cat litter, cat toys..."

"Yeah, yeah."

"Speaking of, I better get back to her before I have to change and head out."

"He's not picking you up?"

"No, I wanted to drive."

"In case you need to flee," Meghan amused.

"That's exactly what your brother said."

"Haha, that's funny. See, he's managing expectations. You'll be fine. Okay, have fun!"

"Bye, Meg." Hadley hung up the phone, untangling the cord from her fingers and waving at Hazel on her way to the stairwell. Once back inside her apartment, Hadley took a look around, eventually spotting Littlefoot hidden in the corner. "It's okay, girl. It's just me."

Hadley sat on the couch, pulled a blanket over her legs and grabbed *Little Women* to continue reading. A few minutes later Littlefoot stood up, arched her back in a big stretch, and walked over to the couch to curl up next to Hadley's leg. Hadley sighed, realizing the silence no longer felt loud, it was once again relaxing. She was able to protect her independence while having a companion to share her love and life with. Settled in, she lost track of time until two hours later her internal clock jolted her. Littlefoot must have sensed the panic because she jumped off the couch and retreated to the corner. "Sorry girl. Didn't mean to scare you," she said, frantically navigating her apartment, suddenly very nervous and very out of time.

"Are you going to be okay by yourself? Should I cancel?" Littlefoot, who was back on the couch, responded with a meow and rolled to her side. "You're no help. You only like Josh because he helped get you rescued." Hadley shook her head when she realized she was already turning into that person who had full conversations with their pets. She walked back over to her mirror and applied mascara and pulled the top half of her hair into a high ponytail. She pursed her lips, staring at her Goodwill navy fitted sweater dress that landed mid-thigh. She tugged at the oversized turtleneck before she shrugged and walked toward the front door. She felt a sudden need to circle back to check her reflection one last time, unsure why it mattered. Once she decided she looked good enough for this non-date date, she gave Littlefoot a gentle back scratch and headed out.

Josh was already sitting at the table when she arrived. She rubbed her sweaty hands against her knit dress as the hostess guided her to the table. "Hey," Josh looked up at her as she pulled out her chair to sit. "Oh shoot, I should've grabbed that for you."

"That's okay," Hadley waved him off.

"You look great."

"Thank you," Hadley blushed, despite herself.

"The waiter came around before you got here so I already ordered a drink. Can I get you one, too?"

"Water's fine."

"Are you sure?"

"Yeah, but I am hungry. How about an app instead?"

"Sounds great. Do you like bruschetta? Or they have fried calamari that's pretty good."

"Don't laugh but I don't think I've had either of those before."

"Okay, not to worry. Let's see, do you like tomatoes?" Hadley nodded. "Okay, let's go with the bruschetta then."

"Sounds good." Hadley fiddled with her cloth napkin, folding and unfolding the corner. Moments later the waiter returned to the table and introduced himself to Hadley as he placed a drink in front of Josh. Hadley's breath caught when she realized what it was. *Bourbon.* She'd been to plenty of girl's nights, but no one ever had bourbon. They always ordered the same fruity and fun drinks that her mom used to enjoy. The last time she saw bourbon was when it was splashing out of a tumbler in her father's unsteady hand as he yelled at her to leave.

"We'd like to start with the bruschetta and just water for her." Josh said to the waiter. "Thank you."

Hadley stilled.

"Are you okay?" Josh asked as he took a sip from his bourbon on the rocks.

"I'm – I'm okay."

"Are you sure? You look like you saw a ghost."

"Yeah." Hadley took a deep breath as her eyes welled up. "I'm sorry, I think this was a mistake."

"The bruschetta?"

"No, I mean coming here. I'm sorry, Josh, I have to go."

Hadley set her napkin on the table, ready to push her chair back as Josh interjected. "Hang on, hang on. What's wrong? Talk to me. I can see you're really upset and I'm sorry if I did something."

"It's not you," Hadley dabbed the bottom of her eyes with the side of her pointer finger to avoid letting any tears spill. "I feel so ridiculous right now," Hadley shrugged. "I just don't date."

"This doesn't need to be a date. I already ordered the bruschetta, and it would be a shame to eat it alone. I mean, it wouldn't be the first time, but it would still be a shame." When Hadley let out her own small smile, he sighed with relief.

"I guess…"

With an anxious gulp of his drink, Josh continued, "Only if you want to. The bruschetta *is* really good though and the shepherd's pie here is excellent."

Hadley looked up at Josh as her smile grew. "That's what your sister said."

"She knew we'd get bruschetta?"

"No, that the shepherd's pie is amazing."

"Oh right. It is… worth sticking around for, some might say?"

"Okay." Hadley smiled at the goofy look on Josh's face and forced her shoulders to drop as she blew out a breath. They sat quietly at the table; Hadley's silence was from embarrassment while Josh was afraid to say the wrong thing. As if on cue, the waiter interrupted the otherwise awkward moment to deliver Hadley's water and a long rectangular plate of bruschetta. "This does look good."

"Should we order now, or did you want a minute to be sure?"

"We can order." Hadley was surprised by his patience and understanding, especially since she hadn't given much of an excuse for why she almost bolted.

"Okay, if you're sure." Once Josh saw her nod, he shifted his gaze to the waiter. "Can we get two of the shepherd's pie entrees, please? Thank you." The waiter jotted it down before he walked away. Josh returned his focus to Hadley and thanked her for staying while handing her a small appetizer plate. He pushed the platter slightly toward her, which made it easier for Hadley to grab her own piece.

Hadley took a small bite followed quickly by a second larger bite. "Oh, this *is* good. Tangy but fresh."

Josh laughed. "One of my favorites. It's so easy too. I mean it's bread, tomatoes, garlic, balsamic. But whatever they do with those ingredients is magic."

"Definitely magic." They sat in a comfortable silence as they worked their way through the platter. Josh eyed her plate as a smile formed. "I'm so glad you're not afraid to eat."

"What do you mean?"

"I've been on many first dates–" Hadley's eyebrows shot up causing Josh to choke on his bite. Clearing his throat, he tried again. "I just mean, I've seen a lot of girls, in general, pretend a quarter of a salad was all they needed. It's refreshing to see you're a real human."

"Oh." Hadley laughed. "You'll never have to worry about that with me." Hadley took a dramatic bite and let out a satisfied *mmm,* causing Josh to choke for a different reason.

After a few minutes of focusing on his food, trying to forget the noise he just heard, he decided to press his luck. "So, I don't want to bring up the past or anything..." Hadley looked up at him and cocked her head. "You know, from *before* appetizers."

Hadley laughed. "Oh, *that* past."

"You don't need to answer this, but you really did look upset. I wanted to make sure I didn't say or do anything stupid. I wouldn't want to hurt you – or any of my friends," he added quickly.

Hadley took another bite of bruschetta, chewing dramatically to make sure it was obvious her mouth was full. Josh took another sip of his drink before wiping at the condensation on the outside of the rounded glass. "You didn't do anything."

"Okay..."

"Well, I mean, you did, but not on purpose. It's more of a me thing." Josh nodded slowly. Hadley gulped down her ice water before blurting out, "your bourbon."

"I'm sorry. It was pretty stupid to start ordering for myself before you even showed up. The waiter had come over and I didn't want to be rude to him, but I guess I was rude to you in exchange."

"No, it's not that," she sighed. "My dad, um. Well anyway, he used to drink bourbon – still does – and he's not a nice guy. The bourbon always made him really mean to me."

"Oh, I see why a bourbon showing up to the table would bother you. That must've been rough for you and your mom growing up."

"Actually my mom died when I was thirteen. She had cancer. I think he was a decent guy back then, at least as far as I can remember. Once my mom died, he started drinking nonstop and that's when the anger surfaced. It sucked."

"I'm really sorry. For all of it. I definitely should've asked Meghan to tell me more about you ahead of tonight, but I was planning on just grilling you with 100 questions," Josh smiled. "I can have the waiter take the rest of my drink away."

"No, it's okay. Thank you, though."

"Thanks for telling me. That's a shitty situation."

"Yeah," Hadley shrugged. "So, what about you? Your parents seemed nice when I met them. Meg always has great things to say about them."

"They're the best. They love a little too hard sometimes, but they mean well."

"That doesn't sound so bad," Hadley said as the waiter delivered their entrees. Hadley's mouth dropped at the wide rimmed white porcelain plate set in front of her. The perfectly shaped beef topped with a crispy mashed potato and set in a rich, dark gravy was nothing like the meals she was used to. When she looked over at Josh to smile, she realized he must've handed off his drink. "Looks delicious."

"I can't wait to dive into this. I'm always a member of the Clean Plate Club when I come here."

"My kind of club," she giggled.

Josh spent the next ten minutes talking about his childhood. He shared stories of how his parents hovered and worried a lot but that it all came from a place of love and how Meghan treated him like a babydoll while Liam mainly ignored him. "Meghan's six years older than me and Liam is two years older than her. He didn't care too much about his very annoying little brother. We get along great now, but it wasn't really like that until I was in college."

"It all sounds nice to me. Can I ask how old you are? It just dawned on me that I don't know."

"I'm twenty-seven. I know enough to not ask you that back."

"It's fine. I'm twenty-four." Hadley reddened. "I guess I should've told you how young I was before I agreed to go on a date with you."

"Ah, but it's not a date, right, so you're excused."

"Well played. Just two friends enjoying some meat and potatoes."

"You got that, right. And for what it's worth, you're not too young. You seem really smart and independent. And pretty. Probably the prettiest friend I have, Andrew aside."

"Andrew's definitely prettier than me."

"Is that so?"

Hadley nodded as they both started laughing. They continued the good-natured banter while they cleaned their plates and the caramel apple bread pudding they ordered after.

"I might not eat again for a week," Hadley groaned as they walked toward the parking lot.

"It was worth it."

"So worth it." They walked to Hadley's car first so she could hand him the cat carrier. "Thanks again for letting me borrow this. I stopped on my way home from the shelter to get everything Littlefoot could possibly need."

"No problem. Is she settling in okay? I can't believe I never even asked about her."

"It's okay. Yeah, she's a little timid but seems to enjoy my couch. Curled up like she's lived there her whole life."

"That's so great. Either pets acclimate really well, or they spend a few days hiding in fear. I'm glad to hear it went smoothly."

Hadley smiled as she shut her backseat door and moved toward the driver's door. "Thank you for dinner, it was nice. I'm sorry for freaking out in the beginning."

"That's okay. You wouldn't be the first girl who wanted to end a date with me early," he chuckled.

"Not a date though, right? So, I'm in the clear."

"Right," he nodded. "Have a good night, Hadley." He took half a step toward her but stopped himself, instead pivoting so he could walk to his own vehicle.

"You, too."

Hadley smiled the whole way home. She thought maybe it could've been a date. They spent most of the time having easy conversations and making each other laugh, though it felt different and more intimate than when she did the same thing with Meghan or the girls. She decided if Josh were to ask her again, she'd say yes to a date and give it a try, just to see. He seemed to hear her loud and clear though, so the prospect felt unlikely.

Pulling into her complex, she parked the car and was happy to at least have someone, something waiting for her at home.

Pizza Between Friends

Hadley went to dinner with Josh, as official dates, three times over the next two months before Hadley decided she just wasn't ready. "It's definitely not you," she had told him. "I have a lot to figure out about myself and I'm getting there, just slowly. Trust me, if I was going to date someone, it would be you." Josh was disappointed but asked if they could stay friends. Hadley agreed even though she doubted that was what he actually wanted.

Much to her surprise, one Saturday afternoon Hazel knocked on her door to let her know she had a call waiting downstairs. Hadley explained, again, while they walked downstairs that she'd get a cellphone as soon as she could afford one.

"Hello?"

"Hey Hadley, It's Josh."

"Hey! Sorry to make you wait while Hazel went and got me."

"I guess you really don't have a cell phone. I thought it was just a ploy to stay mysterious." He laughed then cleared his throat. "Anyway, I was in the mood for pizza."

"Okay... so get pizza?"

"Yeah, I mean did you want to have pizza with me?"

"We've been through this, Josh. I like you but I'm just not ready to be dating."

"Yeah, yeah. We're friends and I'm starving. I need someone who isn't afraid to chow down."

"You know I don't *always* clean my plate."

"Yeah, you do."

Hadley laughed. "Listen, after years of frozen TV dinners, real food is hard to pass up."

"So pizza it is. Do you like Franco's on the corner?"

"Love it. And before you ask, pepperoni."

"You know me well. I can bring it over in forty-five if that works."

"Sounds good. Littlefoot will be excited to see you. She was chasing around a feather toy before Hazel's knock sent her under the couch."

"Sounds cute. I'll see you soon."

"Bye." Before heading back to her apartment, Hadley thanked Hazel, who probably couldn't wait to get her senile eyes on the mystery man.

Like clockwork, Josh knocked on her door forty-five minutes later. Hadley let him in and told him to set the box on the counter. She grabbed two plates while Josh shrugged off his sherpa lined jean jacket and stepped out of his sneakers. He was wearing a green and gray crew neck sweater with a worn-in pair of jeans. He looked much more put together than Hadley, who was wearing black leggings with a thrifted oversized crimson Harvard sweatshirt. She padded in her gray wool socks to the couch with her plate of pepperoni pizza.

"Are you going to join me?" She smiled but didn't wait on him to take her first bite. "What is it about pizza that's always satisfying?"

Josh sat on the floor with his back against the couch, balancing his plate on his knee. He looked back at her and smiled. "It's the perfect combination."

"Mm-hmm," Hadley agreed, taking another big bite. They made small talk while enjoying their pizza. After a few minutes, Hadley slid off the couch to sit next to Josh on the floor. "You could've sat on the couch. Friends sit together, you know."

Josh chuckled. "And move Littlefoot? I don't think so."

"Good point." She pointed to Josh's almost empty plate. "Ready for another?"

"You know it." Hadley got up and refilled their plates before she sat back down on the floor. They debated each other on if pizza really was the best food ever created. Hadley countered that the shepherd's pie they ate a few months ago was on the top of her list.

"All I know is growing up my mom made a baked sausage ziti dish that was to die for. I used to beg for it. That might be my actual favorite meal. What about you?"

"My mom made a lot of meatloaf and parsley potatoes. I still crave it."

"Parsley potatoes sound pretty good. Have you ever tried to make them?"

"No, she never wrote down recipes and my father is useless so I never bothered asking." Changing the topic, she asked, "Am I a total pig if I go for a third slice?"

"Glad you brought it up because I also want more. It's my turn to grab the slices, stay put," he said, as he waved his crust at her before he bit into it.

Hadley waited until Josh started walking back and then raised her eyebrows in his direction. "Speaking of Meghan," Hadley said, drawing out her words.

"Were we though?"

Hadley smiled and took a dramatic bite.

"Oh no, what am I about to find out? She's my sister, Had. Please don't say something gross."

"Ohmigod, Josh." Hadley shoved his arm playfully. "I am the last person you'd hear *that* from. You'd have to go to Helen for that."

"Ah, Helen. She's actually quite the sweetheart under all that bravado and lipstick."

"I agree. She's one of the most genuine people I've met. She knows exactly who she is and what she wants."

"And who she wants," Josh laughed.

"Yeah, exactly," Hadley giggled. "Anyway, we're not talking about Helen..."

"Right, right, Meghan." Josh said, biting into his slice. "I'm all ears."

"What's with her and Andrew?"

"What do you mean?"

"Well, Helen's hellbent that they'll end up back together, but Cathleen doesn't buy it. They seem so flirty when they're together. Like they just click. But Meg never seems to bring Andrew up in conversation, and it's not like we don't talk every day. So is it because she actually doesn't think about him or because she *does* think about him but wants to pretend she doesn't."

"And I know this answer because?"

"Because you're her brother, duh."

"Yeah I don't know if you know how siblings work, but I'm definitely not the keeper of her secrets."

"Only child," Hadley pouted.

Josh rolled his eyes. "Okay, fine. Here's what I know." Josh set his empty plate on the coffee table and shifted his body to face Hadley. He rested his right arm on the couch, prompting Littlefoot to roll over against him. He paused to give the little orange cat the attention she demanded.

"Pins and needles, Josh."

"Sorry. Did she ever tell you they were high school sweethearts?"

"She said they got together young, but I wasn't all that sure what young meant to her and I guess I never asked."

"So they fell in love in high school. It's that time in your life where love is the most important thing in the world and you're so sure you'll be together forever no matter what. The reality of your future isn't even a thought. ya know?"

"When I was in high school the reality of my future was *all* I thought about. Love wasn't even a distant thought. I didn't see or get love at home, and I definitely wasn't looking for it in school. My thoughts were mainly about how fast I could graduate and get away." She picked at her crust while she talked.

"That was dumb of me. Of course not everyone is obsessed with love in high school."

"It's okay, I got the point. So they defied the odds and stayed together?"

"Yeah, except I'm not so sure how long they were actually in love with each other. I think Meg loves the idea of love and always wanted to have a family. She convinced herself that she needed Andrew to be complete.

Then they got married, had Amelia, yada yada. Somewhere along the way they both realized something was missing. I think they were just existing together. There wasn't any huge fight or blow out. No one cheated. They were just high school sweethearts who didn't realize they weren't meant to be until it was much too late."

"That makes sense actually. I love how much they get along. Trust me, you might think Amelia is too young to notice, but she's not." Josh nodded, knowing Hadley was speaking from experience. "So, they probably won't get back together then?"

"I doubt it. They're great friends and always will be. And Andrew is stuck being my fake big brother forever. I think I love him more than Meg does," Josh laughed. "But Meg is happier now than she was then. I think once the dust settled she realized she didn't need Andrew to feel complete. She was complete on her own. And now with Amelia? Well, she fills in all the cracks. That little girl shows them the unconditional love they tried so hard to create."

Hadley smiled and nodded. "Well, that answers that. Looks like you did have the crystal ball. Not that I had any business being so nosey."

"That's what friends do best. Any more juicy questions or can I break out the laser pointer I brought and see just how energetic this lazy cat can get?"

"Now that sounds fun." She reached over to where Littlefoot was resting against Josh's arm and scratched behind her ear. "Let's give it a shot." The pair stood up, collected their plates and quickly cleaned up the leftover pizza. Josh grabbed the laser pointer from the pocket of his jacket and they spent the next half hour watching Littlefoot jump and dash all around Hadley's small apartment.

Once Littlefoot was worn out, and the sun started to dip, Josh said goodbye and headed out. Hadley joined Littlefoot on the couch but soon the sun fully set and the apartment grew dark. Hadley got up and turned on the side lamp, before she set out the cat's dinner and refilled her water bowl. She then moved to the bedroom to change into her favorite pair of burnt orange flannel pajamas, ready to call it an early night so she could read from bed. She left the door open so that Littlefoot could jump up onto the foot of the bed when she was ready.

She flipped on the bedside light and picked up *Romeo and Juliet*. With the book on her pillow, she thought about how Josh was right. There was a time in Hadley's life where she believed true love was everything. She read and reread *Romeo and Juliet* almost as many times as she watched *Grease*. She used to fixate on the tender moments, completely ignoring the toxic themes in Shakespeare and the disrespect in *Grease*. She spent nights wondering if her parents were in love. Wondering if she'd one day be in love.

Now? Now she didn't care about any of that. She cared about her freedom and about being happy. From where she was laying, in her small apartment, she found more in life than she ever imagined she would. She had friends, a pet, a job, and a home that felt safe. Hadley sighed then picked up the tattered book to read. At some point Littlefoot jumped up and curled into a ball against Hadley's ankles. With heavy eyes, Hadley whispered good night. She rolled to her side, set the book on her end table, and flipped off the light. She soon fell into a deep sleep, dreaming of what else her future might hold.

Save the Wishes

"Has she really never celebrated her birthday," Andrew asked. He was wearing khaki shorts and a plain white t-shirt that pulled against his lean muscles.

"Not since she was fifteen," Meghan answered, futzing with the arrangement of mylar balloons.

"Since her mom passed away?" Cathleen questioned.

"Couldn't be," Josh considered. "She was only thirteen when she lost her mom."

"Yeah, so I guess her fourteenth birthday she spent with her father and her fifteenth was with Dorothy."

"Did something go wrong there that made her never celebrate again?" Josh questioned before adding, "it's been a decade."

All eyes shifted to Meghan. She wiped her hands against her green floral mini dress and let out a breath. "Yes and no. She loved the farm and Dorothy; I think we all know that by now. But what she hasn't shared all that much is how her father didn't care about that and forced Hadley to get a job that took up every minute of her free time."

"At fifteen?"

"Yeah, the youngest age allowed," Meghan nodded.

"Whatta scumbag," Helen said.

"Total dirt," Cathleen added.

"Exactly. So she had to stop going to the farm. I think it really traumatized her. She only found out last year that Dorothy had been sending her birthday cards for years and her father just never shared them. I only know it's her birthday because I processed her paperwork when she first started at Placers."

"Plus, it's easy to remember the date, so close to Amelia's," Josh added, and Meghan nodded.

"Is this party a good idea?" Andrew interjected. "We're not going to upset her, are we? Send her running?"

"I mean who knows," Meghan shrugged. "Twenty-five is a big year and that girl has been through a lot, especially with losing Dorothy over the winter. She just deserves to be celebrated. She's been a great friend to us. She's definitely made my life easier at work. Amelia is obsessed with Aunt Hadley; Joshy is obsessed with Hadley–"

"Hey, watch yourself. We're just friends."

"Like Andrew and Meghan?" Helen teased with a very dramatic wink.

"No!" Josh said emphatically. "Like friends who were definitely not previously in love."

Meghan laughed. "Responded a little too quickly, if you ask me." Josh rolled his eyes and groaned.

Andrew smirked and draped his arm over Meghan. "Plus, that just makes us *really close* friends."

"Anyway..." Meghan dragged out, slipping out from under her ex. "Let's just keep this lighthearted and fun."

"You got it," they all agreed.

"Quick comment, though. Maybe we don't make the Josh loves Hadley jokes once Stephanie gets here? She's never been a fan of those."

Andrew broke into laughter, slapping Josh playfully on the back. "We got you, bro."

"Yeah, that's what I'm afraid of," Josh sighed. "We've only been dating for three months, just be nice."

"Come on, back to work." Meghan chuckled before she pointed to the clock. "Hadley will be here at two." Meghan looked around the living room, finally satisfied with the display of purple and white balloons. There were a few basic birthday decorations throughout the room and the kitchen table was set with birthday-themed paper plates and cups. There were three boxes of pizza sitting on her stove, creating a delicious aroma along with the lit vanilla bean candles that were strategically placed to make sure the house smelled sweet no matter where you stood.

Fifteen minutes later, the room was ready and they just needed to wait on Hadley's arrival. Helen and Cathleen were sitting on the couch gabbing, Josh, wearing a pale blue Van Halen t-shirt, was whispering into the ear of his giggling girlfriend, Stephanie, and Andrew was chatting with Helen's latest suitor, Gerald. Cathleen's husband took their kids and Amelia mini golfing so the party could start calmly. They would be back in a little over an hour, in time for dessert.

"What does she think is happening, again?" Stephanie asked. She was wearing a short black dress with a matching chunky belt tied tight at her waist and a pair of yellow patent heels. Her blonde hair was blown out to look like Farah Fawcet's and her eyes matched her sapphire earrings. She started dating Josh three months ago and was desperate to break into his sister's close-knit group of friends. She'd of course met Hadley several times. She worried in the beginning over how close Josh was with her and thought it was weird he spent at least one Saturday a month at

Hadley's ordering take out and *hanging out*, especially once she realized just how many inside jokes they seemed to share.

It annoyed her how perfect Hadley seemed. Unlike Stephanie who spent hours getting ready, Hadley rarely wore makeup and although her clothes never seemed new, she stunned any room she walked into. Eventually, though, Stephanie started to view beautiful, innocent Hadley the same way Josh supposedly did, as one of his siblings. It took some self-convincing, but she was getting there. It helped that Josh was always honest with her and overall came across very trustworthy. With time, Stephanie decided to stop letting her insecurities get in the way of falling head over heels for the goofy guy she met in line at the dry cleaners.

"She thinks Amelia wanted to watch *The Land Before Time* again with her."

"For the millionth time," Josh laughed.

"Yeah, Had's a good sport."

Stephanie smiled and nodded. The room grew quiet when they heard the sound of an engine cutting off. They gathered closely in the center of the room, and collectively held their breaths, unsure of Hadley's reaction. You could hear a pin drop when the front door opened.

Hadley was about to call for Amelia but when the door swung open, she was immediately met with wide eyes and big smiles. Nobody wanted to shout *Surprise*, worried that Hadley would turn and leave, so the room stayed eerily quiet. Hadley froze. The strap of her ivory pleather handbag fell from her shoulder to the bend of her elbow, where it stayed.

"Don't freak out," Meghan said gently, taking a step toward Hadley.

"Freak out? I'm not freaking out. What makes you think I would be freaking out," Hadley's words tumbled together.

"We wanted to celebrate your birthday and remind you that it is okay for *you* to be celebrated."

Hadley saw the calm in Meghan's emerald eyes and exhaled. She glanced down at her arm, just now realizing her bag had fallen. She repositioned it on her shoulder and looked back up. She scanned the group in front of her, everyone looked sincerely happy to see her. When her eyes floated to Josh, he winked and mouthed *Happy Birthday.*

She smiled then shook her head confused. "You guys all got together just for me?"

"Of course we did," Cathleen said.

"That shouldn't be hard to believe," Helen added. "We love you."

"Yeah, even *Gerald* came," Cathleen said, over emphasizing his name and nodding her head in his direction.

"Ger– oh, right, Gerald. Hi." Hadley gave Helen a look that let her know more questions were coming.

"A-ny-way," Helen continued. "Today is about you and your birthday. We've all been twenty-five, honey, this one's for you."

"I can't believe this... I don't usually celebrate. I hate when the attention is on me."

"We know," Meghan smiled. "But Josh promised us you wouldn't panic as long as we got the pizza from Franco's."

Hadley's smile grew. "With pepperoni?"

"Obviously," Josh said as he gently squeezed Stephanie's hand, which she had slid self-consciously into his.

"Oh, well then, no panic here," she teased. Hadley closed the gap between her and Meghan and wrapped her into a big hug. "Thank you for this," she whispered. Meghan's muscles unwound as she relaxed into the hug. Cathleen turned the radio on as everyone started to move about and restart previous conversations.

"Wait a minute," Hadley said suddenly. The attention returned to her. "Where's Amelia? She's the whole reason I was lured here in the first place."

"Henry has the kids playing mini golf, then they'll be here," Cathleen smiled.

Hadley nodded and let out a laugh. "Now there's a saint."

"You're telling me."

After they all ate, Hadley sat on the couch between Meghan and Stephanie and let out a gentle groan as she slouched. "I don't think I've ever eaten a normal amount of pizza," she whined. "I'm stuffed."

"Yeah, Josh said the two of you normally eat a whole large pie together," Stephanie giggled.

"Oh. My. God. Are there no secrets around here," Hadley feigned offense. "I don't think we order *larges...*"

"We definitely order larges," Josh countered as he handed Stephanie a paper cup with sprite.

Hadley cringed, turning to Stephanie. "I'm not a total pig, I promise."

Stephanie laughed. "If I could look like you and eat an entire pizza, I wouldn't even need Josh's help."

Hadley threw her arm around Stephanie and joked, "A pizza lover - my kinda girl. But you don't need to look like me to chow down, Steph. You look great." Stephanie blushed, deciding not to mention that she usually opted for salads and salmon over pizza. Hadley might be naturally slender, but Stephanie had to work hard just to keep her fairly average form.

"AUNT HADLEY?"

"That shriek can only belong to one little girl," Hadley laughed. Amelia blew through the front door and ran directly into her arms. Hadley pulled the five-year-old onto her lap and tucked a rogue curl behind her ear. "How was mini golf?"

"Leo won. But only because he's older than me," she complained.

"It's okay not to win as long as you had fun, sweetie," Meghan added.

"I had fun! Is it time for dessert yet? Mr. Henry promised us dessert once we got back for Aunt Hadley's birthday."

"Maybe in a little bit, sweetie, Aunt Hadley was just groaning over how full she was. I think we should give her a little break."

"I'm never too full for dessert." Hadley winked at Amelia. "Why don't you go wash up and we can definitely have dessert."

"You're a bottomless pit," Josh marveled.

"I'm doing it for Amelia."

"Sure you are," he laughed. Josh grabbed Stephanie's hand to help her up from the couch. Hadley watched as he pulled her in to him, giving her a gentle kiss on the cheek before whispering something that made her blush deepen. Hadley and Meghan rolled their eyes at each other.

"Speaking of P-D-A, what's going on with Helen and Gerald," Hadley whispered, looping her arm through Meghan's.

"I have no idea. I don't think she's ever brought a date anywhere before. We'll have to badger her next week at Royal Oak."

"Definitely. She'll tell us anything after a few French martinis." They walked over to the table where Andrew set out new paper plates. Hadley took a seat at the head of the table as everyone else either grabbed a seat or stood between the chairs. Meghan grabbed the tray of homemade cupcakes she made and set them in the middle of the table. She picked up one of the chocolate fudge cupcakes and stuck a pink striped candle into the center. She lit it and placed it carefully in front of Hadley.

As the room broke into song, Hadley stared at the flickering candle. Tears welled in her eyes as the memory of her fifteenth birthday overtook her senses. Dorothy had also baked her a chocolate cupcake, using the same pink candle. *How could that have been ten years ago?* Hadley felt so broken after that birthday. Her world changed for the worse and she swore she'd never celebrate again.

"Hey, are you okay?" Cathleen knelt down and asked. The energy in the room died as everyone watched a tear slide down Hadley's face.

"I told you this was a bad idea," Andrew whispered, anxiously holding Meghan's arm.

"No, no, I'm okay. This wasn't a bad idea," Hadley said, wiping her eyes. "I'm just overwhelmed."

"In a good way, Aunt Hadley?"

"In a good way, Meels, I promise," Hadley nodded. She took a deep breath in and gently blew it out, accidentally blowing out the candle in the process.

"Oh no, you didn't even make a wish yet!" Amelia panicked.

"It's okay, Meels, we can relight it," Andrew reassured.

"No, don't," Hadley interrupted, taking another deep breath. "I don't need to make a wish," she said quietly. "I'm good," she assured, smiling at Amelia.

Meghan smiled from across the table, understanding what Hadley meant. She knew how horrible Hadley was treated by her father. How important the farm was and how devastated she was when she left after her fifteenth birthday. How often she wished for a better future.

"But why don't you want to make a wish, Aunt Hadley?"

"I don't need to make wishes anymore, sweetheart. Look at how good my life is," Hadley smiled. "I think we should save the wish for someone who really needs one. What do you think?"

Amelia smiled and nodded enthusiastically.

"Geez Louise," Cathleen said, breaking the tender moment. "I thought we agreed to keep it *lighthearted and fun*. We'll all be in tears, soon."

A laugh bubbled out of Hadley, which spread around the table like wildfire. With the room full of energy, Hadley felt a gentle tug on her tangerine-colored linen shorts. She looked down to see a noticeably upset Lizzie.

"What's wrong, sweetie?"

"What about the cupcakes," she said with a quivering lip.

"Technically I did blow the candle out so I think that means we can eat the cupcakes," Hadley winked.

Lizzie, Leo, and Amelia let out a collective yip of excitement that caused Hadley to laugh again. She looked around the table at the mixed reactions of happiness, relief, and doubt.

"I am fine, I promise. This has been the best birthday I've had in a very long time. There's only one thing left to do."

"What's that?" Josh asked.

"A wise woman once told me, 'Always eat the cake.' So, eat the cake, we must," Hadley declared before taking a theatrical bite. Andrew handed out cupcakes to the kids before grabbing his own. Everyone else leaned across the table to grab one, eager to taste the rich fudge. The room fell quiet as everyone ate, but once only crumbs were left, the gossip and easy conversation restarted.

It's Okay to be Sad

"So Gerald is just not a thing anymore?" Hadley questioned the following Tuesday as she stirred the Swiss Miss packet in her hot water. She wore a fitted white t-shirt under a mid-thigh lengthened caramel corduroy dress. She leaned against the table facing Meghan, who was already sitting at her desk with a coffee in hand.

"Yeah, apparently your birthday party was a trial run, but he didn't match her social expectations." Meghan placed air quotes around the last two words.

"Oh my god, that's ridiculous," Hadley chuckled.

"*Helen* is ridiculous. I think she's the only hopeless romantic who is also hopelessly afraid of commitment."

"He seemed nice while he lasted," Hadley shrugged as she made her way to her desk.

"I don't know. Andrew told me he shared some weird interests when they were talking."

"Like what?"

"I think he said he was overly into bowling? He kept sharing facts about bowling, famous people who bowl, the best kind of bowling shoes to wear. Just loads of bowling thoughts under that bushy brown hair."

Hadley laughed. "That's so random. It could've been worse. It's not like he was talking about bodies buried in his rose garden or anything."

"Good point. So, I was looking at the calendar and we have a few repeat clients coming in but otherwise the day is up to fate. I wonder if we'll be busy with how sunny it is outside."

Hadley squinted as she considered the odds. "I'm starting a new crossword puzzle so that usually means right when I get in a groove, it gets busy."

"Then figure out the answers slowly because I could use a quiet morning." They nodded at each other and lifted their mugs into the air to silently 'cheers' to the wish for quiet.

While Hadley was tapping the eraser of her pencil against her desk, considering which four-letter word meant 'a kind of watch or time', the phone rang. "Placers Staffing, this is Hadley. Mhm. Mhm. Yes, just your driver's license or a state ID. Yes, we hold open interviews from two until five. Okay. Okay, great. See you then." After saying goodbye and hanging up the phone she looked over at Meghan. "Well, that's at least one walk-in after lunch."

"I can handle *one*," Meghan smiled before sipping on her lukewarm coffee. "*If* it's actually just one."

Hadley was about to make a joke when the phone rang again. "Are you clairvoyant or something?" She laughed before picking up the phone and repeating her standard greeting. "Yes, I'm Hadley," she said tentatively. "I'm sorry, who is this? Okay... I – uh, okay. Thank you."

"What was that about?"

Hadley swallowed hard. Her eyes were glued to the phone still in her hand.

"Whoa, what's wrong," Meghan stood up, noticing that the color drained from Hadley's face. "Hey, take a deep breath. Who was that?" Meghan walked over and knelt next to Hadley. "Hads... Hadley. *Hadley.* Look at me."

Hadley shook her head incredulously, released a deep breath, and set the phone down. She looked over at Meghan with tears in her eyes. "I, uh..." Meghan watched Hadley and waited patiently for her to continue. "That was Wellspring Hospice Center calling me about my father. He's dying." A few tears slipped down her cheeks, but she was too stunned to fully react.

"Oh Hadley, that's horrible. I'm so sorry."

Hadley shook her head in continued disbelief. "She said he's been sick for a while with, um, end stage liver disease. Liver failure. I guess he took a turn for the worse over the weekend and was moved to the short-term wing."

"Did you know he was sick?" Meghan asked gently, her left hand resting on Hadley's leg.

"No. What's with nobody telling me they're sick? I haven't heard from my dad since I picked up my mom's boxes last year, so I guess he didn't bother to mention he was sick. I guess that's why he was packing everything up. I mean it makes sense with how heavily he drank, but no, I didn't know."

"Oh wow. Okay, this is a lot for you to process. How can I help?"

"I don't know. I guess they called here because he lost my phone number and couldn't remember where my apartment was. He only remembered that I worked for an employment agency in this general vicinity. She had to call a few until she got the right one. That's telling of our relationship..." Hadley hung her head.

"She found you, that's all that matters."

Hadley nodded.

"Are you going to be okay?" Meghan walked to the bathroom and returned with a tissue.

Hadley took a tissue and dried her cheeks. "She told me I should go see him. That he probably won't last the week. I don't know what to do, Meg. I haven't seen him or talked to him in a long time. I worked so hard to create boundaries and protect myself against him. I don't know if I can face him now. I don't even know if he wants me to, or if *I* want to."

"That doesn't need to be decided in this moment. Why don't you go home. I can handle a slow day on my own. Relax with Littlefoot and process all of this. I don't think it's fully hit you, but it will."

"I don't want to leave you alone, Meg. Some of these guys are gross. I'll be fine."

"I'm calling Mary. If she can come in, then will you go home?"

"Yeah, okay," Hadley said reluctantly.

Meghan walked Hadley to her car fifteen minutes later once they knew Mary was on her way. "I'll be fine alone for a half hour, Had. This way you don't have to explain anything to Mary, and you can just get home."

"Yeah, I guess you're right. I'm fine though. Are you sure you don't want me to stay?"

"You're only fine because you're in shock. At the end of the day, despite everything he's done, he's still your father."

Hadley let out an audible sigh. "I know. I just... I don't know what to do."

"All you need to do is go home. Put on your favorite sweats, read your favorite book. You'll figure out what to do eventually."

"Thanks, Meg."

***

"I'm home," Hadley announced as she slipped out of her brown heeled loafers and walked toward the couch. Littlefoot, who was curled up in a ball, lifted her head and let out a long meow. Hadley leaned down and tickled under the cat's chin. She let out a quiet chuckle when she felt Littlefoot press her head into her palm, wanting more. "I'm going to shower and then I'll come relax with you."

Hadley stood in her shower and let the hot water cover her. She washed her hair. Washed her body. Washed her face. She waited for tears that never came. She felt... fine. After she dried off, she wrapped her hair in a bun and threw on a pair of blue flannel pajamas. She stepped into white slippers and shuffled to the living room. She grabbed a book of word searches and cozied into a corner of the couch. Littlefoot stood up, arching into a stretch before she walked over and curled onto Hadley's lap. "Don't judge me for wearing pajamas before lunch," Hadley said, tickling behind Littlefoot's ears. "Meg told me to relax so we're going to try."

Knock, knock, knock.

"That's weird," Hadley whispered. "Who could be at the door? Want to come check it out?" she scooped Littlefoot into her arms and walked with her to the door. "If it's a bad guy, you jump, okay?" She left the chain lock on the door but opened it an inch to see who was on the other side.

"Josh? What're you – hang on." She closed the door to unhook the security chain and then opened the door fully. "What're you doing here? Why aren't you at work?"

"I was out checking on some of my local accounts and got hungry."

"And you just knew I'd be home?"

"Possibly."

Hadley narrowed her eyes at Josh as he set a bag with two chicken caesar salads on the counter. "Did Meg call you?"

"Possibly."

"Ugh. I'm fineee."

"Yeah, I know." Josh nodded. "But I also know you've never turned down food before so set the princess down and grab a salad."

Hadley smiled. "You heard the man," she guided Littlefoot toward the couch so she could jump down safely. Hadley and Josh grabbed their salads and sat where they always did, with their backs against the couch, and started to eat.

"It's okay if you weren't fine, you know."

"Yep, I know."

"Okay." After another minute of silence, Josh tried again. "Did I ever tell you about when I was in college and I dated this girl, Daisy?"

"I don't think so."

"Well, the highlight reel is that I dated her for over a year even though she cheated on me with half of Kappa Sigma."

"Ouch," Hadley said, collecting another forkful of salad.

"Yes, but worse than that –"

"Worse than cheating on you with half a frat worth of guys?"

"If you'd let me finish, I'd get to my point." Hadley twirled her fork in the air, signaling for him to continue. "She always had an opinion on what I was doing or not doing. She hated my major, hated my roommate, my clothes... pretty sure she hated me."

"And you dated her, why?"

"She was gorgeous, and I was stupid. The point is she was awful to me. She constantly made me feel like garbage. Long story short, we finally broke up and you know what?"

"You were better off?"

"Yes, I was absolutely better off. But as terrible as she was to me, I was still devastated."

"Ahh."

"I'm just saying, it's okay to be sad over someone who doesn't deserve your sadness."

Hadley locked eyes with Josh and nodded. "It's not like I'm pretending to be okay, I'm just," Hadley threw her hands up in a shrug, unsure how to even describe what she was feeling. It was Josh's turn to nod. "Would you go see him? If you were me, I mean."

"I can't answer that, Hads, you know that."

"Yeah. I know... I'm just afraid I'll go see him and he'll be mad that I showed up. Like the nurse told me to come but did *he* tell her to call me or was she just doing her hospice duties?"

"I don't have that answer, either." Josh said gently. "Do you want to see him?"

"Yes and no. I wasn't there when my mom passed away. I knew she was dying and obviously our relationship was by no means strained so it's different... but anyway... I never said that last goodbye. Same thing with Dorothy. I was totally blindsided and didn't even know she was sick. Maybe it would be good to say goodbye to my dad, despite our issues. Maybe there's a future me who will appreciate it."

"That's a good way of looking at it."

Hadley blew out a breath and slouched deeper into the floor, where they always seemed to sit. She felt drained from the stress of the unknown. She leaned her body against Josh who knowingly wrapped his arm around her. "It'll be okay, Hads. We're here for you."

"What about Littlefoot? I can't bring her. I mean I guess it doesn't matter if I'm just going for an afternoon but what if it's a whole thing and I end up staying?"

"Steph's apartment allows pets so we can bring her there for the night. I'll bring her back over once you're home. This way if you end up staying, or just want a moment of solitude, you won't have to worry."

"Are you sure Steph is okay with that? Shouldn't you ask her?"

"She loves animals and she loves you. It'll be fun for her, I'm sure of it."

"I'm not sure she actually loves me, I see the way she stares sometimes. But if it's actually okay with her, then that might work. Thanks, Josh."

"Of course, Hads. I wish I could stay longer but I am technically on the job right now."

"So you didn't just get hungry and somehow wind up at my door?" Hadley smiled as she stretched her arms out and rolled her neck. She stood up and collected the empty lunch containers as they made their way to the front door.

"Well, technically it's true. I *was* hungry and I *did* wind up here... but we both know Meg played a hand. She was really worried about you."

"I'm okay. Exhausted and confused, but okay."

"I know, you keep saying that." He sounded unconvinced. "My next two clients aren't far from here so it worked out." Josh was recently promoted to Senior Account Manager at an industrial supply company.

He now spent more time on the road visiting clients and keeping up relations than he did sitting in an office making cold calls. He enjoyed the freedom in his schedule, especially on days like this. He wouldn't admit it to Hadley, but when Meghan called him, he was equally worried knowing she was probably sitting in her thoughts.

They lingered at the door. "Thank you for checking on me... and for helping with Littlefoot. I haven't figured out what I want to do yet. But if I do decide to go tomorrow, I can drop Littlefoot off at Steph's on my way. Just please ask her. It's almost never appreciated when a man assumes things."

"Thanks for the life advice. I will ask," Josh chuckled. "Call me or Megs if you need anything, okay?"

"I will." Hadley said as she shut the door. She walked back to the couch and wrapped an afghan around her, settling into place. Littlefoot laid across her chest, purring steadily against her. She spent the rest of the day debating what she should do. Eventually, still undecided, her eyes fluttered into an exhaustive sleep.

My One and Only Visitor

Hadley woke up queasy over the thought of losing another person without so much as a goodbye, and immediately knew she needed to go see her dad. Without giving herself a chance to doubt her decision, she quickly packed a bag with a few essentials and a second bag with Littlefoot's supplies and left.

After dropping Littlefoot at Steph's, Hadley drove for two hours before pulling into a small park near the Wellspring Hospice Center. She grabbed her soft sided Igloo cooler and walked along the concrete path that wove through the grassy fields. When she noticed a wooden bench, she took a seat and closed her eyes. She listened to the robins whistling and the wrens flutelike singing while she took several slow deep breaths. She focused on keeping calm, despite her thumping heart. She came this far. One block from her father.

After a few minutes, Hadley opened her eyes and unzipped her cooler. She reached in and grabbed her bologna sandwich. The cooler also held a reusable bottle with water, the old photo of her mom as a teenager, and the small alabaster figurine her father gave her. She took all three items out, leaning the photo against the bottle and laying the horse figurine on her lap. She let out an audible sigh before taking a bite of her sandwich. In between bites she picked up the horse figurine with her left hand, rubbing her thumb against its smooth surface.

She stared at the photo propped next to her. Hadley's fourteenth birthday was one of the last positive memories she had with her father. On that day, he acknowledged her horseback riding without argument. He shared new stories about her mother. He gave her the photo she was currently staring at and the figurine she was holding. He smiled at her. Was proud of her. Admitted his shortcomings.

"Are you okay?" a shaky voice asked.

Hadley hadn't realized she was crying. "I'm okay," she said with a feeble smile.

"You sure, dear?" Hadley looked at the short old man, hunched over with the support of a cane. His gray hair circled his head like a halo and his skin resembled crumpled tissue paper.

"I'm sure. I must have gotten caught up in my memories."

The old man shook his head. "Happens all the time. Want someone to talk to?"

"Thanks, but I'm okay." She held up the rest of her sandwich.

He looked at the photo next to her, "That you?"

"Oh gosh," Hadley smiled. "No, it's a photo of my mom when she was younger."

"Beautiful lady. You look just like her."

Hadley wiped her eyes, her smile growing. "Oh, thank you. That means a lot."

"My name is Fred. I usually make a lap 'round the park every day at lunchtime. If you feel like talkin', I'm sure you can catch me. I don't move too fast," he laughed.

"That's very kind Fred. I'm Hadley... Thank you." Fred dipped his head at her before slowly walking away.

Hadley shook her head to clear the swirling memories from her mind. She wiped at her eyes again with the sleeve of her shirt before she placed the rest of her sandwich back into the cooler. She picked up the photo of her mom and held it to her chest. *I'll try, mom.* When she felt ready, she tucked the photo of her mom into the front pocket of her lunchbox and slid the horse figurine into the pocket of her olive-colored linen shorts. Before she could change her mind, she walked back to her car and made her way to the hospice center.

Hadley walked up to a large, semicircular desk in the center of the lobby where she saw a heavyset woman with golden hair sitting in a swivel chair. "May I help you?" the woman asked without looking up.

"Hi, um, I'm here to see Michael Martin?"

"And you are?" The woman, wearing a name tag that said Gina, looked up at her impatiently.

"Oh, right. I'm Hadley. Hadley Martin. His, um, daughter."

"Of course," the woman said as her scowl softened. "Michael will be happy to see you."

"He will?"

"Of course, hon. He hasn't had any visitors yet. Are you up to date on his condition?"

"I'm not sure." Hadley blew out a breath. "I haven't seen him in a while but a woman called me yesterday to say he was suffering from liver failure?"

Gina frowned. "Yes. Unfortunately, he's in pretty bad shape. His whole body is shutting down on him. He's fairly lucid but has his moments."

"And he wants to see me?" Hadley questioned softly.

"He asked us to track you down. It's early enough in the day that he should have his wits to him. It's not normally until the evening when he gets confused. If you're ready to see him, I can page a nurse to come escort you to his room."

"As ready as I can be," Hadley said with a weak smile.

Gina nodded. "Okay, dear." She picked up the phone and spoke briefly into it before placing it back on the rocker. "Someone will be out in just a moment."

"Thank you." Hadley stood next to the front desk, and chewed on her bottom lip while she stared at her clenched fists. She debated walking out, feeling an overwhelming sense of dread, but her feet stayed planted. Several moments later Hadley heard the clacking of high heels on the linoleum flooring. She looked up to see a short, dark-haired nurse approaching. She was wearing pale yellow scrubs and held a metal clipboard.

"Hadley?"

Hadley nodded nervously.

"My name is Aida, I'm one of the primary care nurses assigned to your father. I'm the one who called you yesterday."

"Thank you for calling. Honestly, I was so thrown off that I'm not sure I remember everything you told me."

"That's okay, honey." Nurse Aida guided Hadley toward a seat at the edge of the waiting room. "Let's sit for a minute and run through a few things. I don't want you to feel caught off guard again."

"I would appreciate that," Hadley said with a polite smile.

Aida spent the next ten minutes reviewing her father's file with her. She explained after years of severe alcohol abuse, he suffered a stroke six months ago and collapsed while on a job. He spent several days in the emergency room but never fully recovered. It was not long after when he was diagnosed with permanent liver damage and progressively disordered thinking. "If you have no other questions honey, we can head toward his room. I want to make sure you understand he's hooked up to several monitors and IVs. It can be alarming if you aren't prepared."

"I understand, thank you. I guess I'm ready."

They walked together down the endless white hallway. Hadley couldn't decide if they were walking too quickly or too slowly.

"Are you okay, honey?" Aida stopped when she noticed Hadley had turned pale.

Hadley stared blankly, only blinking once Aida placed her hands firmly on her forearms. She backed against the wall and let out a dramatic breath followed by a rapid succession of quick breaths. "I can't do this," she panicked.

"It can be hard to see a loved one decline. I can stay with you in the room if it helps," Aida said gently while rubbing her arms.

Hadley looked at Aida, slowly starting to regulate her breathing. "He's not a loved one," she mumbled.

"Oh?" Aida said, confused.

"I mean, he's my father, but he wasn't great – we didn't have a great relationship..."

"Oh." Aida seemed to understand. "I am sorry, sweetheart. That makes it even harder, doesn't it. Listen, honey, there's no rulebook here. If you want to leave, you can leave. If you want to stay, you stay. Why don't you go inside and if you feel uncomfortable at any point, look back at the door and I'll swoop in and help."

Hadley nodded while inhaling slowly, blowing the air out through her mouth. "Okay," she whispered. "I can do that."

They rounded the corner and soon were outside of her father's room. Aida stood patiently, giving Hadley all of the time she needed before she moved toward the door. "You're sure he wants to see me?"

"He asked for you," Aida nodded.

"Okay." Aida motioned toward the door, letting Hadley know she could enter when ready. Hadley slowly turned the door handle and stepped into the room. She moved quietly toward the bed, noticing how frail her father was. This was a man who once terrified her. Now, at only fifty-one years old, was as thin as a skeleton with a slight droop to his face. His skin was yellowed and saggy and his hair was even thinner than it was a year ago. His brown eyes, once full of hostility, were now dull and almost lifeless. He shifted slightly in the bed, trying to make out who was approaching.

"Nurse Aida?" His voice shook.

"Nurse Aida is outside," she said nervously.

"Oh my..." he tried to push himself up in the bed but failed. He let out a groan before speaking again. "Hadley?"

"Yeah, it's me, Dad."

"My eyes don't work for shit. Come closer, let me see you." Hadley took a few steps closer, afraid to cross an invisible line near his bed. "If I didn't know any better I woulda thought you were Lizzy. Your mother, I mean."

Hadley smiled.

"You're beautiful. I, uh, didn't think you would come."

"I didn't think I would either. Nurse Aida called me yesterday and said you weren't doing well."

He let out a dejected laugh. "Well, based on the non-stop beeping and booping of these machines, I'd have to agree."

Hadley stood there looking at her father, wondering what to say next. "Um, so how do you feel?"

"Like hell. They're giving me a cocktail of pain medicine but it's barely taking the edge off. Guess I'm used to something stronger," he said grimly.

"Isn't that what got you here?"

"That's what they say."

After a long awkward pause, words tumbled out of Hadley's mouth. "I never got to say goodbye to Mom before she died."

"She didn't want you to see her at the very end, Had."

"Yeah, I know. The point is I didn't get that final moment with mom, and it haunted me for years. I had nightmares about how she died. You never told me if it was painful or painless so my brain would just create these awful possibilities and I –"

"She was sleeping."

"What?"

"She died in her sleep. She went peacefully."

Hadley's eyes welled up as she sighed. "That's – thank you. It's just that, uh –"

"You came to say goodbye to me?"

"I guess. Dad, I don't know. We haven't talked in five years except for when I picked up the donation boxes... and you weren't all that welcoming. You never tried to call me or reach out or anything otherwise. It's like you were happy to forget I existed. So then when Nurse Aida called me, I was really surprised. I didn't even know how to feel. Did you want to see me? Did I want to see you? I honestly never thought I'd see you again. I guess I never really thought about this moment."

"Listen, Hads, you have it wrong. I know I'm shit. I drank myself into oblivion every day. I don't remember half of what I put you through. But the things I do remember? They suck. I was devastated when your mom died, and I went from drinkin' with my buddies to becoming totally out of control. I couldn't stop myself and I knew you were better off without me. I'm sorry if I made your life hard."

"Made my life hard?" Hadley said with rising emotion.

"Yeah. I didn't know how to be there for you."

"You didn't even try. I lost my mom and I needed my dad. But you weren't there. And when you were, you were terrifying."

"I know," he said, hanging his head.

"No, you don't," Hadley's anger piqued. "You just said you barely remember. The thing is, Dad, you might not be able to remember but I'm not able to forget. Those years play on repeat in my head. You screaming at me. You breaking things. Destroying the house. Forcing me to get a job then taking all of my money. I used to hide under my covers at night, terrified you'd come slamming through my door. I hated you."

"You hated me?"

"Yeah," Hadley said confidently.

"Do you still hate me?" he asked with a raspy voice.

"I don't think so. I don't know what I feel," she exhaled.

"I know it doesn't mean much, but I'm sorry."

She nodded but stayed quiet.

"I've been sober for six weeks."

"It's a little too late though, right?"

"Yeah. I already did too much damage to my body."

"You did a lot of damage all around."

"That's fair."

Hadley blew out a breath and looked away. "Nothing about this is fair. Mom didn't have a choice. Cancer stole her life. You had a choice. You did this to yourself. To me."

"You're right."

Hadley stared at her father. She expected venom. She assumed he would be cruel and unwelcoming to her. Seeing him lay in front of her, unable to sit up, was jarring. Hearing him apologize? It's what she wanted to hear for years but hearing it now didn't mean what she thought it would. She reached into her pocket and wrapped her hand around the alabaster horse. "It's okay, dad. I'm figuring life out on my own. I have a decent job and a really great group of friends."

"That's really good to hear."

"I even have a cat."

"A cat," he repeated.

"Yeah," Hadley laughed. "Her name is Littlefoot, I got her from an animal shelter."

"You always did love animals."

Hadley smiled and nodded slightly.

"I'm glad you're here. I told Nurse Aida it was a longshot. I don't deserve your forgiveness, just know that I'm payin' the consequences and I'm sorry."

"I wish things were different," Hadley said as a tear rolled down her cheek.

"Me too," he said through a cough.

On cue, Nurse Aida appeared. "I'm sorry to interrupt sweetheart, but your dad's heart rate is spiking. I saw it on the monitors outside."

"What's that mean?" Hadley's voice was coated with a sudden fear.

"It just means he needs to rest. He hasn't talked this much since he got here, and the energy is taking a toll on his heart."

"I'm okay," he croaked. "It was worth it."

"That's lovely to hear but you really do need to rest now. I'll be back in a few minutes with your medicine and to replace your bags." Nurse Aida turned her attention to Hadley, placing a hand on her shoulder before continuing. "You are welcome to come back later or tomorrow. We have an open-door policy."

"Thank you, but I think this will probably be my only visit. Can I just have one more minute?"

"Of course. I'll be back in a few with your medicine, Michael."

Once Nurse Aida left the room, Hadley turned back to her father. "This is a lot for me."

"I know. It's okay if you don't come back but this meant a lot. My one and only visitor. I'm sorry I messed everything up for you."

Hadley placed her hand on top of the collection of bones that was her father's hand. She wasn't ready to forgive him or to say that she loved him. Instead, she rested her hand on his and bit her bottom lip. After a few moments of silence, Hadley whispered goodbye. As she started to walk out, she heard her father clear his throat and mutter, "I always loved you, Hadley." She stopped in her tracks, closing her eyes. She let the words roll through her but didn't turn back around. Instead, she took a deep breath and continued out the door. Then, she immediately rushed down the hallway and toward the front door of the center, desperate for fresh air.

Once outside, she sat on the curb, head between her knees, and let herself fall apart.

A Million Cheers to That

"Thanks again for watching Littlefoot the other day," Hadley said as she grabbed a jalapeno popper from the platter on the table. "I'm not sure why I thought I would be gone for days and not hours, but it was still a help."

"She's literally the sweetest cat. You're lucky I didn't hold her hostage," Stephanie laughed. She balanced a mojito in her right hand and a half-eaten jalapeno popper in her left. Her hair was secured on the top of her head by a pink scrunchie, and she was wearing a ribbed white tank top with a pair of jeans.

"I don't understand how she ended up in a shelter," Helen wondered as she reapplied her cherry red lipstick.

"Yeah," Hadley replied. "Honestly, how any pet gets abandoned is just beyond me."

"I think people don't understand what responsibility and commitment means until it's too late. So they panic," Meghan said, tucking a loose curl behind her ear.

"So true," Hadley nodded. "Anyway, thanks for this, guys. I really needed a night out after last night."

"Please," Cathleen waved her off. "Any excuse to pass bedtime duties to Henry is fine by me."

"Andrew has Amelia tonight, so I was also happy to get out of my quiet house."

"Well," Helen added, gulping her cosmopolitan. "No kids or husbands here but always down for a girls' night." Helen was wearing a low-cut navy blouse with a pair of black pleather shorts. She lifted her empty glass in the air, letting the waitress know she was ready for another. "Anyone else?"

"I'll take another mojito," Stephanie said shyly.

"Yes, girl! Steph showin' up," Helen said emphatically.

Stephanie looked embarrassed as she sipped on the watered down remains of her drink. "I don't know about that. I wasn't expecting an invite so I'm happy you guys thought to include me."

"Oh please, you're one of us now," Meghan said with a wink.

"Josh or no Josh, you always have a place at this table," Cathleen added.

"Totally." Hadley smiled.

"Really?" Stephanie sounded relieved.

"Yeah, of course," Hadley said with a hesitant look. "Why... are things okay with you guys?"

"Oh, yes, give us the gossip." Helen leaned in with eager eyes.

"No," Stephanie said quickly. "That's not what I meant. Josh is perfect."

"Please don't tell him that," Meghan said with an eye roll that made the girls laugh.

"I never had a solid group of girlfriends, so this is new to me. I had a lot of friends in high school but nothing that lasted past graduation. Josh always speaks so highly of you guys, especially you, Hadley," Stephanie said, pointing casually in her direction.

Hadley blushed slightly. "Meg and Josh have become the family I always wanted... needed."

"I totally see that now and it's amazing. If I'm being honest, though, I was super jealous of you at first. Josh just never shuts up about you or about Littlefoot or – well actually he just never shuts up in general."

Meghan spit her drink as a laugh spilled out of her. "He's *so* chatty, right? Worse than Cathleen."

It was Stephanie's turn to laugh. "Yeah, you're telling me. I think I just chose to focus on the moments he would mention you, Hadley. I was creating these scenarios in my head out of my own insecurity." Stephanie's eyes grew wide with her admission. "I don't know why I told you that," she added quickly, wiping her hands down her face. "I only meant to say I'm glad I got over myself and got to know you. All of you."

"I'll cheers to that," Helen said.

"You'll cheers to anything," Cathleen retorted.

Once their drinks were refilled and they placed an order for soft pretzel nuggets, Meghan turned her attention back to Hadley. "I don't want to bring the mood down, but I want to make sure you're actually doing okay."

Hadley put down her seltzer and shifted her gaze to Meghan. "I am. For now, I am. It's been a rollercoaster of emotions. I'm fine one minute, angry another, crying the next."

"Are you happy you went to see him the other day," Cathleen asked.

"Yeah, I am," Hadley said as the waitress approached with the pretzels. "Thank you," she smiled. She grabbed a nugget, dipped it in the cheese sauce, and placed it on the plate in front of her. "Five years is a long time for silence. I guess I saw him that one time last year but that hardly counted. I got to this weird place mentally where I viewed myself as an orphan. Sure, he was technically alive, but to me he wasn't." Hadley blew out a breath, debating what to say next. "I don't know, it's hard to explain. I'm glad I went. I didn't say everything I wanted to say but I said enough of it. It felt like a huge weight off my chest. Like I can breathe easier now."

"I'm glad you had that opportunity," Meghan said.

Hadley took a bite of her pretzel before she continued. "You know what the worst part was? He said he didn't remember most of it. So he has no real concept of how crappy he treated me and everything he did back then. He was totally disconnected from it. When he tried to apologize to me, it didn't feel real. How can he be sorry for something he can't even remember doing or saying."

"That's shitty," Helen said. "There's no other way to describe it."

"Yeah," Hadley said with a small sigh. "I'm glad I went though. I would have regretted it otherwise. Maybe not right away but one day." Hadley looked over at Meghan before continuing. "I probably wouldn't have gone if you hadn't pushed Josh to push me."

"I got you, girl."

"So now what?" Stephanie questioned.

"I'm not sure. When Nurse Aida called me last night to let me know he passed, she explained he had prearranged everything and already had a plot secured next to my mom. They purchased the gravesites together when my mom first got sick. Another thing I never knew. Um, but yeah... he didn't want to have a church service or burial. I guess he thought no one would show up. So, yeah," Hadley said with a shrug.

"What about going to say a last goodbye at the cemetery," Cathleen questioned.

"I don't think so," Hadley shook her head. "I'm ashamed to admit this but I've never gone to my mom's grave. Not since her funeral. I have these really great memories of her in my head and photos of her that I cherish. The thought of staring at a headstone and talking to her that way seems so cold. When I want to talk to my mom, I look at the stars."

"That's beautiful."

"Thanks," Hadley smiled. "I'm not sure what I'll do about my dad. For right now, I don't have anything else to say to him. One day, maybe. But for now, I'm processing it all and getting back to life as I know it."

"Well, I would like to say one last toast before we head home," Helen said. Hadley grabbed her glass, prepared to hear something hysterically raunchy. Instead, Helen lifted her half empty cosmopolitan and said, "There are friends, there is family, and then there are friends that become family. Cheers to creating the best family out of the best friends."

"Jeez, Helen. Way to keep things light," Hadley dabbed her finger against the corner of her eye. "Okay, okay," Hadley lifted her glass. "A million cheers to that." They clinked their glasses together and let out a collective whoop. Hadley finished her seltzer and placed it back on the table. "As much as I would love to stay and suck back more of these fancy waters, I better get home to Littlefoot. Meg, I'll see you at work tomorrow?"

"I'll be there."

"Does anyone need a ride home?"

"Josh is coming to get Meg and me in a few minutes," Stephanie said.

"Yeah, and Henry should be on his way for Helen and me."

"Are the kids okay by themselves?"

"Please," Cathleen laughed. "Do you really think Henry's at home just crushing the dad duties? Those kids are probably running the house at this point."

"Or they are sound asleep because Henry is a saint," Helen laughed.

"Anything is possible," Cathleen said unconvinced. "Either way, the kids are fine alone for twenty minutes."

"Okay then," Hadley laughed. "I'll see you guys soon." She waved goodbye as she started to walk toward the front door.

Once in her car, she let out a deep breath. A smile spread across her face as she thought back to Helen's unexpected toast. *There are worse ways life could have gone*, she thought. She drove home with the windows down, letting the cool night air tangle her hair.

***

Epilogue
Four Months Later

Hadley pushed herself off the old wooden fence, her gut wrenched with memories, and walked back to her car. She took a minute to compose herself before she restarted the drive. She managed to avoid these roads until now, never wanting to know what happened to Dorothy's land. Even though Dorothy told her she sold the farm, she tried to pretend it wasn't real. She saw now that a developer must have come in and taken the majority of land. Identical houses, stacked side by side, filled the land she used to explore. She was delighted to have seen a horse but when looking around there were no signs of a big farm, just a small corner patch of open land. It must have been a pet, probably forced to live on a half-acre property.

She regretted not fighting her dad and not finding a way to continue helping Dorothy. The life that Dorothy built with her husband was reduced to several cul-de-sacs of matching homes. The guilt flooded Hadley's system. She shook her head, frustrated, and focused back on the road. Her thoughts wandered to why she was here in the first place. Hadley's father sold off the house and all of their belongings a few months before he died. She wondered what kind of paperwork she needed to sign. She assumed it had to do with unpaid loans or past due accounts. A man who drank as much as her father surely accumulated debt. She didn't know what the rules were around passing debt down once you die but she prayed it would be something that could be paid off slowly over time.

Before long, Hadley pulled up to a small brick building on the edge of town. The beautiful black metal placard next to the burgundy red main door read "The Law Office of Goldman and Kirk." Hadley took a deep breath, adjusted her pleated gray skirt, and walked inside.

"Hi, my name is Hadley Martin," she said to the woman at the front desk. "I got a phone call from Celeste about paperwork to sign."

"Okay," the young receptionist replied simply. "My name is Jennifer. Let me see if Celeste is free now."

"Thank you."

"Mhm. You can have a seat over there while you wait," Jennifer said, pointing to a short row of black metal chairs. Hadley was about to take a seat when a tall woman walked into the reception area.

"Hadley?"

"Yes, that's me," Hadley said with a smile as she admired the professional look of the woman in front of her. She wore a tailored burgundy pant suit with a black lace shirt underneath and a basic pair of black leather pumps that raised her already tall frame up three inches. She had almond skin and kept her straight ash brown hair tucked neatly behind her ears.

"My name is Celeste. I'm the lawyer for your father's will and estate. I have a few items to go through with you."

Hadley followed Celeste down a hallway toward a corner office. "Estate? I thought my father sold the house before he died."

"That's correct. I mainly tended to his will but there were a few outstanding items that I am also sorting through. Your help today will be appreciated."

"Okay," Hadley said tentatively. They walked into a beautifully decorated office. The cream walls held large, framed pieces of abstract art. The furniture was constructed from dark cherry wood and the chairs were upholstered with expensive looking leather. Celeste pointed toward a chair on the outside of the desk as she rounded the corner and sat in a high-back espresso leather chair, complete with diamond button tufting.

"Oh wow, your view is beautiful, and this chair is so nice," Hadley commented as she sat on a cloud.

"Only the best," Celeste smiled before digging into her filing cabinet. She pulled out a file labeled Martin, M. and placed it open on her desk. Hadley tried to peek at the documents, but the wording was too small for her to read upside down. "Would you like a coffee or water before we get started?"

"No, I'm okay. Thank you."

"Right. Okay, so we have a few things to go through. Like you said, your father sold the house before he passed away. The majority of that profit went to his medical and hospice stay bills. It was also used to pay off any outstanding debt attached to his name. Unfortunately, I cannot account for anything that was left in the house. Generally, it ends up donated, if not claimed." Hadley nodded, waiting for the bad news to hit. "It looks like there was a balance of $5,600 after paying off the debts and services I listed. You are the only name listed on the will, so this will default to you."

Hadley shook her head. "A balance?"

"Yes. I have a release form that requires your wet ink signature and then I will be able to send you home with a check."

"I'm getting money?" Hadley asked incredulously.

"Yes. Like I said, I know it's not much but the majority of the profit from the house went toward outstanding debts and covering your father's time at Wellspring." Celeste spoke matter-of-factly. "I'm sure it's not what you expected, but better than nothing."

"Nothing *is* what I expected," Hadley said with a laugh. "He has no debt?"

"No debt. Are you prepared to sign the release now?"

"Yeah, I can." Hadley's mind swirled. She expected to be buried under tens of thousands of dollars' worth of debt. Having this money will mean she could bump up the heat instead of throwing on a second sweater. It meant not stressing before every girls' night because she could afford to split the bill without dipping into her rent money. Hadley quickly signed the paper. Celeste called for Jennifer to make a copy of the signed paper and had it tri-folded and placed inside a white envelope alongside the check.

Hadley went to push out of her chair, commenting, "This was really unexpected. Thank you for contacting me."

"Not so fast. We have one other affair to coordinate."

Hadley sat back down and ran through a list of possibilities in her head. She couldn't imagine what was left. "Oh, sorry. Okay..."

"I have a trust account in your name. Seeing as you're older than twenty-one, it should have been released to you already."

"A trust? Sorry but there's no way my father had a trust fund for me."

"No, this isn't in your father's name. Hang on, let's see," Celeste trailed off as she looked through the file for the trust paperwork. "The origin is Dorothy Wellington. I assume you are familiar?"

"Dorothy had a trust fund for me?" Hadley's eyes quickly filled with tears. "I'm confused. What does that mean?"

"It looks like this trust was established several years ago. It predates my time representing your father, so I only have what is written. It looks like she sold a farm and 80% of that profit was placed into a trust fund. It was signed over to your father since you were under twenty-one at the time. He should have informed you but I'm guessing he didn't."

"No, I had no idea about this. I'm sorry, do you have a tissue?"

"Yes, of course." Celeste handed Hadley a box of tissues before using the intercom on her desk to request that Jennifer bring in a bottle of water. Celeste sat for a moment and allowed Hadley to collect herself. "I can go through the details whenever you're ready."

Hadley nodded. "Go ahead."

"Here's the deal, Miss Dorothy left you 80% of her profits as a trust. By state law, it became legally yours when you turned twenty-one. I don't have the knowledge as to why your father kept it from you. He had no legal claim to it. Maybe he forgot."

"I doubt he forgot. It's not surprising that he'd hide this from me. I briefly reconnected with her. I wonder why she never brought it up. Probably because I didn't. What does 80% even mean?"

"It shows she sold her farmland to a developer for $3,450 per acre. You were afforded 80% of that total, which is a sum of $579,600. After the tax and fees associated with the start-up of the trust, the awarded amount is $463,680."

"What?"

"463,680."

"Dollars?"

"Yes, dollars," Celeste smiled. "We just need a few signatures on the documentation, with Jennifer as the notary, and you can be on your way."

"On my way with four hundred thousand dollars?"

"That's right."

"Holy shit."

Celeste laughed before calling Jennifer in.

"I'm sorry," Hadley said, slapping her hand over her mouth. "I never curse. I'm shocked beyond shocked. This whole drive down I was convinced my dad was screwing me with an enormous amount of debt. I was ready to fall over at $5,600. Over $400,000 sounds ridiculous. This isn't a weird scam or anything?"

"No, ma'am. It's all very official."

"Wow. Okay." It took all of two minutes for Hadley to sign the paperwork and be handed a second check. "What do I do now?"

"Well, I suggest you get a financial advisor near wherever you live. They can help you organize your money properly. It's ultimately up to you how you decide to spend, save, or invest. The money is fully yours, with no restriction. Well, those are both certified checks, so they will take a few days to clear once you deposit."

"Got it. Wow. I mean, I think I got it." She stood up and blew out a breath. "Thank you for everything," Hadley said as she shook Celeste's hand. "This is life changing."

"Of course. It's always easier when I get to give happy news."

Hadley smiled as she said goodbye and walked out. Once she got into her car, she tucked the envelopes carefully into her glovebox. She drove in complete silence afraid that the music would wake her up from this dream. She drove for three hours, not stopping until she pulled up to Meghan's house.

She quickly got out of her car, locking it twice before heading down the sidewalk. Changing her mind, she ran back to her car, grabbed the envelopes, and walked back toward the house. She knocked incessantly on the front door until Meghan finally answered.

"Is everything okay?" Meghan asked as she opened the front door, not expecting to see Hadley.

"Yes. No? Yes. Can I come in?"

"Girl calm down, yes of course." The pair walked to the living room and settled onto the couch. Meghan stared at Hadley expectedly.

"So... I went to that lawyer."

"Oh no, did you get buried with debt?"

"Nope."

"No? Okay, then what did you need to sign?"

"Well, there was a small leftover profit from the house sale that was put in my name, so I got that."

"Oh wow, that's great," Meghan said with a little clap of excitement. "Now you can get a cellphone!"

"Yes, but that's not all," Hadley said with bulging eyes.

"It's not?"

"No. So, you know Dorothy..."

"Yes, of course."

"When she sold her farm, she took 80% of the profits and placed it into a trust for me."

"Holy moly. Really?"

"Yep."

"What does 80% of a farm look like?"

Hadley handed Meghan the envelope. She peeked inside before jumping to her feet. "Hadley!"

"I know! I don't even think it's real." Hadley pulled Meghan by her hands, so she'd sit back down. "The lawyer told me to get a financial advisor. *Me.* Someone who spent my teenage years hiding three bucks a week in a shoebox under my bed. Someone who wears two pairs of socks instead of turning up my heat. This is unreal."

"Hadley this is amazing. This is the ultimate security in life. What are you going to do with it?"

"I have no idea. I guess find an advisor and go from there."

"That's a good idea. What do you *want* to do with the money though? There's got to be something fun you can do with a little piece of it. You deserve something outrageous and fun. What about a trip to Paris! or Italy? You do love pizza!"

"Get a grip, Meg. I'm more likely to buy a pizza and eat it on the couch than I am to randomly travel around Italy."

"Okay. Well Josh pays for your monthly pizza hangs so there's no point in doing that," Meghan laughed.

"Yeah, don't tell Josh," Hadley laughed. "This whole thing feels insane. My whole life could change. I could do whatever I want. I just don't think I want anything to change. I don't have much but I'm happy for the first time in a really long time."

"Happiness is everything."

"It is," Hadley smiled. "I think I'll just find someone to help guide me on how to save this for the future. I mean, I've always wanted to see where my mom grew up. Montana is a far cry from Paris or Italy, but it would be really cool. Maybe one day I could do that?"

"That's a great idea, Hadley."

"I'd have to put more time and research into where exactly she grew up and all of that. For now, I don't think I want any big changes."

"That's understandable. How about we start by ordering dinner. Your treat," Meghan laughed.

Hadley laughed. "I think I could cover dinner. Chinese?"

"Definitely!" After placing an order, Hadley and Meghan laid on the plush carpet of the living room. They took turns rattling off ways to spend the money, laughter growing with each ridiculous plan they thought up.

"See, this is what I want. To belly laugh on the floor with my best friend. Money can't buy that."

Meghan laced her hand into Hadley's and said "There's not enough money in the world to buy this. You're the best fake little sister I never knew I needed."

Hadley squeezed Meghan's hand. "You're the best fake big sister that I *always* knew I needed."

A minute later, the front door opened and both girls quickly sat up. "Is that the delivery guy just walking into your house?" Hadley whisper-panicked.

"Aunt Hadley!?"

"Ohmigod," Meghan whispered. "I forgot Andrew was bringing her home." Hadley and Meghan broke out into another bout of laughter. "Come here, Meels," Meghan yelled. "Aunt Hadley and I are daydreaming about ways we would spend half a million dollars."

"I wanna play!" Amelia squealed before wedging herself between her mom and Hadley. "I would buy a unicorn!"

"Excellent choice," Hadley giggled. "Tell me more about this unicorn." Hadley rolled onto her side, absorbing every wild idea that
Amelia had to share. While she knew she'd never spend her money on a
giant fairy cottage or a hundred teacup pigs, she did feel a massive weight
off her chest. She was happy knowing she'd never have to stress over the
small stuff. Happy knowing that she found a family that was loving and
accepting. In it for the highs and the lows. Turns out Dorothy was right
all along – everything would be fine.

The End.

Acknowledgements

Thank you isn't really enough to express how grateful I feel, but it's a start, so here we go.

My husband: Thank you for loving me with your entire heart and for allowing me to love you just as deeply in return. With you, everything feels magnified. I cannot wait to see what our future holds.

Corrine, Kyle, and Connor: You are quite possibly the best set of children anyone could ever wish for. Thank you for keeping life interesting and for always being down for a night of Grotto's pizza and scary movies.

My parents: You always reminded me I was capable of even my wildest of dreams. Thank you for blindly believing in me, even during my most stubborn years.

Gina: You are the most amazing sister ever. I am so proud of who we grew up to become and am grateful for our forever-strengthening friendship. Shout out to her company, @eatwellcollective, designed for anyone who needs help healing their relationships with food and body.

Who runs the world? GIRLS: In alphabetical order, as it would be impossible to place you in any other order. Amanda, Carli, Jessica and

LeAnna: I have the most overwhelming love and appreciation for our friendships.

Significant teachers (who may or may not remember me by my maiden name, Consalvo): Rose Sottovia, my second-grade teacher (1996-1997), Lori Freeman, my high school English teacher (2006-2007), and Susan Magee, my English professor at CHC (2011-2012). You all played a significant part in developing my love for writing. You may not have realized you were placing a positive imprint on me, but please know that you did.

Tanya and Sage: You were the ultimate beta readers. While I appreciate everyone who took the time and energy to read early copies of my writing, I wanted to give you both an extra dose of appreciation. Thank you for the incredible insight.

Madison at Love Lee Creative: Your brain is magic. I'm so glad I got to know you and work with you. Thank you for taking my chaotic thoughts and turning them into the most beautiful cover art I've ever seen.

Last, but certainly not least, to everyone who read early versions, and/or the final published novel: Thank you. Your support truly means the world. Stick around, there's more to come!

About the Author

Dana Harp grew up in central New Jersey where a fun Friday night was walking across the street from the only movie theater in town to the only Applebee's in town.

She moved to Pennsylvania after graduating from Chestnut Hill College with bachelor's degree in English and communications. She continued her education by earning her master's level certification in project management from Rochester Institute of Technology and her PMP certification from the Project Management Institute. She currently works in global operations for oncology clinical research; a career she would not trade for the world.

She lives a private life on the bay in Delaware with her husband, their dogs, and her three bonus children. If the sun is out, you can find them on their boat fishing for flounder or tuna, crabbing, or out raking the clam beds (Dana often takes the easy way out for this one and will tan while reading instead).

It was Dana's childhood dream to become a published author. *Growing Up Hadley* actually began as a 10-page short story she wrote at age 19. Now, she's proudly released *Slowing Down Amelia* – the second book in *The Moments That Make Us* series. While both books share the same world, each one stands alone with its own powerful story.

She will always remember that dreams never die, they just lay dormant until you're ready to make the leap. Thank you for reading and making the leap worthwhile.

www.danawritesbooks.com

www.ingramcontent.com/pod-product-compliance
Lightning Source LLC
Chambersburg PA
CBHW031844310726
48972CB00005B/1396